Lance

Inspiration (

MW01593803

Tumbleweed, Texas Tales Book 1

By

A J Hawke

Table of Contents

Lance McTavish, Home To Texas

Inspirational Historical Western Romance

Tumbleweed, Texas Tales Book 1

Lance McTavish is at the height of success when he is blindsided by a loss he didn't see coming. Having just sold his computer development firm in California for more money than he had ever imagined having, he is ready to devote more time to his wife and children. Unfortunately, she has decided to move on to other interests, ones that do not include her husband and children.

Left with an eight-year-old son and a three-month old daughter, Lance realizes what he thought was his life was only in his imagination. Reeling from the shock of his wife leaving with another man and abandoning her children, Lance turns to his family at the Texas Hill Country ranch where he grew up. He packs up his children and heads back home to Texas and his roots. As he begins to settle in at his parents' ranch, he tries to find a way to deal with his pain and sadness. As he tries to rebuild his life, he meets a woman who begins to draw him out of his despair.

Juliana Spencer has a contented life as a county nurse and living on the McTavish ranch. Her world revolves around her adoptive family and the church they attend together. She is unprepared for the upheaval at the return of the eldest son and his two children. Not wanting to get involved with a man about to be divorced, she still finds herself strangely drawn to Lance.

Just when Lance is getting a handle on his new life, his wife returns wanting the one thing he will never give up, his children.

FREE DOWNLOAD

Sign up for information about new releases mailing list

And get a free copy of one of A J Hawke's books.

Click here to get started:

www.AJHawke.com

Chapter 1

San Jose, California

"Lance McTavish, congratulations! Selling Symbiosis Computing Designs is quite an achievement." The heavy slaps on Lance's back were more of the congratulatory praise that had been coming his way all day.

Lance turned toward his attorney, Herbert Hawthorne. "Thanks, I wasn't sure it would come together this quickly. It's a relief to have the sale completed." At thirty-two-years old, Lance did feel satisfied at accomplishing such a hard-fought goal. Now he was ready to grab hold of the good life with his family.

Herbert slapped him again on the back. "Well, you did it. Now take some time off and enjoy your success."

Nodding, Lance indicated his agreement. "I'm leaving as soon as we wrap up this meeting to go home early. I can't remember the last time I did that."

His attorney laughed. "Kiss that pretty wife of yours and hug your kids. Enjoy life for a change."

Lance intended to do just that. Selling his software firm to a multinational conglomerate had taken all of his time for the last few months. Six years it had taken him to build the company with several innovative business and security applications now used worldwide. When the mega software company had offered hundreds of millions, he had agreed to sell.

Almost an obscene amount of money was now in his bank accounts that would set him and his family for life.

Lance moved toward the elevator in the hallway outside the large conference room, where through the glass wall, he could see his management and research teams eating cake and drinking punch as they celebrated. They had worked hard to be at this point of the sale and earn their share of the profit-sharing bonuses. Lance entered the elevator and punched the button for the top floor heading back to his office.

He glanced at his watch. Still early enough in the afternoon to make it home before his wife Chandra arrived from the airport. The thought of her returning from a ten-day business trip to Europe and helping him celebrate the completion of the sale brought a smile to his face. Maybe he would have time to throw the ball with Mark. At eight-years-old, the boy daily wanted his dad to play catch with him. Now maybe Lance would have time.

As he rode the elevator up to his office suite on the twentieth floor, memories of the fourteen-year journey from poor rancher's son in the Texas hill country to owner of a software company he had just sold for eight hundred million dollars swirled around him. Along the way, he completed a master's degree in international technology, started a small software development company, moved to California, married, and became a proud father.

Margie Anderson, who had been his executive administrator for the last six years, sat at her desk outside his office. She nodded at him, gave a smile, and went back to what she was doing on her computer. Her husband was waiting for Margie to join him in retirement. She was a sixty-year-old multi-talented professional who quietly went about making Lance's life easier. Always professional, in her looks and work, hiring her as his executive administrator had been one of his better personnel decisions.

He sat at his desk and glanced at the picture of Chandra. She was truly a beautiful woman. He sighed. She traveled so much these days with her work as an organizational development consultant. Lance felt pride at her success in her career, but regretted the time she spent away from him and especially their son Mark and their baby girl. His own vague sense of guilt for the long hours he had worked the last few months was ever present when he looked at

Mark's picture in his Little League baseball suit. Lance smiled at the cheeky grin on the freckled-face dark haired, eight-year-old face in the photo.

Chandra's traveling had increased in concert with her success at her job. Lance cleared some files from his desk as he thought of his wife. At first her traveling so much after the children were born had bothered him, but he didn't miss her when she traveled these days. Their lives had evolved into two people living together with parallel lives. He had been so fixated on his business and she on developing her career that they seemed to meet only occasionally at home to discuss their schedules. Even their children did not seem to draw them together.

Well, that was about to change. He would now have time to reconnect with his wife and son. And get to know his baby daughter. Sara Hope was still so young that she was just now starting to show her own personality. Lance did not intend to miss the many firsts in her life as he had during Mark's babyhood. All his hard work through the years was now paying off to give him the time he needed for his family. He had to stop the direction his life was drifting if he wanted the close family like that which his parents had given him in his childhood.

Lance packed his laptop into his worn leather backpack along with several files in preparation to heading home. The direct phone line from Margie's desk sounded a soft buzz. He needed to tell her to leave early for once. She would retire at the end of the month and planned to move to Florida with her husband, Fred. He picked up the receiver. "Yes, Margie?"

"Mr. McTavish, a Mr. Jones is here to see you. He doesn't have an appointment, but he insists it's urgent and personal."

Her voice held the formal tone she used when visitors could hear her speak to him. He glanced at his watch. Mark would be home from school in a couple of hours. He wanted to be there to greet him and he wanted to stop for roses for Chandra on the way home. "Tell him I can give him ten minutes." He replaced the phone receiver and looked up at his office door.

A non-descript small, balding man carrying a large envelope entered quickly. Before Lance could speak, the man asked, "Mr. Lance Nobel McTavish?"

"Yes, what can I do for you?" The man's mannerism and use of Lance's middle name puzzled him.

3

The man thrust a large envelope into Lance's hand. "You have been served." The man then turned and quickly left the office.

"Hey, wait a minute. What is this?" The envelope had nothing on it but his name printed in large letters. Lance walked around his desk and looked out the door of his office to see the man disappearing into the elevator.

Margie smoothed her graying hair that was already in place in the French twist she normally wore and looked at him with raised eyebrows. "Is there a problem, Mr. McTavish?" No matter how many times he had asked her to call him by his first name, she had always maintained a formality with him.

"I'm not sure. That was a process server. It's probably more papers to be signed for the sale." Lance turned and went back to stand at his desk, picked up the silver letter opener, and slit the envelop open. Sliding out the thick bundle of papers onto his desk, the first words he read took his breath away: *Divorce Petition*. All of the joy and excitement of the sale celebration left his body, leaving him struggling to breathe.

Taking a deep breath to get his breathing going again, he read the rest of the document. Chandra, his wife of ten years, had filed for divorce. The shock hit as a blow to his chest and suddenly his legs wouldn't hold him. Sitting down abruptly the word slammed him, *divorce*. They had drifted apart the last couple of years, but that she wanted to leave the marriage completely blindsided him. How could he not have known? He read further into the document. She wanted no assets out of the marriage, no alimony. At her insistence, they had kept their assets separate from before the wedding and since he had owned his company before the marriage, it was not part of community property unless she wanted to try to claim a part of it.

He bit the inside of his cheek as he came to the worst part of the document. She was letting him have sole custody of Mark and Sara Hope. Chandra was not even asking for visitation rights. How was he supposed to tell his son and daughter their mother no longer wanted anything to do with them? Lance rubbed his chest where it ached in sorrow for his children and for his own life that was falling apart in front of his eyes. How had it happened and did he have a choice?

Lance found himself driving home without remembering how he got to his Lexus. As he drove up the drive toward the large contemporary house Chandra had chosen, he tried to brace himself to come face-to-face with his wife. Her flight from Germany should have landed a couple of hours ago. Her BMW in the garage was no indication of whether she was home, as she had taken a taxi to the airport. At least he had another hour before Mark was due home from school. How was he going to protect his son from what was coming into his young life?

Rosa Real, who had been housekeeper and nanny since they had moved to San Jose, and Chandra had started working as a consultant, met him at the door from the garage into the hall that led to the kitchen. "Mr. Lance, Ms. Chandra called. She say to tell you to go to your email as soon as you arrive." Although her English was good, there was still a hint of her native Spanish.

From the way Rosa was wringing her hands, Lance suspected she knew something bad was happening. "Thanks Rosa. If I'm not downstairs by the time Mark gets off the bus, please buzz me."

"I will be right here, Mr. Lance. You depend on me."

Feeling sick to his stomach Lance asked, "Where's Sara Hope?"

Rosa waved toward the downstairs nursery just off the kitchen where she tended the baby during the day, although when she was awake Sara Hope was always with Rosa. "She takes afternoon nap." Rosa looked at her watch. "Maybe she sleeps another hour."

Lance nodded. "I'll be in my office if you need me."

Rosa stood quietly and he felt her eyes watching him cross the hall into the foyer as he headed toward the stairs to go to his office down the hall from the master bedroom. Yes, she knew something was up.

Lance took the stairs two at a time to the second floor and then hurried down the hall to his office. After entering and closing the door, he went to his desk and switched on his computer. As it booted up he stared at his hands that he couldn't keep from trembling. Once the computer was fully loaded, he opened his personal email account. He found a new email from Chandra sent at noon when she knew he would be in the celebration in the company conference room. She also knew he never checked his personal email at work. She hadn't wanted him to get it until he was at home and she probably expected him to be much later in the afternoon.

Lance, you should have gotten the divorce papers by now. I've met someone that I want to be with. As soon as you sign the papers and the divorce is final, I plan to marry and move to Europe. Mark and Sara Hope will be better off with you. I never wanted to raise a child. You can have full custody. I have taken all I want from the house and want nothing else from you. The sooner you agree to the divorce and sign the papers, the sooner you can move on with your life. If you fight me on this, I will go for full custody of Mark. You can mail the divorce papers to this P O Box and contact me through this email account. My attorney will be in touch if it becomes necessary.

Chandra

Lance had to read the email through twice before the full impact of it hit him. Out of habit, he hit print and after hearing the whirl of the page printing watched the printer as a copy of the email appeared. What was he supposed to do now? He couldn't think. Mark would be home soon and he had to deal with his son.

Pulling out his cell phone, he dialed Chandra's number. A voice came on stating the number was no longer in service. Shocked again, he stared at the phone. When had he last spoken with her? It was a couple of days earlier. A short phone call to tell him her return date, but all along she had known she would not be returning.

Scrolling down, he clicked on Herbert Hawthorne's cell number. He had just talked to the attorney at the celebration in the company conference hall, but he needed legal advice.

"Lance, I thought you had gone home. What can I do for you?" Herbert sounded in high spirits. He should as he had benefited greatly from the sale of the company.

"Are you in your office?" Lance fought to make his voice sound normal.

"Yes, you need something? I think we've handled all the paper work necessary for now regarding the final sale of the company."

Lance ran his fingers through his hair in frustration. He couldn't believe what he needed to talk to Herbert about. "I just got a shock and I need your help with a personal matter."

"Of course, Lance. What has happened?" His attorney's quiet calm voice on the phone helped steady Lance.

"Chandra just served me with divorce papers out of the blue. I had no warning they were coming. I don't know what to do. She sent me an email saying if I fight her on the divorce she will go for full custody of Mark. If I don't fight her, I get full custody and she wants nothing from me. She didn't even mention the baby. I can't believe this." Lance fought to keep control but heard his voice break.

"Where are you, Lance?" His deep voice was full of concern.

"I'm at home waiting for my son to get in from school. I thought I was also waiting for my wife, but the email says she's not coming home, ever."

"I'll be over to see what papers you've been served with as soon as I can get there. Print out any recent emails from Chandra for me."

"Thanks, Herb. I need your help." Lance couldn't believe how close to tears he was. He hadn't cried since he was a kid.

"No problem. Don't do anything about this until I have a chance to see the papers."

Lance shivered. Panic clawed at the edge of his mind. "I've got to think of something to tell Mark. I don't know how to do this."

"You'll handle it for the best for Mark and Sara Hope. Just don't rush it. I'll be there in twenty minutes."

"Okay." Lance clicked off the call.

Leaving the divorce papers on his desk, he went into the master bedroom and looked around. Nothing seemed out of place, but then Chandra had never been one to leave out her things. He went to her large walk-in closet and opened the door. Most of her clothes were still hanging on the racks. He opened the jewelry case sitting on top of her dresser and saw her jewelry was still there. Then he noticed the ring that had belonged to her mother was gone, but her wedding and engagement rings lay in a slot in the section for rings. After softly closing the case, he caught his image in her full-length mirror.

Staring back at him was a grim faced man that he barely recognized. What should have been a day of celebration had turned into a nightmare and his eyes reflected that. Still trim at 6 feet three inches and185 pounds, as he had been in college, he managed to fill out the conservative blue suit nicely.

With his hair cut short to help tame the dark curly hair, blue eyes that now had a haunted look, and a face his wife and others had told him was good looking, he wondered about the other man. The one his wife was leaving him for. What did he lack that the other man was able to give her?

Feeling miserable, he wandered back into the bedroom where he looked at the pictures of himself and Chandra, and then of Mark holding his newborn sister on his dresser. None of the pictures was missing. Had she not even taken a picture of her children with her? She didn't carry pictures with her as she traveled. The pain in Lance's chest grew. His wife was becoming a stranger to him. Evidently, he did not know her at all.

He went to the large hall closet where they kept their luggage. Opening the double doors, he gazed around at the different pieces of luggage and realized the four-piece matched set that belonged to Chandra was missing. She usually traveled with her computer bag and a large carry-on. Last week when she left for her trip, he had already gone to work. Had that been deliberate so she could leave without his being aware she was taking so much with her? He remembered little things that should have been signs to him of what was happening, but he had been too involved with the sale of the company to pay attention. He couldn't even remember when they had last made love. He had thought their lack of intimacy was temporary and due to the stress of their jobs. Now he wondered.

Chapter 2

Lance's meeting with his attorney did not help him feel any better.

Herb read the papers carefully. "This is pretty straight forward. Unless you want to contest the divorce, all you have to do is sign, file the document, and the divorce takes place. Evidently, Chandra has established residency in Nevada where a divorce can be final in just a couple of weeks after filing. If you contest the divorce, it could drag on for months or years. Chandra isn't asking for custody of the children, alimony, or even her rightful half of any common property. Do you know the man she wants to marry?"

It seems a surreal question to answer about one's own wife. Chandra was already married, to him. Already the sense of her being gone from his life was settling in his mind. Lance took a deep breath, as he acknowledged to himself that he no longer had a wife.

Realizing that Herb was waiting for a response, Lance met the other man's gaze. "I didn't even know there was another man until about two hours ago. I have no idea who she wants to marry, as I thought she was married to me."

Herb picked up the papers and glanced through them again. "It's your choice but my advice as your attorney is to take what she's offering and get it done quickly. Then if she changes her mind about wanting Mark or Sara Hope she has to go through the court and cannot simply come and try to take them."

The thought of her suddenly taking Mark or Sara Hope away from him left Lance with a twist in his gut. No way was he giving up his children. "So you think it's a done deal? She's not coming back?"

Herb gave him a sad, kind look. "I know this isn't what you wanted or planned. With these documents prepared and with her already moved out of the house, I think you need to assume your marriage is over. Count it a blessing you get to keep your children. I'm assuming that is what you want."

"Oh yes, Mark and Sara Hope are the most important things I can salvage from this mess and soon I have to think of a way to share with my son that his mother has abandoned him." Lance ran his hand over his face. He wanted to weep as he thought of what this was going to do to his son for the rest of his life. Pulling the papers toward him, Lance picked up the pen Herb had laid on the documents and signed his name declaring his intent to end his marriage. With a shudder, he then pushed the papers back to Herb. "Do what you have to do but get this official and as legally tight as possible. I don't want there to be any doubt I have custody of Mark and Sara Hope."

Herb put the documents back into the long envelop and into his briefcase. "I'll get right on it. You're fortunate I am also an attorney of record in Nevada. If I can get your Response to the Divorce Petition filed by Monday, the divorce will be final in a few weeks if Chandra makes no other demands. I'll get you temporary custody papers so you can take Mark out of school or take the children across state lines. If Chandra contacts you, don't discuss the divorce, custody, or finances with her. Let everything go through me."

"Thanks Herb. I'll follow your advice. You've never led me wrong in our business dealings and I trust you with this." Lance stood and walked Herb to the front door. The attorney got into his car and drove off.

Lance felt cold even though it was a warm spring day. He still had to face Mark.

Trying to calm his stomach, Lance found Rosa in the kitchen in the middle of preparations for supper.

"Mr. Lance, is something wrong?" Rosa poured a cup of coffee from the pot that smelled freshly brewed. She sat it on the table.

Sitting down, Lance wrapped his hands around the cup of hot coffee. Why were his hands so cold? "Rosa, I've had some bad news and I need your help."

Rosa sat across from him at the table. Her serene look was calming. "I wondered when I saw Ms. Chandra had taken all that luggage."

Lance cocked an eyebrow at her. "You didn't say anything."

She shook her head. "It not my place to question what you or Ms. Chandra do."

"Well, you might as well know. Evidently, Chandra has met another man and is ending our marriage. She emailed me she's not coming back and she had divorce papers delivered."

The small Hispanic woman leaned forward and placed her hand on his arm. "I'm so sorry, Mr. Lance. When will the children leave?"

Lance ran his fingers through his hair in frustration. "That's the worst thing about this. She doesn't want the children. She's left them both for me to take care of. And I've got to figure out what to say to Mark. He's expecting his mother to come home today."

"Oh, no. I can't believe a mama would not want her babies. Will you keep them?" Rosa had tears brimming.

Lance clenched his fists as they rested on the table. "They are my children. I'll never give them up." He had not meant to sound so fierce but the thought of losing his children was not one he would tolerate.

Rosa gave a small smile. "Good. They need their father more than ever now. What will you do? I know you sell your company."

There was only one place Lance wanted to be right now, at home on the Rocking M Ranch in Texas with his folks. He wanted the calm assurance of love and acceptance he always got from his parents and grandparents. Going from the sense of major accomplishment of the morning celebration at his business success, to the afternoon where he was beginning to sense the total failure of his relationship with his wife, Lance started to question everything about his life. Only at home on the ranch with his folks had he ever felt the full contentment of unconditional love. Maybe that was what he needed now in order to regroup and help his children.

"I'm going to take the children and go visit my folks in Texas." Once he said it, he knew that was what he would do as soon as he could get organized. Mark was no problem but three-month-old Sara Hope required a lot of care,

care that Rosa had been providing. "Rosa, can you come with me? Can you come to my folks' ranch and continue to take care of Sara Hope and Mark for me?"

Rosa gazed at Lance's face as if trying to read something there. "I come, but only after I visit my children and grandchildren."

"I can handle the children for the trip and for a few days after we get there. I don't want to put too much of a burden on my mother. She already has a full life. I may stay for several weeks or months. I'm not sure what I will do." Thinking about a future as a divorced man got his stomach to cramping again.

"You take it one day at a time and trust God to help you. First, you must deal with Mark. I hear his bus stopping out front." Rosa rose to place Lance's empty cup in the dishwasher.

Lance's hands were sweating and he wiped them on his slacks. He owed Mark the truth but how did you tell an eight-year-old that his mother no longer wanted him?

Lance stood and started moving toward the foyer.

Mark blasted into the house through the front door. "Rosa, I'm home!" The shout echoed through the ground floor of the house.

Almost immediately Sara Hope's crying could be heard on the baby monitor. Lance left the care of the infant to Rosa, as he met his son in the middle of the foyer.

Mark dropped his school backpack on the shiny wood floor and leaped at his father. "Hey, Dad, what are you doing home?"

Lance hugged his son to him and held on tight. "I wanted to see my favorite son."

Mark laughed. "But Dad, I'm your only son. I have to be the favorite."

"You think so, huh?" Lance set the boy down and ruffled his dark, curly hair.

"I'm glad you're home from work, Dad. Can we pitch the ball?" The infectious grin in the open, trusting face of the child was hard to resist. Lance remembered taking him to a baseball game when he was four and baseball became his son's favorite game. It still was his favorite sport. It had been too long since Lance had played ball with his son.

"Sure, son, we'll play catch for a while until supper. Now pick up your backpack and take it to your room, change out of your school clothes, and get the ball and mitts."

"All right!" Mark pumped the air with a fisted hand, grabbed the backpack, and ran up the stairs to his room.

Lance didn't want to tell his son that his mother was not coming back and take away that spark of light in his eyes. But, he had it to do. Mark was expecting his mother to be home today. Sighing, Lance went upstairs and changed out of his suit and into a pair of jeans and a black tee shirt. He put on his flat-heeled lace-up boots he hadn't worn lately because Chandra always had a negative comment about his 'cowboy' boots. Well, her opinion no longer mattered as to his fashion taste. Maybe he would do a run through one of the western ware stores with Mark and get his son a pair of boots. After the final lace-up on the boots, Lance sat back and considered all the decisions he had made in the last ten years in order to keep peace with Chandra. The sense of being freed almost left a tinge of guilt. Had he wanted this divorce?

"Dad!" Mark's shout up the stairs got Lance moving downstairs. He had a lot to think about, but for now, he was going to play catch with his son.

As he entered the kitchen on the way to the backyard, he spotted his baby girl lying in her play crib, where Rosa kept her when she was busy at the stove. Lance picked up the squirming baby and kissed her on the forehead. "Hi, little Miss Sara Hope." He had always called her by both her first name and her middle names. Chandra had been against it, wanting to call the child, Sara. But to Lance, the baby was Sara Hope. The infant gurgled and smiled the toothless smile of pre-teething, all drool and crossed eyes. Lance hugged his baby girl close and laughed. "I love you, sweetheart."

The backdoor slammed as Mark barreled into the kitchen. "Dad! Come on. It's going to be supper soon."

"Hold your horses, son. I had to say hello to your baby sister." Lance laid his child back down in the crib. He turned, grabbed Mark around the waist, and carried him out into the backyard like a sack of potatoes. The boy squealed and laughed. When was the last time Lance had played with his son? How much of his son's laughter had he missed?

Rosa called them in to supper after an hour of play. The running around and laughter felt good and for a while Lance was able to forget the talk he had to have with Mark. He would wait until time for bed and then as gently as he could he would tell his son. It would change the boy's life in a fundamental way. Lance would have done anything to protect Mark from the loss if he had the power. But powerless was how Lance felt this warm late spring evening.

After they ate the fried chicken, potatoes, gravy, and vegetables Rosa had prepared, Lance got Mark's attention as the boy tried to find the last bit of meat from the chicken leg. "Go take your shower, Mark. Then maybe we can read something together before you go to sleep."

Rosa reached around Mark, grabbed his napkin, and wiped his hands and face. "Don't touch anything until you get to the bathroom. I don't want chicken grease on the stairway rail."

"Yes, ma'am." Mark scooted out of his seat and ran for the stairs.

Lance watched him go with an indulgent smile. Didn't the boy know how to walk? Everywhere he went was at full speed ahead.

Rosa looked from Lance to Sara Hope who started to fuss. "You want to give Sara Hope her bottle while Mark showers?"

Lance gazed at her with surprise. It had been weeks since he had fed his baby girl. "Yes, I would like that."

Rosa placed the child in the curve of Lance's arm. "You go take her to the nursery and sit in the rocker. I'll bring a warmed bottle."

With his finger tapping Sara Hope's soft little cheek and nose to get her attention, he carried her up to the nursery. Settling down in the recliner rocking chair, he accepted the warm bottle, burp pad, and light blanket from Rosa.

"I'll finish in the kitchen and then come help get Sara Hope settled while you tend to Mark."

"Thanks, Rosa, for knowing I needed to spend some time with my daughter."

Rosa smiled and nodded. "Holding a baby is soothing to the soul." She left the door open to the nursery as she went back downstairs to the kitchen.

Lance touched Sara Hope's lips with the nipple of the bottle and the baby grabbed hold with her gums. She began to suck the warm formula greedily. It had always been a regret to Lance that Chandra had never wanted to breastfeed either of her children. Maybe that was part of the reason she didn't have a strong enough bond to either child to want them with her. Lance gazed into the perfect little face of his beautiful blue-eyed daughter and shook his head. He did not understand how Chandra could abandon them. He kissed the baby's dark curls that took after his own.

"I love you baby doll. You are my precious little one and I'm going to do everything I can to keep you safe." He brushed away a single tear that escaped down his cheek. Was his grief for his children or was it for himself? He loved the woman he knew as his wife. The woman who abandoned her children was a stranger to him.

Sara Hope looked up at him with pure innocence and trust, and lowered her eyelids, framed with long dark eyelashes, as she drifted off toward sleep. Lance wiggled the bottle to keep her awake long enough to finish the formula. If he didn't get her to take all of it, she would be awake in the middle of the night for sure.

Lance looked around the nursery. It contained the top-of-the-line nursery furniture of a crib, dresser, changer, glider rocker with ottoman, recliner rocker, bookcase, armoire, and nightstand. All of the furniture matched and was made from solid walnut. Baskets filled with stuffed animals were in the corners of the room. Whatever his baby needed was provided. He was thankful that he could give what his children needed materially. It was just too bad that he could not give them a mother who cared.

Rosa came in and smiled at Lance holding his sleeping daughter. "I'll get her to bed. You go visit with Mark."

"Thanks Rosa." Lance handed his baby gently over to Rosa. Hopefully, the child would sleep most of the night. Both the master bedroom and Rosa's bedroom were connected to the baby monitor that sat on the chest next to the baby bed.

When he entered Mark's room, he had to grin at the contrast to the serene atmosphere of the nursery compared to the all-little boy room into which he now stepped. Clothes and toys made a minefield of the floor and bright colors of the books and toys strewn everywhere added to the sense of brightness.

"You get your shower taken?" Only in the last few months, had Mark started wanting to take a shower like his dad.

"Yes, sir, I even washed behind my ears." Mark grinned at his dad from where he lay on his bed surrounded by books, toy cars, a baseball glove, and bat.

"And the teeth brushed?" Lance returned the grin.

"Check!" Mark gave him a salute.

Lance had to laugh at the little imp. Setting down on the bed with his back to the headboard, he took off his boots, pushed some of the stuff onto the floor, and stretched out next to his son. "Mark, we need to talk."

"Sure, Dad. What do you want to talk about?" Mark pushed his books aside and gave his full attention to his father. "Is it about Mom not getting home today? You know she was supposed to be back today."

Lance nodded, a lump growing in his throat. "I know."

"Why couldn't she make it? Did she call?" Lance heard the pain and disappointment in his son's voice.

"Mark, you know how sometimes you have a friend and you play together a lot, but something happens and then you don't want to be with that friend so much?" Lance silently prayed that he was not going to botch this up.

"Like when Jimmy Sutter and me got mad at each other and weren't friends anymore?"

"Yes, something like that. Well, your mother has decided that she doesn't like me anymore and wants to live somewhere else." Lance held his breath as he waited for Mark's response.

Mark frowned and glanced at Lance. "Did you have a fight? Why doesn't she like you anymore?"

"I want to be honest with you, son. I don't know why she doesn't like me anymore. We didn't have a fight. Your mom just emailed me that she wasn't coming home and didn't want to be married to me anymore."

In a whisper, Mark asked the question Lance for sure did not know how to answer. "Does she not want to be my mom anymore? Did I do something bad?" Tears were starting to pool in his son's eyes.

Lance wrapped his arms around Mark and held him close. "She will always be your mom. Just for now, she wants to live somewhere else. It's not because of anything you have done. You're a wonderful boy and I love you very much and so does your mom."

Mark was sobbing now with his face buried against his father's chest. Lance didn't know what else to say and so he just held the weeping child.

After a while, Mark spoke in a sad soft voice. "Does this mean Sara Hope and I will have to go live somewhere else with Mom? Are you getting a divorce?"

Hating what he needed to tell his son, Lance clenched his teeth. Forcing himself to stay calm for Mark's sake, he told him the truth. "No, son, you and Sara Hope are staying with me. Your mom has started the process toward a divorce. I don't have a choice in it. I do have a choice of whether you all stay with me and I want you very much."

"Okay, Dad, we'll stay with you."

Lance brushed a tear away from his son's cheek. "I have some things to do in the next few days and then I thought we might go visit Granddad and Grandmama in Texas for a while. You have another week of school and then summer vacation. We can go stay as long as we want."

Mark rubbed his wet face against his father's shirt. "I'd like that. Could we ride a horse?"

Lance smiled. "I think we can manage that. Rosa wants to go visit her children and then she will come to the ranch also."

"Good. I don't want Rosa to go away, too." Mark's voice had taken on almost a lost little boy sound.

"She's going to be with us. And Mark, I sold my company and except for a few loose ends, I don't have to go to work for a while. You're going to have your old man around every day."

Mark squeezed his arms tighter around Lance's waist. "I'm glad, Dad. I don't want you to go away, too."

"I won't do that. I promise." Lance was thankful that the sale of the business was final with what was happening. His children needed him and he would protect them as much as he could from the ugliness of this world.

Soon the relaxing of Mark's hold on him and his regular soft breathing alerted Lance that his son was asleep. Gently, to not disturb him, Lance slid from the bed and covered the sleeping boy with a sheet. "Sleep well, son, and be in God's care."

Chapter 3

Juliana Spencer drove her short-bed 4x4 red pickup truck up the long lane from the road toward the Rocking M Ranch. She enjoyed the drive through the ranch land out to Hank and Olivia McTavish's place. Hank's parents, Walt and Edna also lived at the ranch. Edna, whom everyone called Nana, except Walt, was doing well after the light stroke she had suffered three weeks ago. Juliana had known the older couple for the two years since she had moved to the Tumbleweed, Texas area. The small town of six hundred people was two and a half hours west of Austin. She was the only home health nurse for the immediate area.

Hank and Olivia McTavish had invited her to stay with them and the older McTavish couple when the small garage apartment she was renting in Tumbleweed had flooded and the owner couldn't make repairs. That was three months ago. They had taken her in as if she was one of their children. Paying them rent was something none of the McTavish family would even talk about. Since Nana's stroke, Julianna felt like she was earning her keep and didn't feel as guilty about having free rent.

Driving up the lane toward the barn behind the old ranch house, Juliana saw Hank out in the corral tending to a brown horse with Walt hanging on to the top rail of the fence watching him. After parking next to the old beat up two-tone double-cab brown pickup that belonged to the ranch, she climbed out of her small truck, waved at Hank and Walt, grabbed her medical bag, and bounded up the two steps onto the back porch.

Opening the screen door to the kitchen, she called out, "Ms. Olivia, Nana, it's Juliana."

"I'm in the living room. Come on through." Nana's voice sounded stronger today.

Juliana walked through the large old-fashioned country kitchen and into the living room. She loved this old ranch house. Olivia sat on the couch with her knitting in her lap. Nana sat in her usual spot by the fireplace, in the rocking chair that was surely as old as she was with her Bible in her lap.

"Hey, Nana, how are you feeling?" She sat her bag down on a side table and went to sit in a ladder back chair beside the older woman. She glanced over at Olivia and noticed the lovely pink baby sweater that Olivia was knitting.

"I'm getting better." Nana pointed to the walker at the end of the couch. "That thing will soon be in the past. I'm only using it in case I lose my balance."

"Good for you. When you're ready, let's see how you're moving and then we'll do your exercises." It delighted Juliana to see the progress Nana was making. It has been scary for the family when the stroke happened. Nana was fortunate it had left minimal damage For a few hours, her speech had slurred and her left leg and arm had malfunctioned for a couple of weeks, but now she was doing well with occasional balance problems and a slight drooping of her left foot, the only residual effects. Juliana hoped even that would go away with time. Although physical therapy was not her specialty, Juliana filled in as a physical therapist out here in the country where a home health nurse had to be able to function in many areas.

Juliana had provided physical therapy three times a week since Nana had the stroke. They had become close friends. Juliana loved hearing Olivia talk about her five children. Lance, the oldest, and only one married, lived in California and had a son and baby daughter. Then there was Matt the handsome Air Force Major stationed on an aircraft carrier in the Mediterranean Sea.

Olivia's eyes took on a special gleam when she talked of her daughter, Abigail who at 26 had just graduated from a master's program in counseling with plans to work at the high school level. After traveling in Europe for the summer with a group of friends, Abby was due home within the month. Olivia hoped she would find a position close by.

Juliana had to laugh when Hank and Olivia spoke of their two youngest boys, Logan and Alex. They still looked upon them as children even though Logan was eighteen and a freshman at University of Texas in Austin. Alex was 16 and a junior in high school and was the only one still at home full time. Logan made it home every other weekend to load up on his mother's cooking and to do his laundry. The boys carried the McTavish height, both over six feet and showing shoulder muscle growth. Looking a lot like their dad, they all had dark wavy hair and blue eyes.

Juliana had looked at all the family photos and videos with Olivia and Nana and almost felt as if she knew the entire family. She had become close friends with Abby and the two younger boys, but she had never met Matt or Lance. From the video she had seen made two years ago, both men were tall and big shouldered like their dad and with the slim hips of a rider. It seemed sad to her that Logan was the only one who indicated any interest in the ranch their great, great, great-grandfather had started back in the early 1800s.

Lance, who lived in California, didn't seem to make it home often. He had flown in for a couple of days, without his family, two years ago when Matt was on leave before deploying to the Middle East. Juliana had gotten the idea from Olivia that Lance's wife Chandra did not much like the country life. The look full of longing Olivia got every time she spoke of little Mark and Sara Hope let Juliana know how much she yearned for her only grandchildren. Hank and Olivia would love to see Lance and the children more often.

"You're doing so well, Nana. In another month you won't even know you had a stroke." Juliana gave the older woman her brightest smile. She really was pleased at the progress made. A bad stroke could have been devastating. "Let's get started on your exercises."

Juliana helped Nana move to the kitchen and sit in a straight-back kitchen chair.

Nana pressed her left leg forward against the resistance of Juliana's hand. "Well, you are the one responsible for getting me back on my feet so quick, Juliana. I'll never be able to thank you enough."

"Thanks, but you know you have done all the work. I just sit here and watch." To get Nana's mind off her sense of gratitude, Juliana asked, "Any word from any of the kids?"

As expected, Nana was immediately on to telling of the recent telephone calls and happenings in Matt, Abby, Logan, Alex, and Lance's life. "Matt talked to us the other night through the computer. We could hear and see him. Hank has learned how to do that. It was only for a short time, but at least we got to know he was safe. Abby called from Paris. She was giggling so with her friends we almost couldn't understand her. She is having a delightful time. But I'll be glad when she gets home."

Nana shifted in the chair and under Juliana's instructions began to exercise the other leg. "I cannot believe Logan is finishing his second semester of college. I think he's doing all right. He's almost as serious as Lance was at that age and doesn't talk much. He'll be home for the summer this weekend." Nana paused and frowned. "We don't hear much from Lance. He's in the middle of selling his business and working too many hours. I'm hopeful he'll take some time off soon. For some reason I have had a bad feeling about Lance today. I've prayed off and on all morning. I sense something is not right for him."

Juliana didn't know what to say to reassure Nana. "When will you hear from him? Does he call on a regular schedule?" When she looked at the family pictures on the mantle, Lance's piercing blue eyes and impressive physical look drew her attention.

Olivia shook her head as she walked into the kitchen. "No, he calls when he thinks about it, which isn't too often. Sometimes he'll call me as he is driving home from work late in the evening. Or, he will have Mark call in the late afternoon after school or on Saturday."

Did he know how much he meant to his parents and grandparents and how much they worried about him? He didn't sound like a particularly thoughtful person. Juliana had to admit he was a great looking guy but there was more she expected from a man than just being good looking. Of course, he was off her radar since he was married. That didn't mean she didn't notice how manly he looked.

Thirty minutes later, Juliana patted Nana's knee. "There, all done for today. We'll do another session on Monday. But young lady, I expect you to do the exercises twice a day including Sunday." Juliana grinned to take any sting out of her words. Nana was well motivated toward getting as much control and movement back as possible.

"Don't worry, I'll ramrod the exercise sessions." Hank stood in the doorway of the living room leaning up against the frame of the door with a soft look for his mother.

Olivia laughed and shook her head. "You just think you're going to be in charge of something around here, old man. What are you doing in here in the middle of the afternoon? I thought you were going to ride the fence line."

Hank grinned back at his wife of thirty-five years. "The sorrel mare got a stone under her shoe. It took longer to deal with than I expected and then I spotted a loose railing on the corral fence and got that repaired. Now it's the end of the afternoon and I'm out of the mood to ride the fence line. I'll do it in the morning."

"Well good, you can help start supper." Hank had been helping get the meals since his mother's stroke so Olivia had more time to help her mother-in-law.

Hank looked over at Olivia. "You hear anything from our youngest?"

Olivia smiled and nodded. "Alex called and asked if he could spend the night with Randy. They have an English test in the morning and plan to study together all evening."

Juliana had shared many of the meals and she knew Hank was a fair cook. Because of her work schedule, she was not helping with meals and other household chores near as much as she wanted. Her days were busy seeing patients and driving the long distance between the ranches.

Hank lifted his eyebrows at Juliana. "If you're not too tired I could use a helper for supper. I'm planning to cook my world famous fried steaks and baked potatoes."

Juliana couldn't help but grin at the older man. He was so much fun. "I'd love to help prepare the meal. How about I do the salad?"

"Hey, I'm not dumb. Any help I can get in the kitchen I'm thankful to accept, although I was going to skip the veggies and salad." He walked over to his mother, gave her a kiss on the cheek. "Mom, why don't you lie down and rest while we get the supper ready? You've been up all day and now Juliana has made you exercise for an hour."

"I think I will. I'm tired but I also feel good that I could do the exercises Juliana wanted me to do. That tells me I'm getting better." Nana took Hank's hand and let him help her to her feet. He held on for a moment until he was sure she had her balance and handed her the cane. "You all call me when supper is about ready."

Juliana watched her slowly walk toward the hallway that led to the master bedroom. The older couple had the master bedroom on the first floor with its own bath. Hank and Olivia used the other bedroom on the first floor. There was a study, dining room, living room, and hall bath plus the utility room on the first floor. The upstairs had five bedrooms and two bathrooms plus a sewing room for Olivia. The rambling old ranch house had been built for a large family. Hank and Olivia had more recently finished off the attic, making it a guest room, and adding another bathroom, which they had now designated for Juliana.

Juliana and Hank spent the next thirty minutes preparing supper in the kitchen that had not been upgraded since the 50s, softly talking and laughing to allow Nana a quiet rest. Olivia was in and out of the kitchen as she worked at putting away the day's laundry. Walt came and sat at the kitchen table, entering into the banter. When the table was set and the meal ready to serve, Walt went and woke his wife.

After Hank's short blessing for the food, they enjoyed a quiet meal together. Juliana noted Walt cut up the steak for Nana before he sat the plate in front of her. Juliana was often impressed at the small things the older man did to take care of his wife of almost sixty years. The smiles and looks he got in return spoke of a deep abiding love.

Halfway through the meal, the phone on the kitchen wall rang.

Hank rose and answered it. "Hello, Hank McTavish here."

A couple of moments of silence brought a smile and then a frown. "Hello, Lance. It's good to hear your voice, Son. Is everything all right?"

Hank looked over at Olivia while he listened. "Of course, you and the children can come visit for a while. We would love to see you. You want to speak to your mother?"

He shook his head. "You come when you can. We always have a place here for you and plan to stay as long as you want. Love you, Son, and give Mark and little Sara Hope a hug for us. Goodbye."

Olivia leaned forward. "Lance didn't want to speak to me? What's wrong?"

After he sat back down at the table, Hank put his napkin slowly back on his lap. "He didn't say but something is wrong. Lance wanted to know if he and the children could come stay for a while. He sounded like he had been crying, which is probably why he didn't want to talk to you."

The couple stared at each other as they processed the phone call. Olivia spoke first. "Did he mention Chandra at all?"

Hank shook his head. "No. He seemed to want to get off the phone. They'll be here next Monday."

Nana shook her head. "I told you I had a feeling something wasn't right with Lance."

Walt glanced around the table. The frown emphasized the wrinkles in the weathered, tanned face of the older man. "What do you think might be wrong? I thought he was in the middle of selling his company?"

Hank rubbed his chin. "Let's not guess what might be the problem until Lance gets here and can tell us. No use to worry needlessly."

Olivia nodded. "You're right. We'll just pray for them as always. I don't have a good feeling about this, either." Turning to Juliana, she asked, "Sweetheart, did you get enough to eat?"

Juliana could tell Olivia wanted to change the subject of the conversation. "Yes, the steak was great. There's nothing like your range-fed stock for taste, Hank. Now let me help clean up."

"No, just sit and visit while we clear away. It won't take long." Olivia began to clear the food away while Hank started washing the dishes.

Juliana relaxed and visited with Walt and Nana. She enjoyed this big old ranch house that was showing the need for some extra upkeep. The wood floors needed redone and the kitchen, though big and welcoming, had not been updated in years. Olivia didn't have a dishwasher and her refrigerator looked as if it had been there since her marriage. Juliana had been around ranches all her life and knew it was hard to have extra cash for things like new kitchen appliances unless they died on you. His parents talked as if Lance was doing extremely well with his business, but evidently he didn't share any of the wealth with them.

Hank and Olivia quickly had the dishes washed and the kitchen back in order. Juliana got her bag and prepared to head up to her bedroom. She had some reading she wanted to do after a soak in the tub. "You need anything Nana?"

"No, I'm fine and I've got the old man here to do for me." She reached out a wrinkled hand that revealed a life that had been filled with hard work, and patted Walt on the arm. He patted her back but didn't say anything.

Juliana smiled at them. "I'll see you all in the morning."

"Thanks, dear. Sleep well." Olivia handed her a brown paper sack that Juliana knew contained fresh baked cookies for her to snack on.

"I appreciate the care package. Bye, all." Juliana climbed the two sets of stairs until she was in the large comfortable bedroom on the top floor. Hank had added on some dormer windows when he had finished off the attic, making it bright and airy. At the end toward the full bathroom, Juliana had her bedroom and a large closet-storage room. The other end of the attic was her living room where she had her desk set up. She had thought about getting a TV but liked the quiet. Instead, she softly played her CDs of instrumental music that included the classics. Two books cases were full of her books.

As she soaked in the tub, Juliana wondered about the phone call from Lance. She was worrying along with Hank, Olivia, Walt, and Nana. She was so intertwined with the family she was becoming emotionally invested in what happened to the various members. When she said her prayers before going to sleep she asked God to bless a man, little boy, and baby girl she had never met.

Chapter 4

Lance was able to get through the next few days making decisions and preparing to go for an extended visit with his folks. He wanted to walk away from the house and everything in it that reminded him of Chandra and her betrayal. Reason and the need to provide as much normalcy for the children as possible kept him from too many rash decisions.

Thursday morning found him at the auto dealership. He parked the Lexus and walked among the Ford F-150's. He had always wanted one but Chandra had convinced him he needed a vehicle that reflected a more sophisticated lifestyle. If he was going home to Texas, he wanted to have a truck.

A middle-aged man in a black suit and blue shirt with a matching tie sauntered up to Lance. He reached out his hand and Lance shook it. "Jack Middleton, how can I help you today?"

"Lance McTavish. I'm interested in a Ford F-150 Mr. Middleton."

With a practiced smile, the man replied. "Call me Jack. What are you driving now?"

Lance pointed to his silver Lexus. "That's what I'm driving but I'm ready for a change."

"Well, you came to the right place. You interested in any particular color?"

"I've always wanted a black truck." Lance grinned. It felt so freeing simply to state what he wanted.

"Now that I can help you with. Come this way and I'll grab some keys and we'll test drive some of these bad boys."

Lance spent the next two hours looking at and driving some impressive trucks. He kept in mind that he would be transporting two children in the vehicle.

Jack Middleton rubbed his hands together and asked, "You ready to make a decision today, Mr. McTavish?"

Lance shook his head. "I've got the information I need and I have to consider what I really want. It may take me a day or so. Besides that, I have to confer with my eight-year-old son. I want his input on this transaction."

Jack grinned. "Well, feel free to bring him for a ride."

"I will. Thanks, Mr. Middleton." Lance shook the man's hand after accepting a fist full of brochures and a business card. He didn't plan to buy a truck in California and drive it to Texas. If it was just he and Mark he would have enjoyed a cross-country trip, but not with the baby. No, they would fly to Texas.

When he got back to the house, he called a dealership in Austin, Texas and ordered a Ford F-150 Unlimited with all the specifications he wanted. After arranging for the payment, he requested that the truck be delivered to the airport in Austin upon his arrival. Lance also sent a hundred dollars to Jack Middleton with a note of thanks for his help. After all, the man had hoped for a commission on a sale.

What would his father and grandfather say if they knew how much Lance had paid for the vehicle? It was something he had wanted since he was a teenager. However, Chandra had looked down on the idea of driving a truck. Lance could hear her voice in his head telling him only country bumpkins drove a truck, even as he signed the paperwork for the new vehicle and faxed it back to the dealership in Austin. The truck was big enough he would have no problem carrying both Mark and Sara Hope in the back seat. With leather seats, plenty of headroom and state of the art sound system it was his dream drive.

Lance had no regrets letting go of the Lexus. His company had been leasing the Lexus for him. H would have it picked up by the leasing company the day before leaving for Texas. Now he had to decide what to do with the BMW Chandra had driven. The title was in his name so he would have no problem selling it. Then he thought of another use for it.

Lance arranged for a management company to watch the house and keep the lawn in good shape under the oversight of his attorney. Whether he would return to the house with the children only time would tell. For now, he wanted to get out of town and away from so many memories that were telling him of his failure as a husband, perhaps as a man. He had grown up in a family where divorce was never mentioned, as it was never considered an option. His would be the first in the family. What his folks would think he didn't want to guess.

Lance made a run by the western ware store with Mark after school let out. Lance enjoyed buying jeans, western shirts, boots, and a Stetson for himself and Mark. Mark's enjoyment in the shopping trip almost helped Lance forget why he suddenly felt he could dress his son any way he wanted after so many years of listening to Chandra's insistence that they dress as urban business yuppies to fit in with the country club crowd. Lance was glad to leave that life behind.

"Dad, does this mean I get to ride a pony, now that I have cowboy boots?" Lance glanced at Mark's serious face in the rearview mirror as they headed back to the house.

"I reckon so. Any boy with a pair of cowboy boots just has to ride a pony. We'll see what your granddad has on the ranch in the way of horses." Lance had to grin at the look of happiness that spread over his son's face.

"All right!" Mark shouted and pumped his fist over his head.

Lance wished he could keep the same look of joy on Mark's face. With a sigh, he paid attention to his driving and thought about the upcoming visit to the ranch. How long had it been since they had visited? Two years for himself and four years at least for Mark and it almost embarrassed Lance to admit it. How could he have neglected his parents so? Because Chandra had never wanted to go to the ranch and Lance had been reluctant to go without her. He should have gone himself and even taken Mark. Of course, his folks could have visited more but with Chandra's cool attitude toward the older couple and his dad having animals to care for, Lance understood his folks' reluctance to leave the ranch. Just last month his mom had asked about coming to visit to meet little Sara Hope and Chandra had not too subtly suggested that it was not a good time.

His grandparents had never liked to travel away from the ranch much. An occasional trip to Ft. Worth or Austin to sell livestock was all the traveling his grandpapa liked to do. They had attended graduations but had seemed uncomfortable. Mark barely remembered his own grandparents.

"Dad." Mark's high-pitched voice piped up from the back seat.

"Yes, Mark."

"How long will we stay at the ranch?" Mark's voice was full of eagerness.

"We may stay most of the summer or even longer. What would you think about that?" Lance glanced at Mark in the rearview mirror again.

"Okay. Only who will I play with?"

Lance chuckled. "Don't you worry about that. We'll find some boys for you to go fishing with, swimming in the river, hiking, and even riding a horse."

The slight frown on Mark's face changed to a board grin. "Let's leave tomorrow. It sounds like fun."

After they arrived home, Lance gave all the new clothes he had bought himself and Mark to Rosa to take the tags off and wash before packing them for the trip to the ranch.

Rosa had supper on the table for Lance and Mark. As had become their custom, she had set a place for herself. Lance realized he had had more meals with Rosa than with his wife.

"Mr. Lance, you leave on Sunday?"

Lance looked over at Mark before answering Rosa. "You have half a day on Friday school, right?"

Mark's mouth was stuffed with creamed potatoes. "Right, Dad. At 11:30 we are out for the whole summer."

"Swallow your food before you talk, son." Lance turned to Rosa. "I'll get packed on Saturday and then on Sunday we'll head out for the ranch as soon as we can have lunch. I have a charter flight booked out of the San Jose Airport at two in the afternoon to fly us to Austin where we'll spend the night. I'll have the truck I've ordered delivered to the airport. We'll drive the three hours to the ranch on Monday morning. I may have to stop often because of the children. I'm hoping Sara Hope will sleep for part of the trip."

Rosa nodded. "I will have everything ready and lunch on the table. After you leave, I will finish closing up the house and go to my daughter's place for a week of visit with my family and then I will come to the ranch to help with the children."

"That's workable. I can deal with Sara Hope for a week. Mom and Nana will help me. Just be sure I have enough formula and diapers for the trip. I'll stop on the way to the ranch and purchase what we'll need the first week. And Rosa, I want you to drive the BMW on your trip and to the ranch if you don't mind." Although he had considered the BMW as Chandra's car, it was his to do with as he pleased.

Rosa looked startled. "But I can take the bus, Mr. Lance. That is an expensive car."

Lance laughed. "Yes, it is and it might as well benefit someone. No, I want you to drive it and I would feel better knowing you have a good vehicle for your trip. I'll leave you a detailed map to the ranch. It's not hard to find. If you can get one of your grandchildren to drive with you, I'll pay to fly them back home." He pulled out his wallet and extracted a credit card. "Use this for any expenses for closing the house and expenses for your trip. Charge on it as much as you need."

Rosa took the credit card and looked at it closely. "It has my name on it, Mr. Lance. When did you do this?"

"I had planned to give you your own credit card months ago but never got it done. It came in the mail yesterday. It has a large limit on it so don't worry about using it. It's more convenient for you to use it instead of having to ask me for money to pay for household things." Chandra had always dealt with the household expenses. Why she had never provided Rosa with her own credit card, Lance didn't know.

Putting the credit card in her pocket, Rosa said, "Thank you, Mr. Lance. It will make it a bit easier to travel and I appreciate the trust."

"I do trust you Rosa, both with my money and my children."

Rosa tapped her finger against her cheek as she thought for a moment. "I will call my grandson, Ricardo. He likes to drive and he returned from Afghanistan last week. I'm not sure what he plans to do, now that he is out of the Marines. I think he will like a trip with his grandmother."

Lance nodded. A combat Marine should be able to keep his grandmother safe on a cross-country drive.

~

On Friday morning after having the Lexus picked up by the leasing company, Lance drove the BMW to Mark's school an hour before the children would be free for the summer to watch the end of the year assembly. Mark received a couple of awards. One was for being the most helpful student to the other students. Lance couldn't help but sit a little straighter. He wanted someone to share it with, but it was a reminder that he was a single parent now. He looked around at the other parents who were there for their children.

After the assembly, Lance followed Mark back to his classroom noting the now empty bulletin boards with faded areas showing. Miss Lindal was already getting ready to close up her classroom.

Mark and the other children already packed their things into their backpacks. Miss Lindal stood by the door giving good-bye hugs and receiving comments from the parents.

Lance grabbed the backpack and ushered Mark toward the classroom door. He nodded at Miss Lindal. "Thanks for being such a great teacher for my son. He has been eager to come to school every day this past year. That tells me a lot about your role as his teacher."

The young teacher smiled. "Thank you, Mr. McTavish. Mark has been a joy to teach." She enveloped Mark into a hug. "Bye, Mark. Have a great summer and don't forget everything I've taught you this year."

Mark hugged his teacher back. "I won't. Bye, Miss Lindal."

Lance spent Friday evening playing with Mark and giving Sara Hope attention. He couldn't remember the last time he had devoted so much attention to his children. Saturday was spent sorting through things and setting aside what he wanted to pack. Rosa was a big help in getting organized for the trip.

Sunday morning Lance woke too early and wasn't able to go back to sleep with too much on his mind. He wondered vaguely where Chandra was and what she was doing. Even though she had made it clear that she was done with the marriage, he couldn't come to terms with the idea that he would soon no longer be married. It took some getting used to. Sighing deeply, he quickly tried to put her out of his mind. Dwelling on his soon to be ex-wife brought on a feeling of melancholy that he could do without. Fortunately, Mark hadn't asked about his mother in the last couple of days. Lance could only guess that was a good thing. At least it made it easier on him in dealing with his son.

Lance quickly showered and shaved, and then dressed in a pair of jeans, a western shirt, and his lace-up, flat-heeled boots. When he got down to the breakfast table in the kitchen, Rosa had coffee made.

After sending Mark out into the backyard to play, Lance spent the morning packing what he would need for the plane. In addition to a couple of suitcases for each of them, he had to take the stroller and infant seat for Sara Hope. It always amazed him how much stuff it took to care for a baby. His mother had a baby crib that had been used for the McTavish children for a couple of generations. At least Mark no longer had to have a infant seat with a five-point restraint, although he did have a booster seat that secured him properly with a lap and shoulder strap and so he could see out of the car better.

Carrying down two large suitcases filled with the children's things, Lance found Rosa busy in the kitchen. She had put an apron on over her dark blue dress and had on pearl necklace and earrings having just returned from Sunday services.

He placed the suitcases down in the back hallway ready to load into the BMW.

Returning to the kitchen, he asked, "How was church?"

Giving him a frown, she shook her head. "It was wonderful as usual and you should have been there."

33

Lance fought not to drop his glance, like a little boy being scolded for skipping school. Church was something he had let slip away. He didn't remember making a conscious decision to stop attending, but after he had married Chandra, it was easier to fall into whatever she planned for the weekend than struggle with her over attending services.

"You're right. When I get to the ranch, I'll take the children to Sunday School." He chuckled. "My grandmother will insist on it."

"Good for her. You never listen to me." She placed some bottled water into a box. "Mr. Lance, here are snacks for you boys and bottled water. Here is thermos of coffee that you can refill on journey. Both Mark and you need to drink enough water on trip. And Mr. Lance, just so you know, no water for Sara Hope until she is about six months old, her bottles of formula are all the liquids she needs." Rosa looked over the box she was readying for the trip to the ranch. Her forehead creased with worry. "You sure you want to travel by yourself with the children? Maybe I should fly with you?"

Lance put his hand on Rosa's shoulder. "Don't worry, Rosa. I will take good care of Mark and Sara Hope. Thanks for the tip on the water for Sara Hope. I didn't know that."

"I have put a book on babies in the diaper bag and a copy of Sara Hope's schedule. You should read the book as soon as possible."

Lance nodded. He was too ignorant about the needs of his baby girl having left everything up to Rosa. "Thanks, I'll start reading it on the plane. I know how much you dislike flying. I'd be glad for you to fly with us but is that what you want?"

"No, Mr. Lance. I do not want to fly." Rosa's sharp tone left no doubt what she thought about flying. "My grandson will come this evening and we will visit with my daughter and her family here in California, then Ricardo will drive me on to Texas. After I visit a few days with my two sons and their families close to Austin, we will drive on to the ranch."

"Don't worry about the house, Rosa. I'm not sure yet what I'm going to do. I may put everything into storage except for what I've indicated should be shipped immediately. Herb, my attorney, is going to make sure everything is taken care of and he'll continue to check on the house for me."

Rosa nodded. "I know you have it all arranged. So easy for me to pack my things and others will take care of the house. Go finish your packing and I will have lunch ready in about twenty minutes."

After they ate lunch, Lance loaded their suitcases, stroller, infant seat, and a container of food and formula into the car.

"Mark, come get your backpack." Lance called up the stairs.

"Coming, Dad." He appeared at the top of the stairs. "I was saying good-bye to my room."

Lance held out the backpack that was full of toys and books to entertain Mark on the flight. "That was a good idea. Did you stop in the bathroom like I asked?"

Mark grinned. "Sure did. I'm good to go."

Rosa appeared from the downstairs nursery carrying a wide-awake Sara Hope.

Lance took his daughter into his arms. "Diaper bag?"

Rosa pointed toward the kitchen counter. "It is packed with bottles, formula, change of clothes, and anything else I could imagine you will need."

"Thanks, Rosa. Now you have the maps, credit card, and extra set of car keys?"

"Yes, Mr. Lance. I have everything including the new cell phone. You will call when you land on the ground? I worry about you and the children up in an airplane."

Lance grinned at the frown on the older woman's face. "Yes, Rosa. I'll call so you don't have to keep worrying. We'll be safe in the private jet. It's much easier to fly in than a commercial flight. Try not to be too anxious." Lance slung the diaper bag over a shoulder and hefted Sara Hope higher in his arm. "I'm more concerned about you and your grandson's safety driving halfway across the country."

Rosa laughed. "The only worry about that is Ricardo will drive too fast. But, his grandmama will watch out for that. He is a good driver. Never an accident."

"Dad, can I ride up front?" Mark asked with hope in his voice.

"What do you think?" Lance placed Sara Hope in her infant seat and spent time carefully securing the straps.

"Hmmm, no?" Mark didn't seem disappointed.

"Good guess. Now climb into your booster seat and show me you know how to fasten the seat belt."

Mark put his backpack on the floor of the back seat and climbed into the booster seat next to his little sister. He soon had the seat belt fastened. Lance noticed that his son was almost tall enough not to need the extra height of the booster to see well out the window.

"Good job. Now watch over your little sister while I'm driving. It will take us about forty minutes to the airport." Lance set the diaper bag on the floorboard of the back seat.

Rosa closed and locked the back door of the house before getting into the front passenger seat of the car. Lance clicked the button for the garage door and as it rose, he started the car. "Everyone all set?"

"Let's go to Texas, Dad!" shouted Mark.

Sara Hope looked up at her big brother with a startled look and then gave him a big sloppy grin.

The drive to the airport was easy with normal middle-of-the-afternoon Sunday traffic. They made it in under an hour. After presenting his identification at the gate, they drove to the hanger where the private jet waited.

"Rosa, please stay with Sara Hope here in the car until I have Mark settled. The flight attendant with the plane will get the luggage."

"Okay, Mr. Lance." Rosa waited for Mark to exit the back seat and then she began to unfasten Sara Hope from the restraints of the infant seat.

Lance put his hand on his son's shoulder. "Walk right with me and you do exactly what I say. We don't goof around at an airport."

Mark skipped as he made his way to the short flight of stairs into the private jet. Climbing into the plane ahead of his dad, he immediately made his way to a window seat. "Can I sit here, Dad? Can I?"

"Sure, let me buckle you up and do not undo this unless I tell you to." Lance shortened the seat belt and secured his son into his seat. Mark had flown only once before—on a commercial jet to Aspen. "I'll go get Sara Hope."

"But, Dad, I haven't said good-bye to Rosa." The stress in the boy's voice stopped Lance as he was about to bound off the plane.

Trying to give his son a reassuring look, Lance spoke in a calm voice. "Don't worry, Mark. Rosa will come on the plane to say good-bye. Remember, it's only for a week and then she will come to the ranch."

"Okay." Mark's voice was timid and didn't sound like his normal boisterous self. Maybe the events of the last week affected Mark more than Lance wanted to admit. He sighed at the realization of his responsibility to help his son feel safe in a world that really wasn't.

Rosa was directing the flight attendant about the luggage when Lance got back to the car.

"I'll get Sara Hope, Rosa, if you'll get the diaper bag." He turned to the flight attendant from the plane. "Please, get the infant seat and then we will get it secured in the plane for the baby."

"Yes, sir." The flight attendant grabbed the infant seat and quickly walked toward the plane.

Lance smiled at his baby girl as she looked up at him with big round blue eyes of wonder. Could a baby sense when something different was happening? Lance suspected Sara Hope was taking everything in and waiting until it was time to start letting him know she had had enough change for one day. With the care of one who knew he was carrying a precious bundle, Lance maneuvered up the steps and stepped into the plane with Rosa behind him.

The flight attendant stepped forward and took the diaper bag from Rosa. "Ma'am, let me get this stowed away and then I'll help buckle in the little one. Where do you want her to be, sir?"

Lance looked at the seating arrangement of the four plush, leather seats in the center of the body of the plane with two facing forward and two facing the rear of the airplane. Mark was already in the window seat with his nose to the glass watching the planes landing and taking off.

"Let's put Sara Hope here in this aisle seat facing the rear of the plane. That way I can either sit in front of her or beside her."

Rosa nodded. "That's a good idea. I changed her while you were getting Mark settled. She may want a bottle but as soon as you take off I expect her to go to sleep."

The flight attendant with a tag on her jacket that indicated her name was Tanya spoke up. "Sir, if you give her the bottle as we are ascending she will be less likely to be bothered by the changing pressure in her ears."

"Oh, that's a good idea. I can hardly tell her to swallow. I'll give Mark some chewing gum, which will help him." He made sure the infant seat was anchored tight with the help of the flight attendant and then placed the baby into the seat. Sara Hope looked up at him and gave him a toothless grin. The trust that his children placed in him touched him deep in a place that warmed to their unconditional love.

Rosa sat next to Mark. "Give me a hug and make it a good one because it has to last for at least a week."

Mark wrapped his arms around Rosa's neck and hugged her as if he would never see her again. "Bye, Rosa." His long dark eyelashes were wet from unshed tears.

Rosa hugged him back. "No need to cry, Mark. I'll see you next week."

"You promise?"

"I promise." Rosa gave him a kiss on each cheek and then on the end of his nose. "There that should do you until next week. Take care of your dad and sister."

Rose stood and bent over Sara Hope. She kissed her on the forehead. "Bye sweet baby girl."

Then Lance took her into his arms for a strong hug. "Thank you, Rosa. You take care and use that cell phone."

Rosa patted him on the cheek. "You'll do fine, Lance. I'll see you next week and I'll call before I get there."

She quickly exited the plane and the flight attendant pushed the button to retract the steps and closed the cabin door. "If you will take your seat, sir, and get buckled up, the pilot is ready to leave."

After another inspection to make sure that Sara Hope was safely fastened into her infant seat, Lance sat down next to Mark. "Here is a stick of chewing gum."

Mark took the stick of gum, unwrapped it, and shoved it into his mouth.

"You ready for an adventure, son?"

Mark looked up with his wide grin. "Yes, sir!"

"Then let's go to Texas." Lance met Mark's high five and laughed. Looking out the plane window he saw Rosa get into the BMW and drive away. The plane began to vibrate as it slowly rolled out to the runway. Lance moved to the seat beside the baby, buckled his seatbelt, and had the bottle ready to give to Sara Hope as the plane lifted off and headed to Texas.

Chapter 5

The flight was easier than Lance would have thought possible. Sara Hope was fussy during the takeoff and ascent to their flying altitude. Not too long after they leveled off, she dozed off for a two-hour nap. The flight crew kept bringing Mark various things to keep him amused. By time they landed in Austin, he was wearing a couple of sets of flying wing pins, had a coloring book filled with airplanes, had been served beverages, and had a tour of the cockpit.

"Dad, can I be a pilot and a cowboy?"

Lance chuckled. "Sure, son. There are a lot of cowboys these days that also fly their own planes."

An hour before landing, the flight attendant served Mark and Lance a hot meal of baked chicken with vegetables and chocolate cake. Just before landing Lance changed Sara Hope's wet diaper and as they landed fed her a bottle of formula the flight attendant had warmed up for him. As he put Sara Hope back in her infant seat, he realized he was getting surprisingly good at taking care of a small baby. The Sara Hope fussed at being put back into the infant seat for the landing, but Lance didn't give in and take her out as it was a safety issue.

After the plane came to a stop by a hangar, Tanya opened the plane door and lowered the steps. A tall, lean man, who looked to be about fifty, came toward the plane from where he had been leaning against a big black truck.

"Mr. McTavish?" he asked as he walked up to the plane.

"Yes, that's me." Lance stood at the door of the plane, not wanting to be too far away from the children. "Are you from the car dealership?"

"Yes, sir. That's your truck over there. We just need to have a few documents signed and you're set to go."

"Come on into the plane and we can use the table here." Lance stepped back to allow the man entrance into the plane.

"I'm Dave Snowden and I own Snowden Ford. We do appreciate your business." He sat down at the small table in the main cabin of the plane and started spreading out documents. "Just sign everywhere there is a yellow arrow."

Lance was ready to sign any necessary documents to take delivery of the new truck. He signed at all the indicated places as quickly as he could. Mark kept busy looking out the plane window at all the airport activity and Sara Hope played with the little soft toys hanging on the handle of her infant seat. Either child could start demanding attention at any minute. Lance wanted to be on the road to the nearby hotel before that happened. It was already eight in the evening in Austin because of the two-hour time difference from the west coast.

"That all of the places that need to be signed?" Lance pushed the documents toward Dave Snowden.

Dave gathered the documents up and pushed them into a folder. "Yes, sir, that's it. You should be getting the title and car tags in the mail within two weeks. You have any problems, you call me." He handed Lance an envelope and a couple of sets of keys. "You are now the proud owner of a proper Texas truck."

Lance felt himself grinning so wide it almost hurt. "This is my dream vehicle. I plan to enjoy it."

"Can I be any help getting you all loaded up?" the man offered.

"You sure can. We have this infant seat for the baby and booster seat for my son that we need to get strapped into the backseat. I would guess that you know the best way to do that with this particular truck." Lance unstrapped Sara Hope and lifted her out of the infant seat.

Within minutes, with help from Tanya, Dave Snowden had the infant seat unstrapped from the plane seat, carried it out to the truck, and had it fastened into the back seat, along with the booster seat for Mark.

Lance looked around the plane to make sure he wasn't leaving anything. Carrying Sara Hope, he made his way down the steps from the plane behind Mark who had on his backpack. "Stay right with me, Mark."

"Sure, Dad. I know we have to be careful around airplanes. Hey, is that our new truck?"

"That's it. What do you think?" Lance shifted the heavy diaper bag higher up on his shoulder as he kept a firm grip on Sara Hope. At least the diaper bag was dark leather and did not look embarrassingly feminine.

"All right!" Mark practically ran to the truck.

Dave Snowden grinned at the boy. "You ready for a ride?"

Mark returned the grin. "Yes, sir."

"Then climb on in while your dad gets your baby settled." Dave helped Mark off with his backpack and then Lance and Dave watched as Mark scrambled up into the truck. The wide running board with grip pads helped.

While Lance strapped Sara Hope into her infant seat, Dave showed Mark how to fasten the straps of the big booster seat.

"Welcome to Texas, son. Hope you enjoy your visit." Dave put his big hand out and shook Mark's hand. Then he closed the truck door and stepped back.

Lance had Sara Hope secured. "You all set, Mark?"

"Yes, sir, I'm ready to go."

"Let me double check that we have all of the luggage." Lance put the diaper bag and the box of food that Rosa had packed into the front seat floorboard. All the rest of their luggage he had the baggage handler place in the truck bed under the tonneau cover. Lance gave the airport baggage handler a tip and made sure the tailgate was secured. He had earlier left a tip for Tanya and the pilot of the flight.

After waving a thank you to the pilot and Tanya who stood in the door of the aircraft for all of there help, Lance climbed into his new truck feeling like a kid who just got his most cherished Christmas wish. The smell of new vehicle was a pleasure to breathe in. Lance checked out the directions to the hotel and made sure the rearview mirrors were set.

Dave Snowden offered his hand through the open window. "All the manuals are in the console between the seats. I hope you enjoy your new truck and that you will call on us for your next one."

Lance laughed as he shook the man's hand. "Let me wear this one out first. Thanks for your help and good service."

Dave slapped his hand on the side of the truck. "Anytime."

Lance started the truck, put it into gear, and after making sure Mark and Sara Hope were all right, slowly drove away from the tarmac toward the Hilton Austin Airport. It was a ten-minute drive around the airport to the big hotel. He parked at the covered front entrance and signaled to the valet parking attendant and a porter.

Lance stepped out of the truck and turned to the porter. "Everything from the cab and the back of the truck go up to my room, except the baby stroller base and the booster seat."

"Yes, sir." The valet and the porter soon had the tailgate open and loaded the luggage onto the luggage trolley.

Mark was already unbuckled. "Are we staying here tonight, Dad?"

"We'll sleep here and then in the morning we'll drive to the ranch. We should be there by lunch." Lance made sure Mark had safely maneuvered out of the truck and then he undid the straps holding the infant seat. He lifted it out of the truck with Sara Hope still strapped in it.

Pulling down the carry handle, he lifted the infant seat holding Sara Hope and guided Mark into the big beautiful lobby of the hotel. After signing in they made their way to the elevator for the ride to the top floor and the suite he had reserved.

~

The next morning, Lance glanced at Mark and Sara Hope in the rear view mirror as he drove west making his way out of Austin toward the ranch in the western part of what is called the Texas Hill Country. He spotted a Walmart and pulled into the parking lot.

"Mark, I expect you to stay right with me as we pick up some things here and no asking for a bunch of stuff. Understand?" Lance unbuckled Sara Hope's infant seat and lifted the infant out by the carrier. She was safer buckled in her infant seat. Once they were inside the store, he grabbed a buggy and place Sara Hope in it. She was awake and seemed content to gaze around at all the lights and colors.

"Dad, can I push the buggy?"

"You may grab another one and push it. I'll push this one with Sara Hope and we'll load up your buggy. Go slow and watch out for other people."

Mark was tall enough to do a good job of propelling the buggy down the aisle. "What are we getting?"

"We need to load up on diapers, formula, and wet wipes. And maybe some more of that baby shampoo." Lance pushed the buggy with his daughter with one hand and guided the one Mark pushed with the other hand. "We're heading for that aisle of baby stuff."

Mark looked disgusted. "Is that all we're getting? Just baby stuff?"

Lance chuckled. "Mark, think about it. What if we ran out of diapers out at the ranch? Or, didn't have formula for Sara Hope? How much noise would she make?"

Mark looked at his baby sister and then back to his dad. "We better get lots of diapers and stuff."

It took a couple of minutes but Lance soon found the size of diapers they needed and loaded up the buggy Mark was pushing. The formula was harder to spot but Lance loaded a case of the stuff. He would have to ask Rosa when she got there when Sara Hope would start on regular milk.

With the buggy Mark pushed loaded, and some extra wet wipes and baby shampoo in the buggy Sara Hope rode in, they soon were checking out.

"Look Dad, they got a MacDonald's. Can we get something to eat?"

Lance shook his head. "No, you ate a big breakfast less than an hour ago. We have fruit and snacks in the truck. Besides, you're just reacting like Palov's dog."

"Whose dog?" Mark asked with interest. Any dog was of interest to him.

"Never mind about a dog. I mean when you see the golden arches you automatically want to stop." Lance took his credit card out of his wallet and swiped it through the card reader.

The clerk smiled at Sara Hope in between running their purchases over the scanner.

"But I'm thirsty, Dad." Mark was working up to a good whine.

Lance spotted the case of cold drinks by the check out. He reached in and pulled out two bottles of root beer, which was something he had enjoyed as a kid but hadn't had in years. He placed them on the conveyor belt. "Add these to our bill."

"What's that, Dad?"

"That is root beer. I don't think you've ever had it."

Mark looked with interest at the two bottles. "Is it really beer? I thought we didn't drink beer."

The clerk laughed along with Lance. "It's not alcohol and no, I don't know why it is called beer."

After loading the diapers and formula into the truck bed and making sure the tonneau was fastened shut, Lance secured Sara Hope back into the backseat.

"Buckle up, Mark. You want your root beer now?"

After checking his buckle, Mark leaned back. "Sure, Dad, but I may not like it."

"If you don't like it you don't have to drink it. I'll finish it because I do like root beer." How had he let his son get to be eight-years-old and never have had root beer? Lance opened the bottle and handed it to Mark. "Just take a small swallow to see if you like it."

Mark, approaching the drink as if not sure it wasn't medicine or some other bad tasting stuff, took a small swallow, crinkled up his nose, and then grinned. "I like it. It's good. Can I get drunk from it?"

"No, you won't get drunk from it. It has no alcohol in it." He smiled again. It seemed the further he got from his old life in California the more he was smiling. Or, maybe it was the influence of being with his children.

He eased the truck back into the traffic and headed out of Austin.

~

"How long till we get there, Dad?" Mark yelled.

Lance grinned at the eagerness in Mark's voice. "I figure we can make it in two to three hours."

Maybe Sara Hope would drift off for a nap. Lance needed her to be calm and patient. He would stop when necessary for either child. "Mark, you got a book in your bag?"

"Yes, sir, I got *Lost Island Smugglers* by that guy, you know?"

"You mean Max Elliot Anderson. Why don't you read to me?" Lance had found the books, especially written for boys Mark's age, online and had ordered all the books written by the inspirational author for one of Mark's Christmas presents. Lance and Mark had already read several of them together.

"Sure, Dad." Mark searched in his backpack until he found his book and started reading aloud.

Lance listened as he drove and marveled at how well his son could read. He liked the idea that maybe Mark had gotten his love of reading from his father. There was a long list of books he wanted to read on his laptop. Maybe now he would have time to read just for the pleasure of it.

"Dad! Sara Hope has a problem." Mark's whining shout reverberated around the cab of the truck.

Taking a glance at the rearview mirror, Lance checked out the situation. "Thanks for letting me know, son, but a quieter voice would have worked just as well."

"Sorry, Dad, but it's serious."

Sara Hope was wide-awake and seemed content. Then Lance sniffed the air and understood Mark's concern. The smell of a dirty diaper was over powering the new vehicle aroma. Glancing ahead to the side of the road, he saw a ranch road meeting the highway. It provided more space to pull off the road safely. Why couldn't this have happened ten miles back when they had passed a rest stop? With the odor building, Lance started slowing down and signaling he was pulling over to stop.

"Mark, you wait to get out and only on the side away from the highway. We have to be careful with the traffic."

"Okay, Dad, but hurry. Sara Hope is sure stinking."

Lance had to laugh. The boy wasn't wrong. Lance was out of the truck and quickly walked around to the passenger side. First, he opened the back passenger door and helped Mark clamor out. "You can play from this side of the truck to that fence. Don't climb the fence and if I call you come at once."

"Yes, sir." Mark took off running toward the fence, obviously glad to be out of the confines of the truck.

Next Lance got what he would need to change a very dirty diaper and spread the things out on the front passenger seat. Then he unstrapped Sara Hope from the infant seat. "Come on, baby girl, let's get you cleaned up." He held her up with both hands away from his body, not yet sure how big a problem he had. She gave him a toothless grin and tried to stick her fist into her mouth.

He had gotten her out of the little pink outfit and was working on getting the dirty diaper off with the least damage when he heard a vehicle slowing on the shoulder behind the truck. "Mark, come here right now."

Mark ran back to him. "It's a police car, Dad. Are we in trouble?"

Lance glanced at the police cruiser and then back to his task. The highway patrol officer was going to have to wait his turn. "I don't think so. He's probably stopping to see if we need help." Handing the container of baby wipes to Mark, he said, "Hold this for me so I can grab one at a time."

Mark stepped close, holding up the container. "Sure, Dad."

Lance gave his son a smug look. "Us two strong men can handle one stinky little girl baby, right?"

"Yeah, us strong men can do that, but hurry." Mark laughed.

The crunch of heavy feet on gravel alerted Lance to the highway patrol officer's approach.

"You folks doing okay?" A tall, well-built officer in his forties stepped into view. He was wearing sunglasses in addition to his spotless uniform with his cap with a visor.

Lance nodded but kept working on Sara Hope's little bottom. He almost had her cleaned up. "Yes, sir, we're fine. Just had a minor emergency that couldn't wait."

"My baby sister had the most, stinky, dirty diaper in the whole world." Mark declared swinging around to the officer.

The officer smiled. "Is that right?"

"It sure is. I don't how Dad can stand to touch it. It's the grossest thing you can imagine."

"Now, Mark, it's not that bad." Lance finished putting on the clean diaper and the pink and white polka-dot bodysuit. He then pulled a clean pair of stretchy pull-on pink pants, and finished with a pair of thick pink and brown socks that looked like the baby was wearing little Mary Jane slippers.

Picking up Sara Hope, who was content again, Lance turned toward the state trooper. "Any problem, officer?"

"Not that I know of. Where you folks headed?" The officer was casually looking over Lance, the children, and then the interior of the truck.

"We're going to see Granddad and Grandmama. Grandpapa and Nana will be there too," Mark said.

Knowing that wasn't exactly what the trooper was asking, Lance spoke up. "We're on our way to my folks' ranch just outside of Tumbleweed, over beyond Kerrville and Harper."

The trooper nodded. "I know that area. Some good ranch land. You coming from Austin?"

"We flew in from California yesterday to Austin, spent the night, and started out this morning."

"You got some identification for you and the children? And where is the children's mother?"

"Let me strap Sara Hope back into her infant seat and then I'll get you my identity papers."

"Sure, go ahead and I can tell you need to get that dirty diaper stashed away." The man grinned as he pointed to the rolled up diaper.

Lance took his time to strap Sara Hope back into her infant seat, cleaned his hands with some sanitizer, then got his driver's license out and the legal papers that Henry Hawthorne had prepared for him, showing he had full custody of his children. He handed the license and papers over to the trooper and then turned to Mark. "Go ahead and get in your seat. Buckle up well."

"Yes, sir." Mark scrambled up into the truck and into his booster seat. He struggled with the seatbelt so Lance reached into the cab and helped him secure the straps into place.

The trooper looked through the papers and then glanced up at Lance. "Sir, these are dated just last week."

"Yes, my wife gave me full custody last week. I live in California, but I'm from Texas. I thought with all that has been going on it would be best to take the children to see their grandparents." Lance felt himself tensing up. If the man wanted anything else in the way of papers, Lance had a problem because he didn't have anything else that would prove he had the right to his children.

The trooper gave Lance another long look and then handed the papers back to him. "These seem to be in order. You best be on your way."

"Thanks, officer. I just need to get this dirty diaper into this garbage bag and into the bed of the truck." Lance grabbed the dirty diaper and the wet ones he had used, stuffed them into a garbage bag, and placed the bag into the bed of the truck. The trooper stood and watched him as Lance double-checked both children to make sure they were well strapped into their seats. He then climbed into the cab of the truck and started the engine. He lowered the side window.

The trooper walked up to the driver's side door. "Drive careful. Enjoy your visit to Texas." He stepped back from the truck.

"Thanks." Lance waved as did Mark from the back seat. Putting the truck in drive, Lance noted that the highway was clear and eased the truck onto the pavement.

"Are we almost there, Dad?"

Lance laughed at the well-remembered question he had often asked his own father when they were on road trips. He gave the answer his father had given him. "We'll be there when we get there. Patience, Son." Watching Mark's expressions in the rearview mirror, Lance knew he was seeing a look of frustration that must have been on his own face at that age.

"Dad, why is it so hard to be patient?"

Whoa, that would take a moment of thought to answer. "Well, I guess because we want what we want when we want it. It's hard for a kid to put their wants aside and just wait for something to happen."

"How did you get so smart to know that? Did you have to be patient when you were a kid?"

Lance was glad his son thought he was smart, but he also wondered at what age Mark would figure out his dad didn't really know that much. "I had to be patient all the time as a kid. Remember I'm the oldest kid in my family. There were four younger ones that I had to wait on all the time."

"That must have been hard." The boy sounded so sympathetic Lance had to grin.

He shook his head. "More fun than hard. It's a lot of fun to have brothers and a sister to do things with and to have help with chores."

"But, Dad, Sara Hope isn't much fun. She doesn't do anything but sleep, cry, poop, and eat."

"That's true now, but you wait. In a couple of years you and she will be playing together." Lance could hope they would be friends enough to play together.

"Play with a girl? Yuck! You got to be kidding."

Lance chuckled. Mark was a normal eight-year-old little boy. At what age had Lance gone from not being able to stand girls to doing what he could to get their attention? Not until he was in his teens. He sighed with relief. He had a few more years before he had to worry about that where Mark was concerned.

Chapter 6

Juliana left her bed at six-thirty and pulled on a tee shirt and sweatpants. Strapping on her watch and a holster to carry her bottle of water, she then pulled her long hair into a ponytail and secured it. Skipping down the stairs, she nodded at Olivia who was making coffee.

"You going running?" Olivia asked as she put the can of coffee back in the cabinet.

"Yes, ma'am. It's a beautiful morning to be out in the fresh air." She pointed to the clear light blue of the cloudless sky, she could see out the kitchen door.

"How far will you run today?" Olivia always asked.

"Just to the mail box at the end of the lane, and then back home. That makes about three miles."

Olivia grinned and said her usual. "Better you than me. I'm going to sit and read my Bible and drink a cup of coffee."

Juliana waved, checked her watch, and started down the lane at an easy jog. Listening to the early morning birds, including cooing doves from down by the river bottom, Juliana breathed deep of the fresh, crisp air. She loved living on the ranch. Having grown up on a ranch in the panhandle of Texas where her father still worked as head horse wrangler, she enjoyed this part of Texas and the small town surrounded by hills and ranch land. Going to school in Lubbock at Texas Tech had been great because she got to go home on the weekends, but she preferred living in a smaller place. Her only regret was the added miles to drive home. She missed her parents, two older brothers, and three younger sisters.

When she got back to the ranch house, she showered and then dressed. Before going downstairs, she listened to voice messages on her phone. Grabbing her medical bag and purse, she went to the kitchen and ate the oatmeal and fruit Olivia had ready for her. When she finished eating, she headed out for her first appointment of the day.

Mrs. Peltry was 86 years old and recovering from a knee replacement. She lived on the edge of town. The elderly lady had a bunch of kids, grandkids, and great-grandkids in the area. Someone was always there to help her. However, she didn't seem to know the blessings she had, as she always complained. It was always a relief when a visit to Mrs. Peltry was over.

Juliana made a couple of more stops to check on homebound patients. Next, she drove back to the ranch for her appointment with Nana. The older woman had insisted that Juliana call her by the name that her grandchildren used. Not having any grandparents of her own still living, Juliana was pleased to think of Nana as her grandmother. She was such a sweet loving lady and was always so concerned about Juliana's wellbeing.

The mid-morning sun was bright and the land stretched as far as Juliana could see as she topped the hills on the drive to the McTavish Ranch. She left her window down so she could smell the sweet odor of fresh cut hay.

After parking her little red pickup in the usual area toward the back of the big ranch house, she grabbed her nursing kit, and entered the backdoor into the big kitchen.

"Juliana, good morning, sweetheart." Olivia gave Juliana a brief hug and turned back to the kitchen counter where she put the finishing touches on a big layered chocolate cake with white icing.

"Mmmm. That looks good enough to eat." Juliana couldn't resist sneaking a bit of icing with her finger from the edge of the big mixing bowl.

"I hope so. Lance and the children will be here for lunch and I wanted to make it special. When I get this done, I'm going to start some potatoes to boil ready to mash and start frying chicken. You'll plan to stay for lunch?"

Juliana ate often at the ranch house. Would it be better to let them have their family to themselves today? "You sure, Olivia? You might prefer that it be just your family."

Nana walked into the kitchen from the living room. "Yes, she would and that includes you granddaughter of my heart."

Olivia smiled. "Nana is right. It's too late to get out of it now. You've been adopted into the McTavish family."

Juliana swallowed hard and blinked back tears. She felt warmed with the sense of love and acceptance given her from these two Christian women. "Thanks, I appreciate that." Turning to Nana, she said. "We best get started on your exercises so you can rest a while before Lance and the children get here."

She and Nana spent the next forty-five minutes doing the exercises needed to help the older woman get back her strength and balance. Although her stroke had been considered light, it still left an after effect. Nana was now able to walk about the house without her walker but still used it when she left the house. Yesterday had been her first venture out to church services.

With Nana sitting in a straight back kitchen chair, Juliana had her lifting her leg against the pressure of Juliana's hand. "How do you feel this morning after your outing to church services yesterday?"

Nana's face brightened. "I'm a little tired, but oh, it was lovely to get back to church. I had missed going."

Juliana nodded. "We had missed having you there. Being tired the next day after getting back to your routine is normal, but before you know it, you won't even remember you had a stroke."

"Well, I need to be back to normal, what with Lance and the children coming. I intend to enjoy however long they stay, even if I wear myself out."

Juliana changed to the other leg. "Just thirty leg lifts on this one and then a little walking about the house and then we're done. How long will Lance and his family be here? I'm assuming his wife will be joining him."

Olivia breaded the pieces of chicken and dropped them into the hot grease in the big cast iron skillet. "We don't know how long he'll stay but he indicated at least a couple of weeks. He didn't mention Chandra at all. I'm assuming she's on another one of her business trips." Olivia and Nana exchanged a look that Juliana couldn't interpret.

Nana used Juliana's forearm as a support to help her stand. "Lance hasn't been too forth coming in the last couple of years. It's been a while since we've seen him or his family. We'll have to wait until he gets here to catch up."

Juliana didn't ask any more questions. The two women seemed worried about Lance, but it wasn't Juliana's business. She wanted to stay for lunch just to have a chance to meet this mysterious oldest son. In a way, she felt she knew him, but as a young man living at home, as those were the stories she had heard from his parents and grandparents.

After getting Nana settled in a comfortable chair in the living room, Juliana returned to the kitchen. "May I set the table for you, Olivia?"

"That would be a big help. I had thought to get it done earlier, but between cooking lunch and making sure the bedrooms are ready for Lance and the children, I have been going since six this morning." Olivia smoothed a bit of hair that had gotten loose from the comb keeping her long hair away from her face with the back of her hand that held a meat fork.

"I'm glad to help. Just tell me what to do. You want the apple dishes?" Juliana loved the old pattern of the Franciscan Apple dishes.

"Yes, let's use those. They are bright and cheerful and were always a favorite of Lance's. If it was his turn to set the table that's the only dishes he wanted to use. With Nana and me combining our kitchen stuff, we only have four sets of dishes. It's a good thing this kitchen has so many cabinets." Olivia chuckled.

Smiling, Juliana asked, "How many will be here for lunch?"

"Logan and Alex are both out riding fence and checking the cattle. I packed them a lunch and they won't be in until late this afternoon. So it's just us five and Lance and the children. Sara Hope is only three months old. She won't be at the table unless Lance thinks she needs a bottle. I still have a problem thinking of Lance traveling with such a small baby. When a child he never wanted anything to do with his baby brothers or sister until they were old enough to actually play."

"Sounds like a typical boy. So I'll set the table for seven." Juliana soon had the table set with the colorful cream-colored dishes with the bright red apples and green leaves decorating the edges. Olivia even had a set of the glassware with the same design. Juliana had never before thought about a man having a particular preference for a set of dishes. She stepped back to observe the pretty table. "What else do we need?"

Olivia set the big matching platter on the kitchen counter ready to be stacked with golden fried chicken. "There are roses blooming. A small bouquet would be nice as a center piece."

"I'll be happy to cut some roses for you. I know where the clippers and gloves are."

"Here's a small vase we can use. We don't want too big a bouquet. Hank hates having to look around a bunch of flowers to talk to someone at the dinner table. I learned that early on in our marriage."

Juliana turned to the back porch where she could hear men's voices and a lot of stomping. "I guess that must be Hank and Grandpapa."

Olivia laughed. "Yes, that's their usual way of announcing they are headed in for lunch. At least they try to clean their boots before they come into the house."

Hank came through the kitchen door followed by his father. Both men had on jeans, chambray shirts, and carried straw hats that looked well used. They hung their hats on the wooden hooks by the door and put their work gloves on the shelf above. Their faces were tanned and seamed with creases from a lifetime working in all types of weather. Hank's dark hair was liberally sprinkled with gray and his father's hair was completely gray. Both men looked unusually fit for their ages of 58 and 78.

"Juliana, good to see you. How's my little woman doing?" Walt asked.

"She's doing very well. I'm so happy to see her walking about the house without having to use the walker. That's major progress." Juliana loved the old-fashioned way Walt spoke to and about his wife of fifty-nine years. Next to Walt's six-foot-two frame, Nana was a little woman of five feet two inches.

Hank gave Olivia a kiss on her cheek. "Any word from Lance?"

Olivia leaned against him briefly before turning back to her salad preparation. "Not a word. He'll get here when he gets here. You just have to be patient."

He laughed. "Wow, my words are coming back to haunt me."

Juliana raised her eyebrows in question.

Olivia spoke up. "When the kids were small, anytime we went anywhere at least one of them would be asking Hank, 'when do we get there?' That was always his answer. It got to be a running joke."

"I wonder if Lance says the same thing to Mark. I'm going to wash up and be ready to greet them." Hank headed toward the hall. Walt had already disappeared into the living room.

Chapter 7

The sloping hills covered with live oak trees, scrub cedar, and meadows dotted with cattle became more prevalent. They were getting into the ranch land of the Texas Hill Country. Lance started to recognize familiar landmarks.

He slowed down as they entered the city of Fredericksburg. The traffic wasn't too bad for a Monday morning. Glad it wasn't the weekend when the town could get crowded from tourists, Lance pulled into a McDonald's to give Mark a pit stop before the last leg of the trip. He carried Sara Hope in his arms rather than get out the infant seat. He slung the diaper bag over his shoulder.

"Are we eating here, Dad?" Mark's face was lit up with expectation.

Lance grinned. "No, we're just making a pit stop. Grandmama and Nana will have a big lunch ready for us at the ranch."

"Are we almost there?"

"Only another thirty to forty minutes, okay? You're a good traveler and have been patient."

"Yeah, but I'm getting tired of riding."

After taking care of Sara Hope's wet diaper and making sure Mark washed his hands, they headed back to the truck.

Getting the children back into the truck, Lance gave Mark's hair a quick tousle. "After lunch I'll show you around the ranch and then we can play catch."

Excitement flickered across Mark's face and then concern. "But, Dad, I didn't bring my catcher's mitt or the baseball."

"Don't worry. I'm sure there is all the sports equipment we will need at the ranch. Don't forget your Uncle Alex and Uncle Logan are both home and they have lots of sports stuff. We'll borrow from them until your things arrive."

Lance drove toward the west out of Fredericksburg. As they came up over a ridge, suddenly the land opened up and Lance looked with hunger at the land of his childhood. Memories of his college years surfaced of driving home on the weekend from college in the old truck and cresting this same ridge. He was almost home.

"Mark, look out there. That's land that leads to the ranch. We should be there in another thirty minutes."

"Will Granddad and Grandmama like me?" Mark asked in a high-pitched voice.

"Of course they'll like you, Mark. They love you. Remember when you talked to Grandmama on the phone? What did she say?" Lance hurt that his son questioned whether his grandparents loved him.

"She said she loved me, but what if she changed her mind?"

Lance glanced in the rearview mirror. Mark had a frown on his face and a look of uncertainty. "Why would she do that, Son?"

"Mom did." Mark spoke with calmness and certainty.

What could Lance say to that? Chandra's behavior really seemed as if she no longer loved her children. Taking a deep breath, Lance spoke in a calm, firm voice. "Your grandparents and great grandparents will always love you, no matter what. You can count on it. That's what grandparents do." The frown was still on Mark's face. "You can count on me, too. I promise to always love you and besides that, I like you a lot."

The frown lines started to smooth out. "You do?"

"Yes, I do."

"Well, I kinda like you a lot, too, Dad."

Leaving the main highway, Lance headed up the farm-to-market state road until he could see the small town of Tumbleweed.

"Look Mark, up ahead. That's the town of Tumbleweed where I went to grade school."

"It looks sort of small."

Lance laughed. To a child who had grown up in urban California, he could see where the small town of less than a thousand people, if you counted the ranch families, would seem very small. "It's big enough to have the necessities."

"Where's the McDonald's?" Mark was twisting in his seat to try to look at both sides of the main street of town as Lance slowly drove through.

As Lance glanced at the remembered stores and businesses and the dusty pickups of every kind angled into parking spaces along the sides of the street, memories flooded his mind. There was the little church building where his family still attended. It only held about three hundred people and Lance remembered it being full most Sunday mornings. Did they still have Vacation Bible School the first part of the summer? That would be a great place for Mark to get acquainted with the local children.

"They may not have a McDonald's but look there. The old Dairy Queen is still there. They make the best hamburgers." Lance hoped the hamburgers were still as good as he remembered. The Dairy Queen was where he had hung out with his friends on hot summer evenings throughout high school.

Fifteen minutes west of Tumbleweed, Lance turned onto the crushed Edwards Limestone packed roadway that led up to the big three-story ranch house. "We're here, Mark." Lance swallowed to get rid of a lump in his throat and blinked his eyes rapidly to clear away the moisture that the sight of the ranch buildings evoked. Home. He was home.

Lance pulled the big black truck up beside a little red pickup he didn't recognize. A young woman walked toward the house with her hands filled with roses. Her natural beauty and graceful way of walking struck Lance. Who was she? The question and possible answers floated around in his mind.

Turning off the engine, Lance heard the screen door bang and his mother ran toward the truck. He quickly got out and caught her up in his arms.

"Lance, is it really you?" She laughed and cried at the same time.

Behind her came his father catching them both in a bear hug. "Welcome home, son."

"Where's that baby, Sara Hope?" His mom let him go and turned to the two children in the backseat of the truck.

Giving his dad another swat on the back, Lance turned to help Mark unbuckle his seat. "Mark, this is your granddad and grandmama."

Hank reached past Lance, plucked the boy up, and swung him around. Mark laughed and Hank hugged him tight. "Welcome, to the Rocking M Ranch, Mark. We are surely glad to have you come visit."

Mark looked eye to eye with his granddad. "Me too. I've wanted to come visit and ride a horse. Dad said we could."

"Riding a horse is a requirement for staying here. But, first let me meet this little granddaughter." He sat Mark down on the ground and turned him toward the porch. "Go say hello to Grandpapa and Nana."

The boy ran to the porch where Walt and Nana stood holding on to each other with welcoming smiles.

Lance unbuckled Sara Hope who gazed about with big serious eyes. What was his baby girl thinking? "Here you go, Mom. Meet your granddaughter." Lance lifted the infant up out of the truck and handed her off to his mother.

Olivia gathered the three-month-old baby into her arms. Sara Hope wrapped an arm around her grandmother's neck and laid her head on her shoulder as if recognizing she was in a secure place.

"Oh, Lance, she's beautiful." Olivia kissed the soft, dark curls. "Her hair is just like yours was at this age."

Hank put an arm around his wife and gently rubbed Sara Hope's back. "Sure does look like you, Son, at this age."

Lance looked at his daughter being loved by two of his favorite people. "Really? I don't have a picture of me at that age so I didn't know."

Olivia nodded. "We'll look at the old photos and compare while you're here. For now come meet Juliana and greet Grandpapa and Nana. I'm carrying this little one. In fact, I may not let her go during your entire visit."

Lance had a lot of explaining to do to his parents and grandparents, but not yet. First, he needed to get his children settled. Going back to California wasn't in his plans. Finding a place to raise his children and come to terms with his wife's betrayal was his first priority. And part of that was reconnecting with his family. To think he had had to introduce his eight-year-old son to his father and mother. How had he let that happen?

He carried the diaper bag and followed his mother who carried Sara Hope as if an expert, which after raising five children she was. His grandpapa caught him in a surprisingly strong hug as he stepped onto the porch.

Nana, who looked older than Lance expected and very frail stepped up to him, and as he bent down to embrace her, she kissed him on the cheek. "Lance, it's so good to see you. Thank you for bringing the children."

"I should have come a long time ago. I shouldn't have stayed away so long." Lance felt a stab of guilt at having denied his son the opportunity to get to know his great grandparents. "How have you been?"

Grandpapa let go of Lance and took his wife's arm. "The Lord keeps blessing us. Your nana had a slight stroke a few weeks ago and is still getting around a little slow."

"A stroke! Nana, I didn't know. Why didn't someone tell me?"

Nana smiled. "There was no reason to worry you and I've had Juliana here to help me back on my feet." She turned and motioned for Juliana to come up on the porch. "Lance, this is Juliana Spencer, our good friend from church and the visiting nurse for my physical therapy. I've adopted her as another granddaughter. She lives with us now."

Juliana smiled, passed the roses to her left hand, and held out her right hand. "I'm pleased to meet you at last. I've heard so much about you from your folks and of course from these two."

Lance took her small hand into his and looked down at the beautiful woman with large brown eyes the color of melted light chocolate and a classic face surrounded by blondish brown curls that reached below her shoulders. She wore dark slacks and a knit dark blue shirt with a label that identified her as a nurse with the county. On her feet were low-heeled boots.

"Glad to meet you and I guess thanks are in order for any help you've been to Nana. I'd like to talk later and learn about this stroke."

"I'll be glad to share what I can but your mom and grandmother can tell you everything."

Hank climbed up the three short steps to the porch carrying a suitcase in each hand. "Y'all move on into the house so I can help get the truck unloaded."

Lance started to take a suitcase from his dad. "You don't have to unload, Dad. I can do it."

Hank held on to the suitcase. "You go on in and talk to your mother and get the kids settled. I'll unload your stuff. By the way, that's a nice truck."

Lance grinned. That was high praise. "Okay, Dad, you unload. There's not much really. Most of our stuff is being shipped out."

Nana sat down at the dining table. "Hand me that baby, Olivia."

"You sure, Nana?" Olivia asked even as she carefully placed the baby into the arms of the older woman.

Sara Hope looked up with a solemn expression at yet another new face. Nana began to gently rock. "You and I are going to get well acquainted, Sara Hope. You're my only great granddaughter."

Blowing a bubble, Sara Hope reached up and grabbed the collar of her great grandmother's dress.

Olivia guided Lance up the stairs and down the hall toward the back bedrooms. "I've put you in your old room and in this room I had Hank set up the baby bed. Mark can sleep in here with the baby."

"That'll be great. We don't want to put you all out." Lance set the diaper bag on top of the dresser next to the baby bed. "I've got extra diapers and formula in the truck. I stopped off at Walmart and stocked up."

"Don't worry about that. If we run low, we'll send someone into Tumbleweed to the grocery store." Olivia walked up to Lance and wrapped her arms around his waist. "Thank you for coming home and bringing the children."

This was the second time she had thanked him for coming home. Had she longed for him and the children so much that she felt she had to thank him for visiting? Guilt pushed at him for allowing Chandra's attitudes and preferences to deny these good people their rights to their grandchildren.

"I'm thankful you want me home and will let me bring the children." Lance again felt the beginning of tears. For a man who never cried his emotions seemed so much closer to the surface since he got the news that Chandra had left him.

Hank appeared in the door of the children's bedroom carrying several sacks of things that Lance had purchased that morning. "This looks like baby stuff. You want it in here?"

Olivia took the sacks and glanced through them. She then handed two back to her husband. "This is formula. Take it to the kitchen please."

He took the two sacks and turned back toward the kitchen. "Any chance of lunch anytime soon?"

Olivia laughed. "Yes, we'll eat as soon as everyone can get washed up and seated. It's ready."

Lance grabbed a couple of empty, dirty bottles out of the diaper bag. "I bought some more bottles in that sack there. I need to wash these up and sterilize the new ones. Sara Hope is going to be yelling any minute now to let us know she's ready for another bottle. It's been about two and half hours since I fed her."

Olive gathered the bottles from him. "Don't you worry about things like this. I'm the grandmother here and I'll be taking care of that baby."

Lance kissed her on the cheek. "Thanks Mom, I was hopeful you would feel that way. This is the most I've ever had to care for her. Dirty diapers are not my favorite things."

Olivia laughed. "I can believe that. Now go round up Mark and let's eat."

Lunch, or dinner as they called the noon meal in this part of Texas, was all that Lance had remembered. Watching his son eat his mother's fried chicken, mashed potatoes, gravy, green beans, a salad, homemade rolls, and a chocolate cake with white frosting had been fun. Mark was a very vocal boy, especially about things he liked.

"Dad, this is the best food I've ever eaten." Mark lifted his plate to accept another small piece of cake from his grandmother.

"Well, after all you've eaten I guess we won't be able to take a walk to the barn and see the horses." Lance teased his son knowing his response.

"Yes, we can. I didn't eat too much." Mark glanced at his dad with a frown.

"If you're sure you don't want to take a nap?" Lance also knew the response to that.

"No, I don't want to take a nap. I want to go see the horses. Please, Dad. Can we?"

Lance glanced around the table. "Dad, can you spare the time to show Mark around the place?"

"I would be proud to show you around, Mark." He pushed back his chair and held out his hand to Mark who jumped up and took it.

"Go on grandson and let your granddad show you the ranch. I'll get Sara Hope down for her nap." The baby cuddled up in her grandmother's arm sucking down formula from a bottle.

Juliana, who had not said much during lunch, spoke up. "Olivia, you help Lance with Sara Hope and I'll do the dishes. Then I have to be on my way over to Burnice Pritchard's for her diabetic checkup."

"Thank you, Juliana. You sure you have time?" Olivia settled Sara Hope on her shoulder and started lightly patting her back in preparation of a burp.

Nana stood up from the table with the help of Walt. "I hate to leave the dishes for you Juliana, but I'm feeling a need for a lie down."

Juliana turned to the older woman. "That is exactly what you need to do. After doing your therapy this morning and the excitement of visitors, you need to rest this afternoon. I don't have to leave for the Pritchard's place until two."

Lance stood and started stacking dishes. "Mom, if you want to put Sara Hope down for her nap, I can help with the dishes." It would also give him a chance to ask Juliana about his grandmother's stroke.

Soon Lance and Juliana were the only two left in the kitchen. Lance started filling one side of the sink with hot water. "I'll wash if you'll take care of the food and the drying."

Juliana nodded. "If you don't mind, I know how your mom puts leftovers in her frig."

"I can't believe Mom still doesn't have a dishwasher." Lance dumped some of the liquid soap into the hot water and started washing the glasses.

"I think they hoped to have one installed this year, but with the college tuition going up and not getting the price they hoped on their cattle, there wasn't much left over for upgrading the kitchen." Juliana retrieved a dishtowel from a drawer and started drying the glasses as Lance stacked them into the old dish drainer sitting on the counter with a rubber drain tray underneath.

Lance felt a stab of guilt. He had been making good money for years and now with the sale of his company had more money than he could spend in his lifetime. And, his parents struggled with helping their middle son pay tuition. Where had his head been? Lance kept his head down and scrubbed at the flatware. What must this young woman think of him for not being aware of his parents' needs?

"Tell me about Nana's stroke if you wouldn't mind."

Juliana paused in her rubbing the moisture from a tall glass. "She has given me permission to talk about it or I wouldn't say anything. I think she rather I told you than say anything herself. It was almost four weeks ago. Your folks and grandparents had come to church service that Sunday morning. I spoke to Nana before Bible class and she was fine. Then after services, Walt seemed to be having a hard time getting Nana to stand up. I went over to see what the problem was and noticed that the side of her mouth was drooping and she didn't have control of her left arm. I knew immediately she had had a stroke or a mild TIA."

"What did you do?"

"I called 911 and asked whether it was better for us to drive her to Fredericksburg or wait for the EMTs. They suggested we start driving her and meet the EMTs on the way. I don't know how much you know about strokes."

"Assume I don't know anything and you would be close to right." Lance had turned and was listening to her.

"Okay, well, one of the most important things to understand is the quicker a person gets to the hospital the less damage to the brain. Every minute counts. I told Fred Jones to get his minivan as he had more room than your dad's pickup. Everyone was so helpful and we had Nana in the van and driving down the road in five minutes. I think half the congregation followed us and everyone was praying. We met the ambulance about fifteen minutes outside of Fredericksburg and transferred Nana to it. From the time we realized something was wrong and she was in the hospital was about thirty minutes, which considering where we started from was not bad. The doctors determined it was an ischemic stroke and they gave her a medicine called tPA which breaks up the blood clots in the arteries of the brain. She spent a week in the hospital and then we started physical therapy as soon as she got home. Her speech cleared up in just a day or so but her left leg and arm have taken longer. She may always have a weakness in that leg now. But, she's getting her balance back and doing really well." Juliana laughed. "I'm not sure you wanted to hear all that from the look on your face. Strokes are fairly common for someone Nana's age and she's now on an aspirin a day to hopefully avoid any more strokes."

"No, I wanted to know. It sounds like you were a hero that Sunday morning. Thank God, you were there. Nana looks so frail compared to two years ago when I last saw her."

"You haven't seen Nana in two years?" Juliana's voice told him how surprised she was at that.

"No, I haven't been home in two years. I should have come more often than I have but my . . . ." Suddenly, Lance didn't know what to call Chandra. She was still his wife legally but he was already starting to think of himself as single. "My wife, Chandra, doesn't like the country and preferred not to come to Texas. It became easier to do what she wanted with holidays and vacations. That never included coming to the ranch."

"I'm sorry. I know your family always kept you and your family in their prayers. I'm glad you've come now. Will your wife be joining you?"

Lance turned back to the dishwashing. "No, she won't be coming."

"How long will you get to stay with the children?"

"I'm thinking about relocating back to this area. We may stay for several weeks with my folks and then I may look around for a place to buy." He glanced over at the attractive young woman. She reached up to place a dish in an upper shelf. Her brown hair with streaks of blond hung down her back and swayed as she moved. Lance looked back at the dishwater.

Juliana reached for another bowl to dry. "I'm glad you're thinking of moving this way. Your family will be thrilled. Do they know?"

"No, and I'd appreciate if you didn't say anything. I'm still considering what I'm going to do. Knowing Mom and Dad, they would want us to settle in here and stay. However, I want to get my own place. What about you? How long have you been in this area?"

"I moved here after I finished nursing school. I didn't want to work in a big city hospital and I love to help people who don't have much health care. I grew up north of Amarillo and got my nursing degree from Texas Tech University Health Sciences at Amarillo. I worked for a couple of years in Amarillo while getting my DNP."

"DNP? What's that?" Lance released the drain stopper.

"Doctor of Nursing Practice, I decided to keep going with my schooling until I got to that level. The next step would be to probably go to medical school and I haven't decided if I want to do that."

"Wow, what are you doing working as a county nurse in a rural area? Don't people with those degrees usually supervise in a hospital or teach or something?"

Juliana laughed. "Yes, they do but I wanted to be of real help and besides this way I'm getting to have a much broader experience. I don't like the idea of being a supervisor. I want to do hands-on nursing."

"Good for you. I'm sure glad you're here for Nana." Lance was glad someone was, as he had been AWOL in his responsibilities.

Juliana took the dishcloth and wiped the table clean. She then wiped down the stovetop and counters. "All done. Olivia now has a clean kitchen to start her supper."

"I'd like to ask a favor." Lance waited for her response.

"Sure, what can I do for you?" Juliana washed out the dishcloth, squeezed it out, and left it to dry at the sink.

"Tell me if you see something I can do for Mom or Nana. I have extra funds now and want to help my folks out. But, I'm not sure how to go about that."

Juliana gazed at Lance with a slight frown. "I'm not sure how much help you're talking about, but I do know you have to do it carefully. Your folks are proud people and expect to pay their own way. They won't even let me pay rent. I try to give back by helping out with groceries and such."

Lance nodded. "That is probably why they have never let me know if they needed anything."

"No, I can't see your folks asking for help. They'll just work, make do, share with their neighbors, be content, and thankful for what they have."

"You mentioned Logan's school tuition. Do they still owe on that?"

"I'm sure they do. Logan works for your dad. He is also working for a couple of other ranchers this summer. He got a couple of small scholarships, but it's still expensive to go to college." Juliana smiled. "I should know. I'll be paying off my school loans until I retire."

"The other thing is if you could recommend a doctor for me to have in case one of the children has a need. I hope not to need one, but I'd rather be prepared."

"Sure, I can do that. There are a couple of good pediatricians in Fredericksburg. Well, I have to get going to my afternoon appointments. I'll be back for supper. On Thursday, I'll work with Nana again. We are doing three sessions a week for right now."

"I'll look forward to seeing you at supper. It was good to meet someone who has done so much for my family." Lance surprised himself by how much he wished this pretty nurse were not leaving for the afternoon.

"I'll go tell Olivia and Nana goodbye." She disappeared into the hallway and Lance was left leaning against the kitchen counter thinking about their conversation. Did she have a boyfriend? He couldn't believe where his thoughts were going. What was wrong with him? He was still a married man and she knew it.

Chapter 8

Supper had been fun with Logan and Alex coming in from the range. Lance couldn't take in how much the boys had grown into young men. Both were tall and rangy and with appetites to match having spent a day in the saddle riding fence. They teased Mark and promised to play ball with him in the next day or two. It surprised Lance that Logan and Alex both wanted to hold Sara Hope. Again, he was reminded how much he had missed by not coming to visit his family and how much his son had missed.

As supper was ending, Logan stood behind his chair at the dining table. "You going to be around for a few days, Lance?"

Lance glanced up at Logan. When had his younger brother gotten so tall? "I'll be here a while."

"Great! Maybe you can explain to me how you can make money from a computer program."

Standing next to Logan, Alex was only a few inches shorter. He grinned at Lance with a look that reminded him of Mark. "Hey, that's a good idea. I like working on the ranch but I need more money so I can buy me some wheels like your truck. That's one sweet ride."

"Thanks, I thought so which is why I bought it." Was this tall slender young man an example of how Mark would look in eight to ten years? It was still hard to believe that these two young men had been just boys the last time he had seen them. Another reason for staying in the Hill Country was to get acquainted with his younger brothers.

Logan turned his attention to his dad. "May we borrow the truck to go into town, Dad?"

Before Hank could respond, Olivia spoke up. "This is Lance's first evening home. Shouldn't you boys stick around and visit some?"

"Well, maybe ..." Logan's voice held a disappointed tone.

Lance shook his head. "Don't stay home on my account. The children need to head for bed early and I won't be far behind. It's been a long day. Remember we're still operating on California time."

Hank pulled a set of keys off a hook by the back door. "You know the rules, no one else rides in the truck, and you put some gas into it."

Logan took the keys from his dad's hand. "Sure, Dad, we know the rules. Come on Alex. Let's go."

Alex followed his brother out the back door.

Walt chuckled. "That was quick, Hank. They didn't want to give you time to change your mind."

Lance remembered doing the same thing to his folks when he was in high school. "When he says, go into town, is he talking about Tumbleweed or Fredericksburg?"

Olivia started putting food away. "Oh, they're only going to the Dairy Queen in Tumbleweed. That's where the young people gather in the evenings. They will sit on the hood of their trucks, eat ice cream, and tell tales. You know, like all of you kids have done. They'll be home by nine or ten ready to fall into bed. Hank expects them to be up and working by five in the morning. It makes for a long day."

Lance looked at Mark and Sara Hope. "Speaking of bed, I need to get these kids started in that direction."

"But, Dad, it's still light outside." Mark protested.

"By the time you get a shower, read a while, you'll be ready for sleep and it will be dark."

Hank carried dishes over to the sink. "Olivia, you go help Lance with kiddos and I'll do dishes."

Juliana jumped up and started gathering dirty dishes from the table. "I'll help you Hank."

Lance lifted Sara Hope from her infant seat. She needed changing and a bottle. "Mom, would you mind heating up a bottle for Sara Hope? She can wait until in the morning for a bath."

"Let me feed her and you go take care of Mark.

Mark was asleep by the third page of the book he had chosen for Lance to read to him. Lance laid the book on the bedside table and pulled up the covers around Mark's shoulders. Mark turned over onto his side with a sigh as if he could now totally relax. Lance turned down the lamp until it was dimly lit and would serve as a nightlight. He looked down at Sara Hope in the crib that had been the one for all of the McTavish children. Both children had dropped off into a deep sleep easily.

Entering the family room Lance found his parents and grandparents sitting in various easy chairs. Hank and Walt were watching a baseball game on the old small TV that Lance remembered from his high school years. Dad's birthday was coming up and a big screen TV might be a good gift. Olivia and Nana each had some type of handwork they were working on as they tolerated their menfolk's involvement in the game. He guessed Juliana had already gone up to her room on the third floor. It seemed strange to have such a beautiful woman staying at the ranch. He wanted to get to know her better, but was glad to have just his family to talk to this evening.

Lance sat down in an empty leather recliner that had seen better days. All the furniture in this room was familiar, even the placement hadn't changed much since he had been in high school. He felt transported back in time.

Hank turned off the TV after a nod from his father and turned his attention to Lance. "It's good to have you home, son."

"It's wonderful to be home. I should have come sooner." Lance stared at his tensely gripped hands in his lap. He found it hard to make eye contact with those he knew he was about to disappoint.

"Grandson," Lance looked up at Grandpapa who was leaning forward and stared at Lance like a hawk targeting a prey. "You seem burdened about something."

Lance sighed. His grandpapa had always been tuned into his thinking. Lance had never gotten away with anything with the older man. Glancing around at these wise, good people, Lance wanted to weep. He cleared his throat. "I've got something I need to tell you all." He swallowed down a desire to throw up. He wanted to run out of the room and keep running, anything not to have to tell them of his complete failure in his marriage.

Hank nodded. "Just tell what you want, son."

"I don't want to tell you all but you need to know. I need your help and you can't help me and the children if you don't know." He took a deep breath and plunged in to it. "Chandra has left me and filed for divorce."

Olivia fisted her hand and pressed it over her heart. "Oh Lance, I'm so sorry."

Lance could feel their distress and saw it on their faces. "I didn't have a clue. She went to Germany for a long business trip and the day the sale of my business was final had me served with divorce papers. She has met someone else. I didn't even know she wasn't happy in our marriage."

Hank rubbed the back of his neck. "What does she want?"

Olivia glanced at her husband. "What do you mean? Lance said she wants a divorce."

Lance spoke up. "I know what you're asking, Dad. What does she want as a divorce settlement? Well, she doesn't want anything. Evidently, the man she is with is wealthy. I'm guessing he's European. I don't really know."

Walt slowly massaged his left hand. Lance recalled his grandfather had broken it when Lance was a small boy. He remembered how the cast had fascinated him.

Speaking slowly and softly Walt asked, "What about the children? Since they are here with you ...?"

Lance nodded. "She doesn't want the children. She'll not try for any custody unless I oppose the divorce. So I have already signed the papers. She set up residency in Nevada. I'm not sure how long the divorce takes after the papers are signed, but I'm guessing not long. I signed the papers last week. I don't have a choice. If I don't sign she said she would come after Mark."

Nana turned toward Walt with a distressed look.

He got up and moved over to the chair where she was sitting. Putting an arm around her shoulders, he said, "Now, honey, don't get upset. Lance has done what was the best thing he could do for him and for those babies. He came home."

Taking the handkerchief from her husband, the older woman turned back to Lance. "You all right Lance?"

He wiped his eyes trying to keep a grip on his emotions. "Now that I'm home I will be. This has hit me hard. How could I not have known? And, what did I do wrong to cause Chandra to take such a step? What I really can't get my head around is how she could leave the children."

Olivia got up and walked over to him. "I need a hug."

Lance stood, opened his arms, and gathered his mom into them. "I need a hug worse."

Hank put his arms around both of them. "Son, you know you are welcome here for as long as you need."

"Thanks, Dad. I want to come home. Maybe buy a place nearby. I'm not going to make any rash decisions. I want to spend time with my children and find my center again."

Hank stepped back and made room for his father to move closer to Lance.

Walt took Lance's hands. "You need to get your hands dirty, ride a horse, and get close to the land. Take your time and spend some time thinking about what you want to do."

Lance heard the love and concern from all their comments. For some reasons, he felt worse.

Nana leaned forward in her rocking chair. "Grandson, come here."

He disengaged from his mom's hug and knelt in front of his nana.

She cupped his face with her hands. "You look so tired and sad. After your grandpapa says a prayer, you need to go take a shower and go to bed. Sleep in tomorrow morning and don't worry about the children. We'll take care of them."

"Thanks Nana. I love you so much."

She ran her hand over his brow and smoothed his hair. "It'll be okay, Lance. You're home now."

Walt walked up to the back of the chair where his wife sat. He put his hands on her shoulders. "Let's pray.

Most Holy Father in heaven, we come to you with sadness for our family and especially Lance and the children. Be with them as they find a way to deal with all this. Help us to help Lance and especially the children who have lost their mother. I don't know what to ask for Chandra. We care for her and want what you want for her. Help her to understand her responsibility to her family and especially to her children. Be with us all as we try to do what pleases you. Forgive us our failings and give us peace through the name of Jesus the Christ, Amen."

Lance stood and gave his grandpapa a hug. "Thanks, I haven't heard anyone pray for me in a long time. I need it."

Walt patted him on the back. "Go on up to bed and tomorrow things will look better."

"I think I will. I'm really tired as I haven't slept much lately." He felt drained and felt as if his legs could collapse. All he wanted now was a bed.

After taking a quick shower, Lance crawled into bed wearing a tee shirt and pajama bottoms. He anticipated needing to get up several times in the night with Sara Hope. He had set the baby monitor up in the children's room and his bedroom so he could hear it.

He tried to stop his thoughts that seemed to be going round and round. It was a relief that his parents and grandparents now knew what was going on. Grandpapa's prayer had been comforting and the way he had included Chandra showed how much Lance's family could care for and forgive others. He missed his wife, he missed who he had thought he was as a man, and he missed the vision of what he thought his future would be. Suddenly Lance found himself sobbing and all the tears that had been swimming just under the surface for days came flooding out in a grief that came from a depth of despair and loss.

Chapter 9

Lance woke the next morning to a brightly lit sun-filled room. He stretched out in the bed he had slept in while growing up and that was long enough for his tall frame. Sitting up on the side of the bed, he listened for the children, but the house was quiet. He pulled on a clean pair of jeans and a long-sleeved cotton shirt and made his way to the hall bathroom where he shaved and washed up. Looking in the mirror as he ran a comb through his hair, he noticed that he looked more rested than he had in a week. A good night of sleep was what he had needed.

He listened for sounds of his children again but heard only the sounds of birds chirping in the trees outside the windows. Had Sara Hope slept through the night, or had he not heard her?

After pulling on and lacing his boots, Lance lightly ran down the stairs and then entered the big kitchen. His mom was at the stove and Sara Hope was in a playpen that had been set up in the corner of the room by the table.

"Morning, Lance, you hungry?" Olivia gave him a kiss on the cheek. "Did you sleep all right?"

Lance returned the kiss on the cheek. "I slept great. The best night's sleep in weeks and I'm hungry." He went over, picked up Sara Hope, and nuzzled her hair. "Hi, baby girl."

Sara Hope gave him a sloppy grin as she took her wet finger out of her mouth and ran it down his face. "Mom, did you get up last night with Sara Hope?"

"Yes, I was up anyway and looked in on her. She was laying there wide-awake and the minute she saw me scrunched up her little face and started to cry. I didn't see any need to wake you when I could take care of her. Come sit

77

down and your breakfast will be ready in a minute. You can start with a cup of coffee."

Lance carried Sara Hope with him and sat at the kitchen table. "Thanks, Mom, for the breakfast and for taking care of Sara Hope."

She placed a plate of fried eggs, bacon, gravy, and biscuits in front of him. "You don't have to thank me, sweetheart. It's a joy to be taking care of a baby again. Your children are beautiful. I should be thanking you for such a wonderful gift."

"Yes, Mark and Sara Hope are something good that has come out of the mess with Chandra."

His mom poured herself a cup of coffee, carried it to the table, and sat down. "Let me hold Sara Hope so you can eat."

Lance handed the baby to his mom. "Where's Mark?"

Olivia smoothed the curls on the baby's head. "He's out at the barn with Grandpapa taking care of the horses. He was up as soon as Hank and Walt and ready to go."

Lance shook his head. "I hope he's not too underfoot." Lance wanted his son to have a chance to be around his grandfather and great-grandfather. The older men in the family had so much wisdom to share and being kind Christian men would take care of Mark.

Olivia gently rocked Sara Hope as the baby contently sat in her lap. "Don't you worry about that. His granddad and grandpapa will keep him busy. Tell me about you, Lance. I didn't ask questions last night because I knew it was difficult for you to talk about what is going on with Chandra."

"I'm still trying to get used to the idea that my marriage is over. Thankfully, my business sold when it did. I need to give Mark and Sara Hope my full attention. I still can't believe Chandra left not only me but also the children. What would make a woman do that, Mom?"

Shaking her head and enfolding the baby even closer, she said, "I cannot imagine what she is thinking. I'd never give up one of my children. To turn her back on children as precious as Mark and Sara Hope is beyond my understanding. I can only pray for her to come to her senses. When do you have to go back to California? Can you stay awhile?"

"I sold my business completely. I guess you could say I'm unemployed. A management company is looking after the house. I haven't decided what to do with it, but for now I don't want to be there." Lance got up, poured himself another cup of coffee, and refreshed the cup in front of his mother.

"What will you do, son, if you don't go back to the house in San Jose?"

Lance looked out the big kitchen window toward the soft rolling hills of the ranch. "For a while I would like to take my time and get to know my family again." He watched his mom's eyes sparkle as she cooed back at Sara Hope who was giving her a toothless smile. "Then I had thought about looking around in this area for a place to buy and maybe do some ranching."

His mom looked up at him with an excited expectant look. "You mean, to stay here close to home?"

"Yes, I've decided to come back to Texas and raise my children here close to you all. Mark and Sara Hope need their grandparents."

"Well, we need to be close to you and the children. Have you told your father?"

"Not really. I mentioned it last night. I haven't had a chance to talk to Dad or Grandpapa. I want their advice. I have the money to purchase a place but I'm a computer program developer, not a rancher."

His mom laughed softly. "You may have left for several years but being a rancher is in your blood. You haven't forgotten what you learned from your dad and grandfather, I'm sure."

Lance nodded. "That's what I'm hoping. And I'd like to not rush into anything, so if you don't mind I'd like to stay here for a while."

"Of course I don't mind. If I had my way, you wouldn't even look for a place but stay here from now on. Abby will be home in a few weeks. Although, I expect she'll only be here until she can get a job. Logan is only here through the summer and then he'll be returning to school, the Lord willing."

"Is there a doubt he'll go back?" Lance was surprised, as he knew how important it was to his parents that all their children get a college education.

"Of course, he intends to go back. It's just that college is so expensive. He's working all he can this summer to save enough to register. And we had hoped to have more to give him, but with your grandmother being in the hospital and the extra expense of the longer physical therapy, our cash is being eaten up."

Guilt rippled through Lance as he thought of the millions he now had. However, he had to be careful how he shared it with his folks. Their independent spirit was strong. "What do you mean extra expense of the physical therapy?"

"Oh, you know how medical expenses are. They'll only authorize so many sessions. Juliana told us your grandmother would do better if she continued for several weeks after the authorized ones. She offered to do them for free, but that's not right as she has to make a living and is paying off heavy school debts. Nana is like a grandmother to her and Juliana would do anything for her. Your dad insisted we pay her in advance so as not to take advantage of her."

Lance thought of the attractive young woman with the open cheerful face. Even she had tried to do more for his family than he had. "Mom, I've got the funds. Let me pay for any medical care that Nana might need."

"Are you sure Lance? That would be such a help. Let's not tell your grandparents. They worry so about being a burden, especially Nana, but I don't know what I'd do without them."

"As soon as I make some phone calls, I plan to go find out what I can do to help around here. I won't be much good until I can get saddle broke again."

"Well, we keep that good horse liniment on hand to help with sore backsides."

Lance chuckled as he remembered using it after an especially long day in the saddle. "Mom, I need to ask you about something. The children's nanny, Rosa Real, will be coming in a week or so to help. She has been with us since Mark was an infant and has been more mother to them than Chandra. Her grandson is driving her out from California. Is there room for her here or do I need to find her a temporary place in town until I buy a place? I don't want us to crowd you all."

His mom frowned and was silent for a moment. Did she not want Rosa to help with the children?

"Lance, I can help take care of the children if necessary, but it sounds as if Rosa is a major part of their lives. And to tell the truth, with your grandmother being ill I can use the help. We have the room for her here in the house and it will be much more convenient. Do you think her grandson will mind sleeping in the old bunkhouse? It's in fair condition. The boys would prefer to sleep out there because they can come and go as they like and play their music as loud as they want. The only problem is that it's not air-conditioned and for the next few months will be very hot. But for a few nights they'll be fine and we can let Rosa's grandson sleep here in the house where we have air conditioning."

Lance remembered the year his dad had sold his cattle for a good price and had surprised his wife by installing central air and heating in the house. Before that, the summers had been a lot more uncomfortable. "I'll look over the bunkhouse and see what we might do about getting an air conditioner put in. I can understand Logan and Alex wanting to stay out there. I remember wanting to stay out there as a kid but back then we had several ranch hands and Dad wouldn't let me. Now I have Mark, I understand, but back then I didn't understand his wanting to watch over me."

His mom grinned. "Amazing what we learn as we get older. Well, I better get this baby into a dry diaper and down for her morning nap. I've also got to get lunch started."

"Here, hand her over to me. I can change her. Then I'll head out to see what's going on at the barn and see if I can make myself useful." Lance carried his dirty dishes to the sink full of soapy water and washed his breakfast dishes. Leaving them to dry on the drain rack he turned back and hefted Sara Hope from his mother's arms. "Come on baby girl. Let's go get you into something dry."

His mother shook her head. "I never thought to see you so taken with a baby, and a girl at that."

"Why not, Mom? Changing diapers is just a matter of practice. It's been several years but I got to be good at it with Mark. I changed a lot more of his diapers than Chandra ever did. Maybe that should have been a warning to me when she refused to get up at night with him. She would have let him lie all night in a wet diaper. I never could do that. She never intended to have another child but somehow because she had a bad cold and ran a fever the birth control pills weren't effective." He gave his daughter a kiss on her fat soft cheek. "And I can't help but be glad."

"In the midst of your trials, God has blessed you, son. Don't ever forget that."

Lance sighed and nodded. He did feel blessed when he looked at his children and the rest of his family. If only his wife had cared enough to stay around.

Chapter 10

After getting Sara Hope into dry clothes and fed a mid-morning bottle, he left her with his mom. As he started to cross the backyard toward the big barn, Juliana drove up in her little red pick-up.

"Good morning, Lance. What a beautiful day!" Smiling broadly, her whole face lit up with a joy of living.

Lance couldn't help but return the smile. "Yes, it sure is. Is this your first stop of the day?"

She laughed. "Not likely. My patients are mostly ranch people and start the day early. I've already been to three different ranches. I'm thankful that Nana doesn't mind doing her physical therapy later in the day."

Lance liked her sunny disposition and her friendliness. "I have to admit I slept in this morning and I'm just now starting my day. I didn't see Nana and didn't think to ask Mom where she was."

"She was probably lying down. I encourage her to rest both morning and afternoon. Laying on her bed reading or listening to the radio will rest her body in preparation for the physical therapy. Well, I've got to get to work. See you later, Lance."

"See you at lunch perhaps?" Lance really didn't want to let her go. It was foolish but he was attracted to her.

"Yes, I'll be here for lunch. I don't have another appointment until later in the afternoon. I timed Nana's appointment so I could have a break in the middle of the day. Olivia always insist I stay for lunch if I can, and truth be told, I enjoy spending time with your folks." She grabbed her bag and bounded up the steps, crossed the porch, and disappeared into the house.

Lance glanced around the ranch yard and toward the hills and valleys that spread out in every direction from the ranch buildings that set up on a slight hill. He could hear birds singing in the live oak trees that surrounded the ranch buildings. The sky was light blue with a few fluffy white clouds. The air was cool with a gentle breeze from the southwest. Later in the day, it would warm up.

Back of the ranch house was the big barn that had stood for a hundred years. Solidly built from logs from live oak trees with a shed to one side and a big corral to the other side, it was the center of much of the work of the ranch. Within the corral was a long metal trough filled with water piped in from the windmill and stock tank sitting back of the corral. The windmill was turning in the light breeze that was a constant in this part of the country, providing water for both the stock and irrigation. Lance turned his head and listened but didn't hear the sound of the deep well pump that he knew kept water flowing to the ranch house.

Off to the other side of the shed and back among the grove of live oaks was the old stone bunkhouse. It had been the original home place on the ranch. Built of native stone it blended into the landscape. Lance walked toward the old dwelling curious to see how it was doing with the passing of years. He had so many memories of spending time at the old stone bunkhouse when growing up. They had had a ranch foreman then who had let Lance follow him around.

The little porch needed swept but when he pushed open the unlocked door he was surprised to see the little four-room dwelling was clean and still furnished with bunks, couch and chairs in front of the fireplace, a table with chairs close to the propane cook stove, and fairly new cabinets. The front bedroom was crowded with two double beds, a nightstand, and a dresser. Behind the kitchen was the second small bedroom with a double bed and a dresser. Down the hallway was a bath complete with shower stall. As he looked around, he considered how air conditioning could be hooked up. It wouldn't be difficult to get the little house into shape for the boys to sleep in, including a large screen TV and satellite dish.

Lance pulled the door of the bunkhouse closed and listened to the sounds of laughter coming from the barn. He entered to find his son wrestling with a saddle almost as big as he was. Grandpapa and Dad were watching, grinning.

"What's going on here?" Lance couldn't keep the grin from his own face as he saw the delight in his son's face.

"Granddad said if I could saddle this horse I can ride it. But, I can't get the saddle high enough to go on the horse's back."

Lance raised an eyebrow at his dad and then turned his attention to his son. "Did he say you couldn't ask for help?"

Mark stood staggering to hold up the saddle by the patient old horse. "No... he didn't. Can you help me, Dad?"

Moving quickly to catch the saddle before it landed on the dirt floor of the barn, Lance grabbed it and swung it onto the horse's back. "Now, what do you do?" Lance waited to see if his son knew what to do next.

"Granddad, what do I do next?" Mark turned expectantly toward his grandfather.

Scratching his head, he responded, "Well, I reckon we need to put this saddle blanket on to protect the horse's back from the saddle. If we don't then the rubbing of the saddle will give the horse a sore back and that makes them cranky."

Mark looked at the saddle blanket and then up at the big horse. "Horses get cranky?"

The older man chuckled. "You better believe it. And they tell you if they are cranky."

Scratching his head at the edge of his hat just as he had seen his granddad do, Mark frowned. "But shouldn't the saddle blanket be under the saddle?" The boy looked expectantly at his dad for confirmation.

Lance couldn't keep the grin off his face. "Sure enough, son, the saddle blanket goes first. Let me lift off the saddle and you get that blanket hanging on the rails and smooth it on this horse's back." He lifted the saddle off the horse.

Mark grabbed the saddle blanket and managed to throw it onto the horse. He patted the blanket and smoothed it out. "Is that okay, Granddad?"

The older man ran his hand over the saddle blanket and nodded. "That's just right."

Lance put the saddle back on the horse.

Tipping his hat back, Grandpapa cleared his throat. "You going to leave all them straps dangling like that?"

Grinning at Lance, Granddad took pity on his grandson. "Let me show you how to get the saddle on tight so it won't slide on you." He quickly had the saddle clinched on and the stirrups at a length for a small boy.

"Thanks, Granddad. That seems hard."

"You'll learn how to do it soon enough, but it is time to get you in the saddle. Now you remember what I told you about being gentle with old Sally here. She's old but sensitive. Don't be jerking the reins around. Now let's lead her out into the corral and get you in the saddle."

"Yes, sir, I'll remember." Mark grinned as he followed his granddad and grandpapa out into the corral.

Lance quickly pulled his phone out of his shirt pocket and snapped a picture of the small boy and two older men leading the old horse out of the barn. He climbed to the top rail of the five-foot corral fence, hooked the heels of his boots on the second rail, and settled to watch his son's first ride. He felt tightness in his throat as he watched. How could Chandra not want to be a part of something like this?

"Okay, Mark, I'm going to set you up on old Sally." Hank lifted his grandson easily into the saddle. "Slide your feet into the stirrup, letting it catch against your boot heel. Now tighten your thighs against the horse. Feel how secure you are in the saddle."

Grandpapa lifted the reins and threaded them through the small hands of his great grandson. "For now just hold these and get a feel for them. I'm going to walk you around the corral. Old Sally just follows me, but to help you feel better, I'll hold onto her bridle. Ready?"

Mark had a frown and he was sitting stiff in the saddle. Lance kept snapping pictures he hoped captured his son's determination and the older men's kindness as they initiated his son into a rite of passage on the ranch, learning to ride. Mark was older than Lance had been when his father and grandfather had done the same for him. And it had been on a little pony he had been given for his fifth birthday. His mother and grandmother had watched from the porch of the ranch house.

Lance raised the cell phone and snapped a couple more shots as Mark turned and glanced at his father with a huge grin.

After two circles around the corral, Walt let go of the bridle and then stepped off to the side. "Just hold the reins easy and let your body sway with the motion of the horse. That's it, Mark. You're doing good."

Hank sauntered over to Lance and leaned against the rails of the corral fence. "You remember your first solo ride, Son?"

Lance nodded. "Yes, sir, I do. It was on my fifth birthday, on my pony, Chico." He ducked his head. "I'm sorry I haven't brought Mark to the ranch before this. He should have been riding a couple of years ago."

Hank slapped Lance's leg. "You're here now and that's what is important. You got a fine son there."

"Thanks, Dad. More now than ever before, I feel the responsibility to raise my children well. I didn't pay enough attention to my marriage, but I'm not going to do the same to my children."

Hank looked up at Lance, sitting on the top rail. "I don't know what happened in your marriage and I get the sense that you don't either. It's a hard blow for you but now you have the opportunity to do whatever you like with your life. Your mother and me, we'll do all we can to help. We love you, Son."

Lance soaked up his father's expression of concern and love. "Love you, too, Dad. Just wish I had been around to tell you and Mom that more often. But, now I hope to settle nearby and let you spend all the time you want with your grandchildren."

Hank turned his gaze back to his father and grandson. "I plan to spend more time with you as well as the grandchildren. I've missed you."

Lance's chest tightened with the sharp edge of regret. He wasn't used to his father being so open about his feelings. He had a lot to make up for but this morning was a good beginning.

"Hey, Dad. Look, I'm riding all by myself," Mark shouted.

Laughing at the exuberant joy in Mark's voice, Lance snapped a couple more photos. The morning riding lesson was a memory maker for all of them.

Walt guided old Sally back to the barn entrance and Hank lifted Mark out of the saddle,

Mark gazed up at his grandfather and great-grandfather. "When can I ride again?"

Hank tipped Mark's hat down. "This ride isn't over yet. A cowboy is not finished with his ride until his horse is taken care of. Now we unsaddle, brush old Sally down, and make sure she has feed and water."

"Okay, what do I do first?" Mark's voice was filled with the excitement from his first ride and he beamed at everyone around him..

Hank handed Mark the reins. "You lead old Sally into her stall and I'll help you take care of her." They disappeared into the barn.

Walt wandered over to Lance. "Let's go walk about the place a bit and I'll tell you all the changes."

Lance jumped down from his seat on the rail and put his phone back into his shirt pocket. "I'd like that, Grandpapa."

"I need to check on the windmill and stock tank. We can start there." The older man led the way beyond the corral toward the big windmill that was softly creaking in the breeze.

"I remember when you and Dad built that windmill after the old one refused to be repaired." Lance shortened his stride to match Grandpapa's slow walk. At seventy-eight-years old, he was still strong and active but he wasn't moving as fast as Lance remembered from when he was a boy.

Walt laughed. "Refused to be repaired is a real good way to describe that old windmill. It had stood and worked for almost a hundred years but one day it stopped. Of course, it would be in the middle of July when it was as hot as blazes. Your dad and me, we went to work and got a new one up and running. We had to or the cattle would have suffered. Even as young as you were, you helped out all you could."

Lance remembered how concerned the men were because it was a dry year and they needed the water the windmill brought up out of the well. "I had just finished my first year in school. I remembered being so proud to work with the grown men."

Grandpapa put his hand on Lance's shoulder as they walked across the pasture toward the windmill. "What now Lance? You thought about what you want to do now that you have sold your company? You going to keep working in computers and start another company in California?"

Grandpapa had always been direct in his talk, getting to the point without beating around the bush. Lance appreciated that, although it could be uncomfortable.

"I'm sort of done with managing a company. I was good at it and it surely did pay off. But, it cost too much time away from the family. I want something different now."

"What would that be?"

"I want to build a home for my children and to get back to my roots. I'm going to look around here in the hill country for a ranch of my own. I've got the funds and I want to see if I can be a rancher like my dad and grandpapa." Lance smiled. "They have a pretty good life and gave me a great childhood. I want to do the same for Mark and Sara Hope."

They reached the windmill and Grandpapa checked the pump and water flow into the stock tank. "You remember how to climb up to the platform and replace the oil?"

Lance gazed up at the platform a good thirty feet from the ground. "You take out the plug, drain the old oil, and flush it with kerosene very carefully. When it's all cleaned up replace the plug from the hub and pour the fresh oil into the gear case."

Grandpapa nodded once. "You do remember. You want to climb up there and get it done? I was going to do it, but I'd rather let you."

Lance chuckled. "You just want someone else to climb up there. Where are the supplies?"

"Here in this storage bin. I dropped off the fresh oil and rags the other day but haven't gotten back to do the job."

Lance again looked at the climb in front of him and worried that his seventy-eight-year old grandpapa had really planned to do it himself. Picking up the bucket he would use to bring the old oil down, he grabbed the quart of fresh oil, kerosene, and rags and placed them in the bucket.

Grandpapa slipped a screwdriver, a part of pliers, and small hammer into Lance's back pockets. "Don't want you to climb up there and then have to climb back for the right tools. Now be careful. You get hit by the blades up there and Olivia and Edna will have my hide."

"How can I get hit by the blades if you turn the wheel out of the wind?"

Grandpapa grinned as he turned the crank to tilt the wheel out of the wind. The blades gradually stopped moving.

Lance hung the bucket over his forearm so he could climb to the platform using both hands. After he checked to make sure the platform was solid enough to hold his weight and didn't have any rotten boards, he climbed up on it, and set to work. It took him awhile to drain the old oil and flush out the casing. He made sure not to overfill with fresh oil and then carefully put the gasket and plug back together. Once he had the oil changed, he wiped up any oil that might have spilled and around every metal part he had touched. Satisfied he had the job done, he wiped his forehead that was dripping sweat. The day had definitely turned out to be a hot one.

He took a minute to look out over the ranch from the height of the platform and reveled in the beauty of the vast western hill country. The ranch was a beautiful place and returning home had been a good thing to do.

"You fall asleep up there?" Grandpapa had his hand shading his eyes as he squinted up at Lance.

"No, just enjoying the view." Lance stuffed the dirty rags and empty oilcan down his shirt, put the tools back into his jean pockets, and picked up the bucket with the old oil. Now he remembered the part of this job he had hated as a kid. Climbing down one handed, carrying a bucket of oil.

"Well, Lance, you going to come on down? It's time for my dinner and your mom is going to ring the dinner bell any minute."

Lance felt his own stomach rumbling. When was the last time he had been hungry after doing a hard physical job? He was hot, sweaty, dirty, and starting to ache from the unusual exertion, but he hadn't felt as good in a long time. Slowly and carefully, he climbed down the tower of the windmill. Once he reached the ground, he couldn't keep from grinning.

"That was fun, Grandpapa, thanks for letting me do it."

"Well, I'm glad you enjoyed it. I'm glad it wasn't me up there with the heat of this day. Let's get back to the house, get cleaned up, and eat." Walt turned the crank to reposition the blades back into the wind, which then began to turn.

Lance handed Grandpapa the rags and empty oil container while he hefted the bucket of old oil. "You all still keep a metal barrel in the shed by the barn for old oil?"

"Amazed you remember that old barrel. We take it to the recycling place in Fredericksburg now to empty it."

"I'll empty this old oil and put away the bucket."

They walked slowly and Lance was careful not to spill any of the oil.

"You know, Lance, you could always stay here on the ranch. You and the children are welcome to make your home here."

Lance took a deep breath, wanting to say the right things after such a generous offer. "Thanks, Grandpapa. I thought of that but I know one of my brothers may want to do that. You and Dad have partnered together so many years and you don't need me to butt in. Since I have the means, I want my own place. And I'd like to help out in some way here, but I don't want to move in directions that will offend."

"What do you mean offend?" Grandpapa stopped walking and stared at Lance.

Lance stopped and looked toward the house and barn. "Well, I'd like to help upgrade some things like in the kitchen and help make it easier financially. I have extra funds I want to use for my family. But, I don't want to come in like I know better than you and Dad."

Grandpapa shrugged and started walking again. "I see what you mean and you're right to be cautious as Hank doesn't want your money. He wants you and the grandchildren to be a part of our family. I won't say that some cash influx wouldn't be helpful. Let me think on it and talk to Hank."

"Thanks Grandpapa."

"And about a place for you and the children, let me ask around and see what might be available. You want to buy or lease?"

They walked to the shed off from the barn and Grandpapa opened the door. Lance entered and spotted the old metal barrel. He set the bucket down, pulled the screwdriver out of his pocket, and pried up the lid. He carefully poured the old oil into the barrel without splashing the oil back onto himself.

"Set the bucket under that shelf for the next job that requires catching old oil." Grandpapa took the pliers and Lance stored the bucket.

"You know, Grandpapa, unless I find the perfect place immediately, the idea of leasing a place is not a bad one. I hadn't considered that. I do want to be sure before I spend a bunch of money."

"That's what I was thinking. And don't feel in a hurry. We want you and the children here for a while so we can get some time together. Especially Olivia and Edna will want to spoil those kids a bit."

Lance grinned. "I think maybe you're right as usual."

Just then they heard the dinner bell from the back porch calling them to come in and eat.

Lance stomped his feet before entering the kitchen from the porch. Juliana was at the kitchen counter cutting a loaf of fresh baked bread.

His mom turned to greet him and waved a spoon at him with which she had been stirring something on the stove. "Lance McTavish, what have you been doing? You're filthy and not two hours ago you left this kitchen in a clean new shirt and jeans and now look at you."

Hank and Mark came into the kitchen from the living room.

Lance looked down at his shirt and jeans. They were covered in dirt and even some streaks of oil. He hadn't realized he had been so messy.

Grandpapa put his hat on the usual hook. "Leave the boy alone, Olivia. He's been doing some honest work."

Hank leaned up against the doorframe. "And what would that be, Pa?"

Grandpapa grinned. "He climbed the windmill and changed out the oil for us."

Lance placed his own hat on the hook next to Grandpapa's hat. "And I did a good job if I do say so myself. The last time I did that I was maybe eighteen years old."

Hank frowned. "I told you I'd get around to that in a few days, Pa."

Grandpapa started walking down the hall toward the bathroom. "And now you don't have to. The boy did a good job with no complaints like he used to do as a kid."

Olivia brushed Lance's cheek with a light kiss, being careful not to brush up against his dirty clothes. "Thank you, dear, for helping out. I always worry if I know they are going to be climbing up that thing. Now go grab a quick shower and then we'll be ready to eat."

Lance winked at Juliana and sneaked a couple of slices of the fresh bread. "On my way." He gave Mark a piece of bread as he passed him and bounded up the stairs.

Olivia laughed and shook her head. "That boy, he was always trying to sneak food."

Chapter 11

Juliana tried not to stare as Lance came into the kitchen from working on the ranch. He was disheveled, sweaty, dirty, and still looked great in a blue chambray shirt, jeans, and lace up boots. Evidently, he had wiped his face with hands covered in oil as he had streaks on his forehead and down one cheek. Why she even noticed she wasn't sure. Every time she thought of the man, she reminded herself that he was married.

She grinned at Mark munching on the slice of fresh-baked bread as if it was a sweet snack. "You like that?"

Mark grinned at her. "Yes, ma'am. I never had such good bread before."

Juliana returned his grin. "It was baked this morning by your great-grandmother."

"You mean she made it? She didn't get it from the store?" Mark seemed bewildered.

"Your grandmother and great-grandmother both cook and bake. Haven't you ever had homemade loaf bread before?"

"No, they make their own bread? Like Rosa makes cinnamon rolls?"

Juliana nodded. "Yes, just like that. You want to help me set the table for dinner?" She almost laughed at the eager look on the little boy's face. She was already coming to love this bright little boy.

"All right. What do I do?"

Juliana spent the next ten minutes teaching the eight year old how to set the table. She noticed that Olivia kept glancing at them with a gentle smile as she worked to get the dinner cooked. Mark acted as if he had been given a treat to be allowed to help place the plates, silverware, and napkins.

Later as they all set around the table passing the heaping platters and bowls of food, Juliana tried to keep her glance away from the freshly showered Lance with his dark hair still damp and curling. After the meal and helping do the dishes, Juliana gathered her things and set off for her next appointments.

In a way, it was a relief to get away from the McTavish Ranch and the strong attraction to a married man. Juliana turned up the radio that was set on the country station out of Fredericksburg to distract her from the direction of her thoughts. Juliana thought over her dating history. She had dated some in high school and college but she had never had a serious relationship. Too much effort and time had gone into schooling, and working to pay for that schooling, to have time to develop anything but friendships with young men. She had always been careful to date only young men she met at church as her mother had always warned her that people tended to marry those they dated. She could still hear her mother's voice. *Date the right young men and you will marry the right young man.* Juliana hoped someday to learn if that was true. However, she was in no hurry to get married, preferring to leave it in God's hands.

~

Wednesday morning Juliana headed to Fredericksburg to do some shopping, on her day off. She worked every other Saturday to accommodate patients who worked and she needed to see on the weekend, mostly patients who had to have IV medication for one reason or another. She liked having a weekday to get some of her own chores done.

Her first stop was the western wear store. Next week was Hank's birthday and she planned to get him a shirt. Looking up from a stack of cotton/polyester plaid long-sleeve shirts, she spotted Lance also searching through a stack of shirts.

"Well, good morning." She smiled as he glanced around at her with a surprised expression.

"Juliana, morning, I didn't expect to see anyone I know."

"This is my day off and I'm actually shopping for a birthday gift for Hank. Olivia told me that he needed shirts and what type and size." She pointed to the two shirts she had picked out.

Lance nodded. "I've been thinking about what to get him. I'm picking up some extra shirts and jeans for Mark and me. I realized we didn't have enough ranch clothes not to have to do laundry every other day. The clothes I normally wore in California for work won't do out on the ranch."

"I hadn't thought about that but I can see how you would need different clothes." Juliana wondered how long he planned to stay with the number of shirts and pairs of jeans she noticed in the basket he carried.

"Maybe you can help me with a few things if you have time?"

"What would that be?" Juliana couldn't imagine anything she could help him with.

"Two things really. The children's nanny is coming next week with her grandson. Mom suggested the boys could stay in the old house but I need to get some air conditioning put in. The other thing I need to get is the ranch house and old house set up with a satellite dish and wired for the internet and wireless. I'm a computer guy and cannot exist without my fast speed internet. Also, I thought I might get Dad a large screen TV and high speed optical connection so he and Grandpapa could watch their sports."

Juliana grinned. "He'll like that. Oh, he may fuss about the expense but he'll love watching his Texas Rangers on a large screen. But, how can I help?"

"You can show me where to go to get some of this stuff and who to call to get someone out to set up the equipment. I vaguely remember there being a local appliance store here in town, but I can't remember where or what it's called."

Juliana stared at Lance for a few moments before answering. This might not be the wisest thing to do but it was something she wanted to do. "I've got a couple of hours free. I'll be glad to go around town with you to show you were to shop."

Lance's face, which she realized had been sad looking, lit up with a smile. "That would be great. Let's check out of here and start with the air conditioning."

After they paid for their purchases, Lance led the way to his truck. "I'll bring you back for your pickup after we finish shopping."

He opened the passenger side door of his truck and made sure Juliana settled into the passenger seat. She wasn't used to having a man being so gentlemanly. After he stowed his packages in the back seat he got into the truck and started it. "Where to, navigator?"

"Let's start at the air conditioning place as you start out of town on Hwy 290." Juliana gave Lance a few directions. She glanced around the obviously new truck. Compared to her little pickup, this was the most luxurious truck she had ever ridden in. She couldn't image what it cost. Taking a deep breath, she enjoyed the new truck smell. Within minutes, they had arrived at the air conditioning store. Nothing was far apart in Fredericksburg.

Lance pulled into a parking place without other vehicles close by.

Before she could get the seatbelt undone, Lance was out of the truck and around opening the passenger door. She took his hand as he guided her onto the cab step and then down to the pavement. Lance closed the door and the cab step retracted back under the truck as he clicked the lock for the vehicle.

Lance opened the door to the store and waited for Juliana to enter into the cool interior. The day was starting to heat up.

A middle-aged man walked up to them. "Hi, I'm Mike. How can we help you folks?"

Lance tipped his hat. "Hi, Mike. Need some help in getting an old rock house air conditioned and heated. Think you can help us?"

"Absolutely, tell me about the place and I'll be able to make recommendations." Mike rubbed his hands together.

Juliana listened as Lance described the old house and the need to get both central air and heat put in quickly. Within thirty minutes, Lance had purchased a central air and heating unit and signed a contract for the installation. He talked Mike into taking care of the special wiring that would be needed, for a price of course. Lance handed over a credit card.

Mike rubbed his jaw. "This is going to cost several thousand."

Lance nodded. "Check with the card company to make sure the charge will go through. Also while you're out at the ranch I want you to do a diagnostic on the ranch house system and make sure it is in good working order."

Mike took the credit card. "Wait just a moment and let me check this out." He walked back to an office at the back of the store.

Lance glanced at Juliana. "Sorry about you having to stand around. This won't take but a few more minutes."

She smiled. "No problem, it was fun to watch someone spend money without worrying about the cost."

"Next I want to go to a store that handles large screen TVs."

"Okay, there's a general appliance store just up the road, back toward town."

"Then after that maybe you'll let me buy you lunch in appreciation for your time. I would like to pass a couple of ideas by you on how to help Logan with his schooling." Lance gave her his full attention and kept his gaze on her face.

Juliana turned toward the back of the store as Mike was making his way toward them. "You don't have to buy me lunch but I'd be happy to go with you."

Mike walked up and handed back the credit card. "Your card is good Mr. McTavish for whatever amount you want to put on it. But, of course you knew that."

Lance put the card back into his billfold. "Yes, I did but I understand you wanting to be sure before driving all the way out to the ranch and doing the work."

"I checked with our technical people and we can start tomorrow. It may take a couple of days depending on how much wiring we have to do." Mike handed Lance a copy of the order.

Lance took the paper, folded it up, and put it into his back jean pocket. "We'll be looking for you. You've got my cell number if you need directions."

Juliana spent the next hour helping Lance pick out two large screen TVs, one for his dad and one to put in the old house ranch house for the boys. Again, he had arranged for installation. Juliana wasn't sure how he was able to get the satellite service to promise to have it installed by the weekend but she suspected that he promised a bonus. He also picked up a microwave for the old house.

After Lance mentioned he wanted to eat some Tex-Mex food, Juliana recommended they stop at Mamacitas for lunch. The restaurant was crowded but they found a table for two.

Lance looked up from the menu at the waitress and then at Juliana. "What will you have?"

"I would like the chicken fajita quesadillas with sweet tea." Julia nodded at the waitress.

"And you, sir?" The pretty, young waitress stood patiently waiting to write down his order.

"I'll have the Sour Cream Enchiladas and an order of Nachos al Carbon with both chicken and beef fajitas." He handed the menu back. "Oh, and sweet tea."

"I'll get your tea now and your order will be out shortly." The waitress quickly made her way to the kitchen.

Lance placed his western hat upside down on the crown in one of the extra chairs at the table. "It's strange how it has been years since I regularly wore a hat. But, the minute I decided to come back to Texas I went looking for a western hat. I remember Dad and Grandpapa telling me to always place it crown down on a flat surface." Lance chuckled. "And to always tip my hat at a lady that I pass on the sidewalk. Those admonitions didn't seem to fit in California but here in the Hill Country they seem to be automatic."

Juliana nodded. "When we go back to our childhood homes, we tend to revert back to old thinking and habits. I walk into my mom's kitchen and the first thing I do is wash my hands at the sink, whether they need it or not."

Lance smiled. "It feels good to be home and fall back into some of the old patterns. I hope to teach Mark and for him to have an opportunity to learn from his granddad and great-grandpa."

"Well, he couldn't have better role models. Mark is a wonderful little boy. I'm really enjoying getting to know him. And, of course, Sara Hope is a precious little bundle of joy."

"Thanks for saying that. To me they're treasures I don't deserve, but I'll do what I can to take care of. That's why I brought them home to Texas after my wife left me."

"Your wife has left you?" She tried not to show her surprise and to keep it out of her voice.

Lance frowned. "I thought you knew. My family knows. She left me and the children for another man."

"She doesn't want the children?" This time Juliana couldn't keep the shock from her voice.

"No, she doesn't want Mark or Sara Hope. If we have to divorce, then I want my children. But, I grieve for them that their mother has abandoned them."

"I'm so sorry, Lance. I'm sure this is a grief for you, too." Juliana fought to keep back tears as she thought of the breakup of a family. "Did you seek counseling before she left?"

Lance sighed. "No, I didn't even know we had a problem until she had already left with another man. I didn't know there was another man. We weren't fighting or even arguing. But, I spent a lot of time at work getting my company ready to sell. She traveled a lot with her work. I'm sure it was mostly my fault, but I just didn't know."

Juliana could hear from Lance's voice and see in his eyes the heartbreak he was suffering. She reached out and placed her hand on his arm. "Would you have tried to save the marriage if you had the chance?"

Lance answered instantly. "Yes, of course I would have. I'd have gone to marriage counseling, quit my work, done anything I could. I love my wife and would not ever have wanted to take their mother away from the children. My first warning was the delivery of divorce papers. I didn't even know where my wife was or how to call her. She didn't even say goodbye to Mark. All I could think to do was come home to the ranch. Come home to Mom and Dad and the family."

"You did the right thing for both yourself and for the children. They will get a lot of unconditional love on the ranch."

Taking a long swig of his iced tea, Lance seemed to close up somewhat. "Enough about me and my problems, I didn't mean to dump all that on you."

"I'm glad you did. Now I understand better how to pray for you."

Lance wiped his eyes with his napkin. The server arrived with their food and after she left the table he took Juliana's hand. "Let's pray a blessing for the food."

After he had said a short blessing for the food and dug into his meal, he said, "I wanted to ask you something about Logan and his schooling."

Juliana sensed he was embarrassed to have been so open with her and wanted to move to other topics. "Sure. What about Logan?"

"I have the funds to pay for his schooling and would have already been doing it, but I was so tied up with my life I wasn't aware of the need. Every time I've called in the last few years, I've always asked Dad how things were going and he always said that everything was fine. But, now that I'm home, and can see some things for myself, I realize they have been strapped for cash for some time."

Juliana nodded. "Yes, they have. Your family works hard but it's difficult to make a living as a rancher. Cattle prices have been down, and then with so many dry years in a row, they had to sell some of cattle at rock bottom prices. Cattle prices are going up but your dad doesn't have many cattle to sell now."

"How can I give Logan money for his schooling without Dad thinking I'm trying to take over? He has never accepted money from me."

"I have an idea that might work. You know colleges accept donations to fund scholarships all the time. You can fund a scholarship anonymously and request the university offer it to Logan. Give it a name like, Hill Country Student Scholarship."

Lance smiled, which took away some of his sad look. "That's a great idea. I can give enough to make it cover all expenses for the next four years and even on to graduate school if he wants to go."

"What about Alex? He only has another year to go before he hits the expenses of the university." Juliana had no idea how much money Lance had to share with his family.

"Don't worry. I plan to do the same for Alex, but not yet. I don't know what university he will attend. Also, I want him to be willing to work just as Logan has been. It's important for a young man to learn to work for what he wants. I'm thankful Dad and Grandpapa taught me to work. It has paid off."

The waitress stopped by the table. "You folks want dessert?"

Lance looked at Juliana with raised eyebrows.

She smiled. "No, thank you. I've eaten plenty."

"No dessert this time but I really enjoyed the meal."

"I'm glad sir. We try to have the best Tex-Mex food in town," said the waitress. "I'll bring your bill."

After paying for the meal, Lance again helped Juliana into the truck. He swung into the driver's side seat and started the engine, but sat as if thinking. He got out his phone and punched in a number.

Juliana waited quietly for him to finish his call. She could hear both sides of the conversation.

"Hello, Herb? Lance here. I have something I need you to do for me."

"Hello, Lance. How are you doing?"

"I'm doing well and the children are okay. We're at the ranch with my folks. Listen Herb, I need you to set up a scholarship for my brother Logan at the University of Texas in Austin. I want it to be full expenses for four years. Start with a hundred thousand, and Herb, I want this to be anonymous and called the Hill Country Student Scholarship. Just have the university send a letter to Logan McTavish informing him of the scholarship in the next week or so."

"Sure Lance, I'll get it done in the next day or two and call you back. Which account do you want this to come out of?"

"Take it out of the special activities fund. I may be taking a lot out of that one as I'm going to be looking for a place to buy here in the Hill Country."

"No problem. If it runs low, we can transfer funds into it. Take care of those kiddos and yourself."

"I will, bye Herb."

Lance slipped the phone back into his shirt pocket. "That's done. One thing off my mind."

Juliana marveled at having enough money to make a phone call and spend a hundred thousand dollars. Knowing what it would mean to Logan and to the family she rejoiced and said a silent prayer of thanksgiving to God that Lance was choosing to spend his money in such a way. "It's great that you are doing that for Logan. He's such a good young man and deserves a break."

"I've missed seeing him grow up and really need to spend time with him to get reacquainted. The same is true of Alex. Maybe this summer I can spend some time with them."

"Speaking of time, I need to be heading back. I need to stop by the grocery store in Tumbleweed. I promised Olivia to pick up a bunch of groceries so she wouldn't have to go into town. This being Wednesday I need to get things done this afternoon so I will be free for Wednesday evening church services." Juliana placed her sunglasses on.

Lance grabbed his sunglasses from the console. "I need to be getting back also. I've left the children in Mom's care long enough. I don't want to take advantage of her."

Juliana laughed. "I doubt Olivia thinks you're taking advantage. Knowing her and Nana, they are thoroughly enjoying the children."

"Well, you're probably right. Their nanny, Rosa Real, arrives next week and will be helping out. Rosa has been taking care of the children since Mark was a week old. Her grandson is driving her to the ranch after she visits with her own children and grandchildren." Lance backed out onto the road and headed back to the western ware store to let Juliana pick up her vehicle.

"Will Rosa be staying on for a time?" Juliana couldn't image having a full-time, live-in nanny. What did such a thing cost?

Lance glanced over at her. "She will be staying indefinitely. Rosa has become as much a caretaker of the children as I am. She has mothered them far more than my wife did. Rosa's willingness to relocate to Texas with us indicates that she plans to stay with us."

Juliana smiled at Lance. "She sounds like an important part of your family."

Lance returned the smile. "Yes, she is a part of our family. Mom said she had plenty of room for Rosa at the house and that she would be a big help with Nana having had the stroke. One reason for getting the old house fixed up is to make room for Logan and Alex to stay out there. Mom says they will love it. Almost like having a place of their own. And Rosa's grandson, Ricardo, will stay awhile."

"How old is this grandson?"

"He must be in his middle twenties as he has been in the military and just returned from the Middle East." Lance pulled in next to Juliana's pickup. "Sorry that your pickup is going to be hot in this heat."

Juliana shrugged her shoulder. "That's the way it is in Texas this time of year. The air conditioner in the pickup works well and should cool it off quickly. Thanks for lunch and allowing me to shop with you. It was fun."

Lance picked up his wallet, which he had thrown on the console of the truck. Pulling out two hundred dollar bills, he handed them to Juliana. "Help me out by using this to buy groceries and anything else you think Mom needs. She won't want to take it from me but if the groceries are already paid for she won't throw them out."

Juliana looked at the money and then at Lance. "I won't lie to her if she asks."

"I don't want you to lie to her. Just tell her the groceries are taken care of and if she insists tell her I paid for them."

She nodded. "That will work. Maybe she'll be too busy preparing supper to worry about the bill when I get to the ranch. I can unload and put away without mentioning the cost."

Lance quickly moved around to the passenger side and opened the truck door. "I should thank you. I wouldn't have gotten the shopping done so quickly without your help. And thanks for the advice about the scholarship." He offered his hand to aid Juliana in stepping down from the big truck and walked her over to her pickup.

"You're welcome. Now we need to be heading back so we have time to be ready for Bible class this evening. I always enjoy it when Walt teaches." Juliana settled in her pickup and started the engine. After making sure the air conditioner was on maximum, she put her pickup in reverse and backed out onto the road. As she started back toward Tumbleweed, she kept a watch in the review mirror as a big black truck followed her. Sighing, she took a deep breath. She was going to have to keep a watch on her heart, as she could become too attached to the tall, handsome man driving it.

Chapter 12

After an early supper, Lance had Mark follow him upstairs. "You need to shower and put on clean clothes. We'll be going to Wednesday evening Bible class in thirty minutes."

"What is that?" Mark unbuttoned his shirt and started taking it off.

Lance felt another jolt of guilt. His son had missed a lot growing up in California without any religious training. "Here on the ranch everyone goes to church a lot. Wednesday evenings you will go to a children's class and I'll go to the class in the auditorium. Your grandpapa is teaching that one. When I was your age, I enjoyed the Wednesday evening class as I got to hear Bible stories and do crafts. You'll meet other children your age and begin to make friends."

"You sure about this, Dad? What if the other kids don't like me?"

"You don't worry about that. They'll like you if you are friendly, polite, and kind. You can do that." Lance knew all the changes in his son's young life were hard. Mark had to begin somewhere at making new friends and this was as good an opportunity as any. "Now, take your shower and get dressed. I need to talk to your grandmother."

Lance found his mom in the living room setting in a rocker feeding Sara Hope her bottle of formula. Nana sat in her chair with her Bible in her lap.

"Mom, are you and Nana going to class this evening?"

"No, son, we're going to stay home. I'll keep Sara Hope while you take Mark with your dad and grandpapa."

Nana took her glasses off. "Juliana has recommended that I take it easy, especially as I'm doing so much physical therapy. She wants me to start back to church one service at a time, starting with Sunday morning. I want to go this evening, but I see the wisdom of not getting over tired. And I am tired after today."

Lance sat on the couch and faced his grandmother and mother. "But Juliana didn't do exercises with you today."

Nana smiled. "Yes, but she left orders for me to do my exercises even on days she doesn't work with me. I would have liked to skip them but I promised. So today I exercised both morning and afternoon and stayed up longer than I have been. Juliana says that is what it will take to get my strength back."

Olivia shifted Sara Hope up to her shoulder and started patting her little back to encourage a good burp. "You go on with Mark and enjoy yourself and we'll be fine here."

Lance rose and gave his grandmother and then his mother a kiss on their cheeks. He then kissed Sara Hope on the top of her black curls. "Thanks Mom. I don't mind taking Sara Hope but it'll be easier with just Mark." He didn't tell her that he felt as anxious about going back to church as Mark did. It had been years since he had been in a church building and he wasn't even sure why he stopped going.

As he went upstairs to collect Mark, he remembered when he was fifteen years old and had made the decision to follow God. He had confessed his sins and been immersed by his father in the baptistery asking God to forgive his sins and became a Christian in the small church building in Tumbleweed. Until going to college and getting involved with Chandra, he had taken part in the worship services, read his Bible, and tried to have the mind of Christ. When had he started walking away from his beliefs?

He went into his room to get his wallet and saw his old Bible on the shelf of books. Picking it up felt familiar and comforting. He tucked it under his arm. Entering the hall, he met Mark coming out of his room dressed in clean clothes and with his hair sticking up.

Pulling a comb from his pocket, he quickly combed Mark's hair into some sort of order. "There, son, you look ready to go."

When they got downstairs, Hank and Walt were at the kitchen door putting on their hats. Lance decided not to wear his. "Dad, Grandpapa, let's take my truck if you don't mind, as Mark's booster seat is already in it. Where's Juliana? She mentioned going to Bible study this evening."

Hank put on his hat. "She left right after supper. She always picks up a couple of the older ladies who don't drive and takes them to class. Juliana is thoughtful that way. Thanks for offering to take your truck."

Grandpapa grinned. "Sure, let's see how that black monster rides." He climbed into the back seat next to Mark and left the front seat to Hank.

Lance glanced at his dad. "You want to drive, Dad?"

"You don't mind? I'd like to see how this truck handles."

The men didn't talk much on the ride into town as Mark kept up a running commentary on what he had done that day and asking questions. Lance was glad he had thought to ask his dad to drive. The grin his dad gave him indicated how pleased he was.

When they entered the church building Hank took Mark off to find his class and Lance followed Grandpapa up to the next to the front row of seats. Soon after they were seated, Juliana slipped into the pew next to Lance.

"Hi Walt, Lance. Did Nana and Olivia stay home?"

Walt had his pocket watch out. "Yes, just like you told her to do. She was tired out this evening. Olivia is also taking care of Sara Hope."

Hank came and sat between Walt and Lance. "I got Mark settled into class. There were five other boys his age there."

An older man that looked familiar to Lance stood in front of the podium. "Let's have a prayer and a song and then turn the time over to Walt McTavish."

Lance listened to the prayer that included a request for the continued healing of Nana. The nearness and fresh lavender smell of Juliana distracted him. The congregation had started the singing of a hymn and Juliana had a pleasant soprano voice. On the other side, Lance listened to the deep bass voices coming from his father and grandfather. It brought back memories of his childhood and youth sitting in this same pew listening to the men of the family sing and wishing he had a deep voice. It had been so many years since he had sung a hymn, he wasn't sure he still knew how, so he just listened to the blended voices.

The Bible lesson Lance heard his grandfather present was from the book of John. Walt taught as if having a conversation with the audience. He read a section of scripture, explained it, and then gave an application to their lives. Lance let the words wash over him and just listened. They seemed to feed something within him that had needed nourishment for a long time. The class was over before Lance realized how quickly the time had flown.

Juliana turned to Lance. "Let me show you where Mark's class meets. I help teach it on Sunday morning and need to pick up some paper."

"Lead the way. I'd like to see Mark's class." Lance turned to his dad. "We'll meet you at the truck."

"Sure, take your time."

As Lance followed Juliana down a hallway of classrooms, several people spoke and nodded. Lance responded with a greeting but didn't stop to talk to them. He wasn't comfortable with talking with people about his situation and knew that the first two questions would be where was his wife and what did he do for a living. Neither question was easy for him to answer. The separation from Chandra was still too raw and people looked at him funny if he said he was retired.

"Hey, Dad, look at what I made." Mark was grinning ear to ear and holding a forked stick with a piece of rubber tied between the two prongs.

"What is that?" Lance asked but he already knew.

"It's a slingshot, like the one David used to kill the giant. I'll tell you the whole story tonight before we go to bed. It was great. The teacher said it came from the Bible."

Mark's enthusiasm was catching. "That's great, son. Now let's get to the truck and meet Granddad and Grandpapa."

Juliana waved to them from where she was talking with a couple of women. Lance waved back and then led Mark out to the truck where he began to tell the two older men about his slingshot.

~

The next couple of days went by in a blur of activities. Lance spent his time between helping his dad and grandpapa with ranch chores and meeting the workmen who came to install the air conditioning and heat unit in the old

110

place and setting up the large screen TVs and satellite dishes. Logan and Alex were thrilled with the plan for them to move out to the old house and the installation of the large screen TV.

At noon on Saturday the family, including Juliana, gathered around the dining table for a birthday celebration for Hank. Lance could tell his dad was uncomfortable with all the attention. After a large meal of all of Hank's favorites, everyone started scattering. Lance followed his dad into the living room.

Hank frowned as Lance finished setting up the remote for the large screen TV. "We don't need a new TV. The old one works fine."

Lance chuckled at how predictable his dad was. "Good, you can let me put the old one into my bedroom. The new TV is your birthday present."

Olivia came into the living room. "Now Hank, you know what we say to a gift, even if it's not one we would have chosen for ourselves."

"Humph. The TV is all right and I thank you for the gift, son. But, that's too much expense." Hank settled down into his spot at the end of the couch as Lance tuned the TV to a Texas Ranger baseball game.

Walt came into the living room and took his usual overstuffed chair. "Will you look at that picture! It almost makes it seem like you're there."

Lance handed the remote and channel guide to his dad. "We can all enjoy it. But, you are in charge of the remote." Lance chuckled. "You may need to remind Mark."

Olivia looked around. "Where have Logan and Alex gotten to?"

Walt grinned. "I suspect they have headed out to the old house. They are worse than two women getting their place fixed up. I'm not sure how much more of their stuff will fit out there."

Olivia sighed. "I'm not sure how I feel about the boys being out of the main house. It's almost as if they are leaving home too early."

Nana reached over and patted her daughter-in-law's arm. "Don't you worry, Olivia. There are two sure things that will bring the boys back to the main house, namely food and laundry."

"You're right. Come supper time they'll come barreling through the back door." Olivia's face brightened up.

Lance noticed that Mark, seated next to his granddad, had his head on the older man's shoulders. It wouldn't be long until the boy was asleep. If Lance had suggested an afternoon nap, Mark would have strenuously objected. However, falling asleep, while watching a baseball game, was not part of Mark's definition of a nap.

Olivia stood behind the couch, patted her husband's shoulder, and quietly said, "I'm going to go nap while Sara Hope is sleeping. You're in charge of Mark."

Hank reached up, covered her hand with his, and gave a squeeze.

Seeing the love between his parents reminded Lance of his loss and he didn't want to think about it. Needing to be busy, he motioned for Juliana to follow him into the kitchen. Out of earshot of the others, he asked, "How about going for a drive with me? Grandpapa told me of a ranch to the west that's for sale. I'd like to drive around it before my appointment with the realtor on Monday."

Juliana cocked her head, stared at him for a moment, and then nodded. "A ride in a comfortable air conditioned truck sounds relaxing."

"Give me a minute to put the baby monitor into Mom's room." It was sitting on the kitchen counter, as Sara Hope was upstairs in her crib. Lance tapped on the door of his parent's bedroom.

His mom softly called, "Come in."

Lance opened the bedroom door and stepped into the room. "Mom, I'm going to go drive around the Smith's place with Juliana. Here's the baby monitor. We should be back before Sara Hope wakes up." He handed the baby monitor to his mom.

"Take your time, Lance. I'll take care of Sara Hope."

"Thanks, Mom." Lance gave his mom a kiss on the cheek, stepped into the hallway, and then closed the bedroom door.

~

Lance slowly drove down the lane to the county road glancing over at the pretty, young woman in the cab with him. He turned onto the county road going away from Tumbleweed. Juliana was quietly sitting across the console from him and gazing out the side window.

"Grandpapa told me that Fred Smith wants to sell his ranch as neither of his two sons wants to be ranchers. It's up the road here and then back about a mile."

Juliana glanced over at him. "I've never been out that direction."

Lance watched for the turn off toward the ranch. "Here it is." He turned slowly under the arch held up by two pillars of native rock and across the cattle guard onto the tree-lined drive leading toward the ranch house sitting on a hill a half mile from the county road.

Juliana leaned forward to get a better look at the ranch house they were approaching. "Wow, what a great looking place. How large is it?"

"Not so large, only about 10 thousand square feet, it has 6 bedrooms, 7 full baths, game room, exercise room, and indoor/outdoor swimming pool."

Lance wondered what she thought of him considering such a large ranch. "It has 2800 acres and is fully set up as both a cattle ranch and a horse ranch. There are several hundred acres under cultivation for hay. There are also the facilities for an equestrian center."

Juliana turned to stare at Lance. "You must be serious about staying in Texas. This is not a small investment."

Lance nodded. "Yes, I plan to raise my children here. I'm done with California and the corporate world. I'm returning to my roots."

Juliana laughed as she surveyed the large house as Lance drove around it. "You may be planning to return to your Texas roots, but this place is not like the ranch you grew up on."

"You may be right. This is a different operation than what my dad and granddad have, but the fundamentals I learned about ranching growing up around here are still the same. This is just on a grander scale."

"I'll say it is a much grander scale. It is a lovely place. Just look at those horses running out in that pasture."

Lance followed her gaze toward a big pasture that led down to the river. A fence kept the herd of horses from the river. He had to agree, it was a good-looking place. He turned onto a ranch road and drove to the top of a hill that offered a panoramic view of the ranch. He got out of the truck and went around opening the passenger door for Juliana to step out. They walked together to a spot where the whole valley opened up before them and they could see all the main buildings on the ranch.

"How many people work on a ranch like this?" Juliana asked.

Lance stood close by her side to use his body to block some of the hot breeze that was blowing dust in from the west. He wanted to protect her. "I'm not real sure yet. Moreover, if I purchase the ranch I have no idea how many will want to keep working for me. It's a big operation and employs a number of people from the area. From what I can see on paper, it's a money making proposition and has a potential for more profit. I'll learn more when I take a tour with the realtor on Monday. I just wanted to get a sense for the feel of the place."

"You mean check out the vibes of the place?"

"Yes, so far it feels good. I get a sense my children could be happy and grow up here. That's what is important to me. Plus, it will give me direction and something to do that I find interesting." Lance noted a truck much like his coming toward them on the ranch road.

Juliana also turned to watch the truck approach them. "Have you always wanted to be a rancher?"

"Not when I was a teen growing up here. All I wanted was get away and see the world. It wasn't working with animals and the life of the ranch I wanted to get away from, as much as the small world of the ranch. I wanted something bigger."

"And now?"

"And now that I've seen the bigger world, I want to come home. The bigger world isn't all that appealing anymore. I'm not sure I can fully explain it."

"I think I understand." Juliana tucked a lock of hair back behind her ear that the hot summer breeze was blowing loose from her ponytail.

114

Lance gazed at the ranch buildings that included indoor and outdoor riding arenas. "I want to develop the equestrian center into an equestrian therapy center for both children and adults. I have a lot of acquaintances in the corporate world I can get to work with me through a foundation and give something back to the community."

Juliana looked surprised. "I didn't know you were into equestrian therapy."

Lance chuckled. "I'm not but I do know how much good it can do for people with disabilities. It is too expensive for most people to afford but I plan to offer it at a discount and even give free scholarships. Through the foundation, I'll hire someone to develop it and manage it. I know several people to contact who will help with that."

A truck with the ranch logo pulled up behind Lance's truck and a man dressed as a working cowboy got out and walked toward them. He was a tall lean man in his forties with a look of a rancher.

"Howdy, folks. I'm George Fritze, foreman for the Two Forks Ranch."

Lance turned to the man and held out his hand. "Lance McTavish and this is Juliana Spencer. Lucille Inger, the realtor, told me it would be all right to drive through the ranch. I have an appointment on Monday for her to show me the place."

Chapter 13

Juliana strolled around the top of the hill surveying the surrounding land while Lance spoke with the ranch foreman. She couldn't get over the grand scale and the beauty of the ranch. How much money did Lance have that he could consider purchasing such a place? She shook her head. It was none of her business how much money he had. It was of interest that he planned to settle permanently in the area. His family would be pleased and she assumed that this land he was considering purchasing bordered his family ranch.

"Juliana, you ready to go see more of the ranch?" Lance called her back to the truck. George Fritze had climbed into his truck and driven down the ranch road toward the ranch building.

She not only wanted to see more of the ranch, she also wanted to get out of the sun and the heat. "I'm ready. What did you think of Mr. Fritze?" Lance opened the passenger door of the truck and made sure she buckled up. She had to give him credit for his consistent good manners.

Lance started the truck and slowly drove along the road looking from side to side as he observed the land. "I was impressed with George Fritze. He seemed to be on top of what is happening on the ranch and what it takes to care for the land in this part of Texas. He indicated that he grew up around Harper. I got a good feel from him. After I tour the ranch on Monday, I'll decide if I want to move forward and part of that will be to talk in-depth with the ranch personnel."

Juliana was intrigued with how one would make the decision to spend millions of dollars. "How will you know whether to move forward? On what will you base a decision?"

Lance glanced over at her and smiled. She liked how his face lit up. The look of sadness retreated but soon returned. "That's a good question. If you asked how I would decide to purchase a software development business, I could give you a clear answer. That's where my brain has been for years." He tipped his hat back and scratched his head. "Of course, I'll look at the profit-cost over the last few years. I'm looking for a place that can support itself. I'll look at the facilities, barns and such, to figure out what needs added and which is in place already. Part of my problem is I'm not sure what type of ranch I want, cattle, horses, or both. I want a ranch where I can make a home for my children and find useful work for myself. I'm not the type of fella to want to sit around and twiddle my thumbs."

"Will you try to get the price down?"

He nodded. "Well, sure. That's part of the campaign when you're purchasing something like this. I'll not be hardball about it. I want to offer a fair price, but I won't be taken. One area that I want to be sure is included is the mineral rights. People try to hold on to them when they sell their land."

"What if you can't come to terms and don't get this ranch?"

"I assume there are other ranches in the area. This may not be the right ranch for me. I'm not glued to this place."

Juliana nodded. "I'm sure you'll know what is best for you and the children. I'll be praying that God will help guide you to the right decision."

"Thanks, I can use the prayers. I have many decisions to make and most of them have to do with Mark and Sara Hope. More wisdom would help me also. Know where I can get some?" He grinned at her.

"Besides listening to God, I suggest you talk to Hank and Walt. They are two of the wisest men that I know."

"When I was a teen, I would have said no way I would ask my dad's opinion. I thought I knew it all. However, it is amazing how much wiser they seem now that I'm older and realize how much I really don't know."

Juliana laughed. "That's the truth. I thought my folks were so clueless when I was a young teen. But every year since then I have learned more and more that it was me that was the clueless one."

Lance laughed with her. "I wonder if that is how Mark and Sara Hope will see me."

"Probably, and the truth probably is, we are all basically clueless, whether we're children or adults." Juliana had a catch in her breath at how good it felt to laugh with Lance.

"Oh, I hope not. Someone needs to know what they're doing." Lance turned the truck back toward the ranch house. "I want to drive around the ranch house once more and then we'll head back home."

"Thanks for letting me ride along. This is a wonderful ranch." Juliana was surprised at how comfortable she felt with Lance.

Lance slowly drove around the circular drive in front of the large ranch house. "You're welcome. You coming along made it more fun for me."

~

Later Juliana drove toward Fredericksburg to have supper and maybe a movie with her friend, Maria. She had met the young woman when Maria Sancho had needed some physical therapy after having shoulder surgery. She had grown up on a small ranch her parents owned halfway between Tumbleweed and Fredericksburg and still lived with her family. She worked at the elementary school in Tumbleweed as a first grade teacher.

As Juliana drove she thought about what Lance had said. He had impressed her by his thoughtful approach to purchasing a ranch. It just reaffirmed his background as a successful businessman. One reason she had called Maria and suggested that they get together this evening was Juliana didn't want to spend the evening with Lance and the children. She was beginning to like the man and his children too much for her own good.

When Juliana arrived at the Sancho house, she parked her car, waved at the younger children playing out in the yard, and waited for Maria to climb into the pickup.

"Hey, Juliana, thanks for the invite. I needed to get out of the house. The kids were starting to get on my last nerve." Maria buckled her seatbelt and put on her sunglasses.

Juliana chuckled. "I can't imagine why you would be bothered by six younger siblings plus your folks in the same house."

Maria smiled and pushed her long black hair back over her shoulder. "You know how much I love my family. Normally through the school year, I get to escape for most of the week. Now that school is out, I'm at home for the duration unless I can get a summer job. There is way too much togetherness with my family these days."

Easing back onto the main highway toward Fredericksburg, Juliana nodded. "I was experiencing the same thing at the McTavish place."

Maria lifted her eyebrows. "Oh and why is that."

"I don't know if you have heard or not, but the oldest son, Lance, and his two children arrived last Monday."

"No, I hadn't heard. Like I said, I've been trapped at home."

"Well, he is relocating back to Texas from California. I don't want to spend too much time with him."

Maria lightly punched Juliana on the arm. "All right girlfriend. Give it up. Why don't you like this fella?"

Juliana frowned. "I didn't say I didn't like him. Just the opposite. He's good looking, very nice, and married."

"Oh, I see."

"What do you think you see?"

In a smug voice, Maria gave her opinion. "You find him attractive but he's off limits."

With a sigh, Juliana agreed. "Yes, he's very attractive and his two kids are absolutely adorable, Mark who is eight and Sara Hope, a three-month-old baby."

"And where is the wife?"

"That's part of the problem. She left him and filed for divorce. I have no desire to get caught up with a divorced man. Too many complications. I'd rather stay single."

Maria turned a puzzled glance at Juliana. "I'm confused. Is he divorced or married?"

"That's one of the complications, he's in between."

Juliana maneuvered the pickup into a parking spot at an Italian restaurant where they had agreed to dine. They were soon seated and ordering their food.

Maria played with the wrapper from her straw. "So...if this guy were unmarried and not getting a divorce, would you be interested in him?"

Juliana laughed. "We're still on that conversation, huh?"

"Yes, we are. Come on and tell me."

"Well, yes I suppose I would be. I'm definitely attracted to him. He is tall, dark, and handsome."

"I can see where being around him a lot might be tiresome."

"No, not tiresome, dangerous. However, it won't be as big a problem much longer. He is looking at the Two Forks Ranch."

Maria gasped. "You mean as in interested in buying it?"

"Yes, he has an appointment Monday with the realtor. I went with him this afternoon to drive around it. What a great place."

Maria wagged a finger at Juliana. "You must have forgotten something important to tell me about this guy, like he's rich. No other way he could afford a place like the Two Forks Ranch."

Juliana grabbed Maria's finger and pushed her hand back across the table. "Yes, he must be rich but that has nothing to do with how attractive I find him."

"What's wrong with him that his wife is divorcing him? It is the wife that wants a divorce?"

"Yes, she's the one who has left with another man. I really shouldn't be telling you all this but I know you won't talk about it. I just need someone to talk to."

Maria smiled. "That's what I'm here for, friend. You will do the same for me if I ever meet a guy, which is so not happening these days. I don't know why I stay in this area. All the good guys are taken."

Juliana shrugged her shoulders and frowned. "It sure seems like it. I keep praying and waiting for the Lord to show me the way. And Lance McTavish is not the one."

"Time will tell." Maria turned toward the waiter, as their food arrived.

On the drive back to the McTavish ranch, Juliana thought of the conversation with Maria. It had been a relief to talk about Lance. She said a prayer of thanksgiving for such a friend as Maria. Someone she could trust with her heart thoughts. And she promised to do the same for Maria. In the coming weeks, she planned to be very busy and not have a lot of time to spend in Lance's presence. It would be hard as he was staying at the house. Retreating to her room was an answer but she didn't want to do that to the point that she ignored the rest of the family. It would be easier once Abby got home in only a couple of weeks.

Chapter 14

Sunday morning was the usual rush to have breakfast and get ready for church services. Even Nana was going to services. Lance was up early with his folks and had time to help get Sara Hope fed and changed into a cute little pink ruffled dress and black patent leather shoes. With a white bow secured on her dark curls, she was too cute not to pull out his phone and take a picture. Mark was also soon dressed in slacks and dress shirt.

Lance dressed in his navy blue suit, white shirt, and striped white and red tie. He decided that his black boots would work with the suit. He remembered his dad and grandpapa always putting on their suits for Sunday services even though for Wednesday evening Bible study they wore jeans and chambray shirts. And here he was doing the same with his son.

When Lance carried Sara Hope downstairs ready for church services, Mark shadowed his father. Lance found his mom in the kitchen packing up the diaper bag with a couple of bottles of formula. "Thanks Mom for taking care of that."

Olivia turned and regarded Lance holding Sara Hope and Mark standing beside him. "Oh my, don't you all look fine. Let me get my camera. It's here in my desk." She quickly pulled her camera out and snapped several pictures with Lance and the children standing on the porch of the ranch house.

Juliana came out and joined the picture taking. "Olivia, you get into the picture, please."

For several minutes as other family members came out of the house, Olivia, Juliana, and Lance were busy either taking pictures or having someone else snap them.

Hank finally called a halt. "Need to get going or we will be late. Juliana, can you take the folks? Logan and Alex, you all can ride with Lance, if that is all right with you, son." Evidently, he wanted his wife to himself for the ride into the church services.

"Sure Dad, one can ride shotgun and the other can ride in back and keep herd on the kids." Lance grinned as Alex ran to his truck and jumped into the front passenger seat. Turning to Logan, he said, "If you snooze, you lose. You can ride up front on the way home."

Logan shrugged his shoulders. "I don't mind riding herd on the kids. But just so you know, I don't change no diapers."

Lance laughed along with his folks and grandparents. Juliana smiled at the young man.

Lance slapped Logan on the shoulder. "Don't you worry, Sara Hope will probably be fine between here and the church building."

The banter between his brothers and Mark continued on the drive to the church building. Lance just drove and listened. After parking the truck, Lance gathered up Sara Hope and the diaper bag as Logan, Alex, and Mark headed into the church building.

Being a relatively small congregation of only about two hundred and fifty people counting the children, they did not have an attended nursery, so Sara Hope stayed with Lance as he made his way to the next to the front pew where his parents and grandparents were settling. Several people spoke to Lance and he tried to remember their names, but most of the people he didn't know or remember. They all seemed to know who he was. Of course, Sara Hope gathered a few smiles and comments on what a pretty baby she was. When Lance sat down next to his mom, she quickly took possession of Sara Hope. He didn't mind as he saw the joy on his mom's face as she claimed her granddaughter.

The Bible class and worship service followed the format he remembered from his childhood. It gave him comfort to be back in the fold of his beliefs and values. As he listened to the preacher, Greg Young, Lance thought about what he wanted his life to be like moving forward. He wanted to be the kind of man his father and grandfather could be proud of and he wanted to provide the guidance that his children needed, including the spiritual. How could he when he was so far from what he needed to be spiritually himself? He glanced over at Nana and saw her head bowed in prayer and holding the hand of her husband of almost sixty years. Lance knew what he needed to do to get back on the right track. Taking a deep breath, he bowed his head and silently prayed for courage, wisdom, and forgiveness.

When the preacher gave the invitation at the end of the sermon and the congregation rose to sing, Lance took Sara Hope from his mom, took Mark's hand, and stepped out into the aisle and moved to the front pew.

Greg Young and John Smith, one of the older elders of the congregation, sat down with him and the children.

"What can we do for you Lance?" asked John Smith who had known Lance from time he was born.

Lance settled Sara Hope on his lap. Mark was looking up at his dad with a frown, not understanding what they were doing.

"I need to ask the church for prayers for forgiveness for not being faithful. I want to get my life right with God and to be a part of this congregation. I didn't write anything out because I just decided as I was listening to the worship service." Lance wondered if that was an adequate statement.

Greg Young quietly asked, "What do you need forgiveness for, Lance?"

Clearing his throat because it wasn't easy to speak, Lance confessed, "I've neglected worship service for years and I've left God out of my life to the extent that my son, Mark, doesn't know God. I know that was wrong. I intend to do different going forward. I've prayed for God's forgiveness and now I'm asking the church."

John Smith leaned toward Lance. "What about your wife? What's going on there?"

Lance didn't want to talk about Chandra with Mark there but these men had a right to know. "My wife has asked me for a divorce and has left me the children. She filed for divorce a couple of weeks ago and if nothing happens, it will be final in a few weeks." He glanced at Mark to see his reaction to the cold statement. Mark looked as if he was about to cry. Lance put his arm around his son's shoulders and pulled him close. "I'm not protesting the divorce as she is already living with another man. I'm sure I'm responsible in some way for the separation and divorce. She never discussed it with me and I never knew we even had a problem until I was served with the divorce papers."

The older man put his hand on Lance's back. "I can't imagine what you are going through, but I think you have made a wise decision to come home and to come back to the Lord. As a congregation we will do all we can to help you to be the man God wants you to be and to raise these children to have faith. We will have a prayer with you and the children. I saw your dad baptize you when you were a lad. I watched you grow in faith until you left home. Now you need to lean on your family, both your physical family and your spiritual family to help you back to where you want to be with God. He is always forgiving and merciful and will forgive you of your sins as you are one of His children."

John stood and faced the congregation as the hymn was ending. "We have one of our own who has returned to us and to God this day. Lance McTavish has come forward with his children, Mark and Sara Hope, to ask God for forgiveness and the churches' forgiveness for not being the Christian man that God expects. He wants to return to the fellowship of Christians and to be a part of this congregation. I know that each one of you can relate to the need to be more faithful and will reach out to Lance and his family. Let's pray."

Lance bowed his head and closed his eyes as he listened to the kind words of the godly man. Although Lance felt sad about the situation of his life, he was relieved to have made the public statement of his need for forgiveness and acceptance. Some might judge him harshly but he couldn't undo his life of the last few years.

From behind him, he heard a sniffling and guessed it was his mom and Nana weeping for him. He hoped it was tears of joy at his return to the fold.

As John completed his prayer for Lance, he stooped down to hug Lance, Mark, and Sara Hope. Greg Young, the minister, also gave him a hug and then stood to give announcements and lead the congregation in a closing prayer.

Lance stood for the prayer with Mark hugging his side with his arms around his daddy's waist. Sara Hope was looking around at the congregation over Lance's shoulder and gurgling with her thumb in her month. At the end of the dismissal prayer, his family gathered around giving him hugs and words of love. Even Logan and Alex came up to him and shook his hand.

Juliana came next giving him a sideways hug. "Welcome home, Lance." She stepped away before he could respond.

Olivia took Sara Hope and Logan took Mark toward the back of the church building as many in the congregation came forward to greet Lance and welcome him back into the congregation. Finally, Lance made his way to the back of the church and exited the building with his family.

Walt took Nana's arm as they maneuvered the two steps down to the sidewalk. "Let's get home to dinner and an afternoon nap."

Lance smiled. "Sounds good to me, Grandpapa."

Chapter 15

Monday morning Lance left the children with his folks and drove back to the Two Forks Ranch to meet with Lucille Inger. The realtor was a tall trim gray-headed woman with a broad Texas accent. Lance marveled at how much jewelry she was wearing. Rings, bracelets, large earrings, and several gold necklaces adorned the woman.

She waited in her Cadillac as he drove up in front of the ranch house and then exited her vehicle to meet him. "Good to see you again, Mr. McTavish. You ready to look at the best deal on a ranch in Texas?"

He grinned. "Call me Lance, Ms. Inger."

"Well, I'm Lucille." She dug around in an enormous purse she had slung over her shoulder. "Let me find the keys to the house. Here they are."

As they walked up onto the porch, she began to tell him the details of the ranch and house. Lance glanced around with interest at the broad entrance that flowed into a large living room with a fireplace at one end. Huge windows allowed him to look out over the ranch buildings and pastures.

"Now the house has six bedrooms, seven bathrooms, a formal living room, dining room, and one of my favorite things about the house is the large country style kitchen with eating area and lounge area. The house has two laundry areas. Down this hallway, there are an office, crafts room, and media room. You can access the patio and outdoor pool from several areas. Downstairs there is a game room and access to the indoor pool. Also downstairs, there is an exercise room and all the exercise equipment stays with the house."

Lance was a little overwhelmed by the rapid-fire description coming at him. "What is the water source for the house and barns?"

"Oh, I'm glad you asked. I sometimes get all caught up in describing the house I forget about those types of things. I have it all written down here in this detailed description of the property. It also details what stays and what doesn't stay. The owners have already moved out and only have a few pieces of furniture left to move. Everything else stays." Lucille handed him a thick folder with various information about the ranch. "And the water source is two deep wells that supply the house and the barns. There are also several ponds and tanks on the property as well as frontage along the river."

Lance took a deep breath, as Lucille seemed to be deciding which direction to go next. "What about the garage?" He could see already that the house was more than sufficient for his family.

After entering the kitchen, Lucille introduced him to a woman in her forties. "This is Louisa Martin who has been the housekeeper and cook here for several years. Louisa, this is Lance McTavish who is interested in buying the ranch."

Louisa dried her hands on a dishtowel. "Mr. McTavish, I'm glad to meet you."

Lance reached forward and shook the hand of the short, plump, fiftyish woman. "Mrs. Martin, I look forward to speaking more with you in the coming days."

Lucille pointed to a hallway that led off from the kitchen. "Let's go through here. The garage is designed for four vehicles and there are storage areas off the garage as well as a work room."

Lance followed her into a spacious garage and then into a workroom filled with power tools. "Are you sure all of this stays?"

Lucille glanced around and nodded. "Mr. Smith is retiring and moving closer to his sons. He didn't want to move any of this." She looked at her watch. "I have another appointment in an hour. I could show you the barns and other buildings, but I think Mr. Fritze can give you a much better tour. He can show you the foreman's house where he and his wife live. There are a couple of rooms in the main barn where ranch hands stay if need be. There are two other smaller houses for the ranch workers. But most of the men who work on the ranch live on nearby ranches or in Tumbleweed. And then there is the guest house out back of the main house."

Lance walked out of the garage and gazed over the ranch lands and the stock grazing in the pastures. He turned back to Lucille. "When can Mr. Fritze meet with me?"

"If it fits your schedule he said he could spend most of this afternoon with you. Here is his cell number. He said to call when you are ready."

"I need to get back to my folks, check on my kids, and have lunch. I'll plan to be back by two this afternoon to meet with Mr. Fritze."

Lucille reached into her purse and pulled out a pair of sunglasses. "That should work well. I'll leave the house open so if you want you can wander back through it. If you have any questions after meeting with George call me, otherwise I will plan to talk to you tomorrow. I don't want to rush you, as this is a big property to consider. I want you to take your time and be sure about what you want to do."

Lance walked her to the car and opened the door for her. "Thanks Lucille. I'll know more what my thoughts are about the ranch after I talk to Mr. Fritze."

~

When Lance turned onto the lane leading up to the McTavish Ranch house, he spotted his BMW. Therefore, Rosa and Ricardo had made it to the ranch. He looked forward to seeing them and to knowing that there would be help for his mother in caring for his children.

As he parked the truck next to the BMW and climbed out, Mark came running from the barn. "Dad, Dad, Rosa is here! Come see and she's going to stay." The boy's face split into a grin that showed his joy. It tugged at Lance's heart that his son was more excited about his nanny's arrival than he probably would have been if his mother had shown up.

Lance caught Mark up in a hug. "When did Rosa and Ricardo get here?"

"Just after you left. They got up early this morning and drove from Austin. I'll go tell Granddad that you're back." Mark took off running back to the barn.

Lance shook his head, that boy only had one speed. He headed for the house, crossed the porch, and entered the kitchen.

Rosa sat at the table holding Sara Hope. "Lance, so good to see you."

He bent down and gave her a kiss on the cheek. "How was your trip? Did the car do okay?"

Rosa smiled. "The trip was wonderful. Ricardo loves that car. Now he wants one. My niños and nietos are all doing well. It was so good to see them. However, I'm so happy to be here with you and the children."

Lance's mom turned from the stove where she was stirring gravy in a large black skillet. "I told Rosa how good it was to see her and how you and the children had missed her. Sara Hope took one look and didn't stop wiggling until Rosa took her. As much as I love my grandchildren, it is still a blessing to have some help with their care."

"Where's Ricardo?" Lance grabbed a small piece of roast chicken from a platter on the counter.

"Stop that and wait for dinner. I'm about ready to ring the bell. Ricardo went with your dad to the old house to get settled with Mark trailing along behind. They probably went to the barn after as Mark wanted to show Ricardo the horses." Olivia poured gravy from the cast iron skillet into a large bowl. "Rosa, I have to say, I am really impressed with Ricardo. You have a wonderful grandson there."

"Thank you, Mrs. McTavish. This trip was good for us. I spend more time this week with Ricardo than I have in several years him being away in the military. I'm so thankful he made it home safe from that terrible place."

"Call me Olivia, please. Nana is Mrs. McTavish. Lance, go ring the bell on the porch and then when Mark comes if you will see that he gets washed up for lunch."

"Yes, ma'am." Lance ruffled the curls on Sara Hope's head and grinned at Rosa. "Now I will have two women ordering me about."

Rosa glanced at Olivia, and then back to Lance and beamed. "And you probably need us both to keep you in line. Now go do as your Madre told you."

Lance stepped on the back porch hearing his mom and Rosa softly laughing in the kitchen. He rang the big cowbell that hung at the end of the porch. He remembered from his childhood hearing the same bell call the men into the house for meals. If someone rang the bell continuously it was the sounding of an alarm, but three strong clangs of the bell meant food was ready.

Mark came running out of the barn, followed by Hank and Walt. Ricardo, a tall, strong looking young man followed. He walked with a military bearing, straight and smooth. His black hair, dark eyes, and tan skin gave away his heritage. When he smiled at Lance, it was his grandmother's look.

Lance stepped forward and held out his hand. "Welcome to the McTavish ranch, Ricardo. How was the drive from California?"

Ricardo grinned and shook Lance's hand. "Long. It is close to 1700 miles. It took three days driving as I didn't want to tire my abuela too much with too long a days. If I had been by myself I could have driven straight through."

Lance nodded. "I'm glad you took it easy for Rosa's sake. You're here a couple of days earlier than I expected. Did Rosa get to visit enough with your family?"

"I think so. My brothers' homes are crowded and busy. My abuelita seemed anxious to get back to you and the children." Ricardo pulled his shady Brady down to protect his eyes from the bright sun light.

"Let's get inside and have some dinner. It's good that you all made it okay. I'm assuming you had no problems with the BMW." Lance followed his grandpapa up onto the porch as he walked beside Ricardo.

"No, sir, no trouble. That is a fine automobile. I really enjoyed driving it although Lita kept telling me to slow down. I didn't speed much but she likes to go slow so she can watch the country side."

Lance noticed that Ricardo had no hint of accent but he did use the Spanish word for 'little grandmother' and used the informal term 'Lita'. The affection that the young man had for his grandmother was obvious.

Later after all the bowls and platters of food had made it around the table and everyone's plate was full, Olivia asked, "Ricardo, how long can you stay with us? Are you still attached to the military?"

Lance had wondered that himself and was glad his mom had asked.

Ricardo put his fork down and looked at Olivia. "I've been separated from the service due to an injury I got in Afghanistan. I'd hoped to make a career of the Marine Corp but now I have to consider something else."

Rosa was looking at her grandson with a frown. Lance would ask her later about the nature of Ricardo's injury.

Hank spoke up. "Then you don't have to be in a hurry and can stay as long as you want."

"Thank you, sir. I'd like to stay awhile and see some of this country."

"Can you ride a horse?" Walt asked.

Ricardo switched his attention from Hank to Walt. "Yes, sir. I can ride."

Lance wondered what Grandpapa was thinking. Maybe Ricardo would want to help out on the ranch.

As soon as Rosa settled Sara Hope for a nap, and Mark was reading a book with Grandpapa in the living room, Lance headed back to the Two Forks Ranch and his meeting with George Fritze. It was a long intense afternoon of looking at every nook and cranny of the ranch. His head seemed swollen from all the detailed information George gave him about the history, financial activities, and land management of the ranch. Lance could see that the equine center was really a separate business from the ranch operation itself.

Late in the afternoon, Lance and George stood at the edge of the ridge and looked out over the broad valley where most of the ranch buildings where located.

George pointed toward the south. "You can see from here how this ranch is evenly divided by plains and hill tops. There are several nice valleys between the various ridges that contain good soil and large elm, oak, walnut and other hardwood trees. The pastures are either tall native or introduced grasses. On the hilltops and hillsides are rock outcrops, and they are primarily covered by native grasses with cedar, and Spanish oak, and down by the river and lake there are more live oak. Most of the hilltops and ridges are like this one, clay with rubble and rock outcrops. What I like about these hilltops are the long-distance views one gets."

Lance could hear the love for the land in George's description. It reminded Lance of the McTavish Ranch and the feeling of home. "George, if you had the funds, would you buy this ranch?"

George looked at him with a quizzical expression and then nodded slowly. "I surely would. I love this land and I like being a part of the equine center. You asked questions about making it more into an equine therapy center and that strikes close to my heart as I have a grandson who has autism. One thing that brings him joy is when I put him up on a pony."

"I'm a computer software developer. Not a rancher. How can I run a place like this?"

George stared at Lance for a moment. "I suspect the same way you ran the computer software business you sold. What you didn't know how to do, you hired someone else to do it for you."

Lance laughed. "You've got that right. There was always something else coming down the tube that I didn't know. But I managed to get a good team to surround me and make me look good."

"That's the same thing you do here. You hire good, smart people and let them do what they know best."

"George, are you one of those good, smart people? Would you stay on if I bought the place?" Lance held his breath waiting for an answer. He had already figured out that George was the brains behind the success of the ranch.

George pulled his hat off and looked out over the land. "I would stay. I get the feel you and I could work well together. I'd give you a couple of years commitment and then see how it was going. I'd need to know you have the funding for this type of enterprise. We're making some money with the ranch but not enough to give you full return on your investment in a short time period."

Lance nodded. "That makes sense. With the sale of my computer business, I can pay cash for this place and have more than enough left over to keep things afloat. Is that what you needed to hear?"

"Yes, that's what I needed to hear. Would you live on the ranch or would it only be a part time place for you?" George pulled his hat on and tipped it low over his brow to shade his eye from the late afternoon sun.

"I plan to move my children here and make this our full-time home. I'm staying with my folks at the McTavish ranch until I settle on a place of my own."

"Don't mean to be disrespectful but what about a Mrs. Lance McTavish?" George looked embarrassed even to ask such a question.

"Mrs. Lance McTavish is no longer in the picture. She has asked for a divorce and is giving me the children. It will be a few weeks before the divorce is final. Since I'm purchasing a ranch with the funds from the sale of my business, which I owned before my marriage, it will not be a part of the divorce proceedings." Lance was reluctant to talk about the divorce. If he moved forward toward purchasing this ranch those who worked on the ranch would know about it.

George sighed. "I'm sorry to hear that. I know it must be difficult."

"I plan to talk to some people and then Lucille and I will talk about a fair price to offer if I decide to move forward with a purchase. It could well be a month or two before I know whether I'll be purchasing this place. I know that keeps you hanging in a sort of limbo."

"Don't worry about that. I've been assured that Mr. Smith will keep me on until the ranch sells. I know how big an investment the purchase of a ranch this size will be and that it takes time to decide and then the legal stuff. I'll just keep running the ranch and trying to make some money. I'm sure Mr. Smith will appreciate that."

"Thanks for your time, George. I hope to come back tomorrow to look at the stock with you if that fits into your schedule." Lance looked toward the house and noticed that a car was in the back driveway. "Right now I want to go back through the house while Louisa is still there."

George nodded. "You've got my cell phone number. Call me when you're on your way tomorrow and I'll meet you at the big barn."

Lance waved and climbed into his truck. He drove to the house and pulled up behind the compact car that he assumed belonged to Louisa. He walked to the front door and rang the doorbell.

Louisa opened the door. "Come in Mr. McTavish."

"I'd like to speak with you a few minutes if you have time." Lance took off his hat and stepped into the entry.

"Come on into the kitchen and I'll pour you a glass of tea."

"Thanks, it's been a warm day."

Soon Lance was seated at the kitchen table with a large glass of ice tea.

"Mrs. Martin, I'm making an offer on the ranch and wanted to speak with you about staying on as housekeeper. If I do purchase the ranch, I'll be moving in with my two children and their nanny. My children are eight and three months."

"That sounds wonderful. I'll be glad to stay on if the pay stays the same and also if you offer health care?" Mrs. Martin's voice had taken on a question mark.

"Of course, Mrs. Martin. We can talk details if I get my offer accepted. Now tell me your duties here and how many hours a week you work."

They talked a while longer and Lance made notes in a notebook he had started with information about the ranch and the people who worked there.

Lucille came into the kitchen just as he was about to leave. "I was in the area still and George called and said you and he had a good visit with another planned for tomorrow."

Louisa got her a glass of iced tea, then left the kitchen.

Lucille sat at the kitchen table. "I talked to the owner. He is willing to drop his price if you take the ranch as is. No request for repairs for as he said there is always repairs needed on a ranch. Any of the horses and the cattle will be a separate purchase."

Lance stirred his tea. "I'll offer a flat twelve million for land, buildings, and mineral rights. I'd like to have my dad and grandpapa look over the stock for me. Do you think the owner will be open to that?"

Lucille laughed. "I think so. He really wants to sell and knows there won't be many offers for this big a spread. I'll draw up the forms and get them to you to sign by tomorrow. Do you have an attorney locally?"

"No, but I need one."

"I know several good attorneys to handle the purchasing of land. I will give you a list of ones I've worked with and found to be honest and you can choose one."

"Thanks, Lucille, you are making this easy."

"Well, let's see how this goes. You can go ahead and have your dad and granddad look over the stock and make a list of the animals you want to keep. We might as well make an offer for both the ranch and the stock at the same time." Lucille gathered up her handbag and briefcase and headed toward her car.

Lance drove away from the ranch knowing it was what he wanted. Before making a decision, he wanted to talk to Dad and Grandpapa.

~

Once back at the Rocking M, he checked on the children and then he went out to the barn to talk to his dad and granddad. He found them washing some cuts on a calf's legs. He squatted down beside the barn wall and watched the two men work.

"Dad, Grandpapa, I need a favor."

Hank glanced up at his oldest. "What do you need?"

Walt laughed and dusted his hands off. "He's hard up if he needs our help."

Lance grinned at the older man. "Just the opposite. I know where to find some wisdom when I need it. I spent the morning looking at a ranch to purchase. I need some help looking at the stock and knowing what to offer."

Walt came over and leaned against the barn wall. "Really, which ranch is that?"

Lance looked at his dad when he told them. His dad's face went still and stiff looking.

"My, Grandson, that's quite a place over there. You got money for that type of place? The upkeep along will set you back a bit." Grandpapa's voice didn't hold any doubt or censure, just a calm question. One he guessed his father wanted to ask but wouldn't.

"I've got the money. I managed to sell my computer company for several hundred million."

"Well, good for you. But what do you need our help with?" Walt looked over at Hank as if expecting him to say something.

"The owner wants to sell his stock and I would appreciate it if you all would come over with me to look it over and suggest what to offer. I understand he's running both cattle and horses." Lance looked from his dad to his grandpapa.

Finally, Hank glanced over at Lance. "When do you want to do this?"

Lance shrugged. "Tomorrow morning if you all have time. It will only take about fifteen minutes to drive over there. George Fritze, the foreman, said he could meet us any time."

Walt pushed away from the barn wall. "We're about through doctoring this calf. Supper will be called any time now. Any reason we can't go in the morning, Hank?"

Hank stood and wiped his hands on a rag. "I guess not. We can talk more about the place this evening after supper."

Lance felt on edge that evening as he sat in the living room with his parents and grandparents, talking about the Two Forks Ranch. His dad and grandpapa knew more about the ranch than he had expected. His grandpapa asked the questions. Lance could tell that his dad was listening closely. There seemed to be more tension in the room than usual and it seemed to be coming from his dad.

After his mother and grandparents has gone on to bed, Lance was alone with his dad. "Tell me what you really think about me coming back here and buying a ranch, Dad."

Hank looked at his oldest son before responding. "With the way you've been gone, never visiting much, I just assumed you didn't care for the ranch or ranching. You haven't come to see your mother in over two years. Now you turn up with your kids and a bunch of money and say you're all gung-ho about living in the Hill Country and ranching. It shouldn't surprise you I'm a little unsure about how sincere you are."

The disapproving note in his father's voice shouldn't have surprised Lance. Everything his father had said was true. Lance ran his fingers through his hair. How could he tell his dad how he was feeling when he was still so numb from the changes in his life? "I deserve your skepticism. I was wrong to stay away. I still can't understand how I let Chandra influence me so much as to turn my back on everything that I'm just realizing was my foundation. I can't really blame her as I had choices. I simply made the wrong ones." Lance rubbed his face feeling strangely close to tears. "But for the sake of my children and my own sake, I want to try to be a better man. Maybe one that you can someday be proud of."

Hank looked doubtful. "But why here? Why ranching? You've never shown an interest in it before."

Lance searched for the words to try to bridge the gap between himself and his father. "For all the different things I've done and years I've been away, whenever I thought about the best times of my life, it has always been here on the ranch. When I left, it wasn't that I was rejecting the life you all gave me as a kid, but I wanted to see what else was out there. Then I just sort of ended up lost out there. Chandra so disliked anything to do with my upbringing and the ranch that I hid from her how much it still meant to me. Over the years, I have taken all sorts of ranch magazines, read books on ranching, watched films of the west. It was never the lifestyle that I turned my back on. It wasn't a conscious choice but rather a giving in to keep Chandra happy. Obviously I couldn't even do that."

Hank shook his head. "So there's no hope of her coming back? No way you can repair your marriage?"

"She's already with another man. As soon as the divorce is final, she plans to marry him. I'm not real sure I even want her back now. It still hurts to think my marriage is over but I have to move forward for the sake of Mark and Sara Hope. I have to work to give them the life that is best for them. Even if she wanted to come back, would that be the best thing for the children?"

"I don't know, son. I'm having to fight my anger at her rejecting those two precious children. How could any mother do that? And I'm having a problem letting go of my resentment of the hurt you've given your mother. How do you think I felt when I sat at Christmas dinner and saw your mother's face as she counted her children? You were missing and it grieved her. I know as a Christian I've got to forgive you but it may take some time. If you've got the money and want to buy a ranch close by, that will be great for your mother. But I can't help but fear that you will tire of country ways and soon take the children and go back to the city. Then I will have to try to console my wife again." Hank looked out the window at the dark night with a face edged with grief.

Lance felt sick at his stomach as he came face to face with what he had caused. His mother had never said anything through the years of how the separation was tearing at her heart. But he could hear it in his father's voice and words. Not only had his mother grieved but also his father. Lance searched his father's face for a sign of forgiveness and felt another layer of guilt. "What can I say, but I'm sorry. I never meant to hurt you all so. Please forgive me for being so thoughtless. I promise to be a better son."

Hank sighed and rubbed his face. "I do forgive you, son, but I don't trust you. Only time will help me there. Tomorrow your grandpapa and I will go over to the Two Forks Ranch and give you our best advice. You make your decision based on what is right for you and your family. I'll be praying about it and asking God to help me have the grace to forgive and trust."

Lance wanted reach out and give his father a hug but wasn't sure how it would be received. Instead, he looked him in the eyes and made him a promise. "Thanks, Dad, and I promise I will try to be worthy of your forgiveness and trust."

Hank stood and returned Lance's regard. "It's getting late. In the morning after breakfast, and we have the animals taken care of, your grandpapa and I will go look at some livestock with you."

Lance stood and again wanted to reach out to his dad, but waited for the older man to make the first move. Instead, his dad headed for the stairs and Lance was left with a guilty, letdown feeling. "Good night, Dad. God bless," he said softly.

Chapter 16

Lance spent the next couple of weeks helping his dad and grandpapa on the McTavish Ranch and going through the process of purchasing the Two Forks Ranch. Mark had made friends with several of the boys at church. Every day or so he was either going to someone's home to play or having boys coming to the ranch. Sara Hope was gaining weight and starting to play for several minutes with various toys or objects. Lance was also pleased that she was starting to sleep more through the night. He didn't have to get up with the baby because Rosa took care of her, but he seemed to sense when she was awake and liked to go in and spend the few quiet minutes in the dimly lit room until she went back to sleep. As he studied her serene little face as she relaxed into sleep, he thanked God that she was his.

He and Ricardo pitched in to help out on the McTavish ranch. Lance tried to come up with ways to help his dad and grandpapa that didn't involve throwing a lot of money at the problems. Ricardo showed himself to be a good rider and quick to learn how the older men wanted things done.

In the late afternoon, Lance and Ricardo rode their horses to the barn after spending several hours riding fence. They had cleared brush and scrub pines and cedar from along the fence line. Getting rid of the scrub pines and scrub cedar was a continual job on the ranch to help maintain good pastures.

Lance brushed down his dad's horse that he had ridden for the afternoon's work. "Ricardo, in a week or so I should have the papers signed and take over Two Forks Ranch. You interested in working for me? At times I would ask you to come back here to the Rocking M Ranch and help out."

Ricardo stepped back from the horse he was brushing down. "I'd like that. I like this part of the country and don't really have plans. I've thought about going back to school and finishing my degree. I took classes while in the Marine Corp and only have a few more college credits to go. And I like the idea of spending time with Lita."

"Great, we'll talk more about it later. I'm heading in to take a shower before supper."

Ricardo nodded. "Sounds like a good idea. Between the smell of the horses and the hot afternoon, we both can use one." He let the horse into the corral and then took the path to the old ranch house.

Lance walked into the kitchen to find his parents, grandparents, and two brothers sitting around the table. He pulled up a chair and sat down. "Some sort of family meeting?"

His mom pointed to a letter Logan was holding. "We are all trying to understand this letter that Logan got today from the university."

"Nothing wrong is it?" Lance couldn't imagine what was in the letter for all of his family to look so serious.

Logan slid the letter over to Lance. "Here, you read it."

He picked up the letter and saw that it was a notification that Logan had been chosen for a full scholarship for the rest of his time at the university. Catching himself before he grinned, he said, "This is great, Logan. Congratulations."

"Thanks, but how did I get chosen?" Logan shook his head as if in disbelief.

"It says here that you were chosen for your leadership and scholarship for the past year. Shouldn't this be a good thing? You all had me worried something bad had happened." Lance looked around the table and smiled.

Olivia was the first to return the smile. "You're right. It is a blessing from God and we need to be thankful rather than questioning the why."

Hank nodded. "You're right. It is a blessing. I've felt bad, Logan, that we couldn't just give you the money for your schooling. Maybe now you can give up one of your three part-time jobs and relax a bit this summer."

Alex punched his brother on the arm. "As long as it isn't your part-time job here. You're not going to leave me with all the work."

Logan raised an eyebrow. "All the work? Since when did you start doing real work around here."

Julianna walked in as they all started laughing and talking at once. Lance tried not to be too obvious as to how she got his attention every time he was around her. She sure did look pretty with her hair in a ponytail and her face lit up with a smile.

Nana patted the empty chair next to her. "Come sit down and hear Logan's good news."

Juliana gave the older woman a hug and then sat down at the table. "Great, I could use some good news."

Olivia glanced over at her. "A hard day?"

"Yes, Mrs. Spandler died this morning."

"Oh, I'm sorry to hear that. And the family had called you in earlier?"

Juliana sighed. "Yes, I got there about an hour before she passed. There was no use to call an ambulance. Her heart finally gave out. All the family had gathered and knew it was coming. She was such a lovely old lady and I'll miss her. After visiting someone and working with them in the home week after week, you begin to feel as if they are your family. At 98 years old, she was like a great-grandmother." She smiled at Logan. "Now tell me about your good news."

Logan glanced at Juliana and frowned. "Somehow or other I managed to qualify for a complete scholarship for the next three years at the university. It says here that it covers tuition, books, fees, board, and room. Can you believe that?"

She nodded. "Yes, I can believe it. You worked hard your first year at the university and I'm glad someone recognized it. What great news! "

Lance nodded slightly as she glanced over at him. He stood, went over, and slapped his brother on the back. "I'm glad for you, little brother. Now I'm going to go get a shower before supper."

Olivia quickly got up and headed for the stove. "Oh my, I almost forgot the chicken baking in the oven. You all would have had a fit if I let supper burn."

Lance looked into the children's room and found Sara Hope in her crib kicking her feet and then deciding to suck on her toes. "Hey, baby girl. Did you have a good nap?"

Sara Hope gave a sloppy grin.

"Now you keep playing with your toes while I get a quick shower." He stepped into the hall where he almost ran into Rosa who carried a big stack of clean, folded baby clothes.

"I'll get Sara Hope up and changed. It smells as if supper will be ready shortly."

"Thanks, Rosa."

Lance walked back into the kitchen thirty minutes later feeling refreshed from a cool shower and clean clothes. He saw that Juliana had also changed from her work clothes into a brightly colored pink and white summer dress and sandals without hose.

Hank was speaking into the phone. "No, Abigail, I'm glad you called. Someone will be at the airport in Austin tomorrow to meet you. Don't worry. It's no problem." He pulled Olivia close to him with an arm around her shoulders. "Your mother and I are just glad you're almost home. Just be safe."

Lance saw tears in his mother's eyes in spite of the look of joy on her face. Another McTavish child was coming home.

"I love you, too. Bye, baby girl." Hank hung up the phone and then quickly placed a gentle kiss on his wife's lips. "She's almost home. Her flight got into Washington, D.C. this morning. She and her friends have toured the capital and will catch a flight early in the morning into Austin."

Olivia patted her husband's chest. "Just one more night and then she'll be home and we can both stop worrying."

Lance spoke up. "I'm needing to go into Austin on some business. You want me to pick her up at the airport?"

Hank glanced at Olivia. "You want that ride to the airport in Austin or greet her here?"

Olivia frowned. "I've a lot to do and I want to have a good meal ready for Abby. Lance, if it's no problem for you to go that would probably be best."

"I'll be glad to go. It will give me a chance to get reacquainted with my little sister."

Mark piped up. "Can I go with you, Dad, can I?"

Lance needed to stop by his attorney's office. Earlier in the day, he had gotten a phone call from her. There were papers he needed to sign regarding the divorce. Lance just hoped there wasn't a problem. Also, he might have to wait on the plane's arrival. "Not this time, son. Besides, you have a riding lesson with Ricardo in the morning."

"Oh, right. I forgot. I'll just not go." Mark quickly decided. His riding lessons were the top of his to-do-list these days.

Olivia went to take tea out of the refrigerator and poured it into the ice-filled glasses. She was smiling and singing softly to herself, *Happy days are here again.*

Lance grinned at how happy his mother was each time one of her children came back to the nest, even if temporarily.

~

The early morning drive from the ranch into Austin had been relaxing and given Lance a chance to think. His life had changed so much in the last month. From living in a metro California area, running a large corporation, to being a single dad about to buy his own ranch in Texas, it was a lot to deal with. With the GPS it was easy to find the law offices of Hillary Summers in downtown Austin.

Entering through the double glass doors into the reception area of the law offices, Lance was greeted by a young, smiling receptionist. "May I help you?"

Lance wondered if she had been hired for her bright cheery voice that offered a pleasant welcome. He noted that her nametag simple had Tammy on it with no last name.

"I have an appointment with Hillary Summers. I'm Lance McTavish."

"Just one moment." Tammy picked up the phone on her desk and pushed a button. "Ms. Summers, your 9:30 appointment is here, Mr. Lance McTavish." She listened a moment and put the receiver back on the phone base. Then she rose from behind the desk and started toward the inter offices. "Please follow me, Mr. McTavish."

Lance followed the young woman down a wide hallway past several offices with closed doors. She stopped at the door at the end of the hallway, opened it, and stepped back to let Lance enter.

Before closing the door she asked, "Should I bring coffee, Ms. Summers?"

A stern looking woman in her mid to late forties came around a big desk and held out her hand to Lance. "Hilary Summers and you must be Lance McTavish. Would you care for some coffee?"

Lance shook her hand and smiled. "That would be great. I left the ranch early this morning and need some coffee after driving for a couple of hours, Ms. Summers."

She nodded at Tammy and the young woman quietly closed the door as she departed. "Please call me Hilary and may I call you Lance?"

"Of course."

Hilary waved Lance toward a comfortable looking leather chair in front of her desk as she returned to her seat behind the desk. "I feel like I know you, Lance, after speaking to you several times on the phone but it is good to put a face to the voice."

Lance nodded and smiled. "Same here. It worked out well for me to come into Austin today as I'm picking up my sister at the airport after lunch."

"Good. I'm glad it was convenient. We have several things to go over. First, I'll share with you the happenings on your divorce. Second, we'll get John Stoffer to meet with you to talk about the purchase of your ranch."

"I'm fortunate that my business attorney was able to refer me to you all. I trust Herbert Hawthorn and so I trust his referral."

Tammy entered the office carrying a large tray with a coffee pot, sugar and creamer, two cups with saucers, and a plate of pastries. She poured the coffee for both Hilary and Lance and then quietly left the office. Lance put a dab of cream in his cup and grabbed a large bear claw.

Hilary slid a couple of folders from the side of her desk to just in front of her and then opened the one on top. "I've known Herb for years and I'm glad to help out one of his clients. He spoke highly of you." She had a no-nonsense look about her and she spoke in a low commanding way. "Let's get into your divorce settlement." She handed him a folder with several documents in it.

Lance didn't want to take them. He didn't want to be here talking about a divorce. It still seemed surreal that it was even happening. His hand trembled slightly as he took the folder.

She gave no notice that she had seen the trembling. "Read those over and I'll answer any questions. What we are doing is making sure that everything that needs to be in the divorce degree is there, both to property and the custody of your children."

He opened the folder and stared at the first document DIVORCE PETITION. Chandra and his full names were listed plus the terms of the divorce. Lance looked up at Hilary. "Is this what the final divorce will look like?"

She nodded. "Yes, when both you and Chandra have looked it over we will move toward the meeting with the judge and the final decree. After the judge signs that and Chandra's attorney files it at the clerk's office, the divorce will be final. If there is anything you want different in the divorce settlement now is the time to say so. However, when you sign the papers in the next few weeks, you will have agreed to the terms of the divorce. Look everything over but I can tell you that everything you asked for is there. Chandra agreed to no division of property, no alimony, and she wants no custody of the children. Since you did not contest anything, the judge will usually sign the papers and they will be filed with the court the same day. Her attorney should be very pro-active to help her get a quick divorce."

"And the only reason I have to sign anything is because there are minor children involved?"

"Yes, otherwise, she could divorce you and have the documents mailed to you." Hilary kept her gaze on his as she tapped her fingers on the desk. "I'm concerned about her giving up the children so easily. It would have been better if she gave up her parental rights but that is not required when giving full custody to one parent. Within the month you will no longer be married, Lance. I know that is not what you want but it could have been a long drawn out court case with her demanding half of everything you have and custody of the children."

Lance shifted in the chair. "Can she come back and demand custody?"

"I'm afraid so. As long as the children have not reached their majority, she can always try for custody. However, she is the one who abandoned the children and you, and it will be hard for her to do, but not impossible. The more time that passes, the less you have to worry about. The only problem I see about this divorce is that I question if she set up residency in Nevada, but she had planned ahead and maybe she did. I did find out the time you thought she was working in Germany last month she had really been in Nevada. She completed the required Cope class online just as you did."

The three-hour online, required parenting class had been painful to complete for Lance as it highlighted all the different difficulties that the children might suffer from their parents' divorce. How could he learn all he needed to know in just three hours? Why had Chandra even been required to take the class, as she obviously no longer wanted to be a mother.

Hilary must have seen something in his face because she reached across the desk and patted his hand. "I had copies made and you can take this folder. When you get the divorce decree and the custody papers in the next month or so, I would carry that with you so you always have proof that you have sole custody. It's needed whenever you enter them in school, take them to a hospital or doctor, or take them out of the country."

Lance cleared his throat that threatened to close up on him. "Thanks Hilary. Make sure you bill me as needed. Also, let me know what you need to be on a retainer after the divorce is final so I can call you if I have questions or any legal problems concerning the children."

"That's a good idea. Your situation is very unusual and you never know for sure what another person will do. Now, if you don't have any other questions I will hand you off to John Stoffer."

Lance followed her out of her office and down the hallway to another one. She introduced him to a younger man in his mid-thirties, tall with the broad shoulders of someone who worked out regularly.

John Stoffer greeted Lance with a handshake and an open smiling face. "Howdy, Lance. Have a seat." His Texas accent was strong.

Hilary patted Lance on the arm as she turned and headed back toward her office. "Call me if you need anything, Lance."

In Hilary's office, Lance had felt a terrible weight around his heart and an awful sense of finality. John's greeting smile and hearty voice seemed to lift his spirit somewhat.

The two men spent an hour going over the papers for the purchase for the Two Forks Ranch. Lance felt he was getting good advice from the attorney but he still tried to think of anything that might need addressed before the closing. In addition to the land and the buildings, Lance was purchasing 180 head of breeding cattle and three bulls. George Fritze had explained the four pastures system for the cattle for rotating grazing they had used for several years on the ranch.

One of the things that had impressed Lance with George was his insistence on proper management of the land. Lance's dad and grandpapa had suggested he purchase only thirty-five of the horses on the ranch that included a stallion with an impressive bloodline. The breeding mares numbered twenty-nine and the other horses were working stock for the ranch.

John leaned back in his chair. "Any other questions Lance? I don't want to rush you. This is a huge purchase and you want to be sure about it."

Lance took a few moments to think. "Not about the price. When can we have the closing and where?"

"I think we can have the paper work all done by Friday. I'll get several of my staff on it. We will double check everything to make sure we have every document ready for the closing. I suggest we have the closing out at the ranch. I will bring someone to help and a printer so we can print any changes out. Either Lucile or I can act as notary. The sellers are eager to get this done and have promised to have their attorney there, ready to sign. The present owners have collected everything they want from the ranch that is not part of the sale. Anything left behind is yours to do with as you please." John grinned which lit the room up. "You and your children can move in over the weekend."

Lance cocked his eyebrow. "Sounds good. Call me about the exact time for the closing on Friday and we will get it done."

Chapter 17

Lance had an hour to get to the airport, park, and find the gate for Abby's incoming flight. He looked forward to seeing his baby sister. It had been a while since he had seen her. He had offered to fly her and a friend out during one of her school vacations but she had mumbled something about not coming until the folks could come.

He found the gate with fifteen minutes to spare, stood against a wall, and watched the crowds go by. Compared with the airports in California and other places, the Austin-Bergstrom International Airport was easy to navigate.

Here he was unemployed, soon to be unmarried, and the single father of two children. Much had changed since he had even talked to Abby on the phone. He hoped he could recognize her. It had been two years ago, during his brief visit home since he had last seen her.

Finally, they announced the arrival of Abby's flight and soon people where flooding out of the jet way from the plane. In the middle of the debarking passengers, he spotted her in the midst of several other young people. They were talking and laughing as they slowly made their way following the flow of the crowd. Abby stood out in the crowd, as she was a tall, willowy very pretty girl. Her dark auburn hair was pulled back into a ponytail and she was wearing a bright red pullover shirt and jeans. The shirt set off her dark brown eyes. Lance could hardly believe this beautiful young woman was his little baby sister.

She was glancing back and forth and Lance could tell the moment she spotted him. Her face lit up with a huge grin and she started moving toward him.

"Lance, you came," she yelled above the crowd.

Lance pushed off from where he had been leaning against the wall and met her halfway. She dropped the heavy looking backpack and threw herself into his hug.

"Hey Abby. It's good to see you. My, don't you look pretty."

Abby grinned. "You don't look bad yourself big brother. Did you bring anyone else with you like your kids, or Mom?"

"Nope, just me. I had business to attend to this morning here in Austin and Mom wanted to stay home and cook up a banquet for your return." He grabbed the backpack that was as heavy as it looked. "What do you have in here, your school books?"

Abby laughed. "No school books. I'm done with school for a while. Finishing my master's degree is as far as I'm going for a while. Do you realize that I have been in school for twenty years? I started when I was six and now at twenty-six I plan to do something else for a while. Like get a job and pay off school debts."

They had been walking down the concourse leading toward the baggage areas and the front entrance to the terminal. "How much luggage do you have? I drove my truck to have enough room." Lance hefted the backpack from his hand to his shoulder.

Abby punched his shoulder and laughed. "I only have one checked bag and I only needed that one because I brought gifts back to the family. All my clothes and stuff are in the backpack."

"Wow, I'm impressed. You were gone for almost six weeks. I didn't know women could travel so light."

"Well, I knew I had to carry whatever I took and my friends and I rode the trains that normally don't have many porters. We traveled light and fast."

Lance gazed at her bright, animated face. He remembered this perky little sister. She hadn't changed except in her appearance. Instead of a gawky pre-teen, she was a very attractive young woman. Lance noticed that several pairs of men's eyes followed them as they walked past. He was surprised at how protective he felt for Abby and he glared back at the stares. His beautiful little sister seemed totally unaware of the admiring glances she was getting.

"So you enjoyed your European trip?" Lance asked as he grabbed a luggage cart as they approached the baggage carousels.

Abby watched the luggage making the rounds on the carousel. "I had a great trip. Thanks to the folks and you sending money for graduation. I probably should have used it to pay on my school loans, but I couldn't resist the chance at a once in a life time trip with my friends."

Lance gave her shoulders another hug. "I'm glad you took your trip. Your school debts will get taken care of." He would help her get out from under the debt. It should never have existed. His feelings of guilt rose as he realized again, how much he had neglected his family. His baby sister should not be worrying about debt as she started out in her career.

Soon they collected Abby's bag, found his truck, and were merging onto Hwy 71 West.

Abby patted the soft leather of the passenger seat. "Sweet ride, cowboy. Have Logan and Alex stolen it for a joy ride yet?"

He laughed. "Not yet but I'm keeping an eye on them. Hey, you hungry? We could get a quick bite. As you know, we have a two and half hour drive to the ranch. Mom's preparing a huge supper but I skipped lunch."

"Sure, but only if we stop for Tex-Mex. A couple of tacos and maybe a burrito would be great with a Dr. Pepper."

As they neared the city limits of Austin, Lance spotted a small Tex-Mex restaurant and pulled over. "This look okay for you?"

Abby gave it a look and grinned. "And here I thought you city types would just pull through a Taco Bell and throw the tacos at me. This looks perfect."

Lance climbed out of the truck and was met by Abby at the front of it before he could make it around to open her door. She made him laugh and after the morning he had spent with the attorneys, was a breath of fresh air.

The little restaurant was almost empty as it was past the noon hour rush. They ordered light meals and Dr. Peppers.

Abby took a big bite of her burrito and closed her eyes. "Hmmmm. This is so good. Europe had nothing like this."

Lance had to agree. As he ate, he enjoyed watching the gusto with which Abby attacked the food. Twenty minutes later, they were back in the truck and heading toward the west.

"Okay, big brother. I've waited long enough. What's going on with you? Mom and Dad have talked about you and the children for several weeks but no mention of Chandra. Whenever I've asked, they tell me we will talk about it when I get home. So, what is it we need to talk about?"

Lance turned and looked out of the truck window. He didn't want to tell her what was going on, but she would find out anyway. He glanced back over at her. She sat turned toward him with a waiting look.

Taking a deep breath, he told her about Chandra leaving and filing for divorce. "I picked up the papers that I need to examine for the final divorce decree this morning from my attorney. It's the oddest feeling but I'll soon no longer be married."

Abby had tears in her eyes. "Oh, Lance, I'm so sorry. I know this isn't what you wanted. But I don't understand. You mean Chandra doesn't want anything to do with Mark and Sara Hope?"

Lance sighed deeply. "No, and I'm glad. I love those two kids and they're mine. If I have to be divorced, then this is the best outcome for me. Of course, I'm sorry Mark and Sara Hope are going to have to deal with their mother's rejection. I'll do whatever I can to make it up to them."

"So what are you going to do, start another software company? I can't imagine you won't be doing something, although Mom and Dad said you sold your business for enough money to retire. But you're too young to retire."

Lance grinned at her. "You're right. I need something to do. I've done my bit with computers. The other thing I did this morning was make an offer for the ranch west of the Rocking M Ranch."

Abby's eyes widened as her eyebrows rose. "You did what? But, that is the Two Forks Ranch. It is huge and has that gorgeous equestrian center."

He nodded. "That's the one. It's probably too large for me and the children. I'm hopeful I can make a home there. Their nanny, Rosa Real, moved out here with me. Her grandson, Ricardo, is also going to be working for me."

"What do Mom and Dad, Grandpapa and Nana think about you coming back to Texas?"

Lance chuckled. "What do you think they think? I'm returning with two grandchildren."

Abby nodded. "Right. They are thrilled beyond words and are spoiling the kids rotten. But what do you know about running a big ranch like that?"

"I know a lot. Remember where I grew up, the same as you did. Plus, I can hire people to run the place and do the real work. And don't forget Dad and Grandpapa will be just a few miles away with any advice I need."

"I go away for six weeks and the whole place changes. Good thing I didn't stay the whole summer. I'd have come back to find you a big rancher, with a new wife, and a passel of kids."

"Whoa, there. There won't be a new wife for a long time, if ever. I can hardly stand to think of myself as divorced yet. Give me some time." Half the time he still thought of himself as married. Just because Chandra had gone away didn't seem to change that he thought of himself in concert with her.

Abby placed her hand on his arm. "I'm sorry, Lance. I'm being thoughtless. You must still be reeling from all that has happened."

Lance appreciated her try at comforting him and reeling was a mild word for his reaction to the catastrophic upheaval in his life. "It's a lot to deal with and part of it is realizing that I am the only one parenting the children. I have to do right by them. Thank God, I had a home to come back to and family that will be there to help out."

"You know it, Lance. We will all have your back. And I look forward to the next several weeks as I look for a job and get to know my little niece and nephew."

Lance felt a warm love for his little sister as he thought about how blessed he was to have such a caring family. "Mark and Sara Hope are blessed to have you for an aunt, Abby." She grinned at him with the impish look that he would always associate with his little sister. He couldn't help but grin back.

The rest of the trip back to the ranch went quick as they talked more about his new ranch, the children, Abby's trip, and her plans for the future.

As he drove up to the ranch house, he said a silent prayer of thanks that he had been able to go pick up Abby by himself and that they had had the time together to get reacquainted. All that he needed now was for Matt to come home and his family would be complete.

"Oh look. There's Juliana's pickup, Lance. She's home. I can't wait to tell her about my trip. Don't you think she is wonderful? I love it that she lives with us."

Lance agreed with her assessment of Juliana but was able to keep his response subdued. "Yes, Juliana is a special person. I've enjoyed getting to know her. And she has sure helped Nana."

"Helped Nana? What happened to Nana?" Her expressive brown eyes showed her immediate concern for her grandmother.

"You didn't know? Nana had a stroke about five weeks ago. It must have been about a week after you left. She's doing great. It was a light stroke and Juliana has been working with her to help her get back to normal." Lance didn't want to mar Abby's homecoming but she would find out about Nana anyway. Better to tell her the truth.

"Well, why didn't Mom and Dad tell me? I would have come home immediately."

"Think maybe that's why they didn't tell you?" Lance suspected that his folks had not informed him or Abby because of their stubborn sense of taking care of things themselves. For them not to have told Abby made sense but they should have told him. He might have been able to help. Lance rubbed the back of his neck. The fault was his own as he had not been in communication enough for his parents to know he would have wanted to help.

Abby sighed. "Yes, that's why. They wanted me to have my trip. I bet Nana forbad them to mention it to me. Is she really doing all right now?"

Lance pulled the truck to a stop next to Juliana's little pickup. He reached over, took Abby's hand, and squeezed it. "I promise. Nana is doing great. Except for getting tired easily, you would hardly be aware she has had a stroke. And we owe that to Juliana's care."

The screen door banged open as the family, led by Mark, came tumbling out of the house. All talked and laughed at once as they took turns grabbing Abby and hugging her in a joyous welcome home.

Lance swung Mark up and hugged him close. "Hi, son. How was your day?"

Mark gave a hard squeeze around his dad's neck. "It was great. Ricardo said I would soon be able to ride by myself. Then I can go work the ranch with you, Granddad, and Grandpapa."

"Did you help take care of your sister?"

"Yes, sir. I gave her a bottle this afternoon with Nana's help so Grandmama could make two of the best-looking lemon meringue pies you ever saw. She makes the crust and everything. She said that was Aunt Abby's favorite." He pointed to where Abby was ruffling Alex's hair and teasing him about having grown another inch just since she had been gone. "Is that Aunt Abby?"

Lance set Mark on the ground. "Yes, come meet her. She can't wait to meet you."

"She knows about me?" Mark sounded amazed.

"Of course, she knows about you. You are her only nephew and she talked about you as we drove from the airport." He walked over to Abby, holding on to Mark's hand.

"Abby I want to introduce you to your nephew, Mark."

She took one look at the little boy, reached down, and pulled him into a hug. "Mark, I'm so glad to see you again. I remember the time when you were a little boy and came to the ranch for a couple of days. I only saw you for a little while because I had to go back to school. I bet you don't remember that."

Mark returned her hug. "No, I don't remember but Dad said that you are his favorite little sister. Only you're not little."

Abby and the rest of the family laughed. "No, I'm a grown woman now and I'm so glad to meet my favorite nephew again."

159

His mom slipped an arm around Lance's waist and hugged him tightly. "Well, I'm glad you all made it in safe and in time for supper. Let's go in, get you settled, and eat. Juliana is taking care of the biscuits for me."

Abby took Mark's hand and started for the kitchen door. "Come on Mark. Let's go see Juliana and then your little sister."

Mark trotted along with her with a happy grin.

Lance's mom patted his chest as Abby and Mark disappeared into the house. "You all right, son?"

He nodded. "Just seeing the grin on Mark's face, and my knowing my children are loved and cared for, makes it all right."

"Not just the children, son, you are loved and cared for also. Is it done?" His mom spoke in a quiet soft voice of love.

He knew what she was asking. "No, but almost. It should be done in a few more weeks. Something I never dreamed would be a part of my life and something I would never have willingly brought into the family."

"I know. But when it's done we'll just look forward."

Lance gave his mother a strong hug. "Thanks Mom, I love you."

She patted his cheek. "I love you son so very much. Now let's go in and have a joyful homecoming for your sister."

When Lance entered the kitchen with his mom, he saw Abby and Juliana hugging, laughing, and jumping around. Obviously, theirs was a close friendship.

"Juliana, I can't wait to tell you all about my trip. The only bad part is you weren't with me." Abby pursed her full lips into an impressive pout.

"Maybe the next trip I'll be able to afford to go. Did you take more pictures than you emailed to us?" Juliana glanced at Lance and smiled.

"You better believe I took a lot more pictures and everyone in the family is going to have to see them." Abby looked around at her family and grinned.

Logan gave her a soft punch on the arm. "Is that a threat?"

Hank tugged at her ponytail. "Sounds like it to me."

"You all leave the girl alone. I want to see all her pictures." Olivia gazed at her only daughter with eyes that shown with a deep love. "Now you girls go get Abby settled and I'll call everyone to supper soon."

Lance watched as Abby and Juliana made their way up the stairs. Logan and Alex followed behind carrying her bag and backpack grumbling about the weight.

Hank and Walt wandered into the living room where a baseball game was on the large screen TV. Soon Lance could hear the noise of the game as his dad turned up the volume.

"What can I do to help you, Mom?" Lance noticed that Mark and Ricardo had disappeared and only Mom, Nana, and Rosa were busy in the kitchen getting the supper ready.

Olivia looked around at their preparations. "I think we have this in hand. It would be helpful if you would check on Sara Hope. With all the noise I'm surprised she hasn't let us know she's awake from her nap."

"When did she go down for her nap?" Lance asked.

Glancing at the clock hanging on the wall above the refrigerator, Rosa said, "I put her down about two hours ago. You better see if you can get her up so she'll sleep tonight."

Lance nodded and headed upstairs. Entering the children's room, he found Sara Hope laying in her bed kicking her legs in the air and cooing to herself. "Hey, baby girl."

The moment she heard his voice she turned her head and gave him a sloppy smile. Her drooling was definitely worse these days. His mom said it was because she was starting to get her baby teeth. He got the stuff together and soon had her wet diaper changed. He then dressed her in a little sundress but left off the little sandals. The afternoon had turned hot and even with the air conditioning, it was a little warm in the house from the Texas afternoon heat.

Abby came in and stood smiling at Sara Hope. "Is this who I think it is?"

Lance handed Sara Hope off to his little sister. "Sara Hope, meet your Aunt Abby."

"Oh, Lance, she is beautiful." Abby nuzzled the baby's neck and Sara Hope grinned.

Lance grabbed a bib and fastened it around Sara Hope's neck. "These days it's not safe to go without one of these as she's starting to teeth."

Abby ran her finger around Sara Hope gums. "I can feel two little nobs. You know you need to be ready with a soft little cold ring for her to chew on."

Lance cocked his head. "You can feel the teeth coming in?"

"Of course, big brother, didn't you know that. And sometimes when it is hurting her, having something soft and cold to chew on will make it feel better." Abby seemed familiar with holding a baby and confidently led the way downstairs carrying her little niece. "Juliana went up to her room to shower and change. She'll be down soon."

Lance wondered if he blushed as he tried to act as if he hadn't been looking down the hall for Juliana. Why did the woman have to be so attractive and nice? He would have to be careful or Abby would get the wrong idea and start teasing. How strange was it to be thinking about another woman when he had yet to receive his final divorce papers? Had his marriage meant so little to him? Or, had the marriage been ending over the last year and he hadn't even noticed.

"Hey, Lance, where did you go?" Abby was standing at the bottom of the stairs waiting for him to follow her into the kitchen.

He descended the stairs two at a time. "Sorry, I've got a lot on my mind."

Abby nodded. "I can believe it with all that is going on, especially the momentous occasion of my return. When can I see the new place?"

Lance was thankful that she had drawn him away from his depressing thoughts. Talking about the ranch that was soon to be his home was much more pleasant.

Chapter 18

Juliana was thrilled to have Abby home and wrapped her up in a hug. They had been good friends from the first time they met at church two years ago. "Welcome home. I missed you."

Abby hugged her back hard. "I'm glad to be home. But how could you miss me with all that has happened since I left a month ago. Lance has moved back, now as a single dad about to be divorced." She sighed and a frown appeared. "I can hardly believe it and then Nana has a stroke and no one bothers to tell me, not even my best friend."

Juliana nodded. "It has been busy and eventful. With Lance here with the children, Ricardo, and Rosa, the house is bulging at the seams. But that is about to change with his purchase of his ranch. Don't worry about Nana. She is doing great, just moving a little slower and getting tired easily."

Abby smiled brightly. "I'm so thankful you were here to help her. You must tell me about everything that has happened."

Logan dumped the heavy backpack on the bed as Alex rolled the heavy bag into the bright bedroom that had been Abby's since she was a child. "You can tell Abby everything this evening. Mom should have supper on the table in a few minutes. Glad you made it home."

Abby surprised her not so little brother with a hug. "Thanks for bringing my backpack up the stairs, and I'm glad to see you, too."

Alex gave her a quick hug and stepped back out of reach. "About time you got home, Abs. I've even had to deal with the baby."

"No way, you taking care of a baby?" Abby's laugh was full and carefree. "This I have got to see."

Alex grinned. "Well, maybe just feeding her a bottle. I always hand her off to Lance when Sara Hope needs a diaper change."

Juliana watched the banter between the sister and brothers almost with envy. She missed her own siblings. In a break in the conversation, she said, "I'll see you downstairs. I'm going to freshen up and then I'd better go see what I can do to help."

Abby gave her another quick hug. "I'm going to wash my face and hands and be right behind you."

Juliana changed into a tee shirt, jeans, and sandals. She admitted to herself what she really wanted was to get back downstairs and see Lance, as she skipped down the stairs and entered the kitchen.

The extra leaves were soon on the table and it was set for twelve. Soon everyone gathered in the kitchen and found seats. After everyone was seated, Hank asked Walt to say the prayer for the meal.

"Before I say the prayer I want to say how glad I am to see you home safe, Granddaughter. And, Lance, do you have something you want to tell us?" Walt sat quietly waiting for Lance to look up from his plate.

Clearing his throat, he looked around with a grim expression. "I think what Grandpapa wants me to let you all know, as my family, is that the divorce papers are being finalized. I will probably get the final divorce papers signed in the next month." Lance glanced down at Mark and pulled him close. "As we continue to adjust, we need your prayers."

As Juliana listened to Walt's prayer for his family and for the food, she tried to take it in that Lance would soon no longer be married, but a divorced man. Walt ended the prayer with his usual asking God to keep Matt safe and bring him home soon. Juliana cut a quick glance at Lance to see him staring at his plate with a look of sadness that was heartbreaking. The idea of the divorce being final soon didn't seem to give him any kind of peace.

Grandpapa filled his plate and then gazed at his grandson. "Lance, how goes the purchase of Two Forks Ranch?"

Lance smiled at his grandpapa. "I signed the final purchase offer with the attorney this morning. He expects to have the closing on Friday out at the ranch, as the owner is motivated to sell. Unless there is a problem we can move in starting on Saturday."

Olivia fisted her right hand and laid it over her heart. "Oh Lance, so soon?"

Lance smiled gently at his mother. "We'll be just next door and I expect you to be there with us, helping us get settled in. Rosa and I will need all the help we can get."

His mom nodded. "I know and I'll be helping. It has been so lovely to have you and the children here. But I know you need your own place, to make a home for the children."

Mark looked up at his dad. The boy had been too quiet since the news that his parents were soon to be divorced. "We're moving?" His voice was small and more childlike than usual.

Juliana wanted to get up and go hug the little boy. She couldn't image what was going through the boy's mind. She watched as Lance pulled Mark into his lap.

"Remember I told you about buying the ranch next door and that if we bought it, it would be our new home?"

"Yes, sir. But I didn't know that we would have to leave Grandmama and Granddad and everyone else."

Lance hugged the little boy and kissed the top of his head. "We aren't leaving them. We're getting more bedrooms and bathrooms. Don't you want a bedroom all to yourself where you can have all your things? You'll have a bedroom and Sara Hope will have her own bedroom. Plus, Rosa and Ricardo are moving with us."

Ricardo reached out and ruffled the boy's hair. "We need to move so we can get you your own horse and continue our riding lessons."

Lance grinned at Ricardo. "You think he's riding well enough to manage his own horse?"

"You bet he is. Mark here is going to be an exceptional rider. He's a natural horseman."

Mark straightened up a bit in his father's arms. "That's because you are a great teacher Ricardo."

Walt slapped the table. "It's time for the ballgame on that wonderful huge TV. But, Mark you might want to go to bed a little early tonight because I plan to come watch you ride in the morning. I want to see what a great horseman my great-grandson is becoming."

Olivia stood and carried her plate to the sink. "You men go watch your ballgame and we ladies will do the dishes. You want to dry, Abby?"

Abby got up and gave Lance and Mark a hug. "I'll be glad to dry dishes. I've missed that for the last month."

Lance lifted Mark off his lap and gently pushed him toward the living room. "Go on and save me a seat for the ball game. I'll see if Sara Hope needs a change." He picked up his baby daughter from the day crib that occupied the corner of the kitchen. "Yep, a change is in order and I might as well bathe her as well."

Before Juliana could stop herself, she said, "I'll help with Sara Hope."

He patted Sara Hope on the back, as he looked around at all the people moving around. "That would be great. I can always use help."

"And what am I supposed to do while you take care of the baby?" Rosa was laughing, taking any sting out of the question.

Olivia answered the question, "Why don't you sit and drink a cup of coffee and watch us do the dishes. You have taken care of that baby for the whole day and got the laundry caught up as well."

Juliana followed Lance up the stairs as she heard Hank, Walt, Ricardo, and Mark all shouting at the TV over the noise of the ballgame.

Lance had Sara Hope's left ear pressed to his chest as he covered her right ear. "One thing about being here for the last several weeks is that Sara Hope has gotten used to a lot more noise and people about."

"And that is a blessing as every one of those people loves her to bits."

Lance glanced back at Juliana as he entered the children's room. "I hadn't thought about it like that, but it's true. My children do have the blessing of so many people surrounding them with unconditional love. I find myself caught up in the sadness that their mother has abandoned them, when I should be thanking God for all the friends and family that love them."

"With the enormity of the divorce and their mother not wanting them, I'm sure it's hard to keep a focus on the blessings God has given you." Juliana wasn't sure she should say anything but Lance is the one who had brought it up.

Handing Sara Hope to Juliana, Lance opened the drawer of the dresser and pulled out a sleep sack, a baby washcloth, and towel. He grabbed a diaper from the changing table and some lotion.

"You plan on changing her in the bathroom after her bath?" Juliana couldn't help but ask.

"Sure, I always do." Lance seemed puzzled.

"But there's hardly room in the bathroom."

"I usually just put a towel on the floor and change her there after I dry her off. Well, what would you do?"

Juliana started removing the little sundress over the baby's head. "I would wrap a towel around her and bring her back in here where it's easier to change and dress her. The bathroom floor has to be hard on her."

Lance looked at his daughter and then the things in his hands. "You know, I think you might be on to something. I wish I could have had more parenting classes. I'm sort of unprepared for raising a baby girl. Mark is old enough that I know more what to do for him. Thank God, I've had Rosa. Chandra never did get into taking care of the children."

Juliana didn't want Lance to think she saw him as a bad father. "I didn't mean to imply you didn't know what you were doing with the children. I'm amazed at how well you do. You're a great father, Lance, and don't ever let anyone tell you different." She had spoken more fiercely that she had meant to do.

"Thanks for those kind words. Seems like I'm constantly questioning whether I'm doing the right thing or not. Let's do it your way and see how Sara Hope responds."

After a lot of laughing and cooing at Sara Hope, they got her bathed and dressed for the night. Juliana sat and rocked her while Lance went downstairs to the kitchen to warm up a bottle for the baby. He then sat on Mark's bed and watched Juliana rock and feed Sara Hope her bedtime bottle.

Chapter 19

Lance couldn't take his gaze from Juliana as she sat in the rocker gently talking nonsense to Sara Hope as she fed the baby. Sara Hope watched Juliana with wide eyes as she sucked at the nipple on the bottle of formula. Juliana and Sara Hope seemed to belong together. Lance swallowed and took a deep breath as he felt himself close to tears. Why couldn't someone like Juliana have been the baby's mother, rather than someone like Chandra who could turn her back on the beautiful child?

Juliana hummed a hymn and rocked gently. Sara Hope's eyelids started to droop and soon she was asleep. Juliana removed the almost empty bottle and handed it to Lance. "I'll rock her a few more minutes to make sure she is sound asleep and then lay her in her bed."

Lance went to the crib and pulled the baby blanket covered in pink bunnies to the end of the bed. "You want me to take her?"

"No, I can lay her down without much disturbance. Is the baby monitor set?" Juliana gracefully rose from the rocker and placed the sleeping baby in the crib. Sara Hope pursed her lips as if still sucking and settled into a deep sleep.

Lance checked the baby monitor and made sure it was on. He then stood side by side with Juliana as they gazed at the sleeping baby. "Thanks for the help. Sara Hope responds positively to you."

Juliana glanced at him. "You're welcome. She's a precious baby and I enjoy helping with her. Both your children are treasures to be guarded."

"You're right. Even with the sadness of today, I need to focus on the treasures that have come out of the disaster that was my marriage."

Lance had to keep himself from sliding his arm around Juliana's shoulders and hugging her for her kind words and support. He needed to remind himself that she was just a friend, and he should keep his distance. "I better get downstairs and corral Mark."

Juliana stepped toward the hallway. "I need to get to bed as tomorrow will be busy. Good night, Lance."

He watched her head up the stairs to the attic bedroom and then turned toward the downstairs. A strange sense of loss filled him as if something worth keeping was just out of his reach.

~

The week passed quickly with Lance spending part of each day with George Fritz learning about the running of the Two Forks Ranch. He spent hours in discussion with his father and grandfather getting as much input as he could about ranching in the Texas Hill Country.

Abby frequently went with Lance to Two Forks. She wanted to know everything about the new place, especially his plans for the equestrian complex. He had decided to hire someone to develop the center and make it a non-profit foundation apart from the ranch. He put in a call to an old friend who was working as an equestrian therapist at a large center in California.

Saturday morning Lance woke with realization that he was about to embark on a new phase of his life with the coming move to Two Forks. As he lay in the familiar small bedroom that had been part of his childhood world, out the bedroom window the dawn was breaking over the ranch land. This place had always been safe for him. He had never doubted for a moment that he couldn't come home again. As much as he looked forward to the challenge of making Two Forks Ranch a home for his little family, a part of him wanted to stay in the safe cocoon of his parents' home. However, he couldn't go back to the security of his childhood. He needed to be looking forward toward making that same security for Mark and Sara Hope.

Swinging his feet onto the floor of the bedroom, he said a quick prayer for the Lord's guidance as he moved forward. Then he headed toward the shower and the start of a busy day.

When he reached the kitchen after looking in on Mark and Sara Hope, who were both still sound asleep, he found everyone else gathered around the table with a huge country breakfast placed down the center. Even Juliana was up early and dressed in comfortable clothes.

Lance pulled out his chair and glanced around at his family and friends. "All right, what is going on? Why is everyone up so early?"

Grandpapa grinned and took Nana's hand. "You didn't think we would let you move all by yourself? We're having a moving party. You get to tell us all what to do today."

His mom smiled at him. "All but Nana and me, we're going to hold down the fort here by keeping Mark and Sara Hope and preparing lunch for everyone. Rosa needs to be at your place to help arrange the children's rooms and get herself and Ricardo settled."

"Thanks, Mom and Nana, that will be helpful. The vans arrived yesterday evening with the stuff from the house in California. Empting them will be the first step and then we can get bedrooms set up and beds made." Lance looked around at his parents, grandparents, brothers, sister, Rosa, and Ricardo. The image he had had of trying to do everything himself today faded away as he realized he was not alone.

Hank grabbed Olivia's hand on his right and Abby's hand on his left. "Let's pray for the food, eat a great breakfast, and then go get Lance set up in his new home."

The day flew by with Lance feeling like a general ordering his troops around as they unloaded the two vans of furniture and personal items from the California house. Lance had had everything moved except for the personal items Chandra had left behind. He had kept her jewelry and a few other items in case his children wanted them at some later time, but all of her clothes she had not taken he had boxed up and shipped to her address in Nevada. Whether she wanted the things was not something he felt a need to ask her. He just knew that he didn't want them.

Over time, he would replace some of the furniture that was not a style that he particularly wanted or thought fit into the new place. Especially the formal living room furniture that was too modern, all chrome and hard edges. However, he had not had the time to shop for what he wanted. Maybe Juliana would help him with the shopping. He shook his head. Where had that thought come from?

Lance looked around at the master suite where he had replaced the furniture. He had ordered an oversized bed out of Dallas that did not have a footboard and was long enough that he could stretch out his full six-foot-three length with room to spare. The other reason he had wanted a new set of furnishings in his bedroom was he wanted to remove any reminder of Chandra. He didn't try to reason out why he had ordered an his-and-her chest of drawers set.

Rosa and Juliana worked, with the help of Ricardo and one of the men from the moving company, to place the furniture into the bedrooms Lance had chosen for the children.

Lance wandered into Sara Hope's bedroom.

Rosa sat in a rocker with a moving box in front of her. "Mr. Lance, good you come to make a decision. These are all things belonging to Mark and Sara Hope when tiny infants. They are good things but Sara Hope has outgrown them."

Lance knelt down beside the box and lifted out a tiny little outfit that fitted a newborn. "Let's store them away and we can decide what to do with them later. If they are in good condition, we can donate them. I don't see that we will have any use for them again." Knowing that his marrying days were over, and Mark and Sara Hope would be all the children he would ever have left his chest with a hollow feeling. However, that was how it would be.

Closing the box, Rosa nodded. "There is much storage space in this big house. Juliana, hand me that marker so I can label this box and then, Lance, you can set it in the hallway."

Juliana handed the marker to Rosa. "There are a couple more boxes that have toys for small children that I suggest you store with that box. You can get them out as Sara Hope reaches an age to play with them."

Lance looked to where she had pointed. "I guess we never got rid of anything and I didn't realize it." And he had thought he and Chandra might have more children. "I'll leave you two to finish up here and I'll go make sure everything else is placed where it needs to be. The vans have been emptied and as soon as we no longer need the movers' help they will head out. The last step is to bring over everything at the Rocking M and get the children settled here for the night."

Rosa patted Lance on the arm. "You go supervise and we will finish in here. We are almost done and Olivia plans for us to eat supper at Rocking M. We can bring the children over after supper and get them settled. Mrs. Martin has stocked the kitchen with food. She is off tomorrow but will be back on Monday morning."

Lance wandered down the hall to the kitchen and Mrs. Martin unwrapping dishes out of boxes. "How's it going?"

She grinned at Lance. "Like any moving day. The unpacking is easier than the packing for me. Although the previous owner left kitchenware, with what you have moved here, this will be a wonderfully equipped kitchen to work in. I asked Rosa where she wanted the dishes and her suggestions were in line with my ideas so it's going well."

Lance didn't really care about the arrangement of the kitchen stuff, but he did want to keep both Rosa and Mrs. Martin happy. "Thanks, you're being a big help today."

"I can come back tomorrow afternoon, after church, if you need me." She continued to unwrap a set of tall glasses as she talked.

Lance shook his head. "No need. Tomorrow we will try to get settled but Monday morning is soon enough to finish up the move. I plan for us to be here for a long time and we don't have to rush with everything."

Mrs. Martin placed her hands on the counter and met his eyes. "That is a wise attitude. You take time tomorrow to be with your family and help the children settle. We can have this place in order by the end of the week."

Later that evening after supper, Lance loaded up Mark and Sara Hope in the truck. He had asked his family to keep the good-byes low key. Having made the decision not to show Mark the new house before the move, Lance now questioned if that had been wise. His thinking has been that he wanted Mark to see the house with all their things in it and his bedroom set up. With the family standing on the back porch waving good-bye and reassurances that they would meet at church services the next morning, Lance drove toward their new home at the Two Forks Ranch. Rosa and Ricardo followed them in the BMW.

"Are we spending the night at the new ranch, Dad?" Mark's eyes were wide open as he turned his head from side to side, trying to see everything at once out the windows of the truck.

"Yes, Mark, I told you that. Remember?"

"Oh, yes, you told me last night that tonight I would have my own room. Does it have a bed?"

Lance glanced in the rearview mirror at his son. Mark's expression was serious. "Of course, your bed from the old house and all your toys are now in your new room. You'll like it."

"Okay, I've never had a new room before. Well, maybe if you count the one at Granddad and Grandmama's place."

Lance nodded his understanding. "I keep forgetting you have never moved before, son. You are handling it like a big kid. It's not always easy to make changes."

Mark looked surprised. "Is it hard for you, Dad?"

"It is in some ways, but I look forward to the life we will have here in Texas. I especially like that we will be living on a ranch and so close to your grandparents."

"Yes, that is a good thing. I like Granddad, Grandmama, Grandpapa, and Nana." Mark's grin was back and the concerned look faded away as Lance drove through the archway onto the ranch and the big house appeared in front of them.

Lance opened the garage door with the automatic opener and parked in one of the open bays. Ricardo pulled the BMW alongside.

As Mark climbed out of the truck, he spotted his bicycle leaning against the garage wall. "Look, Dad, my bike!" He ran over to pat his bike as if it was a long lost friend. "Did you know it was here?"

Lance laughed as he unbuckled Sara Hope from the infant seat. She gazed at her brother with an intent look, almost as if she was wondering what he was shouting about. "Yes, Mark, I knew it was here. All your things are here."

Rosa climbed out of the BMW. "Let me have Sara Hope and then you can guide Mark about the house. Ricardo, please bring all my things to my room." She took Sara Hope and disappeared into the house with Ricardo following his grandmother carrying two suitcases.

"Come on, Mark. Let me show you your new home." Lance held out his hand for Mark to grab.

"How long are we going to stay here, Dad?"

"I'm hoping not to move again. That's why the house is so big. I'm hoping it will be big enough for when you get big. You know you will take up a lot of space." Lance teased his son, but it was still the truth. "Now, there are some new house rules and I will not be tolerant if you break them."

"What does tolerant mean?"

"That means if you break a rule, there will be a consequence." Although, Lance couldn't think what some of the consequences might be. He would have to work on that.

Mark looked up at his dad with trusting eyes. "What rules?"

"These rules are to keep you safe and there will be no excuses. First rule is we have swimming pools one outside and one inside the house. There will be locks on the gates and doors to that area of the house. You are not allowed near a pool unless an approved adult is with you. You break that rule and there will be severe consequences. That goes for the exercise room also. The second rule, you do not leave the house without permission and you never leave the yard around the house without an adult with you. That especially goes for the barns and water on the ranch."

"Wow, Dad. I never had so many rules before."

Lance nodded. "That's because we didn't have a swimming pool before and there are too many ways to get hurt on a ranch. As you get older and bigger, there won't be so many rules. There is a third rule I forgot to mention. You never leave with anyone you don't know, whether from this house, the church building, the Rocking M Ranch, or when you go to school. And I'm sure to come up with some more rules."

"I know about stranger danger, Dad. You've told me before not to get into a car with a stranger." Mark spoke with the assurance of an eight-year-old about to be nine.

Lance gazed at his son, such a gift. But he knew the child did not have a clear understanding of the dangers out in the world and he didn't want Mark to really know the truth about what evil could be out there. His job was to keep his son and daughter safe but still raise them to have wings. Walking into Mark's room, Lance questioned if he was up for the job. At least now, he was near his folks and could call for help.

Mark ran and jumped onto his bed and started bouncing. "Look, Dad, my bed and all my toys and books and things." Mark sounded as if Christmas had come early.

Lance grinned at his enthusiasm. "You have a large enough bedroom for your things and a large closet." Lance opened the door to the walk-in closet and then walked across the room to open the door to the full bath including a bathtub and separate glass enclosed shower stall. "And your own full bathroom."

Mark followed his dad into the bathroom and looked around. "Is this just for me?"

"Yes, son, it is all just for you. You know that means more area that you have to keep straight and clean. I expect you to help take care of your things and be responsible. Like no wet towels on the floor, if you spill it, you mop it up, and if you break it, you have to tell Rosa or me."

"Just like in California." Mark nodded sagely.

"Yes, just because we moved doesn't mean things have changed." Lance laughed at Mark's attempt at a wise look.

"Except Mom may not find us here in Texas."

Did Mark not understand that his mom was not coming to Texas? Lance took a deep breath. He had to answer carefully because he would not build a hope that was not there.

"Your mom knows where we are and if she decides to come to Texas she will know how to find us."

Mark looked up with hope in his eyes. "Mom knows where we are? When is she coming?"

Lance walked with Mark back into his bedroom and sat on the bed, pulling Mark to sit beside him. "Listen, son, I hope sometime your mom will come visit. You remember my telling you that she has decided she wants to live somewhere else besides with me? So she is getting a divorce."

Mark nodded. "I know what a divorce is. Like Joey Rosenfelt back at my old school. His parents got a divorce. His dad moved away and then his mom got him a new dad. Are you going to get me a new mom?"

How to answer so an eight year old understood? "I'm not planning on that anytime soon and maybe never. For right now it is just you, Sara Hope, Rosa, and me."

"And Ricardo, Granddad, Grandmama, Grandpapa, Nana, Uncle Logan, Uncle Alex, Aunt Abby, and Juliana are all our family. Right, Dad?"

Smiling at Mark's citation of everyone important in his life, Lance hugged his son. "That is right. Now we need to get you and Sara Hope started to bed and in the morning we will go to church with the family. Mom wants us to eat Sunday dinner afterwards at the Rocking M."

Mark's face lit up with a grin. "Good and then I can go visit the horses and chickens at Granddad's ranch."

After getting the children settled, Lance took a shower and climbed into his new bed. Thinking over the day, he said a prayer of thanks for the new home and that he had his children with him. Sometime in the night, he woke and felt a small boy climb into bed with him. Without saying anything, he wrapped his arms around his son as the child drifted back to sleep.

Chapter 20

Juliana made her way into the kitchen hoping for her first cup of coffee of the day. There she found the family already gathered around the breakfast table. "Good morning, all." She restrained a yawn.

Olivia got up from the table and poured Juliana a cup of coffee. "Morning, hope you slept well after all the activities of yesterday." She gave Juliana a good morning kiss on the check as she sat the cup of coffee down.

She took a sip of the hot brew before answering. "I did sleep well but the house seems unusually quiet this morning."

Walt laughed. "That's what wrong. I knew something was different. It's too quiet with Lance and the children gone."

Olivia shook her head. "They are not gone, only moved. They are only four miles away."

Hank patted her hand. "And they will meet us at church services."

Nana sniffled into her handkerchief. "Well, it feels like they moved a long way away. I had gotten used to having them here."

Walt put his arm around her shoulders. "Now, honey, it's a lot closer than that California."

Juliana had to agree with Nana. She missed knowing Lance was sleeping just downstairs and she missed the cheerful talk of the lively eight year old. And she looked forward to seeing the sweet face of little Sara Hope at church services. Getting too attached to that little family was not a good idea.

Juliana's cell phone rang and she pulled it out of her pocket. "Hello."

"Juliana, this is Pricilla. Lucy's car won't start. Can you pick us up for church services?"

"Sure Ms. Pricilla. I'll stop by for you first as usual. See you in a bit."

"Thank you dear."

Olivia moved around the dining table refilling coffee cups. "Pricilla needs a ride?"

Juliana held up her cup for a refill. "Yes, Lucy's car won't start again. So I will stop by and get both of the old dears."

Nana covered her cup letting Olivia know that she didn't want a refill. "That car of Lucy Graham must be a hundred years old. I'm amazed that it runs at all. And maybe that's a good thing. Lucy was eighty her last birthday and I'm not sure how well she sees."

Walt leaned back with a satisfied look and an empty breakfast plate. "As long as she is just driving around Tumbleweed, she should be okay. Everyone knows to watch out for her in that big boat she calls a car. Thanks, Juliana, for picking them up for church."

"No problem. It's not far out of the way and only takes about ten minutes. They are both so sweet." She really didn't mind stopping by and taking them to church services. It was the least she could do. She didn't even mind that the sweet old dears always told her all about their children and grandchildren, often repeating themselves.

Thirty minutes before time for the Bible class Juliana pulled up in front of Pricilla Miller's little house. The front yard was ablaze with flowers. Juliana got out and went up to the porch to make sure that the old lady maneuvered the two steps off the porch.

"Juliana, you look pretty as a picture. I like your hair down around your face." She placed her hand around Juliana's winged arm.

"Ms. Priscilla, you always say I'm pretty, but thank you. Now watch your step." Juliana helped her settle in the pickup and handed her cane to her.

It only took five minutes to drive the few blocks to Lucy Graham's house that had a similar look as Priscilla Miller's place. Both houses were built in the fifties and had four rooms and a bath. Both had porches and flowerbeds.

"I'm coming. I just need to grab my purse and Bible." Lucy called out the door.

Juliana waited in the pickup as Lucy was much more agile than Priscilla.

Soon Lucy came hurrying to the pickup and opened the passenger door. "Morning, Pris and Juliana. Isn't it a beautiful day? Thanks for coming for us. I went out to start the car this morning and it just sat there. I guess I'll have to call Jeb Brown over to take a look."

Juliana smiled at Lucy. "Morning yourself and coming by to take you all to church is no problem. I'm glad I can do it." Jeb Brown owned the local service station and was the only mechanic in town. She hoped he could repair the old car, as she knew Lucy could not afford a new one.

Bible class went by quickly as Juliana taught the children. Mark had acted as if it had been a month since he had seen her when he entered the classroom. It warmed her heart to think she had come to mean something to the little boy.

After class, he waited for her to see the last of the children out of the classroom and gathered her things. "Can I sit with you, Juliana?"

"Sure, Mark, unless your dad wants you to sit by him."

Mark looked up at her. "He can sit on one side and you on the other."

Juliana laughed. "Yes, that will work."

They approached the usual McTavish pew and found Walt and Nana already seated. They greeted and hugged Mark. Soon the pew and the one behind were filling up with the family including Ricardo and Rosa. Last to arrive was Lance carrying Sara Hope.

"Hey, Dad, sit here by me and Juliana." Mark called out.

"Okay, son, but soften your voice in the church building. Morning, Juliana." His glance seemed to linger on her as he settled into the pew with Sara Hope on his lap.

Juliana smiled and nodded as the song leader announced the first song. She had not realized how anxious she had waited for his appearance. Now seated together, she felt herself relax and turned her attention to the worship service.

After services, she gathered her old dears and drove them home. Then as she drove back to the McTavish Ranch, anticipating Lance and the children being there for Sunday dinner, she thought about her reaction to seeing Lance, Mark, and Sara Hope after just one night of them moved into their own home. She needed to think about it and pray that God would protect her from coming to care too much for Lance and his children. It was perhaps a blessing they had moved to their own place. The separation might not be a bad idea for her own heart.

As she drove up to the ranch house she spotted Maria Sancho's compact car parked next to Lance's big truck. Juliana had forgotten she had invited Maria for Sunday dinner earlier in the week. Maria attended early church services in Fredericksburg.

Juliana entered the kitchen and found Maria helping Abby set the table. "Hey, girlfriend, glad you made it."

Maria set the last plate down and then turned to give Juliana a hug. "Thanks for the invite. I couldn't wait to see Abby and hear all about her trip."

Abby laughed. "And see all my photos. The family is already getting tired of hearing about my trip."

"Well, I want to hear all about it so I can pretend it was me that got to go." Maria's voice sounded a little wishful.

Juliana gave her another quick hug. She understood the desire to get away, especially for Maria who lived with her large family in close quarters. "Maybe if we save our nickels and dimes we can go traveling."

Abby clapped her hands. "We need to plan a girl's road trip, even if it's only to San Antonio for the three of us."

"That sound like a great idea," Maria responded.

Stomping sounded from the back porch and Logan came into the kitchen followed by Alex and Ricardo. They had changed out of their Sunday clothes and were now wearing their work clothes. Their cowboy hats soon landed on the hooks by the door.

Logan reached out and pulled a strand of Maria long black silky hair. "Hey, Maria."

She batted his hand away. "Stop that, Logan. Behave yourself or I'll tell Nana."

Juliana smiled at their playfulness. Although the threat to tell Nana was an effective one as no one wanted to upset her.

Maria and Ricardo seemed to be staring at each other. Juliana realized they had not met before now.

"Maria, let me introduce you to Ricardo Real. His grandmother, Rosa, helps take care of Lance's children. Ricardo, this is my good friend Maria Sancho. She lives between here and Fredericksburg."

"Glad to meet you, Maria. Can I pull your hair like Logan?" His grin lit up his whole face.

"Not if you want to be friends," Maria returned his grin.

Juliana looked at Abby who smiled back. Hmmm, Ricardo and Maria seemed to be making some sort of connection.

"Abby, please ring the bell and call the men to Sunday dinner," Olivia asked as she placed a big platter of roast beef on the table that was now loaded with a huge platters and bowls of food.

Grinning to herself, Juliana maneuvered herself and Maria to sit across the table from Ricardo and Lance. She preferred that to sitting next to them, as she was able to watch Lance without it being as obvious. He seemed to watch her also.

After sitting at the table eating and talking for a couple of hours, the men shooed the women into the living room and the men proceeded to do the dishes. Rosa took Sara Hope upstairs to change her and to get her down for a nap. The baby was already resting her head on Rosa' shoulder and her eyes had the droopy look of a baby about to nod off.

Lance came into the living room. He sat on the arm of the overstuffed chair where Olivia was seated. "Mom, Rosa and Sara Hope are napping upstairs and Mark is getting a lesson in roping from Alex and Logan. Okay if I leave them here while I go drive around my new place?"

Olivia patted his arm. "Of course, you know you and the children are welcome here any time you want."

Glancing at Juliana and then to Abby and Maria, he asked, "Anyone want to go for a ride?"

Juliana looked at Maria and then Abby. They both nodded.

Abby jumped up off the couch. "Let's go, girls. My big brother needs to show us his new digs."

Juliana laughed, as the Two Forks Ranch was hardly something she would call simply new digs. "I'm game. How about you, Maria?"

"I am dying to see the ranch. I've heard about it all my life but I've never been there." Maria followed close behind Abby out to Lance's truck where Ricardo removed Mark's boaster seat and placed it on the porch next to Sara Hope's infant seat.

Lance threw the keys to Ricardo. "You drive so I can look. Maria, why don't you take the passenger seat up front and I'll ride with Abby and Juliana."

Before Juliana knew how it had happened, she found herself seated between Lance and Abby in the rear seat of the truck.

The next couple of hours they spent driving over every mile of road and track on the Two Forks Ranch with several stops to look out over the land. Ricardo and Lance kept up a running dialogue about different aspects of the ranch and its management. Juliana, Abby, and Maria generally just tagged along and chatted girl talk.

As they drove back toward the ranch house, Lance asked, "Want to stop and see the house? It's still a mess as we aren't completely moved in but there are cold drinks in the refrigarator?"

Abby responded before Juliana could suggest they get back to the Rocking M. "Sure big brother. I could do with something cold to drink."

Ricardo took the circular drive at the front of the house and stopped by the steps leading to the porch. He quickly jumped out and made it to the passenger side before Maria could undo her seat belt and open the door.

As Lance held the truck door open for Juliana to descend from the vehicle, she had to smile at Ricardo and Maria. Yes, there was something about the glances they were giving each other. Taking Lance's hand as he graciously helped her exit the truck. "Thanks, Lance."

It seemed to her that he held her hand a couple of moments longer than necessary before he released it. "You're welcome." He then led the way through the front door of the house and welcomed them into his new home.

Lance motioned Ricardo toward the living room. "Why don't you show Maria the house while Abby and Juliana help me get us something to drink? They have both been through the house."

Juliana smiled at Maria. "Go ahead. Just don't get lost."

Ricardo took Maria's hand and led her off. "I'll take care of her."

Abby punched Lance on the arm. "What are you doing, Lance? Trying to play matchmaker?"

Lance raised his eyebrows at his sister. "What do you mean?"

Abby led the way into the kitchen. "I think it's a good idea. They make a cute couple."

Juliana followed Abby into the huge kitchen as Lance waved her to go in advance of him. "You never know. They're both single."

Lance eyed them. "You're both single. Who are you interested in?"

Laughing, Abby started taking cold drinks out of frig and setting them on the counter. "Well, I'm still waiting for a fellow to come along. I can't speak for Juliana."

Embarrassed at the question because the first name that came to her mind was Lance, Juliana opened cabinet doors until she found the glasses. Setting them by the cold drinks on the counter, she stole a quick glance at Lance. She found him staring at her, which didn't help. Feeling heat rising from her neck to her face, she knew she was blushing. Seeking something to say to relieve the moment she asked, "Have you made anymore plans about what to do with the equestrian center?"

Abby set some napkins on the counter. "Good question, Lance. It's too grand and expansive not to be used."

Lance sat on one of the stools across from her at the kitchen counter. "I've got a plan for the center and some people I plan to contact to help me with it. It'll take some time, but I plan to turn it into an equestrian therapy center. First, I have to get some legal things going to set it aside as a non-profit organization. Actually, it'll be separate from the ranch, although I plan to keep ownership of the land." He grabbed a Dr. Pepper and poured it over the ice Abby had put into the glass. "I've got someone in mind to contact to be the director of it for me."

Juliana was impressed with the concept. "That sounds great but doesn't something like that take a lot of money?"

After taking a swig of his Dr. Pepper, Lance nodded. "Yes, it does. This is why I'm going to use my contacts from the business world to raise funds for it. I'll put funds toward it but mostly I plan to fund it from corporations and rich friends."

Abby pulled a tray out of the cabinet and put the ice filled glasses and bottles of soda on it. "Here, Lance, carry this into the living room so we can sit comfortably."

He put his drink on the tray, carried the tray into the living room, and sat it on the coffee table in front of one of the couches.

Abby and Juliana sat in leather chairs and Lance relaxed on a couch.

"Juliana, what do you think about a therapy center?" Abby asked.

"It's a wonderful idea. It can be of help to people in so many ways, not only the ones needing the therapy but to their families. Often I think the loved ones hurt as much as the ones with the problems. It's so frustrating to love someone and not be able to help them."

Lance looked at her with a solemn look. "That's what I'm hoping to accomplish, for not only those in need, but help whole families."

She gave him her full attention. "What sort of needs are you thinking about?"

"I'm thinking about children that need this sort of therapy to give them self-confidence and maybe just some fun. The other major groups I hope to offer help are injured vets and other adults with injuries. I don't know all that can be done with this sort of facility but I also thought maybe a week of camp for underprivileged children. The people I hire will know and be able to advise me."

Juliana could hear his sincerity in his voice. "You've thought a lot about this."

He nodded. "Ever since I started making such a good income, I've wanted to find ways to help others. Of course, I plan to give through the church but I've been so blessed that I'm able to expand into other areas."

Abby gave her big brother a look of love and admiration. "I'm so proud of you, Lance. You done good." She gave him a wink.

Lance hung his head as if embarrassed by her declaration. "In some ways, I've done okay, but in others not so good."

Juliana felt for him as she saw the look of sadness. She had to agree with him he had done well financially and in raising his children. Something had gone seriously wrong with his marriage. Not that she blamed him alone for the damaged marriage, but surely there were things he could have done to selvage it. Juliana didn't know what those things might have been, as she had never been married.

Ricardo and Maria were laughing as they came ambling back into the living room.

"Are those drinks for us?" Ricardo asked as he sat next to Maria on one of the couches.

Lance nudged the tray toward them. "Sure. Maria, what do you think of my new home?"

"Wow and double wow! It's great. It's big but not too big. I don't know whether to be more impressed with the size of the place or by the exercise room, pools, or the views." Maria's voice was filled with excitement and energy.

Lance laughed. "So you like it?"

"Oh, yes sir. It's lovely."

Ricardo glanced over at her and grinned. "She especially was impressed with the master bedroom. She claims that it's as big as her family's house."

Maria batted him on the arm. "Well, it is."

Soon Abby started gathering up empty glasses and soda bottles. "You may be right, Maria. I can't image one man needing all that."

Lance took the tray and headed to the kitchen. "I need my space."

187

Abby giggled. "I guess you're right considering how big you are, big brother."

He stopped and looked back at her. "I can't help it if I ate my Wheaties and got bigger than a midget."

Abby threw a pillow from the couch at him. "I'm not a midget. I'm just the vertically challenged one of my siblings. I'm taller than most women. It's just that my brothers are giants."

Juliana spoke up to avert continuation of the brother and sister banter, although she found it charming. "We need to head on back if we're to make Sunday evening services."

Chapter 21

A couple of weeks later, Lance stopped by the Rocking M before heading into town. He needed to pick up supplies at the hardware and feed store. In addition, he had to stop at the grocery store to fill a list of groceries for Louisa and of course replenish the supplies of diapers and formula.

Offering to pick up groceries was a small thing he could do for his mom. The more he settled into his new home and life, the more he realized how much he had missed by not being closer to his family. So far, he was thoroughly enjoying living and working on the ranch. There wasn't much he missed from his old life.

His step was lighter as he crossed the porch and entered the kitchen. "Hey, Mom, I'm going into town for supplies. Want me to pick up anything for you?"

Turning from the sink where she was washing yellow squash from her garden, Olivia raised her cheek for a kiss. "If it's no trouble there are some things I need. Abby said she would go into town later and pick them up for me, but she's up in Juliana's room on the third floor studying for her licensure exam."

Lance grabbed an apple from the bowl of fruit on the table. "When is her exam and where?"

Olivia dried her hands on a kitchen towel. "She hasn't decided exactly when to take it. We aren't pushing her to get a job immediately. I want her to have a time to enjoy the summer at least. She'll have to start looking in the fall because of her student loans coming due. I think all exams like that are taken in Austin." She picked up a piece of paper on the counter and read over it.

Then she added several items to the list. "Here's what I need. It'll be a help if you can do the shopping for me if it's no bother."

Lance took the list and stuck it into his shirt pocket next to his other ones. "No bother at all, I'm picking up stuff for us anyway. Rosa wants me to pick up some baby cereal. She says that Sara Hope is getting old enough to start eating food. I'm glad Rosa knows about these things or I would just keep giving her a bottle."

Olivia patted his arm. "I'm glad you've got Rosa also. She's a wonderful lady. That baby is growing up so fast. I'm thankful you brought her and Mark home so we can watch them grow."

Lance pulled her into a hug. "I'm thankful to be here also."

"How are you doing, I mean how are you really doing?" The concern in his mother's voice and the look of love she was giving him filled a need in him.

"I'm doing okay, Mom. I know what you're really asking and I'll be honest with you. When I let myself think about things, I'm sorry for where I am in my life in a way. I never wanted to be a divorced, single father. I'm sorry I failed Chandra, although I'm not sure what I should have done differently. But you know, even with that I'm happier than I've been in years. I didn't know how much I was missing home until I came back to the Hill Country. Of all your children, Mom, you don't have to worry about me. I'm doing okay."

Olivia hugged him and kissed his cheek. "I'm so relieved to hear you say that. You know me. I worry about all my children."

He returned her hug. "With two kids of my own, I have a better understanding of parental worry. I know Mark and Sara Hope are doing fine, but I still worry I'm not all I need to be as a father. Now I better get on the road and get to town."

As he drove into Tumbleweed and parked at the one grocery store in the town, he wondered how he could go about paying off Abby's school debt. He would ask Juliana what she thought about it. Filling his shopping cart from the lists and adding some things of his own, he wondered why he was so drawn to Juliana. He had not thought of Chandra much at all in the last week but Juliana was constantly in his thoughts. He kept telling himself that he was taking his kids over to the Rocking M several evenings a week so they could visit with the grandparents and great-grandparents. However, he was honest enough with himself to admit he timed the visits for when Juliana would be there. They didn't talk a lot but he felt better being in the same room with her. Going back home after the visits, his loneliness returned. Was that what the rest of his life was to be?

He stopped by the feed store that was also a hardware store and owned by Morgan Jones, the tall, burly owner. In his late fifties, he had inherited the store from his father. It was filled with all sorts of tools and hardware that catered to the ranchers. A big part of Morgan's business was ordering supplies for nearby ranches that he did not carry on a regular basis. The ranchers could pick up their orders when they came in and save a trip to Fredericksburg or even Austin. Lance wanted to give Morgan as much of Two Forks business as possible as a way to support the business.

Morgan stood behind the counter. "Howdy, Lance, how's it going?"

Lance tipped his hat at the older man. "It's going well. Just a lot of work. I've got a list of stuff here we need out at the ranch. George told me we could order some of it through the Internet, but that you had the experience to know the best sources and would get the best prices for us."

Morgan took the two-page list and scanned it quickly. "I try my best. This all looks doable. You got anything urgent on this list?"

Lance tilted his hat back and scratched his head. "Not that I know of but if there is I'll have George give you a call."

"I'll get right on this. Thanks for your business."

"Morgan, you save us time and effort. We need to thank you." Lance was happy to support some of the small businesses in Tumbleweed. He tried to keep as much of the ranch business with the local people as possible.

Lance headed back toward the Rocking M to deliver his mom's groceries. Shaking his head and chuckling, he wondered at himself being content to be a grocery delivery boy. Just before the turnoff onto the lane to the Rocking M Ranch, Lance's cell phone started ringing. He pulled it out of his shirt pocket and glanced at the caller. Seeing that it was Hilary Summers, his divorce attorney, he punched receive.

"Hello, Hilary." Not wanting to drive and talk on his cell phone, he pulled over to the shoulder of the road and stopped the truck.

"Lance, you got a minute to talk?" Hilary was as usual to the point and abrupt in her speech.

"Sure, Hilary, what do you need?" Lance felt his gut clench up. Getting a call from Hilary brought him back to the reality of his situation.

"Now, I don't want you to panic but we need to talk. I'm already on my way to your place. But I wanted to give you a heads up."

Lance felt his chest tighten as a faint fear of what she was going to say rose. Something was wrong, because Hilary would not be driving two hours out to his place for a small matter. "Okay, what's going on?" He tried to keep his voice calm.

"I've had a disturbing call from Chandra's attorney. She's refiling to get custody of Mark."

Glad that he had pulled over and stopped, Lance stared out the windshield of the truck unable to breathe.

"Lance, are you there?"

Taking a breath, Lance was able to respond. "I'm here. Tell me she can't do that, please, Hilary."

"Sorry, she can do that. You remember me telling you I was uneasy about her giving up custody but not her parental rights?"

"I remember you saying that but how can she come back and say she wants custody of Mark. She abandoned him. And what about Sara Hope?"

"Evidently she only wants Mark. We have to prepare, and prepare quickly. Her attorney said he was going to file in the next day or two. I'm hoping we can file first."

Lance wanted to hit his head against the steering wheel and scream. Taking a deep breath to try and stay calm he asked, "Where will the hearing be? What judge?"

"That's why I want us to hurry and file first so we can keep this in Texas and hopefully in Gillespie County. I've worked cases in your county before and know the judges."

"I don't understand. Where else could the case be filed?" Lance was at least glad he had Hilary to depend on as he was out of his depth when it came to dealing with child custody.

"We could always appeal, but since the divorce petition was filed in Nevada it might land there. If we make some filing before her attorney does, we can force it to be in Texas. The best argument we have for that is the child resides in Texas. Look, Lance, I know you have questions. I'll be there in about an hour and then we can sit down and go over everything together."

"Okay, you know the way to the ranch?" Lance wanted answers now but Hilary was right. It would be better to be able to sit down calmly and talk it through. He hoped he could do that as he his heart was racing and he was near to hyperventilating. He worked at getting himself under control. For him to have a panic attack wouldn't change anything that was happening.

"Yes, I have directions and should be able to make it with no problem. If you don't mind, please have some coffee and a sandwich ready for me. When I got the phone call from Chandra's attorney, I grabbed my papers and started driving your way."

"I'll let you go and will see you in an hour or so." Lance got off the phone before he started saying or doing something he would regret. He banged the steering wheel with his hands and barely refrained from screaming out his frustration. How could Chandra dare think she could go off, leave the kids, and then suddenly want to have custody?

Lance started the truck and drove on to his folks' place. Until he knew more, he didn't want to tell them but he needed their prayers and support. He carried the groceries for his mom into the kitchen and found his parents and grandparents seated at the table eating lunch.

He sat the groceries on the counter and turned to his family. How could he tell these people who cared so much about Mark that they might lose him?

Dad got up and came over to him. "What's wrong, son?"

Lance wanted to cry but instead he gave his dad a strong hug. "I got some unsettling news and I want you all to be praying."

Olivia fisted her right hand and laid it over her heart. "Oh, Lance, something has happened to one of the children."

He quickly moved over to her, knelt down, and gave her a hug. "No Mom. Mark and Sara Hope are okay for now."

Walt took Nana's hand. "Just tell us what is wrong, Grandson."

"I got a call from my divorce attorney and she said Chandra is going to try to get custody of Mark. Hilary is driving over from Austin right now for us to discuss what we need to do." Lance glanced around at the four concerned people. He hated to bring this kind of worry to them. "I would try to deal with it and not burden you all with this, but I need your prayers. I don't want to lose my son." He blinked and stared at the ceiling to keep his tears from falling. More than anything, he was scared.

Dad placed his hands on Lance and Olivia's shoulders. "You did right to tell us. Let's pray right now.

Father, hear our pleas for help and be with Lance as he has to travel this road. Let your will be done. We ask for whatever is best for Mark, Lance, and Chandra and let the good triumph and the evil be defeated. In the name of Jesus the Christ, Amen."

Lance stood and embraced his dad again. He felt the strength in the arms of the man who had always been there for him. "Thanks for that prayer and I know you all will keep praying for us."

Walt stood by waiting for his own hug. "You know we have your back, Grandson. Do you mind the rest of the family knowing?"

"I don't mind the family knowing, but I don't particularly want this to be a time of gossip about the family." What would Juliana think of him being in a court battle for his son? Lance was prepared to fight in any way possible to keep Mark. "I'm not sure yet what to tell Mark. How can an eight-year-old little boy understand his parents fighting over him?"

Nana shook her head. "Until you talk to your attorney and you know what is what, you shouldn't say a word to him. You'll have to tell him but give him whatever days of childhood you can before he has to start hearing ugly truths about the situation. And when you do tell him you must tell him the truth."

Lance was surprised at his grandmother's declaration. She was usually so quiet and soft spoken. "Okay, Nana, I'll follow your advice. I'm going down an uncharted path here. Well, after dropping that news on you, I'll head on home and be ready to meet Hilary."

~

Arriving at Two Forks Ranch, Lance found Mark seated at the kitchen table waiting for lunch. "Hey Dad, hurry up and sit down. I'm hungry."

Lance set the bags of groceries on the kitchen counter and left them for Louisa to put away. "Have patience, Mark, I'll be there shortly. Where is Rosa?"

Mark rolled his eyes. "Sara Hope had to be changed. Rosa said to wait for her."

Lance gave Louisa the grocery receipt. "I think I got everything on the list plus some. Please put this in the folder of household expenses."

"Yes, sir. I'll take care of the groceries. Do you want iced tea or a cold drink with your lunch?"

"I'll have iced tea. And Louisa, I have a business meeting in about an hour with my attorney. She'll need a sandwich and some coffee. Have it on a tray and we'll meet in my study."

"Sure thing, Mr. Lance."

After washing his hands in the small half bath off the kitchen, Lance sat across from his son.

"Why are you staring at me like that, Dad? Do I gots something on my face?"

Lance gave a small smile at his son's English but he didn't correct him. "I didn't mean to stare. I'm glad to see you. How was your morning?" So he wouldn't say something inappropriate, he needed to get Mark talking. With the fear and panic so close under the surface, Lance felt his control slipping.

Mark immediately launched into a detailed description of his latest riding lesson with Ricardo. "You have to watch me ride next time. Ricardo says I'm coming along. Dad, what does coming along mean exactly?"

Lance reached over and ruffled Mark's hair. "What does coming along mean? It means you are growing in your understanding and ability. You know, getting better and better. It's a good thing. Ah, here comes Ricardo and I'll ask him what he meant."

Ricardo and Rosa came into the kitchen from different directions. After they sat at the table, Lance asked Mark to say a blessing for the meal. Not able to eat much because of the turmoil in his gut, Lance listened to the banter between Ricardo and Mark about the riding lessons. If only he could freeze this moment with his son. Mark was obviously a happy, contented boy thrilled to be learning a new skill.

Lance rose from the table. "Rosa, I need to speak with you in my study."

Rosa glanced up at him with a look of surprise. "Of course, Mr. Lance. Mark, after you finish eating I want you to go to your room, rest, and read for a while."

"Okay, Rosa, I don't really need to rest but I got a book I want to read."

Rose followed Lance into his study where he indicated for her to sit in one of the chairs in the sitting area as he sat in another one.

In simple terms he told her what was happening. "I would appreciate it if you would take Mark and Sara Hope over to my folks and keep them there this afternoon. I need to concentrate on dealing with my attorney and I don't want Mark to accidently hear what we're talking about."

"Oh, Lance, I'm so sorry. I will pray for you and the children. May I tell Ricardo?"

"Yes, you can tell him but ask that he not talk to the other people working on the ranch. Until I know more what I'm dealing with, I don't want to have to respond to people's questions."

"I understand. 1 get ready and take the children to their grandparents now. Perhaps you call when you are ready for them to come home?"

Lance stood and gave Rosa a hug. "I'll do that. I don't thank you enough for what you do for the children and for me. But I know I can count on you to be here with us, no matter what happens."

Rosa reached up and brushed his hair back from his forehead where it had a tendency to fall. "You are like my own son and those babies are like my own grandchildren. I will do all I can for them."

Lance watched her walk out of the study with a growing feeling of gratitude for her love of his children and concern for him. Sighing he turned back to his desk and tried to think what he needed to do while he waited for Hilary. He forced himself to concentrate of bringing some of his financial files up to date. Even with a large accounting firm handling most of his accounts, there were still decisions he had to make.

~

Hilary arrived with a banging door and definite sound of her heels on the marble floor of the entryway. Lance met her and led her into his study. Turning to Louisa, who had let Hilary into the house, Lance asked Louisa to bring the tray of food to the study.

Hilary placed her purse and briefcase on the small conference table in front of a window from which one could look out over the Texas ranch land. "Let's sit here. There's room to spread some papers out and for me to eat. Thanks for the food, I'm starved."

"I appreciate you coming all this way. I could have met you halfway." Lance sat in the leather chair opposite his attorney.

"I thought of that, but this is fine. We need to make some decisions and then I need to get some papers to Judge Whitlock in Fredericksburg. I want to file a petition by the end of the work day at the court there."

Louisa softly knocked on the study door and then entered carrying a large tray, which she placed on the conference table. "You need anything else, Mr. McTavish? The glass of iced tea is for you and there is a full thermos of coffee fresh made."

Lance looked over the tray of sandwiches, fruit bowl, little cakes, iced tea, and coffee. "Thanks Louisa. If we need anything, I'll let you know."

Louisa nodded and left the study, softly closing the door behind her.

Hilary took a plate and helped herself to a sandwich. "Okay, let's get down to what our options are."

For the next two hours, she gave Lance a rundown on what the law in Texas allowed when it came to child custody disputes.

Lance ran his fingers through his hair for the tenth time. "So basically I can file a petition for Chandra to be restrained from taking Mark without a

197

hearing. And I can petition the court to rule that any filing for the change of custody for Mark be held in the court in Texas. But until she actually files there is nothing to do about actual custody."

Hilary poured herself another cup of coffee emptying the pot. "Exactly, with the way the divorce settlement is written now, you will have sole custody for now. She can't visit, pick Mark up, take him out of state, or anything else without your permission."

"Do you think she would try to do that?" Lance tried to think back to what he knew of Chandra. Would she try to kidnap Mark?

Hilary shook her head. "Not with her attorney giving us notice they're going for custody. However, if she calls and ask to visit with Mark or take him for a visit, I suggest you refuse and call me immediately. We can arrange a visit away from the ranch with both you and I supervising if that is what you choose and if Mark wants to see his mother. You must be careful to do nothing to indicate you recognize any change in the custody without a judge ruling on it."

Lance nodded. "Do you think Chandra and her attorney will move quickly on this?"

"Yes, that's why I need to print out these documents and head to the courthouse in Fredericksburg. I want the order declaring any filings that have to do with the children's custody have to be done in Texas."

Lance gave her the wireless password so she could print from his printer. Within thirty minutes, she had several documents printed and repacked her briefcase with the files and her laptop computer.

"Lance, I cannot promise you what will be the outcome of all this. I can promise to do the best I can for you. Try not to worry too much and just keep living day to day. This could take weeks and months or it might be decided in a week." Hilary spoke in a confident forceful voice. "I'll get these filed and then we wait."

"I appreciate that you are here for me and the children. I also trust you know what you're doing and I'll try to follow your advice." Lance extended his hand and shook Hilary's hand firmly.

Watching Hilary drive away, he checked his watch. It was only the middle of the afternoon, although it seemed later to him. Hilary had kept them focused on what they needed to accomplish. He returned to his study and saw that Louisa had already removed the tray and dishes. What should he do with himself for the rest of the afternoon? He could hardly think with the turmoil in his mind. The ringing of his cell phone saved him from an immediate decision.

"Hello."

"Hi, son, it's your mother."

Lance had to smile, as he had read the caller I.D. and of course knew the sound of her voice. "Hi Mom. Are the kids okay?"

"Of course, they're fine. Sara Hope is napping, Mark is outside playing, and Rosa is teaching Abby and me how to make some wonderful Tex-Mex food. I don't want to disrupt your meeting with your attorney."

"Don't worry about that. She has already left."

"Oh good. If you don't have stuff to do there that's pressing, could you and Ricardo come over and help your dad?"

"What does he need help with?" Lance took a deep breath. He hoped his dad needed help with something that would take some physical labor. That might be what he needed to do to get rid of some of his anxiety.

"Part of the back pasture fence has come down and the cattle are scattering. He had sent the boys to Fredericksburg to pick up some supplies for giving the cattle their shots starting tomorrow. That only leaves your dad and grandpapa to try to get the fence back up in this heat." His mother's voice sounded calm so it wasn't an emergency.

"Mom, does Dad know you are calling me?"

After a moment of silence, she answered, "No, he doesn't. But he needs help if he's to get that fence back up by dark and I worry about him and Grandpapa working so hard out in this heat."

"Don't worry, Mom. I'll grab Ricardo and we'll be over to help as quickly as we can."

"Thanks, Lance, and plan to have supper here this evening. The children are fine and Rosa and I are already preparing it."

"Okay, I'll see you in about thirty minutes."

"Bye, son. I love you." His mother ended the call before he could tell her how much he loved her. He was glad she had called. One reason for living so close to the home ranch was to be able to help when his folks needed him.

He quickly called Ricardo's cell and told him to get ready to head over to the Rocking M to repair the fence. Then he called George to let him know what was going on. He thought about asking George to send over some of the men from Two Forks Ranch, but figured that the four of them could handle it. The men on Two Forks Ranch had their hands full just trying to keep up with such a large ranch.

After telling Louisa not to prepare supper for them and to leave a little early if she wanted, Lance went to his bedroom and changed into old jeans, a long sleeve blue chambray shirt, and his oldest pair of boots. Putting up fencing was a hard, dirty job that was especially hard on clothes. He also grabbed a couple of bandanas.

Ricardo was already loading tools into the bed of the truck when he got to the garage. "Are you ready to go do a hard afternoon's work?" He looked on a shelf and found a couple of pairs of heavy work gloves.

"Sure, Lance. It can't be harder than going on patrol in Afghan in July." Ricardo grinned as he settled his hat. "We just need to be sure we have plenty of water."

Lance handed a pair of the gloves and a bandana to Ricardo and then tied a bandana around his own neck. Even with his hat on the Texas sun was going to be brutal. The temperature was rising toward a hundred degrees with no clouds and very little breeze.

As Lance drove the truck over to the Rocking M, Ricardo asked, "What's the problem with the fence?"

"I'm guessing that thunderstorm that rolled through last night may be a factor. Maybe a tree or two came down. The straight line winds with the storm were strong for about fifteen minutes."

Ricardo tipped his hat back. "I knew it rained last night but I didn't wake up. That's a first since I've been back in country. I usually am wide awake at any little noise."

Rosa had shared with Lance the problems that Ricardo was having with PTSD since his return from the war zone. He had confided to his grandmother that he was having nightmares, difficulty sleeping, felt anxious, often startling at unexpected loud sounds like a backfire on a car, and experienced panic attacks. The symptoms were severe enough that the Marines had given Ricardo a medical discharge. Lance also suspected that Ricardo had other injuries from his time in the war zone but the young man never spoke of them. He seemed to be able to do the work on the ranch okay. Lance had decided to let Ricardo tell him if he needed lighter work.

Lance stopped by the ranch house and checked on the children. Olivia, Abby, and Rosa were busy in the kitchen that smelled amazing.

Olivia waved a wooden spoon at him. "Go on Lance but look out for Mark. And take that sunscreen lotion with you. He may need to get out of the sun. If he's starting to sunburn, send him back to the house."

"Okay, Mom, how are Dad and Grandpapa fixed for water? Do I need to take more?"

"It wouldn't hurt. Do you have an insulated water jug?"

Lance nodded. "I'll fill it from the outside faucet." The water being pumped up from the house well was cold and clear tasting.

Quickly he and Ricardo got the five-gallon jug filled with water and loaded it back on the truck bed.

Mark came wandering up to them. "What you doing, Dad?"

"Ricardo and I are going to go help repair fencing." Mark's face was red from the heat but he wasn't sweating. Lance realized he better get the boy out of the afternoon heat. "You go on into the house and get cooled off."

"Can I watch TV?" Mark's face had a hopeful look.

"Yes, but ask your grandmama if the program is okay for you to watch."

"All right!" Mark ran toward the house.

"Ricardo, I'll drive and you jump out to open and close the gates." There were three gates between the barn and the back pasture. The ride was bumpy and Lance drove slow to not damage the truck over the rough terrain. Soon they spotted the two older men by a section of fencing that was down. Two trees were down across the wires and Hank and Walt were busy sawing and chopping limbs off the trees, as they had to be cleared first before they could start putting the fence back up.

Lance brought the truck to a stop and climbed out with Ricardo following.

Hank stopped where he was chopping smaller branches off the tree with an ax. Rubbing a sleeve across his face, he asked, "What are you two doing here?"

Lance grinned at his dad. "We were just driving by and saw two fellows that might could use a hand. Tell us what to do."

Walt set the chainsaw down. "One of you fellows grab this chainsaw and I'll start dragging limbs out of the way. We got to get these two trees out of the way before we can start repairing the fence."

Lance put on his gloves and picked up the chainsaw. "Ricardo, why don't you help Grandpapa."

Soon all four men were back at work with the sound of the chainsaw blocking any ability to talk to each other. A couple of hours later the last of the tree limbs were pulled out of the way.

Hank examined the fence. "It appears at least ten of these posts need to be replaced and then the wire put back up."

Walt took a handkerchief out of the back pocket of his pants and wiped his sweating face. "Did we bring enough from the storage shed?"

"I think so. Ricardo, climb up into my truck and count the fence posts. And then you and Lance can start unloading them." Hank turned to his father. "Let's start clearing these old fence posts out of the way."

Lance started taking the fence posts from Ricardo as he handed them down one by one. It reminded Lance of when he would work with his brother Matt, his dad, and grandpapa back in high school. His dad would order them about and expect the work to be done. Lance and Matt had not argued then and Lance didn't argue now. Especially since his dad and grandpapa worked as hard or harder than they expected Lance and Ricardo to work.

Lance stopped by the water cooler and refilled his water bottle several times, as the heat of the day sapped the moisture from his body. He poured water onto the bandana he was wearing around his neck and put it back on sopping wet. It did help cool him down a bit. He encouraged Ricardo to do the same. Soon his dad and grandpapa were also getting water out of the big cooler as their supply of water gave out.

The sun was getting low on the horizon by the time they had the fenced repaired. Lance was hot and tired. Muscles were starting to ache that had not had so much use in a while. The thought of the hot meal prepared by his mom and the other women set Lance's stomach to growling.

Hank put the last of the tools into his truck. "You all go on and get washed up for supper. We'll be right behind you."

Lance and Ricardo climbed into Lance's truck and started the slow drive back across the pastureland to the ranch house.

Ricardo rubbed his shoulder and grimaced. "Now that was an afternoon of work."

Lance glanced over. "You okay?"

"Yeah, just some aches from some old injuries. Nothing a time spent in the hot tub won't fix. It feels good to be able to help your dad and grandpapa."

"This is one of the reasons I'm pleased at how close my place is to the home ranch. So I can be of help at a moment's notice." It also helped to relieve some of the guilt he had about neglecting his folks through the years. He wished he could find ways to help more but he needed to go slow.

Lance and Ricardo went to the old house and washed up. Since his dad's truck was parked by the barn and the boys were not in the old bunkhouse, Lance figured Logan and Alex were already at the main house waiting for supper. His two younger brothers were growing up into responsible young men. He had yet to hear a serious complaint from either one about how much they worked. What would his dad and grandpapa have done without the boys' help?

Lance was tired and looked forward to a shower but he and Ricardo washed up enough he felt like they could sit at table with the rest of the family without offending.

As they entered the kitchen, they were hit with the aroma of Tex-Mex dishes.

Abby bowed at the men. "Come on into the Rocking M Tex-Mex Cafe. For your dining pleasure tonight e have iced hibiscus sweet tea, sour cream chicken enchiladas, cheese enchiladas with beef and queso sauce, chicken chili rellenos topped with tomatillo sauce and raisins and pecans on the side, beef and chicken soft shell tacos, refried beans, and rice."

Lance grinned at his mom, Abby, and Rosa. "Wow, you all have been cooking up a storm and all of my favorites."

Rosa laughed as she patted his arm. "Lance, everything I ever cooked for you seems to be your favorite. And Ricardo is much like you.'

Olivia laughed. "You seem to have figured Lance out. He likes to eat, and Logan and Alex are right behind him. Of course, they haven't had any of your cooking before."

Later Lance pushed back from the table with a sigh. He had eaten more than needed but everything had been delicious.

Olivia got up from the table and pulled a huge pan of hot sopapillas from the oven. She set it in the middle of the table. "With butter and honey, we have a first rate dessert. Abby and I helped but Rosa did most of the supper. So be appreciative."

Hank caught Olivia around the waist with his arm and looked at Rosa. "Thanks for teaching my lady here some different twists on some good eating. This is a wonderful fest."

Rosa blushed at the compliments coming her way. "Oh, Mr. Hank, these are just common dishes at my table. I am glad to share with Olivia and Abby."

Ricardo grinned and shook his finger at his grandmother. "Lita, don't forget to keep sharing these dishes, especially with your favorite grandson."

Rosa caught his finger and wrapped her hands around his. "I never forget my favorite men."

Lance caught Juliana's eye as the bantering was going on. He smiled at her and delighted to see the warm gleam in her eyes. They hadn't had an opportunity to talk but he had sensed her attention as the meal had progressed.

As everyone started to disperse after the meal, Ricardo and Mark followed Logan and Alex into the living room where they soon had a baseball game going on the TV. Until the baseball season ended, the Texas Rangers would be the first choice on the TV.

Lance cleared his throat and spoke to those still sitting around the supper table. "Just to bring you up to date, my attorney, Hilary Summers, informed me that Chandra has decided to go for custody of Mark. We went over everything and afterwards Hilary went to the court in Fredericksburg to file a petition to block Chandra." He looked around the table at the concerned faces. "It looks as if I have a fight on my hands, and it is one I may not win."

Olivia took Hank's hand. "What about Sara Hope?"

"Chandra doesn't want the baby at this time, just Mark." Lance rubbed the back of his neck where it had ached since he got the call from Hilary.

Walt patted Nana's arm. "What can we do?"

Lance shook his head. "Not much, as it is up to a judge now. Well, of course, you can pray. I know that is what you'll do anyway. I would ask that you help me keep Mark's spirits up and also to help me. It may be several weeks before we go before the judge and I want to keep things as normal with Mark as possible."

Juliana spoke up in a hesitant voice, "Can she just come and take Mark?"

Lance gave her his full regard. "She can try, but legally unless she has a piece of paper that says otherwise, signed by a judge, she cannot take Mark without my permission." He looked over at his mom and then Rosa. "That means that if one of you is keeping Mark and Chandra shows up, you call me. If you cannot get me, you call 911."

Olivia looked at Rosa and then at Hank. "We'll keep both children safe. You don't have to worry about that."

Glancing out the window over the kitchen sink at the gathering darkness, Lance suddenly felt the tiredness in his body and mind. "We need to gather up the kids and get home. It's their bed time and mine."

Chapter 22

Lance struggled to tie his tie and finally managed to get it into semblance of a Windsor knot. He glanced at his image in the mirror and saw a tanned, healthy looking man. Living on the ranch was good for him. With the heat of the summer, he wouldn't put his suit coat on until he arrived at the church building. Throwing it over his shoulder, he headed out to find the children.

Going to the door of Mark's bedroom, he looked in to see his son putting on a summer short sleeve pullover. "You about ready to go, son?"

"I just need to comb my hair, Dad. You look dressed up."

Surprised that the boy would notice, Lance grinned. "Well, we are going to church."

"Why do we go to church so much here in Texas? We never used to go." Mark fell in step with his dad as they headed toward the kitchen.

"Don't you like going to church?" Lance asked. Since being back home in Texas, he had found going to church services and especially meeting his family there, reassuring.

Mark looked up as if not sure how his statement would be received by his dad. "I guess I do like it. I like the classes and the other kids. I like the singing. But I sometimes get bored with the preaching."

Lance laughed. "Guess I would say you're a normal kid then. Don't tell anyone but sometimes if I'm tired, I find the sermons a little boring. But then I start paying more attention and following along in the Bible and they get more interesting."

"Okay Dad, I'll try that."

Lance wanted to reach out and ruffle his son's hair but refrained as Mark had just combed it into some semblance of order. "Let's check on Rosa and Sara Hope and see if they are ready to head to church."

After the church services, everyone gathered in the kitchen at the Rocking M for Sunday dinner. Lance looked around the table at his favorite people in the world and hoped they would keep building on the tradition of these meals. He especially liked that Juliana was seated across the table from him. She returned his smile as Hank asked everyone to bow their heads for the blessing of the food.

Immediately after the prayer, bowls and platters of food passed from hand to hand.

"Dad, can I have two pieces of fried chicken?" Mark looked with intensity at the big platter of chicken that was heading his way.

Lance grinned at his tanned, freckled-faced son. "You afraid there won't be enough left for seconds after Ricardo, Logan, and Alex take their share of the chicken?"

Mark returned his grin. "No Dad, I'm worried about you taking all the chicken."

Everyone around the table started laughing.

Grandpapa forked a big piece of breast meat onto his plate. "I guess Mark has been observing what happens around the table. You are one of the biggest eaters here, Lance."

Lance ducked his head and then looked around the table. "Well, considering that I am physically the biggest one here that makes sense to me."

Hank was holding the platter of chicken for Mark to spear his piece. "Lance, you never answered Mark's question, one or two pieces?"

"Son, start with one and then if you're still hungry you can get a second piece. Don't forget your grandmama has peach cobbler for dessert."

Olivia daintily held a piece of corn on the cob between her hands. "How did you know we have peach cobbler? Have you been dipping into the dessert?"

Lance laughed. "No, Mom, I haven't gotten into the peach cobbler, but I could smell it baking as I came up on the porch." He appreciated how much more fun meals were here at his home place than they had ever been in California. Lance looked around the table and realized that everyone there was relaxed, smiling, and enjoying themselves.

Near the end of the meal, Olivia and Abby rose from the table to start dishing out the hot peach cobbler and ice cream. Juliana and Maria cleared the plates and silverware. Hank got up, grabbed the iced tea pitcher, and started around the table refilling the glasses.

Lance felt like there was something he should get up and help with but instead he listened to his grandpapa talking about expected beef prices in the fall.

Everyone settled back at the table to enjoy the peach cobbler made with fresh peaches picked just days before. Lance's phone rang and he slipped it out of his pocket. It might be George needing him for something at Two Forks. When he looked at the caller ID he realized it was Chandra. Pushing his chair back from the table, he rose and headed out onto the back porch.

Once out of hearing of anyone in the house, he answered the phone. "Hello."

"Lance, it's Chandra. How are you?" She sounded bright and cheerful just as she had sounded on the phone throughout their marriage.

"I'm doing well. How are you?" Lance answered hesitantly. Why was she calling now and after all these months of no contact?

"Listen, I'm calling because I want to see Mark. I'm going to be in Austin later this week and want you to bring him to visit me."

"You want what?" Lance barely kept himself from shouting into the phone.

"I'm his mother and I have a right to see my own son. Don't be difficult about this or you'll regret it."

Lance took a deep breath and then answered slowly. "I will contact my attorney, who will contact your attorney. Until I know differently from a judge, you'll not be visiting with Mark."

"Don't be that way, Lance. You used to be such a nice guy."

"That was before my wife blindsided me with divorce papers and abandoned her children. Don't call me again. Go through the attorneys." Lance hung up. He clenched his hands into tight fists, wanting to hit something.

"Dad, who was that?" Mark was standing just inside the kitchen, looking out through the screen door.

Lance didn't want to tell his son but he also didn't want to lie to him. "I'll tell you in a little while. But right now I need to make another call."

Mark had a frown on his face and looked uncertain. "Okay, Dad." He turned back into the house.

Lance walked across the backyard to his truck and got into it. He started the truck and turned up the air conditioner. Looking at the face of his phone, he tapped on the icon for his attorney.

She answered on the second ring. "Hello, Lance. What's going on?"

"Hey, Hilary. Well, you guessed it. Something is going on." He repeated what had transpired on the call from Chandra and then said, "I couldn't believe she would act as if we had been speaking every day. It's been months since we spoke and that was before she left me."

"I think you can assume she is trying to set up a scenario where she can claim to have wanted to see Mark but you refused. You did right telling her to take such request to her attorney. You didn't out right refuse did you?"

Lance ran his fingers through his hair. "I refused unless a judge orders it. What do I do if she shows up?"

"You ask to see the court order that gives her a right to see Mark. However, in the mean time I will talk to the judge and ask him to be ready to move on a hearing as soon as she makes a request for a change of custody. I haven't seen one yet. I think this is maneuvering for a better position. But it tells me that she's coming for custody and we need to be ready."

"So what do I do?" Lance needed to do something, anything to stay in control of the situation.

"Just keep on doing what you have been doing. Live a good life and take care of the children. We'll deal with the court case when it happens. Just be patient, Lance."

"Okay. What should I do if she calls back?" Lance didn't want to deal with Chandra directly. It was bad enough to be having to talk about it with an attorney.

"Don't talk about any details. Just say again that this is to be handled between the attorneys. Don't just ignore the calls because that can be used against you."

"Thanks, Hilary, and I'm sorry for having to disturb your Sunday afternoon."

Hilary laughed. "No problem, Lance. That's what you pay me the big bucks for. Call at any time you have a need for me. Talk to you later."

Lance ended the call and put the phone back into his pocket. He looked toward the house and saw Juliana crossing the backyard toward his truck. In the bright summer sun, she looked cool, serene, and beautiful in a pale pink full-skirted dress. After just hearing from his wife, he should not be noticing how attractive Juliana was but it was difficult, as she looked so good.

Juliana opened the passenger door and climbed into the cab. "You okay, Lance?"

He reached forward and adjusted the air conditioning to provide cooling for the passenger seat. "I'm okay. Why do you ask?"

Juliana leaned on the door and faced toward Lance. A tiny frown was showing between her eyes. "When you looked at your phone, you turned pale and almost as if you were shocked by who was calling."

He took a moment to answer as he thought about how closely she was watching him. "I was shocked. It was a call from my soon to be ex-wife. It's the first time I have heard from her since before she left me."

Juliana sat quietly and waited. So it was up to him whether he wanted to share or not. She wasn't demanding with her words, but her concern was evident by her expression and by her coming out to the truck.

"She wants to see Mark. She wants me to meet her in Austin and bring him to her."

"Are you going to do that?" Juliana's voice was soft and serious.

He shook his head. "No, not now and maybe not ever. I talked to my attorney a minute ago and she agreed with me. Only when, or if, a judge requires it, will I subject Mark to the uncertainty of going back and forth between parents. Chandra had revealed what type of parent she is by abandoning the children in May. Now she wants to demand her rights? Not at Mark's expense she won't." He realized he was getting louder and louder and more heated in his response. "I apologize, Juliana. I guess I'm more upset than I realized. I don't mean to yell at you."

Juliana gave a small beginning of a smile. "Better that you yell at me than Chandra or even at Mark. I don't doubt that you want to yell at someone for having to deal with all of this. Go ahead and yell. I can take it."

Suddenly much of his anger drained away, leaving a sadness. Why couldn't Chandra have been more like Juliana? "Thanks for understanding. I really want to go into the middle of the pasture and scream out at a world where little kids have to be a battleground between parents. They don't deserve this."

"And you do? No one deserves being caught up in the midst of such problems, but that is the world we live in. Difficult things happens and we have to decide what kind of people we're going to be in the middle of it. But you have an advantage over Chandra from what you have said."

"What would that be?" Lance didn't feel like he had much of an advantage over anything. What he felt was out of control. Chandra, attorneys, and the judge had control of what would happen to his son.

"You have the Lord and a supportive family. That doesn't mean you will always get what you want. But you will always have a way to cope with what happens. You can be at peace knowing you are under God's concern."

How could she say that with such confidence? Lance was wishful for the confidence that God would always be with him. "I guess I need to work more on that because right now it seems God is pretty far away. I probably shouldn't say that. It's not that I don't believe what you're saying, it's just hard to see it at this moment."

"Hindsight always makes it easier to see how God is working in our lives. In the moment, it's hard. What's next?"

Lance gritted his teeth and felt his frustration rising. "That's what so difficult. Chandra hasn't filed for custody yet. All I can do is wait to see what happens. I guess I'm learning I'm not really a patient man. If I were, I wouldn't be seated here, complaining."

Juliana reached over and laid her hand on his arm. "What are friends for if not to be a listening heart when frustrations come? I'm your friend and I don't mind listening."

Lance wanted to reach out and pull her into a hug, but it was not appropriate. However, just the feel of her hand on his arm was comforting. He had a friend in the midst of all of the turmoil that his life was becoming. "Thanks, I'll remember that. I appreciate you making the move to come and listen."

"What will you tell Mark?"

Lance shook his head. "I'm not going to tell Mark yet. Let him have his summer fun."

Juliana cocked her head to the side. "What if Chandra shows up? Shouldn't you prepare Mark for that?"

"You're right. I have to tell him something. What I'm going to do first is alert all the adults around him. He won't be leaving the house without someone with him. Wish I had someone to assign to being with him during the day. I can make sure to be with him in the evening and night, but the day time is difficult with all I need to do around the ranch."

"You really are concerned she might show up and take him."

"I am. The way she left me was so unexpected and so well planned out, I now know she is capable of doing just that." He tried to keep the sound of his fear out of his voice. If Chandra got ahold of Mark and left the country, Lance might never see his son again. He couldn't live with that.

"Would it ease your mind to hire someone you trust to be with him in the day time?"

"Yes, but I'm not sure how Mark would take having a nanny at his age."

Juliana chuckled. "Well, don't call the person a nanny. How about a companion or friend?"

"Where would I find such a person?" Lance didn't want to bring in a stranger.

Looking thoughtful, Juliana tapped her chin with a dainty finger. "What about Maria? She's been looking for a summer job and still hasn't found one. She's dealt with her younger siblings and her third grade students. She would be perfect. Mark already knows her."

"Maria? Yes, everyone on the ranch knows her. Thanks, that's a great solution. We had better get back inside. The folks will begin to wonder what's going on." He glanced over at Juliana as they headed back into the house. "Would you take me to see Maria this afternoon after I get the children home and down for naps?"

Juliana nodded. "I'll call her to make sure she's home. It'll be good for you to see where she lives and meet her family. They're really nice people."

"Let me get the family home and change clothes. I'll come by and pick you up."

"Great, I'll be ready."

~

An hour and half later, Lance stopped by his parents' ranch where Juliana was waiting on the back porch for him. The drive to the Sanchos' place only took twenty-five minutes.

Juliana pointed to the turnoff from the highway. "Drive slow, please. You never know what child or dog will be running in front of the truck."

"Sounds like an active household." Lance pulled the truck to a stop between an old double cab truck and a compact car that had seen better days. "Does one of these vehicles belong to Maria?"

"Yes, that old car. She gives so much of her pay to her parents and paying off schools loans, there hasn't been money to get a new car. That's why she has tried so hard to get a summer job." Juliana waved at the children playing in the front yard of the small home.

Flowers were blooming in flowerbeds along the front of the house. In the distance toward the back of the house, he could see a large garden plot. Although obviously poor, the people who lived in this house made an effort to make it a home. Lance appreciated that.

"What does Maria's father do?"

"He works for the city of Fredericksburg with the street department. Her mother works as a seamstress for one of the cleaners in town. Both of Maria's parents come from families that have been in Texas for generations. Maria is the first one to go to college. She's hoping to help her younger siblings to go also."

Maria came running out of the house and opened the passenger door of the truck. "Can we take a ride while we talk? There are too many listening ears in the house."

Juliana climbed out and got into the back seat. "You take the front seat Maria as it's you and Lance that need to talk."

Lance waited for the girls to fasten their seatbelts and then pulled out of the lane and back on the highway. "Where should we drive?"

Maria turned and looked back at Juliana. "We're not far from the west side of Fredericksburg. There's a little place to get drinks and ice cream."

Lance speeded up the truck and headed that direction. "Sounds good. As we drive I need to tell you my situation and then if you're interested I want to make you a job offer."

Looking puzzled, Maria nodded. "Okay, I'm listening." She turned and glanced back at Juliana, and raised her eyebrows as if in question.

Juliana kept silent but winked at her.

Lance proceeded to explain his wife leaving and abandoning the children. He went on to describe the situation with his soon to be ex-wife coming back threatening to get custody of Mark. "What I need is someone who can be with Mark through the day and make sure no one can approach him without me knowing. Rosa has her hands full with Sara Hope and Mark is an active little boy. I don't want to force him to spend his summer stuck in the house."

"Is there any danger to Mark or someone taking care of him?" Maria's voice was calm as if asking about the weather.

Lance shook his head. "I don't think so. It's more a matter that he's too young to be put in a position where he would have to refuse his mother. I'm concerned if she showed up he might go with her not knowing he shouldn't.

If she should take him and fly out of the country, I might never see him again. I may be paranoid but I'd rather err on the side of caution."

Maria kept her eyes on Lance's face as if trying to read behind the words. "I can understand that. What would you want me to do?"

Lance looked into the rearview mirror. "Juliana, if you have anything to say, please jump in."

"So far you're telling Maria what she needs to know."

He glanced over at Maria and then paid attention to the road in front of him. "What I need is for you to come to the house each day by 7:30 am. Mark may or may not be up but I often leave the house by then and head out somewhere on the ranch. In the mornings, Mark likes to go to the barns and greet the horses. Two or three mornings a week Ricardo gives him a riding lesson. Do you ride, Maria?"

"I used to ride a lot back in high school. My uncles rode in the local rodeos and I would ride as a flag carrier. When I went to college I sort of slacked off."

"Good. It shouldn't be too difficult to get back on a horse then. What I'm saying is I will need you to be ready to ride out with Mark on some of the trails around the ranch. Ricardo will be in charge. Then in the afternoons, I encourage Mark to stay around the house in the worst heat of the day and swim. He's a strong swimmer but at his age, I don't allow him near the pool without an adult. Juliana said you are a certified life guard."

Maria grinned. "Yes, sir. Going horseback riding and swimming hardly seems like work."

Lance grinned back at her. "The work will be to keep up with Mark. He's a busy energetic boy. There may be times that I would want you to drive Mark over to his grandparents. I'll pay you six hundred a week, plus provide a car and cell phone."

"When would you want me to start?"

"Tomorrow, if that's not too soon."

"No, that's not too soon. I can begin then."

"Good, I'll have Ricardo pick you up in the morning and bring you out to the ranch. You can drive the car home tomorrow evening. Juliana, anything I've left out?"

Juliana smiled. "No, I don't think so but maybe you should ask Maria if she has any questions."

Lance caught her eye in the mirror. "Good thinking." He winked at her and then looked over at Maria. "So, any questions?"

Maria giggled. "No, sir. If I have any tomorrow I'll feel free to ask."

Lance felt relief to know that Maria was willing to come and keep an eye on Mark. "Call me Lance, Maria. That's what I prefer."

"Okay, Lance. Oh, just up there to the right is the ice cream place."

He pulled the truck off the highway and parked. Soon they were seated around a table, eating ice cream, and talking about horses and riding. Lance had never had so much fun hiring an employee before.

On the way back, they stopped to let Maria out at her home and accepted an invite to meet Maria's family. They were the sort of people he considered the backbone of society. Hard working, religious, and family oriented, they appreciated what they had and were generous to share with others around them. Lance and Juliana's visit was short and soon they were on their way to the Rocking M Ranch.

Lance felt reluctant to leave Juliana at the Rocking M, as he had enjoyed the afternoon with her and Maria, in spite of his worries. There was a comfort and peace being around her quiet and serene presence. Did she ever get mad or frustrated? He shook his head. She was not his and could never be his, but it didn't stop his thinking about her.

Chapter 23

Lance worked in his office where he could hear Mark and Maria out in the pool. Lance had given the okay for Maria to bring a few of her younger brothers and sisters with her to work, which gave Mark several playmates. Maria had been working for two weeks and Lance was pleased with how well she fit into the flow of the household. Rosa and Louisa had both been pleased that she was helping out with Mark. Ricardo seemed exceptionally pleased with having Maria about the ranch.

As Lance read documents pertaining to getting the equestrian therapy center organized, his cell phone rang. After glancing at the caller ID, he grabbed it and clicked receive. "Hello, Hilary."

"Lance, glad I caught you. Well, the request for change of custody was filed."

His stomach clenched and his grasp on the phone was hard enough almost to break it. "Is it filed in Texas?"

"Oh, yes, and in Gillespie County. It will be in Judge Whitlock's court, which is good."

Hearing that something was good about the situation helped ease Lance's anxiety. "Okay, Hilary. Now tell me what isn't good." He had become acquainted enough with his divorce attorney to know she liked to give good news and then hit him with the bad news.

"You may or may not see this as bad news but they're petitioning for immediate supervised visits until the judge can rule on the custody request. I think the judge will agree. The hearing will be Friday and you need to be there with Mark."

Lance yelled into the phone. "Mark will have to be in the courtroom for the hearing?"

Hilary quickly responded in a calm voice. "No, he'll not be in the courtroom, but he has to be assessable for the judge. And if the judge rules that Chandra can visit with Mark, you have to have him there for that to take place."

"Sorry, Hilary. I shouldn't yell at you. I'm kinda agitated by all this." He ran his fingers through his hair for the tenth time since the beginning of the phone call.

Hilary's voice was softer as she said, "I know all of this is very stressful. I wish I could give you some guarantees but I can't, not with a child custody case. It can go all sorts of ways. And Lance, you need to prepare Mark so he'll understand what's happening."

Lance sighed, as that was the last thing he wanted to do. He could hear Mark, laughing and yelling amid the splashes of the children jumping into the pool. "I hate to tell him any of this but I understand."

"Okay. I need to see you in Fredericksburg at the courthouse by eight o'clock Friday morning. The hearing is set for ten that morning but we have some things to discuss before we meet in front of the judge. Can you have someone come with you to be with Mark while we're in the hearing?"

"My problem will be keeping at least some of the family from being there. It could get crowded. I hired a companion for him for the summer to supervise his play, etc. He'll feel comfortable with her and I'm sure my parents will be there as well as my grandparents."

"Good, it won't hurt for the judge to see an extended family."

"What about Sara Hope? Does she need to be there?"

"Do you have someone who can keep her at the ranch? I don't suggest that you bring her, as she's not named in the custody petition. If Chandra, or the judge, wants to include her, we'll ask for a separate hearing at a later date. Let's not tempt Chandra by her seeing the child without a court order."

Relieved but concerned by the thought of another custody change, Lance asked, "You think that's likely?"

"I have no idea if it's likely or not, I know it's possible. Let's worry about one thing at a time. First, we need to get through the hearing on Friday."

"Okay, we'll be there at 8 o'clock on Friday at the courthouse."

"Good, I'll meet you inside the front entrance. There are meeting rooms in the courthouse for attorneys. I'll have one reserved. It'll also be a place where Mark can wait. Now, if you have any questions, call me. See you on Friday morning."

Lance barely had time to say bye before Hilary ended the call. He liked she didn't waste any time with chitchat but he wanted to hang on to her calm, confident voice as he was feeling very unsure of himself. How to talk to Mark so that he knew what might happen? Lance barely refrained from hitting the wall with his fist. What was this going to do to his eight-year-old son? It was unfair to the child. However, with people such as Chandra and her soon to be new husband, Lance wondered if life could ever be fair.

Not able to get back to the work he was doing, Lance wandered over to the window that looked out over the pool area and watched the children enjoying their swim time. As he watched Mark, he couldn't tell if his son's obvious happiness was because of the swimming or because he had several children near his age to play with. Probably both. Lance loved how his son threw his head back and laughed from the bottom of his lungs. And in the next day or so his father had to take away that joy.

~

The call from Hilary had come on Tuesday, Lance only had two days to talk to his folks, Maria, and especially with Mark. Wednesday morning he drove over to the Rocking M, having called ahead of time to ask that the family gather. His mom suggested he come over early for breakfast. So at six-thirty Lance drove up to the back of Rocking M ranch house and parked with the other vehicles.

Entering the kitchen where the smell of bacon frying and biscuits baking hit him, he stepped up behind his mom and kissed her on the cheek. "Morning, Mom."

She reached around with her one free hand and patted his cheek. "Morning, sweetheart. Is it about the custody hearing?"

He smiled. His mom had always known how to get to the point. "Yes, I'll tell everyone at the same time if that's okay."

Logan and Alex came stomping in from the back porch. Even though there was room for them to stay in the big ranch house now that Lance and his family had moved, they had voted to continue to stay in the old house.

Logan, who was almost as tall and muscular as Lance, grabbed him around the waist and lifted him off the floor. "Hey, big brother, I can't believe you're up this early."

Lance laughed as he gave his younger brothers hugs. "You two are ones I'm surprised to see up this early."

Alex grinned. "Well, Mom has kinda made a rule that if we want a hot breakfast we'll be here when it's served."

Juliana entered the kitchen and waved a hello. She went to the big coffee pot, filled two mugs with coffee, and set them down on the table that was already set for breakfast. "Set down and enjoy a cup of coffee, Lance."

Olivia turned to her and said, "Juliana, if you'll check on Nana. Logan, make yourself useful and ring the bell for breakfast. I don't know what's keeping your father and Grandpapa."

Soon everyone had gathered around a table laden with food. Hank gave Lance a sharp look and reached for Olivia's hand. "Let's pray for the food."

Lance barely heard the prayer as he tried to sort out what to tell his family. That he could count on them to be there for him, he had no doubt. However, the outcome of the custody hearing was likely to be as hurtful to them as to him and Mark.

Most everyone had cleared their plates when Walt cleared his throat. "Your mother said you had something you needed to talk with us about. Why don't you go ahead as soon as we refill our coffee cups."

Just as Juliana was finishing filling everyone's cup, Abby wandered in looking like a little girl who had just woken from a deep sleep. Yawning she accepted a cup of coffee from Juliana and sat at the table. "Morning, everyone. Sorry I overslept. What did I miss?"

Lance smiled at his little sister. "You didn't miss anything but one of Mom's great breakfasts." He looked around the table and found everyone watching him. "So here's where we are with the custody situation. Chandra has filed for a change of custody for Mark and she's asking to see Mark before the final custody hearing. The judge has set a hearing for this Friday morning at the courthouse in Fredericksburg. Both Mark and I have to be there along with my attorney."

Olivia placed her right hand, fisted above her heart. "Will Chandra be able to take Mark on Friday?"

Lance frowned when he saw the gesture that had become a signal from his mom of distress. "The judge may let her take him but hopefully only with a supervisor with him. She won't be allowed to leave the area with him. I'm hopeful that if the judge does allow supervised visitation it will only be for a few hours, but it may be for a day or so."

Hank sat his coffee cup down and took his wife's hand. "So help me understand this. This Friday is only a hearing to get visitation. Then there will be a hearing later on the custody?"

Lance nodded. "Yes, sir."

"Do we know when that second hearing will be?" Hank squeezed Olivia's hand.

"It should be within the next week or two. Hilary doesn't think the judge will let it drag on for long." Lance hoped not as his anxiety was starting to affect his being able to get other things done. Once he told Mark what was going on, Lance could only imagine how the stress would affect his son.

Walt waved his hand to encompass the ones around the table. "What do you want us to do? I plan to be in the courtroom at the very least. It's not a closed hearing is it?"

Lance wondered why he had not thought to ask Hilary that. "I didn't think to ask Hilary. I'll call her later today. I do need some of you there to help keep Mark entertained if the hearing goes on for a while. Hilary doesn't think Mark will be called to speak in open court but the judge may want to talk to him." Lance took a deep breath as he could hardly speak about the possibly of what the judge might decide. "And if the judge does grant visitation it could happen on Friday. Mark might not be able to come home with me. I know Hilary is going to ask for supervision but the judge might change that. What I fear most is that Chandra, if she gets her hands on Mark without supervision, might leave the country with him." He glanced around the table at his brothers. "Logan and Alex, I'd like to ask you all to be there and watch the exit of the courthouse. I'm probably being paranoid but I'm also scared. I may not be able to stop a court hearing but at least I can do something to make sure that Chandra goes by the rules."

Logan glanced at Alex who gave a nod and then at Lance. "We'll be there. Don't worry. We'll have your back."

Lance gave a nod to his younger brother. "I had no doubt I could count on you all. Grandpapa and Nana, if you feel up to it, I would appreciate it if you all were in the courtroom with Mom and Dad and you, Abby. Juliana, will you be able to be there?"

"I can plan to take the day off from work. I'll be there. What can I do?"

"I'm asking Rosa to stay at the ranch with Sara Hope. Would you stay with Mark at the courthouse? Maria will stay with him but I'd appreciate it if you would also be with them."

Juliana shrugged her shoulder. "That will be easy to do. We'll keep him entertained."

Lance slowly glanced around the table at each one. "It helps to know I have all of you at my back in this battle. I'm doing my best to fight this in a righteous way. I know all of you will keep Mark and me in your prayers. I'm trying to be content with however it plays out, to trust God that all will turn out for our good in the long term, which is hard for me." Lance felt the push of tears and swallowed hard to maintain his control. "I need to get back to the house. I want to be with Mark as much as I can for the next few days. Grandpapa, would you lead us in a prayer. Pray for me as I try to explain this to Mark later today."

Everyone took the hand of the one next to them and bowed their heads. When the prayer was over Lance noticed that several had tears in their eyes. As he got ready to leave, everyone insisted on giving him a hug and a word of encouragement.

Driving back to his ranch Lance thought over his meeting with his family. He felt better now he knew they were aware of what was going on. He had really wanted to ask Juliana to be with him during the court hearing. That was a bad idea in many ways. The last thing he wanted to do was give

Chandra the idea that he was interested in another woman, even though if he was honest with himself, he was interested. That was as far as he would let himself go in thinking of Juliana. Knowing she would be in the courthouse with Mark was a comfort. Now he had to figure out when and how best to tell Mark about the hearing.

When he got back to the ranch, he found Rosa rocking Sara Hope. "She doing okay?"

"Oh, yes, just a little fussy this morning. She didn't sleep well last night and I'm hoping she will drop off to sleep for a while."

With her little head lying on Rosa's shoulder, Sara Hope was solemnly staring at Lance. As usual, he wondered what she was thinking. He reached over and stroked her soft plump cheek. "Hey, little one. You doing okay?" The baby blinked and then with a sigh closed her eyes.

Lance pulled up a chair. "Can we talk and not disturb her?"

Rosa rocked slowly and patted Sara Hope's back. "Yes, I think she sleeps now and if we speak soft it won't bother her."

Lance gave Rosa a short version of what was happening. "Since this hearing doesn't involve Sara Hope, I want you to stay here at the house with her while we go to the hearing. I'm going to tell Mark this afternoon and we need to be ready to help him cope with all this."

Rosa shifted slightly in the rocker. "I will take care of this baby. And Mark will be okay as long as he is sure of your love, Lance." He had noticed that when they were around other people Rosa always referred to him as Mr. Lance. In private and moments like this, she spoke to him in the same tone of love and concern as she used with Ricardo.

"How can I make sure he knows I love him when I let something like this happen to him?" Lance took a deep shuddering breath.

"You will know what to say. Who has been with him all this time if not his father? Mark is a smart boy and he will not be fooled." Rosa's voice was full of an assurance Lance wished he had.

Later that evening, Lance went into Mark's room after the boy had taken his shower and climbed into bed. Seeing his son sitting up in his bed surrounded by books, toys, and stuffed animals, he had to grin. "You got any room for me to sit down on your bed and talk?"

Mark returned his father's grin. "Sure Dad. I can just shove some of these off." And shove he did.

Lance stepped over the toys and stuffed animals now on the floor and sat next to Mark, leaning back on the headboard of the bed. Pulling Mark up beside him and cuddling him close to his side, he asked, "How was your day?"

"Great, Dad. I rode Ginger at a trot and Ricardo said I did good."

"Hey, that's great. Just think, three months ago you had never ridden. Now look at you." Had it been only been two and half months since Chandra had left him? It seemed a lifetime ago.

Mark glanced up at his dad with a smug look. "Does that mean I get a horse all my own. You know my birthday is next month."

"Nice try." Lance ruffled his son's hair. "I have something serious I need to talk to you about."

"Okay, what is it? Did I do something bad?"

"Not that I know of. You got something to tell me?"

Mark grinned. "No, sir."

"Well, alrighty then. Seriously, I've something to tell you. You know when your mom left and we moved here, I told you she wanted you to stay with me?"

Mark nodded, suddenly no longer playful. "Sure, Dad."

"Well, she has decided she wants to see you and for you to maybe go live with her. She has asked a judge here in Texas to let her do that. We have to go talk to him in Fredericksburg on Friday."

"Do I have to go live with her?" Mark's voice was full of alarm.

"I'm not sure. I've asked the judge for you to stay with me. But you have to realize we have to do what the judge says."

"Then let's tell the judge that I want to stay with you."

Lance almost smiled at the eight year old's simple conclusion. "Don't you want to see your mother?"

Mark shrugged his shoulders. "I'm not sure. She didn't want me before. Maybe she will change her mind again."

"That's always a possibility but she's still your mother and the judge gets to decide where you live."

"Why, Dad? He doesn't even know me. Why does he get to choose?"

"Because when parents argue over their kids a judge gets to decide the outcome."

"I didn't know you were arguing with Mom."

"I'm not really. But now she wants to take you away and I'll do what I can to keep you close. I love you, Mark. Don't you ever forget that." Lance kissed the top of his son's head.

"I love you too, Dad. I'll tell that old judge I want to stay with you."

Lance wondered how to make sure his son understood neither he nor Mark had any control over what the judge would decide. "Mark, listen. On Friday, the judge may say you need to go with your mom and visit for a while. There'll be someone from the judge's office with you and then you'll come home."

Mark gave his dad a worried frown. "But Dad, I'll miss my riding lesson with Ricardo. Why can't Mom come here and watch me ride?"

"That's a good idea. I'll suggest that to the judge on Friday morning. But he may not think it's a good idea and like I said we have to do what the judge says."

"I'm afraid, Dad. What if the judge says I can't come home?"

Lance felt the stinging of tears as he heard his son's fear and felt helpless to protect Mark from the hurt of the divorce and custody fight. He again kissed the top of Mark's head and hugged him close. A tear he couldn't hold back trickled down the side of his face. Fighting for control, Lance said, "Let's pray for the judge, your mom, and for us that God will guide us through all this."

Mark nodded. "We learned a verse in Bible class this evening. You want to hear it?"

"Sure, let me hear it. God's word is always useful."

"For God did not give us a spirit of timidity, but a spirit of power, of love and of self-discipline. 2 Timothy 1:7. The teacher told us that word timidity means fear and she said we didn't have to be afraid much because God will protect us. Isn't that a good verse, Dad?"

Lance swallowed and hoarsely said, "That's a perfect verse. I'll read it again before I go to bed. Now I need to let you get to sleep. Tomorrow Maria's brothers and sisters are coming again to play. You'll like that."

Mark's voice was full of enthusiasm, as if what they had been talking about was no longer important. "I really like them. They're lots of fun and they are teaching me Spanish. Isn't that great? Soon I'll be able to know what Rosa and Ricardo are saying when they speak Spanish."

Lance chuckled softly. "Should we tell them you'll soon be able to understand them?"

Mark grinned. "No, sir. Let's have it for a surprise."

Lance stood and helped Mark scoot under the covers. He bent down and kissed Mark on the forehead. "I love you, son."

His son wrapped his arms around Lance's neck. "Goodnight, Dad. I love you, too." He then planted a smacking kiss on Lance's cheek.

Lance lay awake long into the night thinking about what was about to come. He kept the refrain of the Scripture verse he had learned from his son going in his mind.

Chapter 24

Juliana was finishing up with the physical therapy for Milo Simpson when Greg Young knocked on the ranch house door. The preacher was dressed casually in jeans and long-sleeved shirt unbuttoned at the collar.

Mildred Simpson, who was short, plump, and cheerful, went to the door and greeted him. "Come on in, Greg. Juliana is helping Milo get back on his feet after that hip replacement. The fool seems to think he should be out rounding up cattle in spite of being seventy years old."

Milo walked into the living room using a cane with Juliana close behind in case he lost his balance. "I've two more months before I'm seventy, woman. Quit rushing me. Hey there. Greg."

Greg grinned at the two older members of the congregation. "Hey there yourself. I expected to see you lounging around in your chair there."

Milo grinned. "Well, that's where I'm heading if Juliana will quit torturing me."

Juliana laughed for she loved this couple who were forever bantering at each other. They had celebrated their fiftieth wedding anniversary in June. "No more torture for today, Milo. You've done well and deserve to rest awhile."

Mildred stood by the kitchen door. "I was just about to get us some coffee and slices of fresh butter pound cake Olivia sent over with Juliana. Can I get you a cup, Greg?"

"Sure, that sounds great. Just don't tell Crystal. If she finds out I had cake, she won't let me have dessert at supper." He sat down on the sofa.

Juliana sat in a wing-backed chair across from the preacher. "I find it hard to believe sweet Crystal would deny you anything."

He laughed. "You're probably right. She'd let me have dessert every evening, but my waist line won't tolerate it."

After a slice of Olivia's delicious pound cake and small talk with the Simpsons and Greg, Juliana took her leave of the couple. "I'll see you next week, Milo. Keep up the walking and the exercises I showed you."

"I'm gonna be on it, Juliana. I got a new hip and I plan to use it."

Greg took his leave at the same time and walked Juliana out to her pickup. "How's it going out at the Rocking M?"

Juliana put her bag in the cab of the pickup and then leaned on the door. "It's stressed at the Rocking M. I guess you heard what's going on with Lance and his children?"

He nodded. "Lance called me and asked that the church be praying for them, which we will."

Juliana knew that was true. "It's so sad. Lance seems such a nice person. I still don't understand how his wife could have left him."

Greg looked thoughtful. "May I ask you a personal question?"

Surprised by the question, Juliana saw no need to refuse. "Sure. What do you want to know?"

"What are your feelings about Lance and his children? I mean you personally."

"That's a hard question to answer, as I'm not real sure I know. I like Lance and enjoy his company. I adore those two kids. Mark is so bright and lively and Sara Hope is just a little doll. Who wouldn't love a baby like her?"

Greg raised his eyebrows. "Maybe her mother, which is a sad statement. Are you guarding your heart as far as Lance is concerned?"

Juliana looked up at the preacher whom she knew cared about her. Greg and Crystal both had reached out in friendship when she had moved to Tumbleweed almost two years ago. "I'm doing my best. Lance is still a married man and then he is going to be a divorced man. I had promised myself when a teenager that I would wait for a godly Christian man who was without lots of baggage. And I know that is not Lance. Having the two children is not baggage, but having an ex-wife is."

Greg patted her on the shoulder. "I'm thankful that you're thinking things through and realize the seriousness of getting too involved. I don't want either you or Lance hurt. I think he has been hurt about as much as he needs."

"What do you mean? As much as he needs?" Juliana was puzzled. No one needed to be hurt with a marriage breakup.

Greg looked out over the ranch land. "I don't think Lance would mind me saying this. He had let his life drift in a direction that separated him from God. He didn't take the spiritual leadership that he should have taken in his family. I'm not saying he deserves what happened, but it took what happened to wake him up. It's too bad it took his wife leaving to do it. He has a second chance to do things right. What all that will involve I'm not sure. And those kids now have a better chance of knowing God because of what has happened and that's a blessing coming out of the hurt."

Juliana gazed at Greg for a few moments before responding. "I see what you mean. We all sometimes have to have a sharp reminder of what is truly important. For myself, I place a high priority on being righteous before God and I plan to continue that path."

"You're going to be okay and so is Lance. Well, I've got to move on and check on Priscilla Miller and Lucy Graham before I head home. It was good to see you, Juliana."

"You, too. Say hello to Crystal for me."

Greg moved off to his own compact car. He waved as he drove off down the ranch road. Juliana was not far behind him.

The chat with Greg replayed in her mind. What really were her feelings for Lance? To say she cared about him was true but was it all of the truth? If only she could have met him at a different place in his life, before Chandra. Wishful thinking never made anything different. At least she could pray for him and tomorrow morning she would be at the courthouse in Fredericksburg to lend her support in any way she could.

Later that evening Maria called. "Hey, Ricardo has offered to pick me up in the morning. He suggested that you ride over with us. He's going to drop

231

off the BMW for Hank, Olivia, Walt, Nana, and Abby. Logan and Alex are driving Hank's truck. Ricardo said you all could drive here and we can take my car on into Fredericksburg, leaving your pickup here. What do you think?"

Juliana chuckled. "We should have just leased a bus for everyone. I assume Lance will be driving over in his truck with Mark, which is good as they need that time together."

Maria sighed. "Yes, that's what Lance told me this afternoon. He also had Rosa pack a bag for Mark in case the judge ordered him to go with his mother for the weekend. Oh, Juliana, this is so hard. Lance looked so sad when he was talking to me. I wanted to promise him everything would be okay, but I couldn't. It may not be."

"I know. I want to do the same thing. I assume you suggested Mark bring a backpack of books and toys for tomorrow. We may not need it, as the hearing may be short. But I have known of these things going for hours when you count in the wait time before your hearing is called."

"I'm glad you're taking off work and will be there with me. I can keep Mark busy but I need you to keep me encouraged."

Juliana responded, "I'm not sure who will be encouraging whom, as I'm kinda down about all of this myself."

Hearing Maria yawning, Juliana quickly said goodbye. "I'll see you in the morning. Now say your prayers and go to bed."

Maria giggled. "Yes, Mom, and the same to you."

Sleep did not come easy that night. Juliana hoped Lance and Mark were able to sleep. Saying an extra prayer for them, Juliana finally drifted off to sleep.

Chapter 25

Morning had come too early for Lance, as he had set his alarm for five am. They needed to leave by seven to meet Hilary at eight. Lance showered, shaved, and dressed carefully. He wore his dark blue suit with a white shirt. The tie he picked out to wear was a subdued blue and white stripped silk. He needed to give as solid an impression as possible to the judge. Lance grunted. Everything revolved around the judge. Lance had never met him but his dad and grandpapa both knew him. That Judge Theodore Whitlock had grown up in the area Lance considered a positive, but exactly how the judge would view the case was the huge unknown.

At six-thirty Lance woke Mark up and got him moving toward getting dressed. Mark had showered the night before and only needed to wash his face and brush his teeth. Lance had Mark to dress in slacks and a short-sleeved dress shirt, and his dressy leather loafers.

"Why do I have to dress up so much, Dad?" Mark stood patient as Lance combed his hair. "And why are you in a suit? It's not even Sunday."

Lance managed to smile. He didn't often wear a suit although he had been wearing one to church services on Sunday mornings. "We want to dress in a respectful manner because we're talking to a judge today. There are times we need to dress up to show we respect the person we're seeing and a judge is such a person."

"Dad, do we have to go see the judge?" Mark sounded younger than usual. The soft hesitant voice seemed sad to Lance compared to Mark's usual boisterous voice.

"Yes, we do, and we're going to be okay no matter what happens. Now don't mess up your hair and come on to the kitchen for a bite of breakfast before we leave."

~

Lance didn't recognize any of the vehicles as he drove up and parked at the courthouse in Fredericksburg. It was not quite eight o'clock in the morning and his folks would not be arriving until closer to ten o'clock when the actual hearing was scheduled. As he and Mark clamored out of the truck, Ricardo pulled the large maroon-colored mini-van, Lance had bought for Maria to drive, into a parking space nearby. With the size of her family, and driving Mark around, Lance had decided she needed a vehicle that would accommodate all the people who might need to ride in it. Plus, it was a safer vehicle than a smaller car. He hadn't told Maria yet but he planned to sell the minivan to her at a low price when she was no longer working for him. She needed it for her family.

Mark was quick to give Juliana and Maria hugs as they stepped onto the sidewalk in front of the courthouse. "I brought games, books, and some toys in my backpack. Dad said to so I wouldn't get bored."

Maria returned Mark's hug. "The backpack is so you won't get bored, but I see that your dad is carrying it."

Mark grinned. "Well, he grabbed it."

Lance handed the backpack off to Ricardo. "You hang onto this so I can carry my briefcase." Lance noticed with appreciation that Ricardo had also worn a suit, dress shirt, and tie. Maria and Juliana were dressed in pretty dresses they usually wore to church. He felt a warmth at the effort they were making to do what they could to support him and Mark.

Juliana gave Lance a smile. "Do you know where we need to settle? And can we bring drinks and food into the courthouse?"

"I have a rough idea where we're to meet my attorney. I'm not sure about what you can take into certain parts of the courthouse, but there's a coffee shop next door."

Ricardo draped Mark's backpack over one shoulder. "Why don't the girls and I take Mark to the coffee shop and get a drink and snack and you find out where we need to be and when."

Lance nodded. "Good idea. Mark, Maria is in charge. I'll go find out what is what and give you a call, Ricardo. Do all three of you have your cell phones?" He looked around at them and got a nod from each one. "After I go into the courtroom I won't be able to communicate by phone, but up until then we can stay in close contact."

After checking his watch and noting he had ten minutes to make the meeting with Hilary, Lance gave a wave and started up the steps into the courthouse.

After going through security, Lance soon found the conference room on the second floor where he met Hilary at the door.

She looked down the hall and then at Lance. "Where's Mark? Didn't you bring him?"

"He's at the coffee shop next door with Maria, Juliana, and Ricardo. I didn't know if there would be a place for him to settle until we have our talk this morning. When it's closer to time for the hearing they'll bring him up. I didn't want Mark sitting in the hallway in case Chandra shows up."

Hilary cocked an eyebrow. "Good thinking. I'm assuming Chandra will show up. If only her attorney shows up, that may be a negative for the judge or it may not. There's no way to tell." She led the way into the room that held a large conference table with leather covered chairs surrounding it.

She and Lance settled at one end of the table and Hilary began to go over what might happen in the hearing. "The main thing is for you to set and look interested and confident. No grimaces, frowns, and no comments unless the judge directly asks you a question. You want to look serious but not angry. Calm is important. Any questions?"

"How likely is the judge to allow visitation?" Lance knew she could only guess but he asked anyway.

"There's more than a good chance he'll allow some level of visitation. How much is the question. You need to prepare yourself and Mark. It may even be for several days at the worst and only a couple of hours at the least."

Lance struggled to take a deep breath. "You really think he might give Mark to her for a week or so? She could take him anywhere and I might never see him again." How could she sit so calmly with the possibility of such a horror happening? He had to calm himself before he tried to talk to Mark.

After they had discussed more of the legal aspects of the case, Hilary said, "You need to be prepared that anything is possible in a child custody case. We have to wait and see what happens. I do think the judge will give some sort of visitation. No use to borrow trouble before it gets here. Now why don't you get Mark to come on up before the others start arriving. It's only nine and you have an hour before the hearing. I'll go check and see if Chandra, or her attorney, has arrived yet. You wait here until I come to get you just before we need to enter the courtroom."

After Hilary left with her briefcase, Lance took a moment to pray and then phoned Ricardo for them to make their way to the conference room.

When they arrived, Lance met them at the door. "You all please find a bench to sit on in the corridor while I speak to Mark for a few minutes."

Ricardo glanced over at Maria and Juliana. "Sure, Lance. We'll be right out here when you need us."

Mark followed his dad over to the conference table. After climbing into one of the leather chairs, he asked, "Is Mom here yet, Dad?"

Lance sat next to his son and in a soft voice he responded, "Not that I'm aware of but she and her attorney should be here soon. You won't see her until maybe after the hearing." Trying to drink in all he could of the sight of his son, he had to swallow and look up at the ceiling to keep back tears that threatened. "Mark, I want to talk about what might happen at the hearing. Do you understand why we have to be here today?"

Mark looked up at him expectantly, "Sure, Dad. You told me Mom wants me to come visit her and maybe live with her. You want me to stay with you. And because you and Mom can't decide we need to let the judge decide."

"Your mom is living with another man, Mark. You'll be visiting both your mom and this man. His name is Henri Fontaine" Lance hated he had to explain such a thing to his son. It was taking away part of Mark's innocence and bringing such ugliness into his life. Lance wanted to break something and yell at Chandra for doing this to their child.

Mark drew circles on the polished conference table with his finger. "Will he be my new dad? I don't want a new dad. You're my dad and I want to live with you at the ranch with Sara Hope, Rosa, and Ricardo. Do I have to go visit Mom? Why can't she come visit us?" He raised his gaze filled with such sadness that Lance was fighting tears again.

"She doesn't want to be around me any longer, Mark. However, she wants to see you. She's your mother and she loves you." Lance hoped Chandra loved Mark. He would really hate it if they were going through all of this and she didn't really love her son.

"Can I tell the judge that I don't want to go visit Mom and that she needs to come visit us?" Mark asked with a hopeful note in his voice.

"I'm hoping the judge will ask what you want, but he's going to make the decision based on what he thinks is best for you. Here's how I'm expecting today to go. You will wait here with Maria and Juliana while I go with my attorney to talk to the judge. He may ask you to come into the big room, called a courtroom, to talk to you. Or, he may want to talk to you in his office. Then you may or may not come back here to wait for his decision. If he decides you need to go visit your mom, you and I'll say goodbye and then you'll go with your mom. It'll be okay and you'll soon be back home." Lance could only pray he was telling Mark the truth.

"I'm scared, Dad." Big tears started rolling down his face.

Lance pulled him into his lap and hugged him tight with both arms. "I know it's scary. I'm a little scared myself. You'll be okay and so will I. Just remember I love you no matter what. Even if someone tells you I don't love you or don't want you, you remember it's a lie, okay?"

"Okay Dad and I love you too."

Lance slipped a cell phone and charger from his pocket. "I got you a cell phone for your own. If your mom asks if you have one you don't lie to her, but it might be best if your mom didn't know you have it. You can keep it in your backpack. You know my cell phone number but on this phone you only have to dial this icon and it will call me. Every night you need to put it on the charger."

"Wow, my own phone. I thought I had to wait until I was older to have my own cell phone."

Lance chuckled. "Well, this is a sort of an unusual case. Now if you don't have any questions let's get the others in."

After Ricardo, Maria, and Juliana converged around the conference table, Lance sat back and watched his son interact with them. Lance wondered what else should he be telling Mark to prepare him for possible separation from what he was familiar? How did Lance prepare himself? All too soon, Hilary was at the door motioning for Lance to follow her to the courtroom.

"Stay here with Maria and Juliana. Love you, son." Lance gave Mark a hug and kissed him on the forehead.

"Love you too, Dad." Mark looked at his dad like a little lost puppy.

Lance motioned Ricardo to come with him. "I'd like you to be in the courtroom in case I need to send a message to Maria and Juliana."

"Sure, Lance, I'll be glad to do that." Ricardo gave Maria's arm a squeeze and strolled out the door behind Lance.

They followed Hilary down the hall to the door to the courtroom. Since Lance had gone into the conference room, the hallway had filled with people none of whom looked happy to be in the courthouse.

Hilary paused before opening the door. "Chandra and her attorney came in just before I came to get you. They should already be seated at the front of the courtroom. You should greet her with a nod but don't engage her in a conversation. You never know what might get said or how that might be used later by her attorney. Okay?"

Lance nodded his understanding. He wiped his palms on his pants legs and swallowed hard. Stepping into the courtroom, he looked straight ahead and followed Hilary. Ricardo stopped at a row of seats where Hank, Oliva, Walt, Nana, and Abby were seated and sat in an empty seat next to Abby. Almost immediately, Lance spotted Chandra as she was turned toward an older man seated at a table at the front of the courtroom. Her hairstyle was different, but otherwise, she looked the same. Her hair looked more blond than red and she was dressed in a green suit that showed off her slender form.

Her makeup was to perfection and Lance again had the thought that his wife could have been a modal as she was so gorgeous. Somehow, the physical beauty no longer stirred him as it had in the past. Now he was searching her face for some sign of a deeper level of maturity. One that would help her make decisions for the best of their children instead of her own desires and wants.

She caught sight of Lance and met his gaze with a cool look of recognition and small nod. He tried to do the same but wasn't sure he could match her sense of cold uncaring. *Why did you leave me, Chandra?* The refrain of the unanswered question filtered through his mind as he took his seat beside Hilary at a table across from Chandra and the older man he assumed was her attorney. Would there be any answers to his questions of why she had left him and preferred another man? Why their marriage had fallen so low that they were in this courtroom to decide how to divide their children? Lance's inner questions stilled as the judge entered the courtroom amid the instruction from the clerk for all to rise and the hearing began. Judge Theodore Whitlock was in his sixties, tall with a full head of gray wavy hair and a full mustache. He walked and talked like a military man. Looking down from his podium desk and in his black robe, he was the full image of a no-nonsense judge.

Chapter 26

Juliana turned to Mark as soon as Lance left the conference room. "Let's get out the deck of cards and play either Crazy Eights or I Doubt It. You choose, Mark."

Mark immediately opened the backpack and started digging for a deck of cards. "Okay let's play Crazy Eights and then play I Doubt It. You play too, Maria."

Juliana chuckled. "Now wait a minute. Who said we could play both games?"

"You didn't say I had to choose just one game, Juliana," Mark responded.

Maria giggled. "He's got you there, Juliana. I'm going to watch you, Mark. You're too smart."

They spent the next two hours playing several card games with Mark winning as much as either of the young women. Juliana had trouble keeping her mind on the games as she found herself wondering what was happening in the courtroom. "Let's take a break and go to the restroom. I'm glad there's one attached to this room. We don't have to wander the hallway looking for one and maybe miss your dad coming back."

Mark had just taken his turn using the restroom when there was a knock on the door. Juliana opened it and saw Lance's attorney.

"The judge wants to see Mark and talk with him."

Juliana turned back to Mark. "Leave your things and go with Ms. Hilary, Mark."

Mark looked at Maria. "Do I have to go?"

Maria shrugged her shoulders. "That's what your dad said. Remember he said that the judge would want to speak to you. Go on, Mark. It's okay. I'll watch your stuff and makes sure that no one takes it."

Mark scooted down from the large conference room chair and slowly walked to the door. As he stepped out into the hallway, he let Hilary take his hand and waved with his other hand at Juliana

Juliana went back to the conference table and sat down. She grabbed a tissue out of her purse feeling as if she would let go with a bucket of tears any minute.

Maria patted her hand. "Let's say a prayer and try to keep our spirits up."

Juliana swallowed down the tears that threatened. "You pray for us, okay. I'm not sure I can."

"Sure." Maria took Juliana's hand and then expressed a prayer for guidance and for God's will to be done no matter the result of the custody hearing.

Juliana hugged her good friend after the end of the prayer. "I'm sorry I'm getting so upset. But the whole thing is just so sad to me."

"I know. I have so enjoyed the last several weeks. It hasn't seemed like a job at all. Just spending time with Mark and bringing my siblings over to play, I've come to care about Mark and about Lance."

"I need to give it into God's hands better. But, I keep wanting to tell God how this should all work out." Juliana felt guilty she wasn't being stronger spiritually.

Maria looked thoughtful. "Well, you're not alone in that. I keep remembering what Joseph told his brothers after he revealed himself to them. I think it is in the last part of Genesis. He said that what his brothers had done was meant for evil, but God meant it for good. The only way that could have happened was for Joseph to have stayed faithful to God. That's what we need to do is stay faithful and let God work all of this out the way he wills."

Juliana hugged Maria again. "How did I get so blessed as to have such a friend as you?"

"The same to you, my friend. We've both been blessed."

Juliana wondered how Lance felt about what was happening. Was he able to see potential good coming out of the hurt of the divorce and custody battle? She hoped he had at least that much comfort.

After two more hours of waiting, Ricardo came back to the conference room.

Maria jumped up and hurried over to him. "What's happening?"

Ricardo shook his head. "It's not good. The judge is letting Mark's mom take him for the weekend. Lance asked me to get Mark's things and take them to the courtroom. It should be over in another few minutes and then I guess Lance and his attorney will come back here."

Juliana had trouble taking her next breath. This was not too unexpected but it was still bad. What must Lance be feeling if she felt this bad? Was he going to lose his son?

Ricardo gave Maria a sideways hug and grabbed the backpack and suitcase with Mark's things. "I'll be back shortly." He quickly left the room closing the door softly behind him.

Juliana and Maria hugged and both reached for tissues as tears threatened.

"We need to get control and be ready to be supportive of Lance. He must feel awful about seeing Mark leave with Chandra even for a couple of days." Juliana wiped her face with the tissue.

Maria hiccupped halfway to a sob. "I know but I'm going to miss that little guy. You don't think Chandra will try to take him away and not bring him back after the weekend?"

Juliana sat back at the table. "I hope not but who knows what she'll do. Lance told me he was completely blindsided by the filing for divorce and especially by her leaving the children with him."

"At least she hasn't taken Sara Hope yet. Oh, you don't think she'll come back and want the baby? That would just be more awfulness." Maria sounded ready to start wailing.

"Let's calm down and wait to see what will happen. Only God knows at this point." Juliana took a couple of deep breaths to calm herself down. Lance didn't need to come back into the room and find two hysterical females.

Chapter 27

"Chandra Martin McTavish will take custody of the child, Mark Michael McTavish for the next forty-eight hours and return the child to his father, Lance Nobel McTavish at 10 o'clock Monday morning here at this courthouse. For no reason is Chandra Martin McTavish to leave the state of Texas with Mark Michael McTavish. To do so will be considered by this court to be in violation of this court order and will be designated as kidnapping. This court will reconvene at 1 pm on Monday for final custody judgement. This court is adjourned."

Lance sat down after the judge left the courtroom not able to force himself to move as Chandra and her attorney followed the court clerk back to the judge's chambers where the judge had left Mark. Lance was not even to be allowed to say goodbye.

Gradually Lance became aware that his attorney stood by his chair waiting for him. He pushed himself up from the table with both hands like an old man. When he turned he found both his mom and grandmama there to wrap their arms around as they stood and cried.

"Lance, let's move back to the conference room where we can talk a minute." Hilary took his arm and they started slowly to move out of the courtroom. Hank, Olivia, Walt, Edna, Abby, and Ricardo followed behind.

Lance had some questions but decided to wait until they had some privacy. Entering the conference room the first person he saw was Juliana. She stood tall and calm with a sadness in her eyes. He wanted to go over to her, put his arms around her and his head on her shoulder, and weep. Instead, he excused himself and locked himself into the bathroom at one end of the conference room. He grabbed both sides of the sink, lowered his head, and wept silently. How long he let himself go to pieces he wasn't sure. Finally, he tore off some paper toweling, wiped his face, and blew his nose. Turning on the cold-water tap, he splashed water onto his face and then tore more toweling and dried his face. After staring at himself in the mirror and seeing a grief that had not been there before, he closed his eyes and prayed.

"Father, keep Mark safe both physically and spiritually. Let him have happiness as he spends time with his mom. Bless Chandra and Henri Fontaine that they will be kind and caring for my son. Help me bear this burden of Mark being gone and bring him back safe. Help me be thankful for what I have, my family, friends, and especially for Sara Hope. Help me to be the dad she needs in spite of my grief over possibly loosing Mark. Oh, Father you know how much I love my children. I ask that I may be allowed to raise them to your glory. In the name of your son, Jesus the Christ. Amen."

The prayer helped him to calm down and he was ready to face his family and friends. What was he going to do with himself? The weekend stretched out long and endless. He just prayed that Mark would be returned on Monday.

When he returned to the conference room, his parents and grandparents were gone.

Juliana stood beside him and quietly said, "Your folks decided to start on home. Your mom wants you to come by and eat lunch even though it's getting late."

Lance nodded. "Okay. I need to ask Hilary some questions and then I need to see Sara Hope."

Ricardo took Maria's hand. "I'll drive Maria home. Why don't you ride with Lance, Juliana?"

"I'll be glad to ride with you, Lance, if that is what you want. I'll even drive if that will help."

Lance stared at her for a moment. "I would appreciate that." He turned to Ricardo. "You two go on and leave. Juliana and I will be along shortly."

Ricardo and Maria each gave him a hug and left the conference room, leaving Juliana and Lance alone with Hilary.

~~~

Juliana sat at the conference table across from Hilary and next to Lance. She questioned whether she should stay in the room but Lance gave no indication he wanted her to leave.

Hilary sorted some papers. "Lance, I know you don't feel like it did, but that hearing went as well as we could have expected it to go. The only thing I wish is that the judge had decided in favor of supervised custody for the weekend. He did order Chandra not take Mark out of the state. I did tell Theo, I mean Judge Whitlock, that you had Mark's birth certificate and passport so Chandra can't take him across the border."

Lance ran his fingers through his already unruly hair. "Yeah, I wish the judge had ordered supervised visitation with me as the supervisor. He did say Mark could call me. Why do you think he said I wasn't to know where they're spending the weekend?"

"Oh, that is obvious. So you won't go and sit out in front of the place for the weekend. That is what you want to do isn't it?" Hilary gave him a severe frown.

"You know me too well already, Hilary. That's exactly what I want to do." He sounded as if he wanted to bite someone's head off.

There was a look of such fury in his eyes that Juliana had to force herself to look at him. Had he arranged to have Chandra followed? Then she remembered the phone he had given Mark. Did it have a GPS in it? Was he tracking his son? Somehow, she had no question that he was. Was it legal? Juliana didn't know, but she understood the sentiment that would cause him to do it.

Hilary stared at them as if she wanted to say something.

Lance broke the silence. "What else do I need to do to get ready for Monday?"

Hilary looked down at her papers and then back up at Lance. "There's nothing I know we need to do. The judge will talk to Mark again after the weekend. Then he'll make his decision. I hope he makes it on Monday but be prepared to have him set another date for his judgement. Now go home and have a quiet weekend with your daughter. I'll see you here on Monday at 9 am. We'll have things to go over at that time."

Lance stood and reached across the table with his hand extended. "I don't know how to thank you for your guidance through all of this. It would be a lot harder if you were not so capable."

Hilary shook his hand. "It's my pleasure and I'm glad to help. I have to be as objective as possible but I really do want you to have custody of Mark. I think it'll be in his best interest."

Lance and Juliana said their goodbyes to Hilary and left her in the conference room reorganizing her papers and making notes.

He handed his keys to Juliana as they approached his truck. "I'll take you up on driving back to the ranch if you don't mind. I'm not sure it would be safe for me to drive the state I'm in."

"Sure, I'll be glad to drive." Juliana soon had them on the highway out of Fredericksburg.

Lance slumped down in his seat and stared out the window. She didn't think he was seeing anything they speeded past.

She heard his sigh and then he said softly, "I can't believe all this is happening. None of it was ever in my game plan."

Not knowing what to say she kept her eyes on the road. He straightened in his seat and looked over at her.

"Thanks, Juliana, for being there. I've come to depend on your calm spirit through all this turmoil."

Juliana glanced over at him. The sadness on his face was heartbreaking. "I'm glad I could be of some help. Did Mark seem okay when he left?"

Lance hit his fist on the seat of the truck. "I didn't get to see him leave. The judge talked to him in his chambers and Mark waited there for Chandra to come. I don't even know who was with him."

No wonder he was so upset. In addition to Chandra getting a full weekend of visitation, Lance hadn't been able to reassure Mark that he would see him on Monday.

"Hopefully, Mark will call you this evening and you can reassure him."

"I can only hope Chandra will let him call. Maybe she won't find out that I gave him a cell phone."

Juliana slowed the truck and paid attention to her driving as they passed through Tumbleweed.

Lance's phone rang and he pulled it out of his pocket quickly to answer it. "Hi Mom. Yes, we're almost to the ranch turn-off."

He glanced at Juliana as he listened. "Okay, Mom, we'll come straight to the house. Be there in a few minutes." He ended the call.

"You're folks are already at the ranch?" Juliana asked keeping her eyes on the road.

"Yes, Abby drove the BMW over to Two Forks to bring Rosa and Sara Hope to the Rocking M. They should be coming shortly." He sounded relieved.

Juliana turned from the highway onto the lane to the Rocking M ranch house. "You need to stay close to your family, Lance. They need you and you need them. You are all concerned about the outcome of this custody battle."

Lance was silent for a few moments. "You're right. I've been thinking only about how all this affects me, my feelings. Others are scared and hurting too. They love Mark as much as I do."

Juliana wanted to stop the truck and put her arms around Lance to comfort him. How scared he must be that he would lose his son. She kept driving and soon parked behind the ranch house. No matter how much she might want to be a comfort to Lance, he was still a married man. What he needed from her was her friendship. Looking in the rearview mirror, she spotted the BMW coming up the lane. "There's Rosa with Sara Hope."

Lance jumped out of the truck and hurried over to the BMW barely giving Abby time to stop the car. He opened the back passenger door and unhooked the straps securing Sara Hope. Juliana followed him to the car and opened the door for Rosa who was in the front passenger seat. Abby came around the car and the three women watched as Lance picked up the infant and hugged her to himself swaying gently as he caressed her back. He had his eyes closed and seemed unaware of anyone else.

Rosa went up to Lance and started to rub his back, murmuring to him in Spanish.

Juliana looked over at Abby and nodded her head toward the house.

They crossed the back porch as Oliva opened the screen door. "Is Lance all right?" She asked softly.

Juliana glanced back at Lance holding his daughter and Rosa giving what comfort she could. "He will be, but for right now I think he needs to feel at least Sara Hope is safe."

Abby hugged her mom with her eyes bright with unshed tears. "I feel awful and don't know what to do."

Olivia kissed her daughter on the forehead. "Just pray and let Lance lead the way. He'll let us know what he needs. I think for now we need to let him be. Let's get everyone together at the table to eat lunch. I've got it ready."

Juliana said, "I'll get the diaper bag and encourage Rosa and Lance to bring Sara Hope into the house out of the sun."

Olivia nodded. "Please do. If I went out there now I would just starting bawling."

Abby sniffled. "I may anyway."

"No you're not. Lance doesn't need all of us being weepy females, as hard as it is not to be." After closing the screen door, Olivia pulled Abby further into the kitchen.

Juliana went back to the car and pulled out the diaper bag. "Lance, your mom has lunch on the table. You need to try to eat something. Why don't you take Sara Hope in out of this heat and sit at the table holding her? Rosa, you need to get out of this sun, too."

Lance looked around as if becoming aware of where he was. "I'm sorry, Rosa. Juliana is right. Let's go inside." He walked slowly up the steps and crossed the porch with Sara Hope cuddled in his arms and with Rosa and Juliana following.

Hank held open the screen door. "Come on in, son. You want me to take the baby?"

"No, Dad. I need to hold her for a while." The bleakness in his voice caused an ache in Juliana's chest. She wanted to give comfort but didn't know what she could do.

Chapter 28

Lance followed Rosa with Sara Hope home to the Two Forks Ranch after they ate the light meal his mom had prepared. She had wanted him to stay with them at the Rocking M, but Lance needed to be alone. After he changed into jeans, long-sleeve cotton shirt, and boots, he checked in with Rosa who was rocking Sara Hope in the nursery.

"She doing okay?" Lance squatted down and stroked the fine hair on his daughter's head.

"She's fine. I should lay her in her bed for her nap. It is just that I want to hold her for a bit." Rosa looked close to tears.

Lance nodded. "I know the feeling. I just need to know she is safe and home. Especially with Mark gone...." His voice trailed off and he had to swallow to keep from sobbing.

Rosa smoothed Lance's hair back from his forehead. "What are you going to do this afternoon? You need to keep busy and no brood."

"I'm going to go to find George and see what's going on with the work around the ranch. Maybe I can find something to do that will take my mind off all that is going on."

"You do that. I'll make sure Sara Hope is okay. You have your phone?"

Lance pulled it from his pocket. "I've got my phone and I'll keep it with me." He kissed the sleeping baby's head, patted Rosa on the shoulder, and then headed out to find George.

Twenty minutes later, he had found George and two of the ranch hands, Johnny Hunter and Pete Keller, cutting brush and mountain cedar from around a fence line and a large pasture. He pulled on his gloves and went to work. In the heat of the hot Texas summer afternoon, he soon worked up a major sweat. Johnny and Pete kept urging him to slow down and drink from the canteen. When it was empty, they refilled it from the 5-gallon water cooler they had on the bed of the ranch truck that carried their work tools.

Both the ranch hands and George left at three to go help with the watering and feeding of the horses and cattle. It also got them out of the heat and into the shade of the barns for a time. They left the water cooler with Lance as he told them he would work a little longer on the cutting of brush away from the fencing. He had intended to stop in an hour or so, but he kept on until almost dark. The hard physical work helped keep his mind away from what might be going on with Mark.

When he finally made it back to the house, Rosa was waiting for him.

"Mr. Lance, you work too long. Look at you, all dirty and tired. I almost sent Ricardo after you but he say to let you alone. That you need to work hard." She fussed with getting his hat and bandana off and then let out a moan. "Oh, look at your poor hands! Oh, what have you done?" She started pulling him toward the table in the kitchen.

He went to the sink and carefully rinsed his hands. "Don't worry, Rosa. I've had blisters before." His hands did hurt along with his back, legs, and feet. He hadn't done as much physical labor in one day since he was a teen on his dad's ranch. And sitting in the chair at the kitchen table felt good, even necessary as his legs wanted to fold up on him.

"Here is your dinner. Eat and then soak in a tub. Then I will bandage your hands." After placing a plate of food in front of Lance and a large glass of iced tea, Rosa bustled around getting a pan filled with cold water and a washcloth. "Here let me have your left hand." She placed a wet washcloth she had soaked in the cold water on the palm and fingers of his left hand.

"Mmmm. That feels good." Lance murmured as he ate, using his right hand gingerly.

After he had eaten, Rosa let the cool cloth rest on his right hand. After a few minutes, she removed it. "You go take a soaker bath and go to bed. I will come up and put medicine on your hands."

Lance smiled at her earnest expression. "Thanks, Rosa. It's just blistered because my hands are not used to hard physical work. But I'll do as you say as I'm beat. I didn't sleep much the last couple of nights. Is Sara Hope asleep?"

"Yes, she didn't have a good nap this afternoon and was ready for bed as soon as I had fed and bathed her."

"I'll look in on her and then go take a bath." Lance went down the hall to Sara Hope's room and stood by her crib.

She was asleep on her back with her arms flung out and above her head with her little fists almost closed. Lance lightly rubbed her soft pudgy cheek. "Sleep deep and know you're safe, baby girl. I love you." He bent down and kissed her forehead.

He glanced at his cell phone as he laid it on the sink counter in his bathroom. He was anxious to get a call from Mark. Lance had called the security company he was using in Austin to track Mark's phone as he drove back to the house. They had told him Mark's cell phone was located at the Four Seasons Hotel in Austin on the 9th floor. So Chandra and Henri were staying in the luxury suite at one of Austin's best hotels. That meant Mark had his own room and would be able to call if Chandra hadn't taken the phone away.

After a long soak in the large bathtub to try to get some of the aches out of his back and arms, Lance dressed in lounge pants and a tee shirt. He had just settled on the bed when Rosa knocked on the door to the bedroom.

"Mr. Lance, you ready for me to doctor your poor hands?" Rosa carried a tray with bandages, medicines, a basin of water, and hand towels.

"Come on in, Rosa. My hands are feeling better." Lance felt uncomfortable having Rosa fuss over him. He had run cold water over his hands after his bath and they were feeling better, although he had to admit to some impressive blisters.

Rosa set the tray on a chair and she sat on the side of the bed. After carefully examining first the left hand and then the right hand, she shook her head. "Just as I thought. We need to drain a couple of these blisters to let them heal quicker and so you have less pain."

"What? They're not that bad." Lance had scarcely gotten started on his protest when Rosa was wiping down the palm of his hand with an antibacterial wipe.

She then picked up a needle she had laid on an alcohol soaked piece of gaze. With just a few pinpricks, she soon had several of the larger blisters on each hand draining. Working quickly and surely, as if she had done this before, she spread tea-tree oil over the blisters and put on a light gaze bandage.

"I'll treat them again in the morning and put a thicker bandage on them. I think you no listen to reason and will try to work again tomorrow." She finished her nursing and gathered her supplies back on the tray.

Lance sat in the bed with his bandaged hands in his lap. "Thanks for the nursing."

Rosa patted him on the cheek. "You are welcome. Now you sleep after your prayers."

Lance smiled at her. It had been a long time since someone had tucked him into bed. After she closed the bedroom door behind her, he glanced again at his cell phone. As if on cue, it rang. He grabbed it wincing at the pain from his bandaged hand and answered the call.

"Hi, son."

"Hey, Dad. You okay?"

Lance closed his eyes at the sound of his son's voice. The ache in his chest eased slightly. "Of course, I'm okay. That's what I'm supposed to ask you. Are you okay?"

"I miss you Dad, and Rosa, and Maria, and Ricardo, and everyone." His voiced sounded wistful.

"What did you do this afternoon? Did you eat a good supper?" Lance thought of a lot he would like to ask his son but knew it was best not to. Like what had his mom told him? Was he enjoying being with his mom? Was Henri treating him nice?

"I went swimming in a big hotel pool, then we ate supper at a table in the hotel apartment. Henri and Mom have a cook that goes with them on

Henri's plane. We had roast beef and stuff. I have a TV in my room and Mom said I could watch it until I got tired and wanted to sleep."

"Did you talk much with your mom?" Lance had a sense that Chandra had stuck Mark in his room after supper to amuse himself.

"Well, we talked some at supper but it's kinda hard."

"Why is that, son?"

"I don't really know Mom much anymore and I don't know Henri at all. When I tried to tell them about the ranch and Granddad and Grandpapa, they didn't seem to listen, so I got quiet. Was that okay, Dad?" The sound of his son's unease about how to talk to his mother caused a return of the ache in Lance's chest.

"You did just fine. It'll get easier as you spend time with them."

"What did you do this afternoon, Dad? Did Ricardo ride the horses like he promised. Are the cattle okay? Did Sara Hope miss me?"

Lance laughed. "Whoa, son. Let me answer one question at a time." He proceeded to tell Mark about cutting the weeds and small scrub brush and trees from the pasture, and then they talked about other things involving the ranch and the people on it.

After a while, Lance heard Mark yawning. "You need to get to sleep, son. Set your backpack next to an electrical outlet, leave your charger in the backpack, run the electrical wire out to the outlet, and then set your phone on the charger. Can you do that?" He heard Mark moving around.

"Dad, do you not want Mom or Henri to know I called you?"

"Mark, if they ask, you tell them the truth. But, I'm afraid if they knew they won't let you call me. If they don't see the phone, maybe they won't think to ask." Lance couldn't believe he was teaching his son how to be sneaky but the thought of not hearing from Mark at least once a day was too hard to think about.

"Dad, I've got the charger plugged into the outlet like you said.

"Just leave the phone on and put it on the charger after this call. Is the phone set to mute?"

"Let me look."

Lance waited, imagining Mark searching the icons on the phone. It amazed him how his eight-year-old son was so calm with using the technology.

"Hey, Dad. It's on mute."

"Okay, we better say goodnight and both of us get some sleep. Let's say a prayer together."

"Can I pray first?"

"Sure, son." Lance listened as his son said his prayers. Even though it took a while, Lance didn't mind at all hearing all the simple, commonplace things that Mark prayed about. His list of things to thank God for took a couple of minutes and included his bat and glove and various foods.

Lance then prayed a short simple prayer, asking God's care for Mark. After ending the prayer, he said, "I love you, son."

"Love you too, Dad. Goodnight."

Lance heard the click of the phone call ending before he could answer. He sat with the phone in his hand for several minutes. He sighed and placed it on his charger on the nightstand beside his bed.

Chapter 29

Dawn was breaking when Lance woke the next morning. He had finally managed to fall asleep for a few hours. His body ached from the work he had done the afternoon before. Facing two more days before he would be able to see Mark, he wondered what to do with himself. The ranch hands had Saturday and Sunday off except for those doing the feeding of the animals. They rotated so they only had to work the weekends every four weeks or so. They would think it odd if Lance spent his Saturday alone cutting brush along a fence line.

The house was quiet as he left and went to the barn. He saddled Millie, the brown mare he liked to ride. She was a big horse and feisty in the early morning. Lance mounted and after he had her settled down headed out on one of the ranch roads. Millie seemed eager for a hard run. Lance rode up to the top of ridge overlooking the ranch buildings and the ranch land beyond. For now, it was cool although the day would heat up later.

Lance sat and watched the day begin and prayed. After a time he headed down the dirt track letting Millie set a fast pace and rode back toward the barn. As he rode the last stretch of the road and turned to go on the blacktop, he slowed the horse and walked her back to the barn. They had been riding an hour and Millie had worked up a sweat. By the time they got back to the barn, she was almost dry.

At the barn, Posey, was busy getting feedbags ready. "Morning, Lance. Millie give you a good ride?"

"Morning, Posey. Yes, it was a good ride. I've walked her for the last fifteen minutes. She should be cooled down some. You mind caring for her now?"

"Not at all. I like to do the grooming and care of a good horse after they've done a good ride." Posey took the reins after Lance dismounted. The ranch hand rubbed the horse on the muzzle and patted her neck.

Lance thanked the horse wrangler and headed for the house. Once there he went to his room, changed into a swimsuit and went to the indoor pool. He swam laps for thirty minutes before getting out of the pool feeling somewhat relaxed.

After dressing, he was ready to head to the kitchen and find something to eat. Louisa had indicated when he hired her that she preferred to work on Saturday and take another day of the week off in addition to Sunday. She usually took Tuesdays off after cooking enough on Monday that all they had to do was heat the food. It has worked well and Louisa was happy.

He looked into Sara Hope's room and found it empty. As he started toward the kitchen, his cell phone rang. Glancing at the phone, he saw that it was a call from Juliana.

"Good morning, Juliana."

"Good morning to you, Lance." Her voice was soft and as smooth as warm honey. "I'm calling to see if you have plans for the day, or, if you would be open to a project."

He liked how she got right to the point of her call. "I'm still trying to figure out something to keep me busy for the day. What project do you have?"

"Well, I'm going over to Jacob Kieffner's place and help build him a barn. Morgan Jones has organized it and raised funds for the material. Jacob's barn burned last month and there's no way he and Olga can afford to build a new one."

"You mean a barn raising, like folks used to do?"

Juliana laughed. "I guess so. Morgan got a contractor to get the foundation and flooring done. It's on the site of the old barn but will have more modern thing like electrical outlets. Morgan has asked everyone in the county to consider coming and helping out. He even has a barbeque place catering lunch for free."

Lance didn't especially want to be around people all day but if he kept busy, he could make himself useful instead of wallowing in self-pity. "When do you want me to pick you up and what should I bring?"

"Can you be here in the next half an hour? I want to get there and get set up before it gets so terribly hot. Bring any hand or power tools for building. Good gloves and long-sleeve cotton shirt, a wide-brim hat, and a couple of bandanas are important for working in this heat. Also, do you have a large water cooler?"

"Yes, I can be there in half an hour, I'll dress appropriately, I'll bring tools, and I will bring a 5-gallon water cooler."

Juliana laughed. "Then I'll be ready when you get here. Your dad, grandpapa, and brothers all left at daybreak and are already there working. Your mom decided that she needed to stay home with Nana who wanted to go but Walt wouldn't let her in this heat."

Lance had to smile at the idea of his nana building a barn but knew she was feisty enough to try. "I'll see you in half an hour."

"See you." Juliana's phone went silent.

Lance headed back to his bedroom, packed a backpack with extra clothes, and changed into a blue long-sleeved chambray cotton shirt. He then went to the kitchen where he found Rosa feeding Sara Hope.

Louisa was busy at the stove.

"Morning, Ladies." Lance bent down and kissed Sara Hope on the cheek. For his effort, he got a small fist covered in cereal in the jaw. Grabbing a napkin to scrub the cereal off his face, he grinned at his baby girl. The sloppy smile and squeal he got back warmed his heart.

Louisa turned and asked, "What would you like for breakfast, Mr. Lance?"

"I'd like some eggs, bacon, and toast in about five minutes. I'm in a hurry because I just told Juliana I'd go with her to help build a barn."

Rosa smiled. "That is good idea for you to go help Jacob and Olga. They need a barn and it will keep you busy."

259

Lance should have known Rosa would have known about the barn raising. "You okay to stay here with Sara Hope?" As soon as he said it, he knew how silly a question it was.

"Of course, Lance. Louisa, do you have anything to send with Lance for snacks and maybe a cooler of soft drinks."

"Just as soon as I have your breakfast ready, I'll fix a cooler of snacks and drinks." She set a pan of biscuits from the oven to the table and then dished up a plate full of scrambled eggs and crisp bacon. "No toast this morning unless you insist. I had already started the biscuits."

Lance realized that she had anticipated his being ready for breakfast. "Biscuits are even better." As he took his seat in front of the plate of food, Louisa placed eating utensils and then poured him a cup of coffee.

"Thanks, Louisa. That is under five minutes." He bowed his head in a silent prayer for the food and for Mark. Then he began to eat quickly knowing a good breakfast was the fuel his body needed for the day of work ahead.

~

When he drove up to his parent's house, he saw that Juliana waited on the porch, dressed in a similar blue chambray shirt and jeans such as he was wearing. She had her hair tied low on her neck in a ponytail and she was wearing a wide-brimmed hat straw hat. Her fresh all-American look was refreshing. She slung a large backpack around her shoulder and picked up her medical bag, trotted to the truck, and climbed into the passenger front seat after stowing her things in the backseat.

"Good morning, Lance. It is going to be a great day to build a barn."

He grinned at her. "Just what I had planned to do all week, go build a barn."

Lance backed the truck around to head back down the lane. He waved at his mom who stood looking out of the window over the kitchen sink.

He glanced over at Juliana who had taken off her hat and was leaning forward to let the cold air from the air conditioner flow on her face. "I can crank it up higher if you need me to."

Juliana leaned back and put her seat belt on. "No need. I just wanted to cool down a bit. I wasn't out on the porch more than five minutes before you got here but that was enough to get hot. This is going to be a scorcher of a day to be building a barn. You know the way to Jacob Kieffner's ranch?"

"Sure, I worked some for him when I was about fourteen. Dad would let me and Matt go a couple of days a week to work for Jacob so we could have some ready money. Their sons are in between Matt, me, and Abby age wise. We went to school together." Lance though of some of the fun times they had had back then. "I don't know where the boys are now. I'd be surprised if they stayed on the ranch."

"From what I know, the two older ones don't live around here anymore, but Abe, the youngest one is still at the ranch working with his dad."

Lance nodded. "That's good. Is he married?"

"No, he's still single. I've not heard of him dating anyone." Her voice was so matter of fact that Lance sensed that she had no interest that way. For some reason, it made him feel better and he relaxed his hands that had been tightly gripping the steering wheel.

As they turned off the farm-to-market blacktop highway onto a gravel county road that would take them to Jacob's ranch, he asked, "Who is ramrodding building the barn? I hope it's someone who knows what they are doing."

Juliana laughed. "It better be someone who knows what they're doing and will know how to tell everyone else what to do. I know that Morgan Jones is taking the lead at organizing it, including raising funds. George Fritze is in charge of the building today. He's the ramrod as you call it. From what I've heard he has a lot of experience at construction."

Lance glanced over at her with surprise. "George? As I think about it, he's perfect for being in charge such a project. He never said anything but we don't seem to have time to talk about anything but the ranch work. Today is his day off."

"I imagine most of the people who come to help will be using a day off from their regular work. Morgan is hoping a bunch of people show up. He has had all the material delivered and George has the plans. With enough people who know how to work, a barn can be built in a day if the foundation is already laid."

"You sound as if you were part of the planning." Juliana was more a part of the ranch community around Tumbleweed than he was.

"Yes, I'm part of a loose committee for the project and they asked me to be here today as a nurse in case of injury. I'm prepared for that, as I don't think you can have a large group of people working on such a project without someone getting hurt. I just pray that no one falls off the roof of the barn and gets seriously hurt." Juliana's tone was soft and serious.

Lance wasn't surprised at her being willing to help in such a capacity. He had thought she was going to be part of the community and enjoy a day that would hopefully be fun if full of hard work. But it was much more than that. She was offering her services as a professional nurse. He respected that.

Lance was about to park out in the pasture with most of the other trucks and vehicles, when Pete Keller, one of his ranch hands, yelled and waved him closer to the house closer to the hive of activity going on toward the back of the large backyard.

Pete Keller pointed toward the old ranch house. "Hey, boss. Park up here. George wants Juliana near the house."

Lance grinned as he had thought Pete was trying to butter him up when all along, Juliana was the one considered important enough for special treatment. "Hey, Pete. Are most of the hands here?"

"Yes, boss. All but Posey and August. George had them stay at the ranch and take care of feeding the animals and exercising the horses. They'll keep an eye on things."

Lance nodded at the huge muscular man who had worked at Two Forks Ranch for the last fifteen years. He didn't talk much and was a hard worker.

Juliana led the way to the back porch of the ranch house where Olga had set up a table, a cot, and several chairs

Lance grabbed his tool belt from the backseat of his truck. After strapping it on, he filled the slots with hammers, screwdriver, and other small tools from his toolbox.

He called to a teenage boy he had seen at church service. "Hey Jonah, you mind taking this cooler of water and this one of cold drinks to where they are putting such stuff."

"Not at all, Mr. McTavish. You mind if I take a cold drink? I'm already hot." The boy had an open-faced friendly look about him.

"Take whatever you need and thanks for the help."

George came up to Lance as he tied a bandana around his neck. "Hey, Lance, glad you could make it. We need all the help we can get. How are you with heights?"

"I'm good with heights. Tell me where you want me."

"Work with the roofing crew. Your dad is in charge. Your grandpa volunteered for the roof but I don't want him up on top of the barn. All we would need is for Walt to tumble off and then I'd have to deal with Edna."

Lance laughed. "You're right. Let's keep Grandpapa on the ground."

He gave a wave toward Juliana who was getting her supplies organized. He went to find his dad. They spent most of the morning putting up the 2x8 rafters. With a crew of fifteen men working just on the roof they had the rafters in place and the 2x10 ridge board up by noon.

Most of the men had been at work several hours before Lance had arrived. When his dad called for the noon break, Lance was more than ready. He climbed down the ladder and wandered over to the water hose to wash up. Long tables loaded with food and other tables for people to sit and eat were placed under a canvas tent that provided shade but didn't relieve the relentless heat of the hot summer day. After loading a plate to overflowing with barbeque beef with all the fixings and fried chicken, he sat down at one of the long tables with benches.

Juliana sat across from him and handed him a quart jar filled with iced tea. "So how goes the new career as a carpenter?"

Lance swigged down half of the iced tea before he answered her. "I have been greatly reminded why I went into computers. They have to be kept cool. I have muscles hurting I had forgotten I had. Building fences isn't as hard as climbing around rafters under a Texas sun."

Juliana nodded and responded between bites of fried chicken. "I've gotten a few injuries from hammers landing on fingers rather than where they were aimed. I also had at least two cases of mild heat stroke. George is watching people trying to catch ones who aren't used to the heat. He's being extra cautious and sending people over to rest awhile at the nursing station. Most just needed to take a break and went back to work, but I sent two home."

Lance's eyes glittered in amusement. "Do those misplaced hammers usually involve a thumb?"

"Usually. One was from Ricardo. I don't think he has done a lot of carpentry."

Hank and Walt walked up with loaded plates of food and sat down at the other end of the table. Juliana took Lance's iced tea jar that was now empty and soon returned with a tray of quart jars filled with ice tea. She passed them out to Hank, Walt, Lance, and a couple of other men seated at the long table who had been on the roof.

Hank took a long swig. "Thanks, Juliana. That hits the spot." After he had eaten for a few minutes, he waved his fork at Lance and the other men seated at the table. "The first thing we will put on the roof is 7/16" OSB sheathing. Then Lance you take a couple of men and work behind us to put down the roofing felt. Once we have that on the entire roof we'll start hammering on the asphalt shingles. George will have more men coming up to help as other areas of the barn are completed. By dark we need to have the roof finished."

Lance took fifteen minutes in his truck to cool off with the air conditioning running before heading back up to the barn roof. He had invited Juliana to join him for a few minutes in the truck but she was called to the nursing station.

Just before the sun slipped behind the horizon, Hank hammered the last shingle into place. Lance was too exhausted to acknowledge they had done it. He carefully climbed down from the roof and stepped back to look at the completed barn. There was still a lot of interior work to be done but the bulk was finished. All Lance wanted to do was get home, soak in the Jacuzzi bathtub, and go to bed.

Juliana had already loaded her backpack in the truck and was waiting for Lance. "You look like you've been in the wars. Are you okay?"

Lance grinned. "I didn't fall off the roof, so yes, I'm fine."

"Thank the Lord, no one fell off the roof. I'm proud of the day you put in. This is a blessing for Jacob and Olga."

"In spite of feeling every muscle in my body crying out, I enjoyed it. I only lasted the whole day because I couldn't quit as long as Dad and Grandpapa were still going. Dad sent Grandpapa home a couple of hours ago to take care of the animals. Dad's going to ride back with us."

Hank came walking around the corner of the house wiping his face with a wet bandana. "Y'all ready to go?"

Lance opened the front passenger door for Juliana and the back passenger door for his dad. "You take the back seat, Dad. You can stretch out while I drive you home."

"Thanks, son. I'm not sure my legs will ever be the same after hunching over that roof. You did a good job." Hank hoisted himself into the back seat, stretched out, and put his head back. Lance closed the doors and climbed in behind the steering wheel.

They didn't talk much as Lance drove them to the Rocking M.

Once there Hank climbed out of the truck as if in slow motion. "You want to come in and eat a bite?"

Watching Juliana climb the steps up the porch, Lance responded, "No thanks, Dad. I need to get home and check on things."

Hank waved. "See you at church in the morning, son."

Lance waved goodbye to Juliana and got one back as she opened the screen door to the kitchen. He wasted no time driving on home. Once there he wanted to go hug Sara Hope but realized he was too dirty and needed to clean up before he encountered anyone.

Once he reached his bathroom, he shucked his dirty clothes and headed to the Jacuzzi bathtub. As he sunk down into the hot water, he could feel his muscles start to relax. When he got back to his bedroom, he found a couple of chicken salad sandwiches and a tall glass of lemonade on a tray. Rosa was looking out for him. He had just finished eating the second sandwich when his cell phone pinged. Glancing at the phone, he saw that it was a text from the security firm. The text let him know that Mark's phone had spent most of the afternoon and evening in his room at the hotel. The morning had been spent at the pool area of the hotel. In a way, Lance was glad that Mark had not been out and about in Austin in the heat, but he wondered how much time Mark had spent with his mother.

Getting rid of the towel he had wrapped around himself when he had exited the bathtub, Lance pulled on a tee shirt and lounge pants. Taking his phone with him, he went down the hall to Sara Hope's room. He watched from the doorway for a few moments as Rosa held Sara Hope and rocked while reading to her from a storybook.

Rosa looked up and smiled. "You okay, Lance? Olivia called to tell me everyone on their way home and very tired. Ricardo almost fell asleep over his sandwich. He barely talked before going to bed."

Lance strolled over and took Sara Hope from Rosa. Kissing the baby on her pudgy cheek, he got a giggle from his baby girl. "I'm tired but feel good. We got a barn built with about fifty other men." He bounced Sara Hope on his hip and watched as she pointed to the picture book and in her own private baby talk indicated what she wanted. "You want Rosa to finish the storybook?"

Lance's phone rang and he handed Sara Hope back to Rosa before answering. "Hi Mark. How are you doing?" He waved at Rosa and headed back to his bedroom as he listened to Mark tell of his day. He seemed to have spent most of his time watching TV in his hotel room. Lance told him about the barn raising. Mark kept asking questions about what they had done and who was there.

"You had a lot more fun than I did, Dad." Mark complained.

"Sorry about that. Does your mother have anything scheduled for tomorrow?"

"Not that I know about. I wish Monday would get here so I can come home."

"Me too, son, I miss you." Lance tried to be upbeat for Mark when all Lance wanted to do was jump in his truck and go bring his son home. The visitation was half over but it still seemed to be forever.

They talked a few more minutes and then Lance got off the call. It was good to hear Mark's voice and he was missing him. He wanted to keep the call going but Mark needed to go to bed and so did Lance. The work on the barn had had one good outcome. He had hardly thought about Mark all day. Much better than sitting at home brooding over what he couldn't control.

Chapter 30

Sunday crawled by even with going to church services and Sunday dinner with his folks. His younger brothers and Ricardo had spent the afternoon in the swimming pool at Lance's ranch. Juliana had gone to spend time with Maria and some girl friends in Fredericksburg. Being at loose ends and feeling unsettled, Lance had tried to do some work in his office in between wandering out to the pool and talking to the fellows and then spending some time with Sara Hope. The evening dragged until Mark called and Lance could reassure himself that his son was all right.

Finally, Monday morning arrived and everyone headed out for Fredericksburg again. Lance drove the truck alone and was glad to have the time to pray and gather his thoughts. His mind kept running all sorts of scenarios of what could go wrong. He did not trust Chandra and Henri to do what was best for Mark.

Once he got to the courthouse, Hilary led him back to the same conference room and soon after, Maria and Juliana arrived with Ricardo.

Juliana gave him a hug, as did Maria. "Lance, you look as if you haven't slept much. You doing okay?"

Lance smiled. "I'm doing okay. Just a little stressed. But as soon as I see Mark I'll be fine."

Maria took her turn to hug Lance. "You and me both. I have worried myself sick this weekend. If Juliana hadn't made me go out yesterday afternoon with our friends, I would have sat at home and worried all day."

Ricardo grinned at her. "You should have called me, cariño."

Maria responded, "Like you called me, *nene?*"

Lance was glad they could tease each other and sensed that maybe they were trying to ease a little of the tension in the room.

Hilary sat with her briefcase open in front of her. "Your folks planning to be here?"

Lance glanced at his watch. "They probably left the ranch about twenty minutes ago. I didn't know exactly when we are to see the judge so I suggested they try to get here by nine o'clock."

"Good. Every time we go in front of the judge, I want him to see that Mark has extended family here in Texas. I should go check with the judge's clerk and see if I can find out anything about when Mark will be returned to you." Closing her briefcase, she picked it up and quickly left the room.

Lance was too tense to sit quietly so he got up and began to pace the room. What if Chandra didn't bring Mark back? What if the judge decided Mark needed to be with his mother and let her have primary custody?

Juliana began to hum the old hymn, *When Peace Like a River*. Soon Maria started to sing softly and Juliana joined her in a soft sweet harmony. Lance stopped pacing to stand and simply listen to the words. He felt a calming and his hands relaxed from the fists he had not been aware of making. He closed his eyes and he let the meaning of the hymn flow over him. All he could think to pray was, *Father please give me peace, no matter the outcome of today.*

The door opened and Hilary entered the room. Behind her followed a grinning Mark who dropped his backpack and ran into his dad's arms.

"Hey, Dad. You glad to see me?" Mark's voice was muffled by the bear hug Lance engulfed him in.

"Glad? That is too weak a word. I'm thrilled." Lance laughed from the sheer joy of having his son in his arms.

Hilary spoke up. "I hate to break this up, Lance. The judge wants to see us."

"He wants to give a judgement now?" Lance let go of Mark as Juliana and Maria gathered the little boy up in hugs and kisses.

His attorney nodded. "He has already talked to Mark and Chandra. Let's go."

Lance gave Mark a quick hug and a kiss on the top of his head. "Stay here with Maria and Juliana. We'll be back soon." Lance gave Ricardo a glance and pointed his chin toward the door. "You mind being in the courtroom so if needed you can bring a message to Maria?"

Ricardo smoothed his dark hair down and headed toward the door. "Not at all. Lead the way."

After a quick walk down the hallway and into the courtroom, Lance sat next to Hilary at the same table as on Friday. Seated across the aisle were Chandra and her attorney. Lance noticed his family seated a couple of rows back where Ricardo had joined them.

They only waited for a couple of minutes when the bailiff called out. "All rise for the Honorable Judge Theodore Whitlock."

Judge Whitlock entered the courtroom and sat behind the bench. The court clerk handed some papers to the judge with whispered words. The judge then spent several minutes reading over the papers.

Lance wanted to scream at the judge to get on with it but willed himself to sit still and wait. Hilary looked through some documents she had in front of her as she also waited quietly. Lance wanted to turn and look at his folks but decided being still was the better thing for this moment. He didn't know if the judge had already made his decision or was still contemplating what would be his judgement in the custody of Mark McTavish.

"In the Petition to Amend the Child Custody for Mark Michael McTavish are all present and ready to proceed?" Judge Whitlock asked.

Both attorneys answered in the affirmative. "Yes, your honor."

Lance kept his attention fixed on the judge as several questions when back and forth from the judge and the attorneys.

The judge looked around the courtroom. "Are there any further questions before a decision is given?"

Again, both attorneys answered. "No, your honor."

"It is the judgement of this court that the child Mark Michael McTavish be placed in joint custody. Lance Nobel McTavish, father of the child will have the care of the child for the next fourteen days after which the mother, Chandra Martin McTavish will be granted custody for the next thirty days.

After that, the placement of the child will be thirty days alternating with each parent. The plaintiff, Chandra Martin McTavish, is allowed to take the child out of the country when he is in her custody with each event being granted by the court as needed. All those involved will return to this courtroom within fourteen days for the child to be released to the mother at that time. So judges the court." Judge Whitlock pounded his gavel once, then rose, and left the courtroom.

Hilary turned to Lance. "This is what I expected, although I'm surprised the judge let you have Mark for the next fourteen days."

Lance wanted to pound something. "Doesn't the judge understand that if Chandra is allowed to take Mark out of the country she may not bring him back?"

"I brought that up with the judge in his chambers when I talked to him earlier this morning. He feels it's in Mark's best interest to spend time with his mother. Since his mother is moving out of the country then that is logically where he needs to visit her according to the judge. He did stipulate that Chandra has to provide an approved adult to travel with Mark. He has to be delivered back here to Fredericksburg. We have to wait and see what happens."

Lance glanced over at Chandra and saw her giving Henri a kiss and hug. Henri had a smug satisfied look about him. Why did Henri want Lance's son? Was it just to satisfy Chandra?

Hilary spoke to him. "Lance, go get your son and go home. Make the most of the next two weeks."

"Thanks, Hilary. I plan to do that. You'll look over the ruling carefully for me? Maybe we can set up a time to talk on the phone."

Lance slowly made his way out of the courtroom shepherding his family with him. When they reached the hallway, they started asking questions.

Olivia was first. "Lance, what does it all mean?"

Hank asked, "Do you get to take him home today?"

He wanted to get to Mark and go home. "I'll come over for lunch and we'll talk about it then. For now I want to get Mark and head home."

Fourteen days. That was all the time he had for sure with his son. How much life could he crowd into two weeks? How much fatherly advice could he impart to his son? There was so much he wanted to tell Mark.

Chapter 31

Juliana tried to read her little New Testament that she carried in her purse. She couldn't focus. All she could think about was what was happening. For some reason Lance didn't want Juliana in the courtroom. Trying not to look at her watch every other minute, she glanced up and watched Maria and Mark play tic-tac-toe on Maria's cell phone.

Lance had looked so tired and stressed this morning. Juliana was getting to know him well enough that she could tell from his eyes what mood he was in. This morning had been concern and an edge of fear.

As Mark giggled as he blocked Maria's next move and Juliana felt a lump in her throat at the thought that this precious little boy might disappear from their lives. What was it going to do to Mark to go back and forth between two parents who no longer loved each other? Thank God her parents had given their children the example of a strong, loving marriage. She had always appreciated and loved her parents deeply, but she had never thought that much about what it must be like for children having to grow up in two different families. The pain Lance and Mark must be going through.

Maria nudged Mark's arm. "It's your turn, buddy."

Instead of pulling the cell phone toward him and making his move, Mark glanced between Juliana and Maria. "What's going to happen now? Why are we waiting here?"

Juliana looked at Maria and raised her eyebrows? "Maria, you want to take that question?"

Maria shook her head. "Not really. Why don't you take it?"

Saying a silent prayer for wisdom, Juliana responded. "Mark, you know why we've been coming to talk to the judge?"

"So he can tell Mom and Dad who I should go visit next?"

"That's right. What do you think about that?" Juliana wanted to understand what Mark was thinking and not tell the little boy what to think.

Mark put a finger to the cell phone on the table and spun it around slowly several times before he looked up at Juliana and answered her question. "I guess it's okay. I wanted to see Mom but I missed Dad and the ranch and everything. It was boring with Mom and Henri. I don't think he likes me cause he don't talk to me. He and Mom talk to each other in a language called French and I don't understand it. Mom says I have to learn it. Mom didn't want me to talk about Dad or the ranch or Sara Hope or Rosa or anything. But she did let me watch all the TV I wanted, but I got tired of that and wanted to go outside. Mom said she didn't have time to take me to a park. There wasn't a yard."

Mark had given his views with a somber voice and worried expression on his face. He didn't have his usual animation about him. Juliana wanted to grab him up and take him home to the ranch. Why does Chandra even want Mark? She and Henri didn't seem too interested in spending time with him.

Juliana reached over and pushed his hair off his forehead. "You know that your dad loves you very much and would like to keep you with him all the time."

Mark looked up at her with big sad eyes. "I just wish Mom would come home and we could be a family again."

"Your Dad would make that happen if he could, but he respects your mom's right to choose to be with him or not." Juliana hoped Mark didn't start asking questions about his mom and Henri living together.

The door from the hallway opened and Lance came into the conference room with Ricardo following. Lance was so pale that Juliana was afraid of the news he brought.

Mark jumped up and ran over to his dad. "Can we go home now, Dad? Can we?"

Lance gave him a hug and kissed the top of his head. "Yes, we can go home now. Juliana, you want to ride with us?"

She glanced at Maria and Ricardo. They probably would not mind having the ride home with just the two of them. "Sure Lance, if Mark doesn't mind."

Mark grabbed her hand and started pulling toward the door. "Come on, Juliana. Let's go home."

Lance gave a small smile. "We're coming, son. You don't have to drag Juliana out the door." He turned to Maria. "You coming on out to the ranch?"

Maria nodded. "If that's what you want. I'm fine with getting back to work if you still need me."

"I think it won't hurt. I'm not as concerned about watching over Mark from outsiders, but it will still be helpful for you to be there and supervise the activities, especially the swimming pool." Lance grabbed Mark's backpack and suitcase and looked around for anything they might be leaving behind.

Maria picked up her phone and put it into her purse. "Yes, sir. Ricardo can drop me off at home and I'll drive the minivan on to Two Forks."

"See you all later." Ricardo took Maria's hand and led her out the door.

Juliana was glad Maria still had a job with Lance, as the money was helpful to Maria. Moreover, Juliana didn't mind riding with Lance and Mark. Knowing it shouldn't matter, she couldn't help but feel thrilled at spending time with Lance.

As Lance drove them on the road that led west out of Fredericksburg, Mark chattered about his weekend and asked his dad about the ranch.

"Hey, Dad, did Applejack miss me?" Mark's voice was filled with the expectation that his pony had missed him.

Lance chuckled. "I'm sure he did but you need to ask Ricardo. He spent more time with him."

"I bet Applejack did miss me. I always take him a carrot or apple. He sure likes his apples. I guess cause of his name. Do you think that's why?"

Juliana grinned as she saw Lance roll his eyes at Mark's constant questions. Lance was so patient with his son.

"Hey, Dad, I'm hungry. Can we stop at McDonald's?" Mark strained to look out the vehicle as if in search of the Golden Arches.

Lance nodded and glanced over at Juliana. "We can stop for a snack and bathroom break if Juliana doesn't mind. Your grandmama is preparing dinner for everyone so we don't need to each lunch yet. It's too early."

Juliana twisted in her seat to grin at Mark in the backseat of the truck. "I'm fine with stopping. I could use a cold drink and maybe some fries or an apple turnover. I had breakfast early."

Mark grinned back. "That's two against one, Dad."

Lance chuckled and responded. "Okay, okay, you win. Now start looking for a place to stop."

"There, Dad!"

They stopped at a McDonalds and soon the three of them were loaded with drinks and snacks of fries and apple turnovers. As soon as he was in the driver's seat, Lance started the truck and turned the air conditioner up. Before driving away from the fast food restaurant, he ate a baked apple pie and swigged on a large ice tea. "I was so nervous this morning that I didn't eat much. Now I've got Mark with me, I'm starting to relax and I'm hungry."

"I understand as I was pretty tense this morning myself. Olivia was up early and had started baking. She will have her usual spread ready by the time we get there." Juliana brushed crumbs from her top as she finished her baked apple pie.

Lance put the truck into reverse, backed out of the parking space, and soon had them on the road toward Tumbleweed.

After a few minutes of silence, Lance glanced back at Mark and said softly, "I think he has drifted off. I have a feeling he didn't sleep well the three nights he was gone. I know I didn't."

"If Mark is asleep do you mind telling me what the judge said?"

Lance ran his hand over his face and sighed. "Hilary said this was probably going to be the outcome but I still don't like it. I have Mark for the next two weeks and then I have to give him to Chandra for a month. The judge is going to let them take him out of the country. The judge may trust

Chandra but I don't. Not anymore." Lance's softly spoken words had become bitter sounding.

Juliana kept her voice as soft so as not to wake Mark but kept the tone neutral. "Then we will continue to pray, and I'm sure you'll make the next two weeks good ones for Mark. That doesn't mean sending him off with his mother won't hurt."

"I'm trying to step back and focus on my children. I don't want to look at their mother as an enemy, but with her sitting in the courtroom with the man she ran off with seated behind her ... well, the Lord and I are going to have to do some talking, as I'm not in a very forgiving mood."

What to say to that, Juliana didn't know. For Lance to become bitter and resentful at his soon to be ex-wife was understandable. As a Christian, she knew the ideal was for him to forgive Chandra. But how did one do that? "It's a fine line to walk. You want to give your children the gift of being able to love both their parents. The circumstances will make that difficult."

Lance nodded. "I do want Mark and Sara Hope to be able to love their mother. Every child deserves that. They shouldn't have to make a choice between their mom and dad. I'm going to do my best never to let them hear me utter a word of criticism against their mother. Even this custody thing, if Mark hears me speak of it, I want him to think I'm laying it on the judge and not his mother."

Juliana wanted to take his hand and give comfort. The yearning to reach out to Lance was strong, but he was still a married man. She turned to stare out the truck window at the passing ranch land. It almost hurt to look at Lance and yet still have to keep a distance. But in her heart she knew that was best. The need to protect herself and to protect Lance, had to be her first consideration if she was to maintain a standard that was in line with her conscience before God.

Chapter 32

Lance indulged Mark in whatever his son wanted to do for the next two weeks. Everyday either they went over to the Rocking M for a meal with the parents and grandparents or the family all met at Two Forks Ranch. Lance, Hank, and Walt took Mark fishing in the Llano River and let him float in a tire tube in the river. They took a day to climb the summit trail to the top of the Enchanted Rock and then had a picnic with the whole family at the picnic tables near the park headquarters.

The family reminisced about other trips to the Enchanted Rock State Park when Lance was a small boy. Walt and Edna told of trips to the Rock with Hank when he was a child. After hearing how native people had been on the Enchanted Rock for about 10,000, Mark spent the day looking for arrowheads, but never spotted one.

In the evenings, Lance read to Mark and let him sleep with him. Whether Lance did that for Mark or for himself, he wasn't sure. Most nights Lance lay awake into the wee hours watching his son sleep and praying for his son.

Long before he was ready, they only had two more days before they had to return to the Fredericksburg courthouse and let Chandra take Mark. Lance tried not to think about it but he did tell Mark, as Lance didn't want his son to be unprepared for what was coming next in his life.

Over the two weeks, in between her work, Juliana had been around. But she and Lance had not had any time alone. Lance knew that was best, as he had nothing to offer her but friendship. Juliana had made it clear that she wanted nothing romantically to do with a divorced man.

~

Like the too soon end to the summer vacation for a child, all too soon, they were on their way to Fredericksburg for Lance to give Mark over to Chandra for the next month. Lance glanced over at Mark who had his forehead pressed against the truck window staring out at the passing landscape as Lance drove slowly toward the courthouse on the Monday morning. He had let Mark ride in the front seat using his booster seat as the truck had both a lap and shoulder belt. Mark had grown so much during the summer that he was now almost tall enough to sit up front without the booster seat. When they had first left the ranch Mark had been talkative, but the closer they got to the courthouse the more silent the boy got.

"Mark, are you doing okay?"

His son turned and looked at him with big sad eyes. "I didn't want to say goodbye to Sara Hope and Rosa and everybody. And now I'm going to have to say goodbye to you, Dad. Why can't Mom come stay at the ranch?"

How many times had Mark asked that? Lance swallowed and blinked his eyes a couple of times before he could answer. "I don't know why things have happened like they have. Mom isn't going to come and live at the ranch. I would let her come but she wants to stay with Henri. I can't change that." Reaching over, Lance rested his hand on the back of Mark's neck and head. "I can tell you this. I love you, Mark, and I always will. Whether you are here with me in Texas or you are far away. You are the best son a man could ever want. I'm so proud to tell people that you are my son."

In a soft voice, Mark responded. "I love you too, Dad. I always will."

"And you need to always remember that no matter what happens God loves you too and Jesus is watching over you with the angels by his side. No matter what, you are never alone and you can always pray. You have the new cell phone. It will work in Europe and you can call me anytime."

"I feel like I want to cry but I'm too big for that."

Lance could see that the tears were just ready to fall. "We are never too big to cry. I'll probably cry all the way home today and it'll be okay."

Mark blinked and the tears receded. "You're going to cry? Why, Dad?"

"Because the minute you're gone with your mom, I'll start to miss you."

"But you don't ever cry."

"I do cry sometimes, son, but I try to be brave around you and Sara Hope. That why you don't see me cry much." Lance knew that was true. It was possible that Mark had never seen his father cry. Today might be a first, as Lance didn't know if he could control himself not to let the tears fall when he had to watch his son walk away. The real fear it might be longer than a month separation caused a constant tightness that was almost a pain in his chest.

"Here we are at the courthouse. We might as well go in out of this heat and wait for your mom in air conditioning." Lance parked the truck, climbed out, and got the suitcase out of the back seat. Mark had his backpack with his things to amuse himself while traveling. Rosa had suggested they only pack a few clothes because Mark was growing out of them. Chandra could buy new ones. Mark had especially wanted to bring his cowboy boots but in another couple of months, he would grow out of them. Chandra wouldn't want their son to wear the boots anyway.

When they reached the conference room, Hilary was already there with her briefcase open and papers spread out around her.

"Morning, Hilary." Lance shepherded Mark in ahead of him and rolled the suitcase behind him.

"Lance, Mark. You're right on time. As far as I know Chandra should be here soon."

"Hi, Miss Hilary. I got to ride in the front seat of the truck this morning." Mark propped the backpack in a chair and then climbed up in the next one.

"Well, that's impressive. Are you sure that's legal?"

"Sure, I'm almost nine years old and we have the right kind of seat belts. It was fun." Mark put his elbows on the table and propped his head on his hands as he settled in as if to stare at Hilary for the next hour.

Lance nodded a greeting. "My understanding is that Texas law doesn't really say where in the vehicle a child must ride. I did tell Mark this was a one-time event. Next time he rides in my truck he has to sit in the back seat."

"Ah, Dad. I did okay this morning." Mark crossed his arms and leaned back in his chair.

"Yes, you did. However, I do know it is safer for you to be in the back seat. Today was a one-time special event." Lance managed to use his fatherly laying-down-the-rule tone. What he wanted to do was grab Mark up and run.

There was a soft tap the hall door. Hilary got up quickly and opened it enough to see who had knocked. Lance heard a back and forth of whispering and then Hilary came back over to the conference table.

"Wait here. The judge wants to see me." She gathered up her things and slung her briefcase over her shoulder. "If the judge sends for you, you can ask the deputy to watch Mark as Maria isn't with you."

"I thought we were doing a simple handoff and didn't see a need for Maria to come." The judge asking to meet with Hilary puzzled Lance.

"As soon as I know what's happening I'll let you know." She quickly left the room closing the door softly behind her.

Lance spent the next hour with Mark drawing pictures on the paper tablet his son carried in his backpack. They had started when Mark was only about two years old with Lance drawing animals and plants in different environments. As Mark got older, it had evolved into a game of seeing which one of them could draw the most animals and plants. Today Mark chose the ranch environment and they took turns drawing a different animal or plant. Mark never seemed to run out of energy for the game but Lance started to feel nervous about the length of time Hilary had been gone.

Finally, there was another soft knock on the door. When Lance opened it, a deputy stood in the hallway. "Sir, Judge Whitlock wants you in his chambers. I'm to watch the boy for you. I'm Deputy Marvin Clark."

Knowing it was a useless question, Lance still had to ask. "What's this about?"

"I have no idea. I'm just the messenger."

"I understand. Mark, you do what Deputy Clark asks you to do. I'll be back as soon as I can." Lance kissed Mark on top of his head and ruffled his hair. He then quickly moved out into the hallway.

When he found Judge Whitlock's chamber, he knocked on the door. He heard a deep bass saying to come in. Once in the room Lance saw Hilary seated in front of the judge's desk with her head down.

"Mr. McTavish, please sit down." Judge Whitlock waved to a leather-bound chair next to Hilary.

"Please call me, Lance. What's going on?" Lance glanced from the judge to Hilary and back. Neither one seemed to want to look at him.

Judge Whitlock cleared his throat and looked as if he was about to speak when the door opened and a uniformed officer came in quickly and started whispering into the judge's ear. The judge nodded and the officer left as quickly as he had come in.

"Lance, I've got some bad news for you. I'll just give you the facts as I have received them."

"Okay ...." Lance didn't know what was coming. Hilary wasn't being helpful as she sat in silence and waited for the judge to speak.

"At approximately 8:30 this morning a helicopter took off from the Austin International airport with three passengers and a pilot with a flight plan for the Fredericksburg airport and another plan filed for a return flight for this afternoon. At 9:20 this morning, the helicopter dropped off the radar screen. Various people in the vicinity east of town reported a loud explosion in the sky. The state troopers arrived first on the scene, followed by the fire departments from various communities, and the sheriff's deputy. They are still searching the area but they have located several bodies. According to the Austin Police, those on board the helicopter were the pilot Buddy Engles and passengers, Chandra Martin McTavish, Henri Fontaine, and Harold White, an attorney. All are assumed dead. However, remember this is a first report. The Austin Police seem sure of who was on board the flight. I'm sorry for your loss, Lance."

Lance bent over and pressed his face into his hands. His mind didn't know what to do with the information. *Chandra dead? How could that be?* How was he going to tell Mark his mom was dead?

Hilary stood and rubbed a hand over his back. "I'm so sorry, Lance. I know this is a shock."

He realized he was crying. Images of Chandra as she had been when they first married and had their children flashed through his mind. His wife was dead.

Getting control of himself, he reached into his pocket and pulled out his handkerchief. Wiping his face, he sat up and turned to Hilary. "I need to go to Mark."

She continued to rub his shoulder. "Let's take a minute to take this in and to talk about what is next."

Lance looked at the judge. "You're absolutely sure? There's no mistake?"

The judge shook his head. "No, I don't think there is a mistake. We're still verifying who was on the helicopter, but all the information so far is consistent with it being the flight your wife was to be on. Of course, there will be an inquiry and the coroner will make a positive I.D. For now, I'm putting the custody case and the divorce filing on hold until we get the official death certificate from the coroner. When I have that the custody case will be dismissed. The petition for divorce will be dropped in Nevada as soon as they have the same notice. I'll want to make a formal declaration of you as the sole guardian of the children. But that will come after the coroner issues a death certificate. That shouldn't take long. What may take longer is to determine the cause of the explosion of the helicopter."

Hilary sat down in her chair. "I would like to ask you to issue a temporary custody statement for Lance today. Just something for him to have."

Lance spoke up. "I have the custody papers from the judge in California still. Are they still valid?"

"Do you have a copy handy? I probably have a copy in your file if you don't."

Hilary dug into her briefcase. "I have a copy here." She handed some papers over to the judge.

He took his time to read them over and then said, "I think these are adequate for now, but as soon as the coroner releases his findings I'll have a death certificate issued and then we'll appoint you as the legal guardian of the children here in Texas. There is the possibility of the children inheriting from their mother and other things may come up."

Lance found he was focusing in on what the judge was saying only part of the time. Hopefully, Hilary was catching everything.

Chandra was dead.

"Lance, Lance." He heard Hilary calling his name.

"Yes?" She appeared blurred and vague.

"I think he's in shock. Let me walk him back to his son." Hilary took Lance by the arm and indicated he should stand.

Lance shook himself and focused back on what was happening in the judge's chambers. "Sorry, I don't know what just happened."

Judge Whitlock stood. "That's all right. You've had quite a shock. Go on and take care of Mark. I know how to reach Hilary if I have any more news. For now, you're free to go and take care of your children. I suggest you avoid the press and refer all questions to the authorities."

Hilary held the door and guided Lance by the elbow out of the judge's chamber. "Lance, let's stop by the restroom and you splash some water on your face before you talk to Mark." She guided him to the door of the men's restroom.

Lance entered and stood at the sink. He splashed cold water on his face. Taking several deep breaths, he looked at himself in the mirror as he wiped his face dry. *No more divorce, no more custody battle.* He should be happy at this unexpected outcome. But he had never felt truly negative toward Chandra and a part of him still loved the young woman he had married. All he felt was a deep sadness, both for himself and for his children.

Taking out his phone, he saw that he had a strong signal so he dialed his folks' number.

"Hello." The confident sound of his father's voice brought a new round of tears to Lance's eyes.

"Dad." He managed to gulp out.

"Lance? What's wrong, son?"

Taking a deep breath and swallowing, Lance tried again. "Dad, I got some bad news. There was a helicopter crash and Chandra was killed this morning. She's dead."

"My word, Lance! That's awful. Are you and Mark all right?"

"I'm getting there. I haven't told Mark yet. The judge just told me. They seem real sure, so I guess it's true. The judge told me the custody issue is over and so are the divorce proceedings. So I guess that makes me a widower." Lance took another deep breath. "I don't know what I'm saying. I wanted you all to know because it'll be on the news. I'm going to get Mark and we'll drive back to the Rocking M. Would you tell everyone and have Rosa bring Sara Hope over to your place? I need to see my baby. And tell Rosa not to talk to the press if they call."

"Of course, Son. You drive safe and come on home. We'll be waiting for you."

Disconnecting from the call, Lance felt the push of tears again. Home. Yes, he needed to get home. Home to the ranch, home to his folks. Home to Juliana. First he had to get his son and take him home. Squaring back his shoulders and wiping his face again, he tossed the paper towel, and went out to meet Hilary in the hallway.

"You all right, Lance?" Hilary asked in a low caring voice.

"I'm all right. I need to get Mark and drive home. I feel as if I need to do something about verifying whether it was really Chandra that was killed."

"You need to leave that in the hands of the authorities. They'll take care of that. You have to plan the funeral. Did she have other family?"

He shook his head. "No, that was the thing about Chandra. She was an only child of only children. Her parents died when she was in college. There are maybe some distant cousins but no one else."

"The man she was with, this Henri Fontaine. What do you know about him?"

"I don't know anything except his name. I assume they flew into Austin on his private jet. They may know how to contact his people." Lance wasn't ready to deal with these kinds of problems.

Hilary seemed to notice his feelings. "Don't worry about those kinds of details. The authorities know how to handle all of that. I'll stay in touch with Judge Whitlock and the coroner's office and let you know anything that comes up. Otherwise, pick up Mark and go home"

Lance and Hilary stood outside the conference room door.

He said, "I'm not going to tell Mark here. I'll start for home and tell him as we're traveling. I can always stop by the side of the road if I have to. The best place for him to be is with his grandparents and the rest of the family."

She nodded. "Then I think I'll leave you here. Mark just needs you for now. I'll be in touch. And again, I'm so sorry all of this is happening."

"Thanks for all you have done. The Lord blessed me when I hired you."

They hugged and Hilary went on down the hallway with a wave. Lance took another deep breath and opened the door to the conference room. The deputy was playing tic-tac-toe with Mark. He rose as Lance entered the room.

"Hey, Dad, Deputy Clark is good at tic-tac-toe."

"Thanks for staying with my son. We're ready to leave." Lance started gathering all of Mark's things and put them back into his backpack.

"Where we going, Dad?" Mark slung the backpack over his shoulder and Deputy Clark helped him get both arms through the straps.

Lance picked up the suitcase they had brought full of Mark's things. "We're going home. I'll explain as we drive."

They waved goodbye to the deputy and went out to the truck. Lance quickly had Mark and his things in the truck and started west heading back home. He let Mark sit in the front seat again. When they were out in the country with the highway stretching out in front of them, Lance knew he couldn't put it off any longer. He pulled over at an entrance to a ranch road and stopped the truck.

"Son, I've got some bad news. You're not going to go stay with your mom. You're going to be staying with me and Sara Hope."

Mark looked over at his dad with a grin. "Really, Dad? That's not bad news. I didn't want to go away."

"That's not the bad news. It's why you're not going with your mom. There was an accident this morning and the helicopter she was coming in to pick you up crashed. Your mom was hurt real bad and she died."

Mark's face sort of twisted into a puzzled frown. "You mean I won't ever see Mom again?"

"I'm sorry Mark. She was hurt too severely and she died." Lance didn't know what else to say.

In a tight small voice, Mark asked, "Is it okay if I cry?"

"Mark, it's okay to cry." He unsnapped his seat belt and then got Mark out of his. He pulled Mark into his lap and held him close as his son cried as if his heart was broken. Lance held his tears in with difficulty. Mark's grief was what was important now, not his own. He would grieve later.

After a while, Mark had quieted down to a few hiccups. Lance handed him his handkerchief, which Mark took and loudly blew his nose.

Lance continued to hold his child and rub his back. "We can talk about it and you cry all you want to cry. It's sad when a fellow loses his mom. Your mom loved you and wanted you with her."

Mark sat up and looked at his dad. "She did want me."

"Yes, sweetheart, she did."

Climbing back to the other side of the seat, Mark snapped himself into his seat belts. "Let's go home, Dad."

"Okay, let's do that." Lance buckled up and drove back onto the highway. "We'll go to the Rocking M. Everyone wants to tell you how sorry they are about your mom but how glad they are that you're staying with us."

Mark's face brightened a little. "You think so? They're glad I'm staying?"

"Absolutely."

"Maybe Grandmama and Nana will have dinner made. I'm getting hungry."

Lance hoped that being hungry indicated Mark was past his first shock over his mom's death. Mark had only had the three days with his mom since they had left California. He seemed content with her not being around every day. Lance prayed that meant the grieving would not be so hard on the child. Lance didn't have a clue how to process his own feelings right now. There was shock of course, but still a tremendous relief that he wasn't going to lose Mark. The thought that the helicopter could just as easily exploded on the flight back to Austin was terrifying.

Chapter 33

Lance spotted Juliana's pickup as he drove up the lane to the Rocking M. He sighed almost as if he had been holding his breath. Juliana was home. Close to the house was the BMW. He longed to just sit and hold his baby girl.

"Mark, run on into the house. It's too hot to greet everyone outside here. Everyone will want to hug you and love on you."

"Okay, Dad. I don't understand why, but okay." As soon as the truck stopped, Mark was out the door and running up the porch steps.

Hank held the door for Mark to run into the kitchen and then waited for Lance to enter. As soon as his dad closed the door to keep the cool air in, he swept Lance into a tight hug. "I'm glad you made it home safe, son."

Returning the hug, Lance felt he could relax a bit. He was home and his dad was there to protect him.

"Oh Lance." Olivia was there needing her hug. "I'm so sorry about Chandra. Are you okay?"

Lance let her hold him for a bit. "I'm doing okay and so is Mark. We're just in shock and of course sad."

The next several minutes were spent giving and receiving hugs from Grandpapa, Nana, and Abby. Logan, Alex, and Ricardo gave him their manly hugs of shoulders hitting and hand slapping once on the back. Everyone hugged and kissed Mark as well.

Lance found himself standing in front of Juliana.

She wrapped her arms around his waist and laid her head on his shoulder. "You really okay?"

"I am now. Having family and home to come back to is what I needed after the shock of this morning." He held her in his arms until he felt her edging back and then he let her go. For the little while he held her, it had felt so right.

"What now?" Her eyes were big and questioning.

"Now we go on with life." Where that life would lead them he didn't know but he had a hope.

Rosa came into the kitchen holding Sara Hope. "Oh Lance, Ms. Chandra...."

Lance took Sara Hope as Rosa started crying.

Lance kissed Rosa on the forehead. "We'll talk later after we go home. For now I want to hold Sara Hope for a while."

Juliana came over and held Rosa in an embrace of comfort, patting her back.

Olivia quietly requested, "Everyone take a seat. Dinner is ready."

There followed much scraping of chairs as the family gathered around the long table that was barely large enough for everyone.

Hank tapped the side of his glass with a spoon. "Let's hold hands and Grandpapa will say the blessing."

Walt took his wife's and his son's hands. "Let's pray. Our Heavenly Father, we ask for your blessings to understand how to help each other heal from the death of Chandra. Especially be with Lance and the children in the days ahead. Bless this food and the hands that prepared it. In the name of Jesus, the Christ. Amen."

As platters and bowls passed around the table, the phone rang. Hank got up from the table to answer it.

"Hello."

He listened for a few moments, then asked, "Who is this?"

Again he listened a few moments before he said, "All I can do is refer you to the authorities. I don't have any information. Goodbye."

Hank hung up the phone and it immediately rang again. Ignoring it, he sat back down at the table. "I'm going to let it go to voice mail. Lance, you might want to give George a call and tell him to close the gate onto Two Forks Ranch. The press can be a little pushy."

Lance sighed. Going into the living room still carrying Sara Hope, he phoned George.

"Hello, Lance. Where are you? The phone is ringing off the wall."

"I'm at the Rocking M. I don't know if you have heard, but the helicopter carrying my wife crashed outside of Fredericksburg this morning. All on board were killed. You can expect some media to arrive at the ranch. I want you to have someone posted at the front gate and keep the gate closed."

"I'm sorry to hear about your wife. What about Mark?"

Lance realized that all those on the ranch cared about Mark. "He's with me and he'll stay with me. Rosa and Sara Hope are here at the Rocking M but later this afternoon we'll be back home. I just wanted to call and warn you about the media."

"Thanks, I've already been fielding calls."

"Let all the calls go to voice mail. Then you can sort through whom to respond to. If you need me, call on your cell and I'll answer, as you'll come up on caller ID."

"All right, I'll take care of things. If the media gets too pushy, I'll call the sheriff's department."

"Thanks, George. I'll see you this afternoon." Lance ended the call and made sure his phone was on vibrate. He wanted to be available if Hilary or the authorities called, but otherwise he was going to ignore it.

He patted Sara Hope's back as she rested against his chest with her head on his shoulder. She had fallen sound asleep during the phone call with George. Feeling a need for some space from others, he sat down in the large rocking chair in the living room and rocked his baby daughter. The murmuring of voices from the kitchen was soothing.

In a little bit, Mark quietly came into the living room and Lance pulled him up into his lap and cuddled both his children in his arms. Before long,

Mark had also dropped off to sleep. Knowing the stressful morning the boy had had, Lance was glad his son could escape reality for a while.

~~~

Juliana helped serve the peach cobbler Olivia had baked for dessert. And then looked into the living room. Lance rocking his children in the big rocker almost brought her to tears. She was concerned for Lance and Mark in their grief. Also, for Rosa who had known Chandra for eight years and knew her well, Juliana regretted the sense of loss they all must be feeling. For herself, there was no grief at the death of Lance's wife because Juliana had never met the woman. Was she wrong to be relieved the woman was out of Lance's life? What Chandra's death opened up to the future for herself and Lance was a question only Lance could answer. Juliana had to give them all time to work through the initial shock. But one thing she sure about was how thankful she was that Mark would be staying with his father.

Lance glanced up and their eyes met. He nodded to her and said softly, "Come sit with us for a while."

Taking a chair next to the rocker, Juliana sat and quietly waited for Lance to open the conversation.

Lance sighed. "Holding these two precious ones is the best thing in the world. They give me a reason to be a better man. I want to protect them from every hurt in the world, but I can't protect them from the reality of life."

Juliana nodded. "I know. You're a wonderful father and you may not be able to protect them from it, but you can always be their anchor in that reality."

"That's how I felt driving up to the ranch after this morning. Mom, Dad, Grandpapa, Nana, you, and everyone else here are my anchors. You all help me realize I'm not alone in this."

Juliana didn't know what was best to say and Lance seemed to want to talk, so she gave him her attention and listened.

After a bit, he continued. "From one moment to the next your life can change totally from what you thought it was. Just a few months ago, I was on top of the mountain, having sold my company. Then in a moment, what I thought was my life changed with Chandra leaving me. Then I move here and think all is set and again things changed and I feared I would lose my son. No way did I see this morning coming. Now I have to learn to live and try to protect my children in this new reality."

Juliana glanced at her watch and realized she had to leave soon to see a patient. "For now you need to just live and not try to figure everything out. Give yourself and your children some time to adjust. Let your family love you and let others be a barrier to the events of this morning. Go play with your children and let the world go by."

Lance smiled. "I always feel better about things after talking with you. Thanks for being such a good friend."

"I have to leave for work. Will you be here later?" Juliana didn't want to leave him but her reality was she needed to get to work.

"I'll stay here for a while and then later this afternoon I'll take the kids home. Why don't you plan to come over for supper? I'm going to try to talk the family into coming over to Two Forks for the evening."

"Okay, I'll come by after I finish my appointments this afternoon." She gave Mark and Sara Hope a light kiss on the top of their heads and Lance a squeeze of his shoulder and then she headed for the kitchen. The men had all disappeared and Rosa, Abby, Nana, and Olivia were seated at the cleared table drinking iced tea.

"You want a glass of tea, Juliana?" Olivia asked.

"No thanks, I have to go. I have appointments this afternoon."

~

As Juliana drove to her first appointment, she couldn't seem to get her thoughts going in anything but circles. Lance was no longer married. He was a widower with two children and a fresh grief. What did that mean to Juliana's life? She cared deeply for Lance and the children. What did the happenings of the day mean for her? Driving up the rough country road to the old farmhouse of her patient, she prayed for God's guidance for her and for Lance. She vowed to put these thoughts aside and give her full attention to her patients.

The next few days were quiet. Lance spent his time with Mark and the family either at the Rocking M or at Two Forks. The media hounded them until after the funeral and then went on to the next big story. Lance gave no interviews and spoke not a word to the press.

After work, the day before the funeral, Juliana drove up to Lance's home. Mark was playing out in the yard. After she stopped the car, he ran up and as she stepped out of the car gave her a big hug. "Hey, Juliana."

She returned the hug. "Hey, yourself."

"Grandmama is helping get supper ready. I like for you all to come for supper. It makes it more fun."

"Thanks, Mark. I like being with you."

"I'm going to go play some more before I get called to supper." He took off running across the grass.

Juliana turned toward the house and bumped into Lance. He put out a hand to steady her. "Sorry, didn't mean to startle you."

"No problem. I should look before I starting walking. I was too busy watching Mark run across the lawn. I declare he has grown an inch since yesterday." Lance looked tired and sort of hurried.

Lance glanced over at his son doing cartwheels on the green expanse of lawn. "I think you're right. Did you have any trouble getting in the gate?"

"No, Pete was there to open it for me and I didn't really even have to slow down much."

"Good. The press just won't go away until after the funeral. I've learned that with the press if you don't want to be in the limelight, don't talk to them, ever. Especially don't talk about my family. This is a time I would hope they would respect my privacy and the privacy of my children, but it seems to have opposite effect on the press."

Juliana respected his desire to keep out of the limelight. "They do seem persistent."

"Oh well, soon there will be another tragedy and they will be off to bother some other poor soul. Come on in and let's see if supper is ready."

~

The morning of the funeral Juliana waited with Hank, Olivia, Walt, Nana, and Abby for Ricardo to pick them up in the stretch limo that Lance had rented. He had also rented one for himself and the children to ride in with Rosa. She had offered to stay home with the baby, but Lance decided they all needed to go to the funeral. Sara Hope was too young to remember her mother, but in the years to come, she would learn about her mother and might take comfort that she was at her mother's funeral.

The small church building soon filled with church members and community members who had come to know Lance or were friends with McTavish family. The sheriff and his deputy kept the media out.

As they all filed into the church building, Juliana somehow found herself seated next to Lance. Mark was on his other side with Rosa beyond holding Sara Hope.

Lance took her hand and said softly, "Thanks for taking off work and coming. It means a lot, especially as you didn't even know her."

"But I know you, Mark, and Rosa and this is a hard time for you all. The least I can do is be here."

Greg Young, the preacher, stood in front of the gleaming dark casket and beside a large photo of Chandra smiling at the audience and began the service. With congregational singing, prayers led by Greg and one of the elders, it was a short service compared to some funerals that Juliana had attended. She wondered why Lance had chosen not to give the eulogy but Greg handled everything with a smoothness and kindness that helped move the service along without seeming to rush.

Rosa and Mark both wept during the service, but Lance was dry eyed, as if he had already shed his tears in private. Sara Hope started getting restless and ended up in Juliana's lap. The baby was now six months old and was a hefty baby. In the last week, she had started to sit up by herself and to roll around the floor to get where she wanted to go. Juliana knew Sara Hope would soon be crawling. She already was starting to rise up on hands and knees and rock back and forth.

Juliana lightly tapped Sara Hope's lips to quiet her as she gurgled and blew bubbles. Lance glanced over and smiled at the baby. Sara Hope grinned at him and waved her arms. He then turned back to Mark who Lance had nestled up under his arm. He reached across Mark every once in a while to rub Rosa's shoulder.

Juliana continued to hold Sara Hope at the end of the service as Lance, Mark, and Rosa went up to the casket. Lance was murmuring softly to Mark and had an arm around each of them as they touched the casket. Juliana could only imagine what they were saying as a final goodbye. The rest of the family made their way toward the outer doors and then waited for Lance and the others. Ricardo stood with Juliana as they waited patiently.

Juliana glanced at the handsome young man and softly said, "You're being such a good grandson by staying so close to your grandmother."

Ricardo returned her look as if surprised by the comment. "But of course, she is my Lita and she is sad. She worries she should have known how badly Chandra felt in the marriage and that she was going to leave. Lita was as blindsided by all of this as Lance."

"Rosa is such a kind person. I can see how she would think she should have been able to do something to avert all this pain and hurt."

He nodded. "She thinks of Lance and the children as if they were her own family. That's why I came out with her and plan to stay. She will never leave them, at least while the children are small."

Lance guided Rosa and Mark away from the casket and toward the outer doors. Juliana and Ricardo fell in behind them as they made their way with the rest of the family to the waiting limos for the ride to the cemetery. Lance had decided to bury Chandra in their family plot in the old cemetery at Tumbleweed so that growing up Mark and Sara Hope would be able to visit the grave if that was what they wanted.

After the service at the cemetery, they all returned to Two Forks Ranch with those that Lance had invited. Greg and Crystal Young with their three children, most of the church members, and all the ranch hands from Two Forks shared a meal and visited for a couple of hours. Louisa had brought in several of her daughters and nieces to help with the meal, and most of the church members had brought food.

Juliana wandered about the big living room and dining room talking with various people. She always managed to keep an eye on Lance. A couple of times when it seemed as if someone was cornering him with questions, she went up to him and turned the conversation, allowing him to escape. Finally, the last person had driven away with only the immediate family still sitting around the living room.

Lance came and sat on the couch next to Juliana after seeing off the Young family. It was the only vacant seat facing the huge empty fireplace.

He put his arm on the back of the couch above Juliana's shoulders. "Thanks for helping me out there a couple of times. I didn't want to be rude. But some people don't have common sense."

"I was glad to help. This is a difficult enough day without having to deal with thoughtless chatter. How are you doing?"

Lance smiled sadly. "I'm doing okay. The first couple of days I was really thrown for a loop. I couldn't seem to get my thinking going. After a week, I'm doing better. Glad to get today over so we can start getting back to our regular lives."

Juliana shrugged. "Whatever our regular lives really are. It will be helpful to Mark that he starts school in another week."

"That's what I was thinking a minute ago. It will give him structure, something else to think about, and new friends. He's doing well making friends. Church has helped with that, plus Maria's siblings coming over the last few weeks. He's even learning Spanish from them. I think after we get past today, he'll do all right."

Juliana looked around and noticed Mark was not with them, nor was Ricardo. "Where is he now?"

Lance chuckled. "That Ricardo is a smart young man. He took him out to keep Applejack from feeling left out. I don't know if they'll go for a ride or not with the heat. Mark asked me if it was okay to go out and have fun. I told him that is what his mom would have wanted."

Juliana sighed. "What a thing for a child to have to ask."

Lance gazed into her eyes as she returned the look. "Juliana, not now but in a few days, I want us to talk."

"I'd like that." Juliana felt her heart rate jump. Yes, she wanted to talk.

Chapter 34

Three months later.

Lance tied his tie for a third time trying to get it to look perfect. In a new dark blue suit and white shirt, he had pondered over which tie to wear for his wedding. Was Juliana having some of the same type of difficulties getting dressed as he was? Ever since Juliana had agreed to marry him, he found that every other thought was of her.

The last three months had been exciting as he and Juliana had gotten to know each other better. Going with her up to the Panhandle to meet her family had been terrifying. Her dad had been standoffish at first but Lance had asked him questions about ranching, which was something the older man talked about easily. Juliana's mother and siblings had been thrilled with the idea of the relationship and curious about Lance. By the time they were ready to return to South Forks Ranch, Lance had felt at ease with Juliana's entire family. They were simple, straight-forward people who lived their lives surrounded by their belief in God and their loyalty to each other. Lance appreciated that they were a lot like his family. The wedding was the first opportunity for both families to meet.

Mark came into the bedroom, dressed in a similar dark suit, shirt, and tie. "Hey, Dad, we look alike."

Lance reached for his comb and tried to tame Mark's hair.

Rosa came into the bedroom carrying a small jar. "Mark, I tell you to wait for me. I fix that hair that waves at everyone."

Lance laughed. "Rosa, he has a cowlick just where I do."

She dabbed a little of the cream on the back of Mark's head and combed the hair down. "That's better. Now don't touch your hair. It looks good."

Lance walked around Rosa and whistled. "You look great in that frilly pink dress."

Rosa blushed. "Don't be silly. This is just a fancier dress than I normally wear. You have to dress up for a wedding."

Mark stuck his finger in his collar and pulled at it. "Why is that, Dad? This is not comfortable."

"Don't fidget, Mark. We dress up for weddings because they're an important life event. And we want to help Juliana have a great wedding." Lance was glad she had opted for a regular suit for him to wear and not a tuxedo. He had wanted his brother Matt to be here today but he was still in the Middle East flying planes on and off carriers. Logan, Alex, and Mark were his groomsmen. Lance had bought them all matching navy blue suits.

Ricardo appeared at the bedroom door. "It's time to go, Lance. You don't want to be late for your own wedding."

Lance nodded. "Is Maria here yet to take Sara Hope?"

"Yes, and so is the limo to take us all to the church building."

Maria was going to take care of the active ten-month-old during the wedding ceremony so that Rosa could have a break. Lance wanted both his children at the wedding and especially in the wedding pictures. Maria waited by the front door holding Sara Hope who was dressed in a frilly sky-blue dress with a matching bow in her dark hair. Little black patent leather shoes with little white leggings finished out her outfit. She was starting to pull herself up and hang onto furniture. Lance expected to see her first steps any day now.

Lance kissed Sara Hope and quickly stepped back out of the way of grasping hands that wanted to grab his tie. "Hey, baby girl. Don't you look cute. So do you, Maria. Has Ricardo told you how lovely you look in that dress?"

Maria giggled. "Yes, sir, he has." The soulful look she gave Ricardo told Lance there would probably be another wedding down the road.

With Ricardo's help, they were soon all into the limo and heading down the road toward town and the church building.

It was a warm sunny day for the middle of November in south Texas. No one needed a coat and as they drove up to the church building, Lance saw that everyone was dressed in their church clothes. For the local men to dress up in a suit and tie in the middle of the week was a complement to the bride and groom.

The church building was almost full by the time Lance and his groomsmen walked up and sat on the front pew with Greg Young.

Mark leaned over and whispered to his dad. "What do we do now?"

Lance pulled the boy into a hug. "We wait for the bride, Juliana. And then you remember what to do?"

"Yes, I follow Alex and stand quietly while Mr. Young talks."

"You'll do fine." Lance glanced over at his two younger brothers who both looked so grown up in their new suits. He missed Matt but was happy to have Logan and Alex stand up with him.

There was bustling going on at the back of the auditorium. A group of singers began to sing *One Hand One Heart*. Then Lance saw his dad and grandpapa escorting Olivia and Nana to their spot in the next to the front pew. His mom and nana were dressed up in new dresses. Then Juliana's brothers escorted her sisters and mother to their pew at the front.

At the end of the song, Greg leaned over and whispered, "It's time, Lance." Lance followed the preacher up to the front of the auditorium with Logan, Alex, and Mark following. They stood in front of the arch covered with multi-colored flower and looked toward the back of the building. The group of singers began to sing *Whither Thou Goest* as Lance watched as Maria, Abby, and Cassie, Juliana's sister, walked down the aisle and stood on the other side of Greg. They wore dark blue silk dresses with gathered long sleeves and full skirts that brushed their ankles.

The chorus of singers began to sing the *Bridal chorus* from Lohengrin but with English lyrics that started with *Faithful and true, We lead ye forth, Where love triumphant, Shall crown ye with joy.* The sound of the full chorus singing the powerful majestic words caused such a feeling of joy to swell within him as he watched Juliana enter and begin the slow walk down the aisle with her father. He blinked rapidly to contain the tears that threatened. She was so beautiful. Her dress was simple and elegant. She looked serene with a veil flowing behind her from a crown of flower-trimmed silver. She had chosen to wear her hair down and her face framed by little ringlets. The smile she directed at Lance was full and confident.

Lance returned her smile and said a silent prayer of thanksgiving to God for blessing his life with such a wonderful companion as Juliana. He also prayed to be worthy of and to able to protect the blessings of his soon to be wife and two precious children. As her father handed her off to him, he took her slender soft hand and planned to hold on to her forever.

MORE BY A J HAWKE

For updates about current and upcoming releases, as well as exclusive promotions, visit the author's website at:

www.AJHawke.com

Sign up for the author's Newsletter

Mailing list and get a free copy of

CAUGHT BETWEEN TWO WORLDS

Click here to get started:

www.AJHawke.com

More Books By A J Hawke

Available At Amazon.com

SERIES

CEDAR RIDGE CHRONICLES

Cabin on Pinto Creek Book 1

Joe Storm No Longer A Cowboy Book 2

Colorado Morning Sky Book 3

Colorado Evening Sky Book 4

TUMBLEWEED, TEXAS TALES

Lance McTavish Home To Texas Book 1

Inspirational Contemporary Western Romance

STAND ALONE NOVELS

Caught Between Two Worlds

Inspirational Contemporary Western Romance

Mountain Journey Home

Inspirational Historical Western Romance

For updates on new releases of upcoming books and promotions, sign up for the latest news here: www.AJHawke.com

About the Author

Born in Spur, Texas into a multi-generational Texas family, A J Hawke has traveled throughout the American West as well as other parts of the world and enjoys reading, writing, friends, family, and being a Christian. She writes historical as well as contemporary Inspirational Western Romances. Her approach to writing is to tell a good story, have a happy ever after for her characters, and have as few spelling errors as possible. (If you find one please email the author at AJHawkeAuthor@gmail.com with that rascal's location within the book).